RETURN OF THE
WIZARD KING

THE WIZARD KING TRILOGY

I

RETURN OF THE
WIZARD KING

THE WIZARD KING TRILOGY

I

DARK HORSE BOOKS

Published by
Dark Horse Books
A division of Dark Horse Comics LLC
10956 SE Main Street
Milwaukie, OR 97222

DarkHorse.com

Maps illustrated by Robert Altbauer

Library of Congress Cataloging-in-Publication Data

Names: Corrie, Chad, author.
Title: Return of the Wizard King / Chad Corrie.
Description: First edition. | Milwaukie, OR : Dark Horse Books, 2020. |
    Series: The Wizard King trilogy ; book one | Summary: "After nearly
    eight centuries, the last wizard king seeks a return to Tralodren. But
    doing so requires the manipulation of some mercenaries oblivious to his
    goals. The gladiator sold his soul for revenge. The knight's a bigot.
    The dwarf only cares about regaining his honor. Even the wizardess seems
    too bookish for anyone's good. But they've all been hired by a blind
    seer and his assistant to retrieve some forgotten knowledge kept hidden
    away in some jungle-strangled ruins. Get in. Get out. Get paid. At least
    that's what they thought. Instead, they uncover hidden agendas and
    ancient power struggles threatening to take the world to the brink of
    annihilation"-- Provided by publisher.
Identifiers: LCCN 2019051914 (print) | LCCN 2019051915 (ebook) | ISBN
    9781506716268 (paperback) | ISBN 9781506716312 (epub)
Subjects: GSAFD: Fantasy fiction.
Classification: LCC PS3603.O77235 R48 2020 (print) | LCC PS3603.O77235
    (ebook) | DDC 813/.6--dc23
LC record available at https://lccn.loc.gov/2019051914
LC ebook record available at https://lccn.loc.gov/2019051915

First edition: September 2020
ISBN: 978-1-50671-626-8

1 3 5 7 9 10 8 6 4 2
Printed in the United States of America

THE WIZARD KING TRILOGY

Return of the Wizard King
Trial of the Wizard King
Triumph of the Wizard King

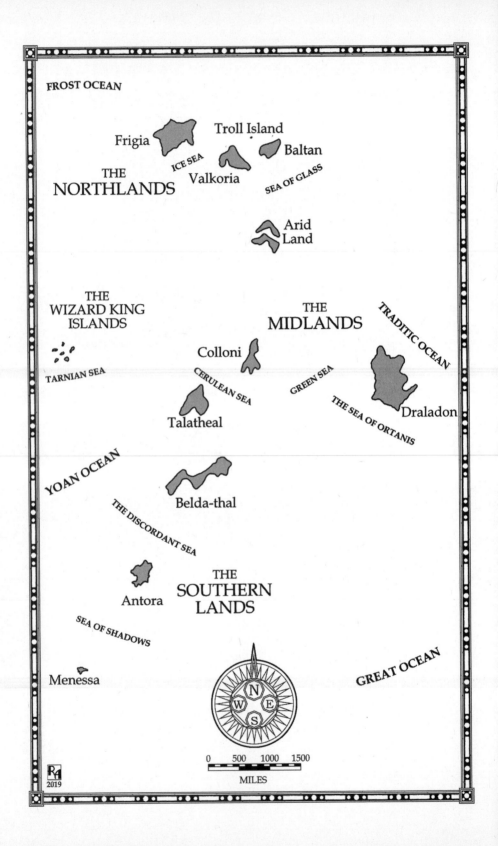

FROST OCEAN

Frigia

Troll Island

Baltan

ICE SEA

THE
NORTHLANDS

Valkoria

SEA OF GLASS

Arid
Land

THE
WIZARD KING
ISLANDS

THE
MIDLANDS

TRADITIC OCEAN

Colloni

TARNIAN SEA

CERULEAN SEA

GREEN SEA

Talatheal

THE SEA OF ORTANIS

Draladon

YOAN OCEAN

THE DISCORDANT SEA

Belda-thal

THE
SOUTHERN
LANDS

Antora

SEA OF SHADOWS

GREAT OCEAN

Menessa

N
W E
S

0   500   1000 1500

MILES

RH
2019

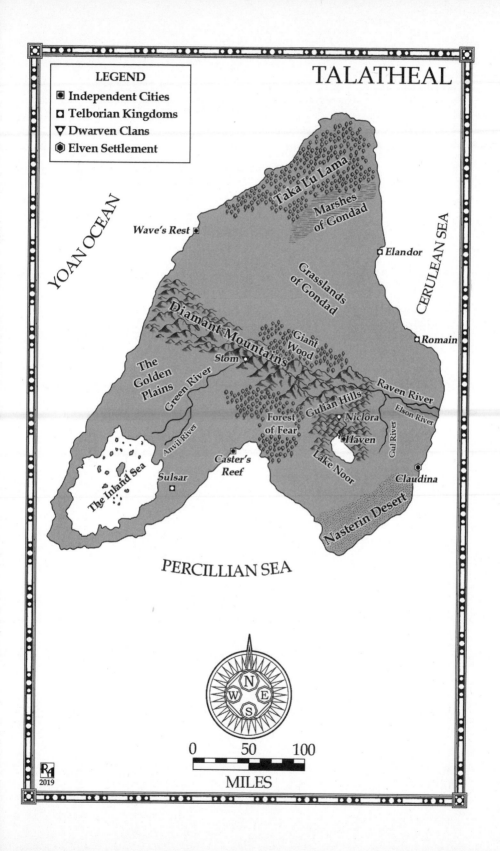

CHAPTER 1

THERE IS ONLY POWER AND THE PATH ONE TAKES TO ATTAIN IT.

—**Raston Tolle, Telborian wizard king**
Reigned 34 BV–6 BV

Valan emerged from the portal's brilliance into the musty chamber. Once through, he turned to face the mosaic fixed into the stone wall through which he'd passed. The white light had already faded, revealing the azure and violet tiles forming the twelve-foot circle. Small and uniform in shape, they'd been crafted into a swirling twist of color—a whirlpool of polished tiles spiraling into some unknown pit.

Turning from the wall, he took in the large chamber. As the portal's lingering glow faded all was lost in a shadowy murk, punctured only by the purple glow from a collection of runes carved into a solid blue marble column, encircled by a wrought iron fence, at the chamber's center. Valan's silver robes reflected part of the runes' light as the mage strode forward, brown eyes seeking out all he could with ardent interest.

As he walked, he retrieved a clear glass globe from the satchel dangling from his shoulder. Aside from what was in the satchel, all his belongings either were in the pack strapped to his back or stuffed into one of the handful of bulging belt pouches swaying with his steps. The mage whispered a word as he tossed the globe in the air. This birthed a flash of sunlight from the now white and glowing ball that hovered above and to the right of his head.

Once his eyes adjusted to the light, he shed his pack and set it beside him with careful effort. This done, he took a few steps forward, the glowing ball following him closely as he did so. With its help, he could now clearly discern where he stood.

Built in a rectangular design, the chamber was about one hundred feet from the base of the stairs opposite him and about eighty feet wide. Its twenty-foot ceiling increased its cavernous feel. It was built from large granite blocks tightly packed one into the other; they formed a near-seamless weave of walls and floor. But as impressive as the sight the stones conveyed was, the real object of interest was that blue column dominating the chamber's center. Ringed with a fence crafted of spear-point-tipped wrought iron shafts, it was a surreal sight in the otherwise empty room.

He'd come a long way for it—searched and pressed himself through more than others might have thought possible. But now . . . His booted heels clopped loudly as he made his way toward the skeletal fence, its gate latched by a worn wrought iron bar that slid into an equally worn clasp. The latch was on the outside, keeping anyone or anything inside the fence from straying too far from the column.

"Finally." With a slight gesture, the gate swung open, squeaking softly. He cleared the twelve feet between the fence and the column with ease, reaching a slender hand for the cold blue marble.

"The Transducer." There was power there. Power to tap into, to use . . . and master. He craned his neck, taking in the majesty of the impressive fifteen-foot structure. Soon enough he'd translate the purple glowing runes stretching its length. It wouldn't be long now.

At the column's base, where he stood, was an eight-foot doorway. He dared a look inside. With the aid of his globe, he discovered a hollowed-out room. It was about six feet in diameter and constructed from floor to ceiling in polished blue marble.

"Everything's intact," he murmured. But any further investigation was cut short by the sound of stone scraping on stone coming from the top of the stairs that snaked up the wall opposite him. The stairs partially flanked the wall and then ducked into an ascending corridor with a brighter opening he took for a doorway just beyond it.

Withdrawing from the fenced area, he watched a soft white line of light slide down the walls parallel with the stairs. Assuming it was some aid in maneuvering the old steps, he was more concerned with who might be descending them. He wasn't expecting visitors.

He whispered another word, dimming the glowing ball's brilliance to the brightness of candlelight, and tiptoed closer to the stairs. Someone was indeed making his way down. Only one person. Good. He soundlessly bounded up the steps two at a time, keeping a few spells on the tip of his tongue. The point where the stairs made their right turn into the corridor beyond was where he met up with his unwelcome visitor.

The pointed ears, claw-like hands, and skin the color of a ripe pear made clear he was facing a hobgoblin. He stood a foot above Valan's six-foot frame and was much more muscled than the mage. But Valan's magic was more than an equalizer, even considering the sword sheathed at the hobgoblin's side.

But the hobgoblin's steel-gray, short-sleeved robe, accompanied by the brown padded cloth vest, wasn't quite right for a race said to be more at home in armor or common dress than robes. The Steel Cross he wore as a belt buckle confirmed Valan's initial suspicions. The twin swords crossed over a round shield was a clear sign this was a priest of Khuthon.

A quick swipe of his hand sent the hobgoblin flying from the stairs and roughly hitting the floor below. While he spoke some Goblin, he didn't need to be fluent to understand the guttural growls that followed were clearly curses of pain. As the hobgoblin swiftly found his feet, Valan cast another spell.

"Agris lorim naslee rah!" A sudden burst of aquamarine energy shot out of his hands. An eyeblink later the hobgoblin was frozen solid, a thin layer of ice outlining his frame. The room was encompassed in a sinking mist birthed by the sudden change in temperature, the icy hobgoblin crackling in the seething fog.

Looking back at the corridor from where the hobgoblin came, Valan found it empty. He waited a moment more—ears tuned for anything while eyeing the daylight streaming in from the new opening with some trepidation. Once confident he was truly alone, he spoke another word of magic, plucked the now dimming globe from the air, and returned it to his satchel. He made his way toward the base of the ascending corridor.

The hobgoblin wouldn't have been alone. Not a priest. So that meant there were others above. But how many? And were they *all* priests, warriors, or a mixture of both? Fishing out a silver medallion from beneath his robes, Valan studied the object carefully, noting the small ancient runes etched around its lip. More than once, the medallion had saved him from death. Many who'd tried introducing him to Asorlok failed—their weapons bouncing off his flesh as if it were hardened iron. The medallion would keep him safe from any physical attack, but if there were any more priests about he could be in for a very real fight.

Replacing the medallion under his robes, Valan ascended the stairs with more spells at the ready. He could feel the change in temperature as he climbed, growing quickly from a damp chill to a warmer and more humid environment. Of course, he knew from his studies the ruins sat in the midst of the jungle of Taka Lu Lama, but it was one thing to have head knowledge of a matter and quite another to experience the thick, semitropical air firsthand. All the better the Transducer was in the cooler chamber below.

At the top of the stairs, he discovered that the opening was a secret door hidden behind a statue, which he immediately crouched beside for added protection. The hidden door opened into a column-lined hallway with a row of statues extending forty feet down along the wall opposite the columns. All of the statues—including the one he hid behind—were of powerfully muscled humanoids and devoid of heads, each wearing unique armor and carved into a variety of military stances.

To his left the hallway turned around a quiet corner with no hint of activity beyond. It was the same on his right. This just left the open door across from him, out of which came the sound of more hobgoblins. Creeping forward, he dared a look inside.

Twenty hobgoblian priests stood in the center of a rectangular area that must have been an ancient temple's altar room. The entire area was lit by the late morning light, flooding in from both the holes in the ceiling and the broken stained glass windows on the wall opposite him. Naturalistic images of vines and roses, birds and serpents lived amid the supporting pillars lining the walls, alongside frescoes and mosaics depicting faceless forms, some in scenes from daily life and others devoutly petitioning headless giants. And while the massive space was impressive, Valan's main interest was with the altar the priests had pooled around.

The granite structure was square, about four feet tall. Its chipped and chiseled surface was host to a crudely formed set of crossed swords resting over a round shield, etched into the stone on all sides. The bloodstains were also recent additions and hard to miss, stirring his thoughts with darker musings even as he noted the stone lectern a few feet from and facing the altar.

On the wall to his left, however, was something more interesting: seven bookcases filled with scrolls and tomes. These stood beside a handful of simple wooden tables and chairs—another obviously recent addition to the room. If any of the items in the bookcases had been found in the ruins, they'd be a great boon for work with the Transducer. Pondering the matter, he observed the score or so goblins working in various capacities: sweeping the floor, tending to the bookcases, and assisting priests.

Goblins were related to hobgoblins—even ogres. All three races had roots in the jarthal, an ancient race said to have been created by Khuthon at the birth of Tralodren. Valan had long studied the various racial lines covering the world. It was essential if he wished to make proper use of the Transducer. In many ways, goblins were similar in appearance to hobgoblins, but with uniformly straight black hair—instead of the hobgoblin's brown or black—and skin the color of a ripe lime. The biggest difference, of course, was their size: goblins were only about half the height of hobgoblins. Even so, they could still be trouble should any of them notice his lurking. But a hobgoblin would beat the goblins to it.

No sooner had a nearby priest turned in Valan's direction than the hobgoblin thrust a thick finger like a spear point right at him. The room teemed with frenetic energy and Valan leapt fully into the open, eyeing

the onrush of goblins while the priests shouted back and forth to each
other in their native tongue. He could ascertain just enough of their
varied shouts to understand they took him for an intruder and that he
should be killed. It was all he needed to know.

"Ackrin-loth gestra!" he shouted as he spread his fingers, expelling a
web of lightning that took care of the closest goblins. He took no notice
as they dropped, convulsing painfully on the floor before entering
Asorlok's gates. His attention was locked on the priests.

A spear crafted of searing red energy sailed straight for his heart. It'd
been lobbed by the lead priest, who continually barked out commands.
Valan instantly sidestepped the prayer made manifest. The weapon
narrowly missed his right shoulder. Wasting no time, Valan conjured and
flung a set of sharp icicles at the priests. They tried to avoid them but
couldn't entirely prevent their sharp points from piercing their flesh. Now
even more enraged, the priests rushed him en masse, weapons tightly
gripped and more curses on their lips.

Valan stood his ground. "Agris larom magalasta urik kane!" Before
the hobgoblins knew what had happened, they'd run into and then
through a translucent, eight-foot-tall, charcoal-gray barrier which
suddenly formed a few feet from Valan's position. To any casual observer
it might have appeared as if the whole structure was made of standing
water, which splashed on and off the hobgoblins as they barreled through.
But that was where the similarity ended.

The priests wailed as the charcoal-gray gel clung to them, eating away
at their flesh and clothing like acid. Even their weapons weren't immune,
sizzling and melting like butter in a hot skillet. One by one, each
hobgoblin fell on his knees, cursing and crawling toward the mage.
Though each was intent on doing him harm, none could make good on
such claims. Their weapons were useless, and no matter how hard they
struggled to wipe it off, the gel would only spread farther across their
contorted bodies. A moment later all were fully on the floor, either dead
or very nearly so. But that wasn't the end.

Valan spun round and found a fresh force of hobgoblins shouting
for his death. The hallway he'd first seen apparently led out of the temple.

Yet while they had the greater numbers, these hobgoblins were common warriors, their status clear by their chain mail shirts and drawn swords. No magic. No priests. Valan smiled and began casting a new spell. This was going to be fun.

· • ·

Hadek didn't know if he should look into the commotion coming from the temple. Content as he was in his personal oasis from the challenging world that was the Basilisk Tribe, the bald goblin didn't feel like leaving it for anything. But as the noise grew and the shouts and sounds of fighting reached him, he knew something wasn't right, and for his own sake he needed to investigate. And so it was he found himself now taking in a most amazing and terrifying sight from where he hid beside a pillar close to the door through which he'd entered, not too far from the bookcases.

A skirmish was underway, and Hadek was glad to stay out of it. What made the matter all the more intriguing was that it all appeared to be related to a single intruder standing at the room's main entrance: a lone Telborian wearing silver robes. The brown-haired human was lean and carried no weapon, but none of the warriors could send him to Mortis. Attacks that should have run him through or sliced off his head instead stopped just outside his frame with a sudden jerk.

All the warriors could do was slice a bit of his robe here and there. His flesh wasn't marred in the least. It wasn't until the Telborian returned the attack that Hadek fully understood the nature of the threat. The human used magic to cut down the hobgoblins with apparent ease. And if seeing him in action wasn't enough to give one pause, then a quick inventory of the carnage surrounding the wizard was all one needed to heed.

The slain priests lay in puddles of their own dissolving flesh and weapons, while the goblins had also taken a beating. Most had been killed, but a remnant of their ranks hung back from the fighting—some even hiding, like Hadek. It seemed a wise course of action given the situation, but it wasn't an enduring one. Eventually the hobgoblins would either die or retreat, and then where would that leave him? Alone with the wizard. And that wasn't good.

Hadek pressed himself deeper into the limited shadows afforded him. If he ran, he could be spotted and killed just as easily as he could in battle. His indecision lasted until he spied Boaz rush into the scene. The chieftain of the Basilisk Tribe was leading a fresh force of warriors into the temple even as the last of those who'd challenged the mage were shaking hands with death. Upon catching sight of each other, Boaz and the mage stood still. Hadek supposed each was taking stock of the other. When they'd finished doing so—a time frame measured in heartbeats—the human addressed Boaz in rough Goblin.

"You can keep throwing your men's lives away or be wise and surrender."

Boaz seemed surprised he'd been addressed in his native tongue. He squared his shoulders and peered around the room. His expression grew dark and he released a snarl of seething wrath when he caught sight of the priests' remains. Hadek tried keeping as still as a statue.

"You can't harm me," the mage continued, "no matter how much you try."

"What do you want?" Boaz eyed the wizard from sole to crown.

"That blue column in the chamber below. You leave me to it and my experiments, and I'll leave you to your lives."

Boaz was still. Hadek was surprised Boaz didn't run him through right there. Or at least attempt it. He didn't take kindly with others trying to prove themselves his better. The handful who had since Boaz became chieftain ten years earlier were quickly shown their place in Mortis.

"And who are you to demand anything?"

"I think your dead priests speak to that," the wizard answered. "The only question that remains is if you'll join them."

Behind Boaz, the remaining warriors, some fifty strong, observed the exchange. The growing unease among them was palpable. They dominated the main hallway extending out of the open room the priests had turned into their makeshift library and altar room. But even the spacious hallway couldn't comfortably afford so great a company of men. And with them blocking the exit, Hadek wasn't able to escape. That just left his secret refuge . . .

"We're many," Boaz replied confidently. "You can't hold back a whole tribe."

Before anyone could act, the wizard brought forth a fat shaft of lightning from the hand he'd directed at the hobgoblian warriors. The men howled in agony as the lightning forked and danced between them. Their deaths were gruesome but quick.

Boaz raised his sword and bellowed, making for the mage like some goring bull. Instantly, the chieftain was lifted from the ground. Hadek could see he was choking. It was like some giant invisible hand had uprooted him and was now crushing his throat. Boaz dropped his sword as he frantically tried to free himself from the phantom vise, but to no avail. No matter how hard he clawed he remained in its grip.

"Now," said the wizard, "are you going to join your men or help me?"

"What do you plan to do?" Boaz croaked.

"I'll need help in my experiments."

"Wh-what sort of help?" Boaz gave up trying to free himself and instead focused his gaze on the mage. Even at a distance Hadek could hear him struggling for breath.

The mage's grin was far from calming. "Test subjects."

"How many?"

Hadek could see where this was going and didn't like it one bit. Thinking it was now or never, he made a dash for the nearby door, drawing both men's attention. Even in his present predicament and distance from the hobgoblin, he could feel the hot ire of Boaz's glare burn into him.

"He'll do for a start, I suppose." Hadek was pulled toward the wizard as if he'd been lassoed around the waist. It was no good resisting. He might as well have been standing in oil as he slid over the stone floor with the greatest of ease. As soon as he reached the mage he dropped to his knees. There was only one option left.

"Have mercy." He addressed the wizard in Telboros—the Telborian's native tongue. The wizard stepped Hadek's way, letting Boaz drop to the floor behind him.

"You speak Telboros?" he returned in the same language.

"Yes," Hadek quickly replied. "The priests taught me so I could help them."

"With what?"

"Those." He pointed at the bookcases.

"You can read too?" The wizard's respect was rising. Out of the corner of his eye, he watched Boaz's previous ire drift into disgust.

"What are you saying?" Boaz demanded in Goblin, forcing himself on his feet. He, like most of the tribe, couldn't speak Telboros. It was the priests who preferred the language when they wanted to keep something private. And, by extension, some of those serving them also had to be instructed to better facilitate their will.

Any other time Hadek would have quickly responded to Boaz's question, but now he felt more emboldened to resist—as if he had some protection he could fall back on. It actually felt good in a way. Though it was really more like hiding behind the flat of a dagger's blade that at any time could show him its edge, for the moment, he welcomed it.

"Yes, I read and write—"

"What's your name?"

"Hadek."

"Hadek?" Boaz's voice was rough from his ordeal but still strong enough to remind the goblin he could be run through if he wasn't careful.

"Rise." Hadek did as the wizard bid. "Your life will be spared as long as you serve me."

"What's he saying?" Boaz nearly cursed as he retrieved his sword, making sure his attention never fully left them.

Before Hadek could answer, the mage spun around and faced the chieftain, speaking once more in Goblin. "That if you value your life as well as your tribe, you'll do as I say. I want all of those scrolls and books moved down into the chamber—bookcases and all. Those tables and chairs could be of use too. And then I'll need those test subjects."

"Do you have a name I can curse?" Boaz sheathed his sword with a frustrated thrust.

"Valan." The mage returned to Hadek, switching back to Telboros. "Come. There's much to be done."

As Hadek followed Valan he tried not to dwell on Boaz's searing stare as he passed. Even as they neared the secret entrance to the chamber it stuck with him. He'd been far from cherished before, but now . . . Now he was certain that outside of Valan's protection he was a dead man. And who was to say how long the mage would be among them, or how long he'd tolerate Hadek's presence? Or if he'd end up being made a test subject after all? What had he gotten himself into?

•●•

"Interesting." Cadrith's words were as dry as his skeletal frame and the threadbare plum robes and gray hooded cloak draped over them. To his left, always at the ready and in reach, rested his staff: a time-seasoned wooden shaft capped with an infant's skull. His attention was locked on the back of a violet glowing skull clutched in a monstrous obsidian hand a few paces from his throne. Its gaze seemed focused on a far corner of the room, hiding its empty sockets from Cadrith's eye while small silver runes burned hot across its sides and front. It was through this skull he'd just finished watching Valan's encounter with the hobgoblins.

"Now how best to use you . . ." He slid back into his polished red stone seat and looked out onto the small room. Besides the throne and the skull there was only a lonely chest opposite him, allowing both it and the scrying skull to always be within Cadrith's sight.

A lone window peered onto the fading twilight outside and the swaying shadows beyond. The occasional breeze rustled a few tapestries, but the centuries-gnawed surroundings were far from his thoughts. When he'd first arrived at the deserted keep after awakening from his longer-than-expected slumber, he'd been mildly curious about the new setting. But it eventually became meaningless in light of his desire to return to Tralodren.

The original strategy had been to wait out the Divine Vindication's removal of magic on Tralodren, taking his time to develop his plans and skills as best he was able. Had he known how long it would be until magic finally returned, he might have reconsidered the strategy. If not for his spell somehow extending his slumber for centuries beyond his original intentions, he'd have had to endure all that time in what had proven to be a dismal situation. It'd been vexing enough dealing with the past five years since he'd awakened; he couldn't even begin to fathom the agony of over seven hundred years staring him in the face.

Why the spell had gone awry he didn't know, but he was grateful it did. If he'd been a more religious man, he would have thanked the gods, but Cadrith knew they'd nothing to do with it. If anything they would have kept him in continued slumber, or just killed him. Either that or one of the local denizens could have just as easily destroyed him had the spell also failed to keep him hidden from sight while he slept. Another reason for the religious man to give his thanks. But awakening, he discovered, was the easy part.

Taking up his staff, he moved toward the window, ancient robes fluttering in the soft breeze. Since entering the Abyss, he'd taken to keeping his hood drawn at all times. There was no reason for it other than it let him pretend there was still something there to cover. It was more a habit now than anything else. A small tongue of azure flame flickered inside each of his eye sockets, which seemed to scan the empty, hilly terrain around the tower he'd taken for his current domain. All was still, but that meant nothing. He'd learned well enough that in the Abyss much of what's seen can be deceptive.

He spied movement in the distance, a dark shape fluttering through the clouded sky. Looking back at the scrying skull, he gave a wave of his bony hand, causing it to return to normal bone—albeit with some carved runes here and there. A moment later, a familiar visitor took a perch on the window's ledge, moving his strong form through it by means of his clawed feet and hands.

"Sargis is eager for some news." Akarin finished making his way inside, forcing Cadrith a few steps back so the nine-foot winged demon had his needed space.

"I'm sure he is." Cadrith watched the demon case the room, his yellow eyes in stark contrast to his blood-red skin, bald head, and black bull-like horns curving out from his forehead. "But I'd be better able to make progress without so many interruptions. I told him I'd keep him informed of any developments." The demon's brawny tail swayed from side to side before stilling itself behind him.

To say the lich loathed the pointy-eared minion would be an understatement of the highest order. The demon was nothing more than a lackey of his weakened master, who, like Akarin himself, mistakenly thought himself superior to others. And that arrogance and boldness grew more annoying with each visit.

"He's aware of what you told him." Akarin folded his powerful wings behind him as he found Cadrith once again.

"Then why are you here?"

"To find out what you might have forgotten to pass on since the last time you shared your progress." Akarin crossed his arms and puffed his chest. Cadrith had never seen the demon clothed in anything other than a short-sleeved scale mail shirt. The armor flowed down to his thighs and covered his black silken breechcloth. A thick segmented plate metal belt kept his sword always within reach.

"It's nice to see I still have your master's trust," he said, making his way for the throne.

"Is there any reason you *shouldn't* have it?" The demon raised a bushy black eyebrow.

"You've grown a bit bold, Akarin." He took a seat.

"And Sargis has grown even more impatient." The demon tapped a clawed finger on his muscular forearm. "Do you have anything to tell him?"

"You can tell him I believe I've found our key." Cadrith was once more peering at the silent scrying skull.

"He might want to know more than that." Akarin's tail swished as he again looked over the room, focusing on the darker corners now.

"*He* wants to know . . . or *you* do?" Cadrith peered back at the demon.

"Does it matter?" Akarin's smirk pulled back just enough of his lips to show the sharp teeth behind them. When added to his overall physicality, the effect would have been quite terrifying to most. But Cadrith knew a thing or two about theatrics—especially when it came to keeping one's place in the dangerous social order of which he was now a part.

"If you value your life, it does." He glared back, latching on to the demon's eyes. Though it would have been easier to do so if he still had eyes, he was sure Akarin got the intended effect.

"I'll make sure he gets the message," said Akarin, turning to leave.

"Please do. And when you see him, remind Sargis that *I* will contact *him* about anything he should know." Akarin didn't reply, merely leapt out the window and into the spreading night. Cadrith waited a while longer before returning his staff to the side of his throne and casting the spell to reactivate the scrying skull. There was still much that needed doing.

CHAPTER 2

DO GOOD BY YOUR FELLOW HUMAN; DO GOOD BY EACH OTHER.
STRIFE SHOULD NOT BE FOUND AMONG YOU BUT A UNITY,
WHICH WOULD MAKE YOU THE ENVY OF ALL THE RACES.

—The Sacred Scrolls

"Panthora rejoices with you." Sir Dravin, the grand champion of the Knights of Valkoria, addressed the assembly before him. "Today these dedicates are brought closer into her presence than any other warrior." His half plate armor, heavily decorated with panther motifs in keeping with tradition, rested beneath a billowing gray cape embroidered with a profile of a golden panther's head. Clean shaven and broad shouldered, Sir Dravin was in the prime of his life and embodied what one would expect in a man who led a noble knightly order. Those whom he addressed shared the same fair skin with a range of platinum blond to brown hair and lighter-colored eyes. More than a few of the men wore beards, with the knights in attendance clean shaven, as was the custom.

The two-story square room in which they stood was large enough to allow all the occupants who'd come from across the Northlands—parents of the dedicates and knights alike—to watch the thirty dedicates standing in front of the altar steps get inducted into the knighthood. Above them, a bronze candelabra dangled from the ceiling. Its forest of white candles blazed with an abundance of light that illuminated all below in great detail. But it was the altar and the platform upon which it sat that held the most attention.

Rowan Cortak stood with the rest of the dedicates. An hour earlier, the sandy-haired, blue-eyed Nordican had been standing atop the keep, looking out over the growing night sky and recollecting everything that had led him to this ceremony. Now he was in the windowless altar room battling his uncomfortable ceremonial vestments and the profuse heat. The coarse, long-sleeved, beige-colored garments had gray emblems of a pouncing panther stitched on their shoulders, thighs, and arms. All the dedicates wore them as a sign of being set apart for the knighthood. But for Rowan, the heavy garb only served to wring even more sweat out of him. He noted all the other dedicates seemed equally uncomfortable.

He focused on the altar in an attempt to calm his nerves. The small mahogany rectangle was polished to a sheen but plain. On each of its corners sat a panther—carved of the same dark wood and holding aloft the polished granite crowning the sacred object. A golden shield emblazoned with the silver symbol of the faith, which also doubled as the knighthood's crest—a profile of a roaring panther's head—stood upon the altar like a miniature sun.

Sir Dravin gestured for the young men to approach the white quartz steps. "Step forward to receive Panthora's blessing and enter this sacred trust of service for humanity's greater good."

The young men's faces twitched with nervous smiles as they slowly drew near the altar platform, forming rows so everyone was allowed a place on the steps. Rowan found a spot on the third step, just a breath away from the grand champion, and within sword strike of the high father beside him. He also found himself near one of the twin smoking bronze braziers that were stationed on either end of the step, permeating the entire area with their incense. Beside each brazier sat a noble-looking gray marble panther.

Rowan hoped none could see his legs shake nor hear his racing heart and erratic breathing. He'd always pictured himself more calm and noble at his induction, not as scared and excited as he'd become. A quick glance to his right, though, showed even his barrel-chested friend Holvar fared the same. Holvar's quick grin reassured him and even brought a smile to his own lips as the high father began the invocation.

Long white tresses hung from the brilliant gold circlet encompassing the high father's wrinkled brow. And while in some ways his appearance brought a comparison to some wizened old tree, the priest's bright blue eyes spoke of great vitality and spirit—more so than what might be found in men even half his age. The high father wore a brown robe tied with a cream-colored sash that accentuated his thin waist. His shoulders were wrapped in a white cloak embroidered with golden panther motifs, the garment affixed over his left breast by a golden brooch crafted in the shape of Panthora's crest.

"Goddess of all that is right with humanity, hear us." The high father's voice was raspy but strong. "As each dedicate steps forth to swear themselves to you, may you take note. May they find honor in your sight, now and always. May they know your truth and walk in it—in this life and the next."

This said, each dedicate turned toward their left, forming a line which would take them one by one to the high father, who'd speak a brief blessing over them. The dedicate would then take a few more steps to Sir Dravin, where they'd kneel before him and the altar behind him. The grand champion would then tap his sword first upon their left and then the right shoulder, speaking the old oath said to have been entrusted to the knighthood by Panthora herself. Rowan watched the pattern repeat itself a handful of times until Tomas, a dedicate before him, rose from his knighting.

"Approach, Rowan Cortak." The high father's invitation gave Rowan a small start, but he quickly recovered. A few steps later he was before the high father, who extended his left hand toward Rowan's head. "Blessed be the human who seeks for Panthora with a whole heart. Blessed be the human who keeps to her ways. Blessed be the human who honors her, for in his doing he too shall be honored." As the high father spoke Rowan felt all the fear, the excitement, and the rest of the emotional tumult he'd been feeling fade away. Even his sweating had stopped as what felt like a cool breeze flowed over him.

In a daze, he made his way to Sir Dravin, dropping on one knee with a bow of his head. He felt the flat of the blade tap him on his left shoulder. "To Panthora and her order you are now forever bound." He felt the flat of the blade kiss his right shoulder. "Arise, to your new life and duty, Sir Rowan Cortak."

Rowan did so, attempting a subtle search for his parents among the crowd as he made his way from the altar in as dignified a manner as possible. He continued through the double doors opposite the altar and found himself in the much cooler hallway that was already filling with an overflow of knights, family, and former dedicates.

Searching through this growing crowd, his face beamed upon catching sight of a woman with a handful of goose feathers mixed with the locks of her dark blond hair. A set of colorful glass beads encircled her neck, helping her brown cloak and the rest of her hide outfit stand out in contrast. Behind her stood a massive man with tanned leather breeches, matching boots, and a chest covered in a simple bearskin vest. He was taller and more muscled than most other Nordicans in attendance, with a red face burned from icy winds and strong summer sun. A few braids stood apart from his brown hair, which scraped the tops of his shoulders.

Pushing through the sea of bodies as respectfully as he could, Rowan eagerly made his way toward them. When he was within arm's reach, they drew together into a group hug.

"We're so proud of you," said Logan Cortak, Rowan's father.

"I've missed you," Rowan managed to squeeze out, once the initial pressure of the embrace had subsided. It felt good being with them again. In some ways this reunion even surpassed his joy at being accepted into the knighthood.

"I've missed you more." Jenna, his mother, kissed his cheek, dropping a few of her tears in the process.

"Come with me." Rowan started down the hallway, directing his parents to follow. "I'll take you to my quarters. It'll be cooler there, and I can finally get out of these robes."

•●•

"So I took it by its tail and spun it around in the air until it howled like a fiend. Then I threw it into the lake. Best fight I've had all year!" Logan chuckled, a sparkle in his eye.

"And your father thinks he's losing some of his strength as he ages," Jenna said, rolling her blue eyes as she joined in her husband's mild mirth.

"Well, it was only a cub," Logan stated. "I couldn't have done it to a full-grown beast cat, not even when I was in my prime."

"Still, it's quite the feat." Rowan gave his father a hearty slap on the back. "If you keep this up you'll be the strongest elder in the tribe's history."

Rowan's quarters were housed in the upper level of the keep. He, like the rest of the dedicates, was given a windowless room to reside in, but with the aid of the candelabra made from deer antlers that rested on the small table beside the bed, most of the darkness had retreated to the far corners of the room. Outside of a plain table, a chest, and the bed upon which the three of them sat, it was simple and clean. He was looking forward to seeing what sort of accommodations he might get next now that he was officially a knight. This small pleasure was just one of many new privileges awaiting him.

As a test of the discipline the new knights would exemplify, dedicates weren't allowed outside the walls encircling the keep except once a year, when they were allotted a brief family visit. Constant training and adherence to the code were the young men's only pursuits. The visits were permitted to ensure they never completely lost touch with the people they were to serve and protect.

Rowan and his family had suffered through this and survived, but it was taxing on them all. Rowan, particularly in the early years, had felt especially alone. The brief visits allowed him to catch up with most of the tribal issues and stay generally informed on anything else of importance. He was also able to watch the passing years touch his parents with a bit of gray, while reminding himself just how blessed he really was to have such a family. Not all of the dedicates could say the same.

"So when do you want to leave for Hosvir?" He peered again into his parents' loving eyes.

"I doubt we'll see you for some time," said Logan. "You're a Knight of Valkoria now, and freshly knighted at that. You have battles to fight and causes to champion."

"No, Father. I'm sure to get a brief rest before I take up any obligations. Who would order a mission so soon for a new knight—and on the very day of their knighting ceremony?"

Rowan didn't like the way his father was looking at him, nor the sigh that escaped his lips. "You're not your own anymore, son. You have responsibilities you must keep and an oath you've sworn to honor. Your commanding officer will probably have a mission for you sooner than you think." Logan's arm encircled Jenna as she hugged her husband tight. "You have a service to perform. A service not only to humanity but to Panthora as well."

"I'm sure they'd make allowances for someone who was just knighted." He attempted an optimistic rebuttal, but it was a fleeting hope; his faith in his previous plans had been dealt a strong blow by his father's logic.

"Maybe for a higher-ranking knight, but not a new one like yourself. I doubt you'll have much of a say in such things for some time."

"Don't worry." He placed his hand on his mother's arm as fresh tears began sliding down her cheeks. Though she tried, she couldn't hide the flow. "I'm sure I'll be able to stay at Hosvir for a while, or at the very least be posted close to it." He didn't really believe this either but still hoped against hope his words would become reality anyway.

• ● •

"What?" Rowan had been summoned to Fronel's room just a few hours after the ceremony. He'd thought the journey knight wanted to offer his congratulations or perhaps give him some news of new quarters becoming available. What he discovered instead was more than unexpected.

"You're to leave Valkoria at once, Sir Rowan." Fronel's eyes fixed on him, a stoic look on his face. He sat behind a large pine desk, its base supported by four great, carved panthers.

On Fronel's right stood a tall shelf lined with various books and scrolls—records that had been kept of all the knights and their activities over the years, of which Fronel was one of the chief chroniclers. A bright lantern hung above them, shedding enough light into the room to write by, but no more than that. Behind the hulking journey knight, next to a narrow, clear glass window, was a small bronze shield emblazoned with the knighthood's crest—a constant reminder of what was now forever before him.

"It is vital you leave as soon as possible." Fronel addressed the young knight with the dry formality that hierarchy often instilled in ranked officers of any institution.

Journey knights were the midrange administrators of the Knights of Valkoria. Lesser knights, like Rowan, took on the tasks they dealt out. The higher-ranked knights were called champions and served as a sort of council and advisory group to the grand champion—whom all served under—acting in conjunction with the priests of Panthora, the other residents of the keep.

"Journey Knight Fronel, I think there's been some type of misunderstanding. I was under the impression I could have some time with my family." Rowan did his best at keeping his face blank. Somewhere amid the excitement of being part of the knighthood and immersed in his training he'd let himself forget just what he was preparing to become. It was like his father said: he wasn't really his own anymore. He had responsibilities . . . duties to his goddess and order.

"Then you were misinformed, Sir Rowan."

"I see. Will this mission take long?"

"It all depends on your ability to see it through."

"May I ask where I'm going then, sir?"

"You've been chosen to go to Taka Lu Lama."

Rowan knew of the place from his training, part of which sought to educate the future knights on the basic geography of the lands beyond the Northlands, where the knighthood and the Nordicans dwelled. Taka Lu Lama was located in a northwestern pocket of Talatheal. It was a jungle that skirted the northern and western edges of the Marshes of Gondad. A strange terrain to be found in a land given to more temperate climates, but one which had existed even before the days of ancient Gondad. It was also a fair distance away—a few weeks at least—if he had his figures right.

"Reports have reached the grand champion from trusted agents in the field, saying there may be elven imperial movement in the area." Fronel's tone flattened, like a sage reciting figures and dates to his pupil, as he rustled through some parchment pages on his desk. "And from what those same agents have been able to gather there seems to be some interest in exploring the jungles of Taka Lu Lama."

"For what purpose?"

"We're not quite clear, but some reports talk of a few drunken elven soldiers mentioning ruins in the jungles along with information there that might help them rebuild their empire." Fronel ceased his scavenging of parchments and looked Rowan full in the face. "We can't let that happen. We all know what happened the last time the elves were allowed an empire."

"Yes, sir." Rowan nodded, thinking on his training and the stories of the ruthless empire the elves of Colloni had crafted millennia before. That empire was what brought about the Imperial Wars, along with the chaos and sorrow that followed in their wake. One incarnation was more than enough for Tralodren to endure.

"You're to travel to Talatheal, find out if the elves really are seeking to rebuild their empire, and retrieve or destroy the information if it exists. A rather simple task, but one of great importance."

"Surely there are others who could do this mission in my place—other knights more worthy, perhaps." Rowan hoped this might be true. Maybe if someone else was he'd be given some lesser assignment. One closer to home.

"You should be honored, Sir Rowan. Not every knight is given their first mission so soon after being knighted. Have you forgotten the way to excel in the knighthood is through service to the Queen of Valkoria?"

"Forgive my outburst." He took in his feet for a moment, trying to get his warring emotions under control.

"Your boat leaves at dawn. Pack what you can and get to the docks. May Panthora be with you."

CHAPTER 3

So let's cast our sights on the Yoan.
And may Perlosa grace our plans.
And may we return as richer men,
hale and healthy too.
But until we do let us make it through
these waves of icy blue.

—Old Nordic sailing song

Rowan woke to the musky odor of the windowless cabin he'd been given on the *Frost Giant*, the ship to which he'd been attached. He'd been sailing in it for close to two weeks. And while he knew they were making progress, out in the open water it was hard gauging such success. Swinging himself out of his hammock, he wiped the sleep from his eyes, shuffled over to a small bucket of cold rainwater, and splashed himself into full awareness. He donned his pants and shirt over his light gray undershirt then strode out of his cabin and into the cool dawn air.

The caravel was a rather simple vessel with three decks and two masts. From these masts flew deep blue sails striped vertically in a shade of brownish red that reminded Rowan of dried blood. The morning's sun shone clear and bright, free from any trespassing clouds, and the Yoan Ocean was in constant motion. Thankfully it rolled with the ship rather than against it. The crew of forty strong Nordicans dominated the seasoned deck and rigging as the waves carried them and their cargo along their southern trek. They were rugged and tempered from their exposure to the open ocean, wearing dense beards, which protected their faces from the ravages of the salt and wind. Simple drab garments covered their leathery skin. Each also carried a sharp knife at his side and a charm of protection from Perlosa's wrath about his neck.

Rowan knew, of course, such trinkets were more superstitious than anything, but many a sailor swore the goddess of the sea would protect them if they possessed such an amulet, which consisted of a sliver of silver bent into a crescent moon. While it wasn't the same as the Silver Crest used by priests and the true followers of Perlosa, by wearing it the sailors believed they could appease Perlosa without outright worshiping her.

He knew from his training—and now personal experience—that the sailors felt they couldn't hold to just one god, instead keeping to their own miniature pantheon: Endarien, Perlosa, and even Rheminas being common deities upon which they often called. The fact that many still held to such beliefs was a sign of how much work those who honored Panthora had before them in bringing even their fellow tribesmen into the truth.

Rowan watched some of the sailors joke with their mates as they devoured their meager rations of salted fish and dried bread, washing it down with flagons of watered-down wine. This would be their sole meal of the entire day unless they caught more fish. The past two days had turned up nothing, which struck Rowan as odd since they were near the outskirts of Arid Land. He'd heard accounts of good fishing to be had in the area. But empty nets or full, they'd probably make sight of the mountain and pine-encrusted land sometime later that week if the winds held and the ocean continued being kind. Something new to look forward to, he supposed—at least for a few hours.

He strode to the port side of the vessel and peered over the railing. He noticed the ocean had changed from the frosty blue green common to the Northlands to a deep, murky green, often found in warmer climates. He was delighted. The change meant he was all the closer to his destination. Another small ray of hope in his overcast thoughts.

A thumping series of footfalls drew his attention toward the captain as he made his way onto the main deck. The rotund man swaggered over with a reassuring smile about his bearded face. "Don't worry, lad. You won't be on these waves forever. Soon enough you'll go ashore, do what you must, and be back to Valkoria in time to enjoy the Harvest Festival." He gave Rowan a hearty slap on the back. "And there'll be plenty of girls looking for a dance with a knight just back from a mission, I'm sure," he added with a knowing wink.

Rowan looked intently into the horizon. He knew the captain only wanted to cheer up a homesick boy, but his efforts met with limited success. "You're right," he half muttered. "It won't be long at all." He feigned a smile.

"That's the spirit! Can't have a Knight of Valkoria getting glum on his first mission, now can we?" The captain gave Rowan a final pat and slowly waddled his way around the deck, stopping every now and again to look over a few crewmen and examine some of the ship's rigging. Rowan renewed his focus on the water. When he did so he noticed a large black stain swimming into view beneath the emerald waves. He knew dolphins and whales frequented the area along with the greater numbers of fish, but the shape of this shadow was unfamiliar.

"What's that?" he called to a sailor coiling some rope nearby.

The sailor finished his task before making his way to Rowan's side. He bent over the railing and stared into the water, where he spotted the dark blotch moving alongside the ship as fast, if not slightly faster, than the *Frost Giant* itself.

"It looks too big to be a dolphin," said Rowan.

The sailor only grunted as he studied the creature. Rowan followed his gaze and caught sight of a tail and a long neck attached to a reptilian head. A head that seemed to be peering up at them as the dark image continually grew closer . . . and larger.

All color faded from the sailor's face as he rose with a shout. "All hands on deck! Midgard off the port bow!" He ran for the back of the ship, where the weapons were stored, shouting even louder as he did so. "All hands—"

He never finished his sentence. A massive force struck the *Frost Giant*'s port side, sending all on deck to their knees and Rowan onto his back. A deep roar erupted from the starboard, followed by a hissing sound as a large cloud of boiling mist engulfed all those on that side of the ship.

Rowan stared transfixed on his side as the screams of sailors and the sound of sizzling meat issued out of the cloud. Men ran out of the mist in terror, covering their tortured eyes with hands of boiling flesh. Their clothing and weapons had melted away in some parts, leaving behind smoking, dripping remnants. Before he could react, the captain grasped him with both hands and yanked him to his feet. "What are you doing standing about? To arms!

"To arms!" again the captain shouted. "All swords at the ready!"

Rowan watched, frozen, as the crew rushed about, dispensing swords in a frenzied fashion. The captain slapped his shoulder, freeing him from paralysis. "Get your sword! We need all the help we can get, and there's none better than a Knight of Valkoria, now is there?" He pushed Rowan—almost throwing him—to his cabin before running into the fray.

Rowan sprinted into his room, where he tore out his leather armor from the chest beneath the hammock. He tossed aside the bracers, pauldrons, and greaves in favor of the cuirass, which he slapped on his torso while also seeking out his sword. He threw the scabbard to the floor as he pulled the blade free with his right hand, finishing the cuirass' buckles with his left.

He could hear the captain shout as he rushed back on deck. "Keep a level head and away from its breath!" Rowan tried making a quick assessment of the growing melee. He'd been trained to do so but had never really fought in a true battle—and never against a linnorm.

Both captain and crew amassed on the starboard deck, which was now pitted and worn as stone after a sandstorm. He watched as the captain raised his broadsword in challenge while peering over the partially eaten railing. Fear squeezed Rowan's heart when the linnorm rose above the waves. Its maw was huge and elongated with thick, deadly teeth poking out of scaly lips like jagged reefs. It had the long neck and sleek body of some great eel or serpent, along with grayish-green scales speckled with a soft blue. Like most Nordicans, Rowan had been raised with tales of dragons and linnorms, but it was quite another thing seeing one in the flesh.

The Midgard's sea-green eyes seemed to mock him, almost dare him to attack, appearing more intelligent than any simple beast. As the moment extended and the world around him seemed to slow, he thought he could actually see the linnorm's delight in attacking them. It was actually enjoying this. And it was on the heels of that sudden revelation that those same haunting eyes smiled back at him with chilling mirth.

"Perlosa, be merciful," the captain stammered before hurrying and joining the rest of the chaos on the deck. Even as they managed to flee the Midgard's attack, many of the crew quickly jumped back from the eroded railing before an enormous webbed claw knocked them overboard.

"Change our heading due east!" the captain bellowed.

Another shudder ran through the side of the ship, sending water crashing up and over the vessel. The force of the wave knocked the crewmen about—the captain among them—but many of them managed to grab on to rigging or railings, preventing them from being washed overboard. Rowan would have fallen to the deck himself if not for the grace of Panthora, which somehow kept his feet in place. While the sailors regained their footing and attempted to lay in the new course, the Midgard remained fixed in its position, looming over the deck. Under such a dreadful presence all on board scattered like mice before a cat.

"Where's that boy knight?" the captain huffed while righting himself. The question was a cold slap across Rowan's face and made him blush with shame. He'd been standing there the whole time, doing nothing to help his fellow Nordicans—fellow humans—in their time of need. He was a knight now and needed to do better.

He raised his sword and charged into the fray, his eyes on the Midgard's neck towering above the starboard railing of the ship. As he approached, a sailor took a swing and cut deep into the linnorm's flesh, birthing a thin, red river. Those who saw it began to rejoice. But even as the crew took some courage from the act, a crimson burst rained across the deck. So quick was the occurrence many turned their heads to and fro in confusion before realizing the Midgard had struck.

The bold crewman who'd wounded the linnorm was now absent from their midst. A heartbeat later all grasped his fate as they spied a set of helpless feet dangling between the Midgard's teeth. These too vanished with the backward flip of its head that helped its meal slide down its throat. The crew grew ashen and still. Rowan stopped in his tracks, his momentary bravery failing.

The captain urged Rowan on. "Have at him!"

"What can I do against such a beast?" Rowan asked himself just as much as the captain.

"You're a Knight of Valkoria," the captain snapped back. "You're supposed to be better than ten strong men."

Another hiss crackled through the air. More screams arose from the men as the Midgard's acidic breath claimed more lives. Rowan could smell the searing fumes—like burned meat—and feel traces of the linnorm's breath gnawing at his own face and hands, stinging his eyes and making his scalp itch and tingle. He closed his eyes, shutting out the chaos around him. But it wasn't going to get any easier the longer he stood in place.

Taking a deep breath, he raised his sword with a war cry and charged. The linnorm lunged at this new threat, attempting to swallow the young knight whole, as it had its previous attacker. He saw the jaws rush for him. He anticipated the strike and somersaulted low and to the right as the mouth snapped with an echoing clap inches away from his side.

Returning to his feet, he swung his blade and brought it down upon the linnorm's head. He managed to sever a vein, causing a spout of blood to erupt from the wound. The cheers of his fellow Nordicans increased his nerve, allowing him to delve into reserves of courage he never knew he had.

The Midgard howled in pain and reared its head just as Rowan attempted a second blow. The attack fell short as the linnorm raised its head and neck out of range. Rowan could no longer reach the Midgard, but some other crew members, who had now rushed forward, were within striking distance. Their weapons birthed new wounds, frustrating the creature. Rowan quickly joined their efforts, and soon blood flowed freely from the linnorm's neck and head. The crew's combined efforts had severely weakened it. All that was needed was one more solid strike.

Rowan swung in a wild, slashing arc so fiercely that he lost his footing on the blood-coated deck and fell with a wet thud. Despite this, the linnorm suddenly sank into the water with a cascading splash of foam and watery blood, flooding the deck and rocking the vessel. No one dared breathe. When they were convinced the menace had finally gone, the men all gave a great shout while Rowan bent his knee in thanks to Panthora. After his prayers, he looked around the vessel, trying to survey the damage. Scattered about the deck were the wounded, lying on their backs like freshly caught fish. They stared blindly into the sky as their flesh slowly bubbled like a simmering stew.

The captain hollered orders with his clean sword and unmarred flesh plain for all to see. As he shouted, sailors scurried about at different tasks, trying to salvage the ship and keep it seaworthy. Rigging was replaced and pieces of wood from below deck were brought up and nailed into the gaps. Others set about the gruesome task of swabbing the now purplish blood and still smoldering acid from the deck, which had collected into a few small puddles. The rest worked on retrieving the handful of sailors who had been swept overboard.

As he took in the frenzied aftermath, Rowan heard the deep moaning of a wounded crewman near his foot. The man's eyes and nose had melted like lard in a fire, leaving behind an unsettling visage. The crewman's hand clenched at the air as if grasping for the remains of his life. Rowan could glimpse bone and muscle beneath the ruined flesh; tangled cobwebs of veins fell and rose like roots over the sinewy hills of his cheeks and neck.

The fallen sailor grabbed on to Rowan's foot with a death grip. "Kill me," he spat out from bloody lips. Rowan looked on the wreck of the man, his mind torn between respect for human life, as the knighthood taught, and the honor of a mercy killing, embraced by Nordicans in dire situations. But what was his duty? Where was his allegiance? He wasn't a Nordican like these were, at least not anymore. He was Panthora's and she was his. But weren't these still humans—his very own people even . . . And didn't he owe them some basic duties as well? He wasn't ready for this. Yet something in him told him he *was* ready, and this was as prepared as he'd ever be.

He shook his foot free from the dying man's grasp and briskly fled to his cabin. He needed to be away from the moans of the dying, and the stench of acid and blood. Let another deal with the matter. He was sure they'd make the right choice. Right now he just needed to think.

CHAPTER 4

THE SMALLEST OF SPARKS CAN BE STOKED
INTO THE GREATEST OF FIRES.

—The Solarium

Dugan gritted his teeth as the cestus' sharp sting plowed fresh rows across his bruised cheek. Above his left eye a fresh cut trickled down his face, a crimson creek mingling with his streaming sweat to burn and blur his vision. Except for the breechcloth he was naked. The two wide flaps of dark brown fabric covered most of his thighs like a skirt, descending about a hand's breadth from the knee. His cell was spartan and small, windowless with a lone torch for light and an imposing door with a small viewing window he noticed was getting some good use.

"You belong to Gilthanius now," the elf before him said in accented Telboros. "And that means you'll have to perform *better* than expected if you want to keep your life." The remark was followed by another punch to the face.

Dugan was chained to the wall behind him. The links connected to the chafing shackles on his ankles and wrists allowed him some slack, but that slack was made much shorter by the two elven men holding him at each wrist. The elves were members of the guard assigned to keep order, protect, and maintain the arena. As such, each wore a leather cuirass with matching metal bracers and greaves, while their captain, an elf named Balus, had opted for a simple brown tunic, pants, and boots.

The middle-aged, black-haired Balus was taking delight in Dugan's beating, having donned his spiked gloves with dark glee when he and the guards with him first entered Dugan's cell. At his arrival, Balus had beaten Dugan worse than a stubborn mule. Dugan's tan face was now a massive patchwork of bruised and broken flesh. His body was splattered with blood and more bruises. But even though his frame had been nearly broken and his blond, shoulder-length hair was matted with gore and sweat, his green eyes still held a defiant glare.

Elves closely resembled Telborians in physical appearance, save for their pointed ears and inability to grow facial hair. Each had dark brown to dark blond hair and green, brown, or blue eyes. If they covered their ears, they could easily pass for humans. Growing up, Dugan had heard old stories about how there might be more than just one race of elves—like there was more than one race of humans. If that were true, neither he nor those who told him such tales had ever seen them. Probably for the best, given his experience with the Elyellium.

"And so you won't forget your place," Balus continued, cruelly eyeing Dugan, "we're going to give you a small reminder." The comment earned him a round of laughter from the elves beside him.

It was then he noticed the smell of searing metal. It grew more intense as Balus stepped away and was replaced by a stooped elf who smiled at Dugan with an almost toothless maw. He'd the look of one who lived his life close to a forge. He was covered in a light dusting of soot with wrinkles that had transformed into grimy black lines. He also held something else, but Dugan couldn't see it clearly. The two guards pulled him into a rigid stance.

A few heartbeats later, he felt the pain of another blow. The sound of searing flesh filled the room. The elderly elf smiled as the screaming agony of a blistering rod jabbed into Dugan's left shoulder, clawing its way into his skin and burning deep into muscle. He cried out in fury. In his agonized struggles he nearly succeeded at freeing himself. Balus saw this and threw a fist at Dugan's jaw, but Dugan jerked his head to one side. Instead of making impact with his ruined cheek, the elf's hand collided with the stone wall behind him with an audible crunch.

"Tripton's bow!" Balus howled, trying to open his broken hand. "I'll see to it you're treated worse than the *hounds*!" He stormed out of the cell, leaving Dugan to ponder the dizzying pain swirling about his head. The bent old elf turned slowly, inspecting the brand he'd just placed. Once satisfied, he too departed.

This left Dugan alone with the two guards, who still held him fast at the wrists. They let go at the same time, both making a sprint for the sturdy oaken cell door. He let out a howl of anger and pain as he lunged after them, but was stopped by the sudden jerk of his chains before they slammed the door and barred it with a drop of a heavy iron latch.

The iron fetters and chains groaned against Dugan's pulls for release. Laughing, the two guards looked in again through the viewing window at the helpless animal in his cage. So easy to control. So easy to maintain . . . from behind closed doors. Dugan cringed in pain as he stretched his right hand over to delicately inspect the branding. Examining his fingers, he noted how they were coated with a sticky brown liquid.

He drew in a deep breath, but quickly bent over in pain and spasms as he began to cough. This fit lasted for a good while. When it subsided, he noticed a small puddle of blood had chilled on the cobblestone between his feet. The immediate danger having passed, his adrenaline started to wear off, and the full gravity of his beating was revealed in ever greater detail with each passing heartbeat.

Licking his split, bloodstained lips, Dugan whispered, "I won't be broken." Raising his voice, he repeated, "I won't be broken." Then, snarling with the rising rage inside him, he growled, "I'll have my revenge!" To add strength to his words, he hit himself hard on his burned shoulder. The pain was like lightning coursing through his being, causing him to scream as blackness overtook him.

• • •

As he came to, light and sound rushed into Dugan's waking mind like a raging river. He became aware of the thunderous cheering and shouts of the elves in the stands above, the sun glaring down at him, and the white sand surrounding him. Behind him he could feel the hard, gray stone of the arena's inner wall. The oval-shaped barrier encased the only world he'd come to know besides his cell and the twisted passages worming their way under the sandy ground where he sat.

"Dugan?" A voice flitted into his consciousness. A medium-brown face came into his field of vision. This was Laka, a Celetor with whom he'd been fighting for the better part of five years. Laka's amber eyes held some concern, which Dugan rapidly realized was for him.

"You all right?" Laka put a hand on Dugan's shoulder. He spoke Telboros, the chosen language of many of the other gladiators, though they were a mix of various races. Dugan tried to move but stopped as a pain flashed in the back of his skull. "Whoa, there," Laka cautioned. "You hit the wall pretty hard."

It was then that memory returned. He'd been fighting with Laka and four other gladiators against some ogres. Three, if he wasn't mistaken. They'd put up quite a fight—Dugan being thrown against the wall by the final one before he finished the ogre off. In truth, it was a small miracle he wasn't more wounded than he was. The small cuts and bruises he'd received in the fight were minor, and even the banging his head had taken didn't seem too great an injury. Soon enough, they'd mend, and join the myriad of scars, bite marks, and various other wounds crisscrossing his body.

Today's games were for the glory of Founding Day, the day the Elyellium Empire was said to have been birthed by the great Aerotripton. Why they celebrated the formation of an empire when they professed to be a republic, Dugan didn't know. All that mattered was that the twenty-second day of Endaris was an important day for the elves, which called for games—and for Dugan and the rest of the gladiators to shed blood.

"They dead?" Dugan, by Laka's aid, rose to his feet.

"Yeah." Laka let him go once he was certain he could stand. "Remind me not to get on your bad side." Like Dugan, he wore chain mail on his left arm—a sleeve attached to a segmented pauldron held in place by a thick leather strap lashed diagonally down his chest and back. A skirt crafted of metal-studded leather strips swayed from his belt, with a set of leather boots fitted with bronze greaves completing the rest of his attire.

"How you holding up?" Dugan noticed the cuts and scrapes across Laka's frame, focusing on a small but grim gash on his left thigh.

"I've had worse." The Celetor smiled.

"The day isn't over yet." Dugan took stock of the carnage around him.

Scattered like shards of pottery lay the other four gladiators who'd been fighting with them just moments ago. Now they watered the sand with their blood while their spirits departed for Mortis. In some ways Dugan almost envied them. He'd be a liar if he said he hadn't had thoughts of joining them and all the others who'd fallen before them once he got a sword in hand. But then when he did it just didn't feel right. In time he understood what he really wanted was something more than just release from this place. He wanted satisfaction, revenge before departing. But the longer he lived, the more he realized just how elusive that satisfaction had become.

Each of the fallen gladiators wore the same armor as Dugan and Laka down to the identical round shields emblazoned with the eagle crest of Colloni—the very same mark burned into each of the gladiators' left shoulders. Two of them were Telborian, one an elf, and the other another Celetor, although one who hailed from a different region than Laka, as evidenced by his dark brown skin and short curly hair. Laka wore his straight black locks in a more shaggy mass about his head.

Sprawled amid the wreck of life were the three ogres they'd just killed. Ogres always reminded him of large apes, which sometimes found their way into the arena as well, along with a whole host of beasts. Their seven-foot frames, well-muscled bodies, and black, hairy hides only added to this resemblance. While their light brown flesh and faces held some similarities to apes, they were more human than anything else, save for their pointed ears and sharp canine teeth. Dugan had seen ogres with darker skin and brown hair and various mixtures in between, but all were deadly in combat—even more so with chain mail shirts, long swords, and shields, as these three had.

"Keep your eyes on the gates," Dugan instructed Laka while seeing if there was anything he could salvage from the dead. Wiping sweat from his eyes and forehead, he ignored the great crowds around him shouting and screaming in alternating breaths for both his death and his becoming the instrument of another's. He'd learned to push such noise far from him, focusing on the most important thing facing him each time he entered the arena: survival.

"What do you think it'll be this time?" Laka adjusted his grip on his shield and gladius. "I think they're running low on ogres."

"Just something more to kill," Dugan said, retrieving two gladii from the fallen.

"Always with your humor." Laka again sought to make merry between them. It was the Celetor's way—like many before him—trying to find something bright in the dark world that had ensnared them. Dugan knew better. He'd seen more than a score of men like Laka come and go since being forced to fight for the elves' amusement. Soon enough Laka would be dead. Just like he would.

"They should be announcing it soon." Dugan tossed Laka one of the blades, keeping the other to add to the one that waited alongside his shield—both of which he'd dropped upon impact with the arena wall. After retrieving them, Dugan shoved the second blade in his belt and spied out the emperor's box on his right.

Stationed above the wall's oval curve, the emperor's special viewing area was a sight to behold. Made of carved white marble with twin elven soldiers doubling as columns holding up the overhanging roof, it was adorned with golden-lipped ledges over which a red silk banner flowed. Upon the banner was the crest of the great city of Remolos, capital of the Elven Republic of Colloni: a golden eagle with spread wings and white nimbus behind its right-turned head.

In his early years Dugan had nursed a fantasy of leaping to ascend the banner and laying waste to the emperor and his followers before his own demise. But it was a fool's fantasy. The inner arena walls were twenty feet tall—high enough to prohibit anything from coming up while keeping those above them close enough to see all the action. Wisely, the banner was also only three feet in length, keeping any seeking its use as leverage out of reach.

And so it was that he and many like him found themselves contained by the gray granite oval stretching a thousand feet between its concave curves. This was the extent of their world, where even the republic's most common rank and file could stare down at them from above—much farther away than their betters, on the third tier of seats with the women, but looking down at them nonetheless.

"I'm betting it's a horde of buxom women wearing nothing but a smile wanting to congratulate us on a fight well fought." Laka's voice pulled Dugan from his thoughts.

"That wouldn't be much of a show," said Dugan.

"Speak for yourself." Laka smirked.

Dugan glanced up at the box opposite the emperor's. There sat Gilthanius, the manager of the arena, who made it a point to literally beat it into all the gladiators who found themselves captive that he was their master, and they the expendable entertainment. For the first two years in the arena, Dugan had transposed Gilthanius' face onto every one of his opponents, alternating it with Balus' from time to time, until he realized just how little good it did him.

Gilthanius' box was a bit more subdued when compared to the emperor's: a polished granite series of columns and a ledge behind which he sat with a collection of arena guards and various favored persons. Here too the same red silk banner, displaying the crest of Colloni, was draped. Dugan watched the two trumpet players step forth to the edge of Gilthanius' box, ready to blare out the notes all gladiators quickly learned to dread.

A new round of cheers erupted from the bloodthirsty crowd.

"Keep your eyes on the gates!" Dugan joined Laka in darting his eyes back and forth among the eight visible gates built into the arena's wall. There was a gate under Gilthanius' box, one under the emperor's box, and three on each of the longer stretches of wall between them. There were also many more hidden under the sand and in some interesting places one wouldn't think to look—all to add more spectacle—but the main eight were the ones from which much of the action stemmed.

"Here it comes." Laka jabbed his sword toward the rising portcullis under the emperor's box. And no sooner had it opened than a group of figures emerged into the sunlight.

"Lizardmen." Dugan clenched his jaw as the small company hurried toward them. Unlike the two gladiators, the bipedal reptilian humanoids wore only breechcloths and carried painful-looking spiked clubs. "I count six."

"An even split then." Laka drew closer to Dugan.

"Back to back until we can break away." They did just that, backing up to each other while still allowing room for whatever might be needed when swords started swinging.

"You think you're up for this?" Laka didn't take his eyes from the growling alligator-like jaws salivating at the prospect of ripping into his flesh. "That ogre *did* hit you pretty hard."

"We'll find out soon enough." Dugan made a quick study of his foes, noting their sharp, clawed feet and hands and strong, swinging tails that could pound him back against the wall as surely as any ogre's fist.

"I still think the women would have been a better choice."

Dugan didn't blame Laka. Lizardmen weren't the easiest of opponents. No one had really been able to figure out their language, and so they just named them for how they looked rather than anything else. They were thought to be savages, so it amused the masses to have them take the role opposite the more civilized warriors Dugan and Laka supposedly represented. At least they weren't as imposing as the ogres—this batch of lizardmen were only a few fingers above six feet, though Dugan had seen some others closer to seven in times past.

The lizardmen rushed forward, acting as one. Dugan merely stood his ground, waiting for the distance to dwindle. The closer the lizardmen got, the stronger their stench became: a dank, musty smell reminding him of snakes and other reptiles. To the crowds it might have seemed an exciting battle, but to Dugan it was nothing less than another part of the soul-wearying drudgery that had become his life. After five years of repeating the process—emerging from his cell to slay for the masses, then returning to his cage once again—he knew this was the best it would ever get. No matter how often he prayed for relief, if anything was going to change, it would need to come through him and him alone—if he didn't wind up in Mortis first.

Laka struck first, blocking the downward arc of one of the nearest lizardmen's clubs with his shield and then slicing the arm holding it. Seeing that first blood was drawn by the gladiators, the crowd erupted with a jubilant shout.

Together the lizardmen encircled them, making their job easier, as each now faced the three they'd planned for: one to the front and one on each flank. Dugan thrust his gladius at the center lizardman, even as the one on his left tried denting Dugan's shield with his club. His attack was thwarted by the other lizardman's parry, causing Dugan to contend with a series of back-and-forth exchanges between his three attackers, resulting in a stalemate of sorts.

Laka was having better success, attacking low and nipping at his opponents' thighs and waists—drawing both blood and the crowd's approval in the process. And he would have continued such progress if it wasn't for the club that whacked him across the face. The blow was so strong it shoved him back into Dugan, leaving the Celetor struggling for footing and clear vision. But Laka was far from defeated. Gritting his throbbing teeth, he pressed through the defenses of the lizardman who struck him, slicing deep into the creature's entrails.

Again the crowd roared.

Dugan was able to find his opening in a similar manner, jabbing his gladius through the heart of the lizardman at his right before blocking the two attacks from his flank and center with sword and shield. Laka managed to wound the lizardman to his left, but took another smashing blow from a spiked club that knocked him to his knees.

Dugan registered this in the blinks between attacks as he worked himself between his two lizardmen, stabbing the one on his left through the heart before spinning around to cross weapons with the one remaining. A brief series of strikes and counterstrikes were exchanged before he found his opening and severed his remaining opponent's head from his neck.

The crowd went wild.

Dugan spun on his heel, ready for what lay behind him. Immediately, he saw Laka's bloody body prone on the sand, being pounded like some dead mule by the remaining two lizardmen. Without thinking he took his gladius like a spear and chucked it at the lizardman on his right. The blade sailed clear through the creature's chest, jabbing out through the other side. Staggering back and choking, he gave a garbled snarl before falling to his side.

Upon seeing his comrade's fate, the remaining lizardman stopped his pounding of the long-dead Celetor and fixed his sights on Dugan. Removing his shield, Dugan took hold of it as a discus and stood his ground as the lizardman rushed at him with an animalistic cry. He didn't get more than a few steps before Dugan launched the shield straight for him. The lizardman raised his club, attempting to swat it down. This was only part of Dugan's plan. He used the moment of distraction to move in and, reaching under the club, lay hold of the lizardman's hand to break his wrist with a crunching snap.

The club was dropped as Dugan shoved back the same arm, and set his sights on the creature's neck, wrapping his arm around it and pulling with all his might. The lizardman writhed and fought against his efforts but grew weaker and slower as Dugan held fast.

The crowd was brought to its feet.

Dugan gritted his teeth and fought to increase his stranglehold with arms burning with exhaustion. Soon enough the lizardman fell into a slumber-like stillness, allowing Dugan to whip out the extra gladius in his belt and hack off his head.

When his grisly work was finished, the loud blast of horns pulled his attention back to Gilthanius' box. The new set of notes indicated the day of battle was now at an end. Another day of slipping closer and closer into being little more than a common animal trained to entertain his masters. Even though such battles weren't a daily occurrence, he'd be out here soon enough for another elven holiday or event under the hot sun and the bloodthirsty crowds who'd just as quickly cheer his own death as his slaying of another.

Dugan sought out Laka; the Celetor was now more bloody pulp than human. He reckoned Laka died quickly, at least. Dugan wondered if he'd be just as fortunate when his time came. All of those who entered the arena had been trained well and were quite practiced, but in the end it would never be enough. How soon would it be before he joined Laka? How long until he was too old or too slow to stop that one attack that got past his defenses and sent him to the sands just like Laka . . . or even worse?

Catching movement out of the corner of his eye, he took note of the elven slaves sent to cart off the dead making their way inside the arena from the side gates. Dressed in the simplest of tunics and sandals, they were the lowest of the elven rank: Elyellium who had been brought into subjection. But even those, save for a few exceptions, weren't forced into the life of a gladiator, the lowest form of existence on Colloni. The wooden carts they manned were no more than a flat surface fixed between two wheels with two long poles for a man to pull. There was no need for opulence. The dead would be piled on top and dumped in a mass grave—forgotten just as quickly as they were once heralded by the masses.

The procession continued as a small company of guards entered the arena. These ensured the surviving gladiators were disarmed and escorted to their cells or the physicians, whichever might be needed. The old pattern played out before him. For a moment, he felt the heft of the sword in his hand and wondered if he might be strong enough to find some solace in its embrace. He'd been able to hold the blackest of this depression at bay with thoughts of escape and fantasies of revenge, but that would only help him for a little longer, and he knew it.

"Drop the weapon," a guard ordered as he and the nine others approached. The sun shimmered off the nose guards of their open-faced helmets. Each sported a gladius, a few more also having a crossbow at the ready.

Dugan stood still.

"I said, drop it." Dugan ignored him, looking up at Gilthanius' box once more. He could now see Balus leaning over the ledge with a familiar dark sparkle in his eyes. His flowing red cape and gold-trimmed white tunic under his armor were an attempt to look dignified. Dugan wasn't buying it.

"Did that ogre's punch clog your ears?" Balus leered like some poor imitation of a god. "Maybe some lashes will help unclog them."

Something had to change.

"Surrender your weapon or—" The guard never finished his ultimatum. Before he could react, Dugan had launched his gladius up and toward Balus. The weapon hit home in the surprised captain's chest with enough impact to not only dig a good way past his leather cuirass but into his rib cage and beyond. A shocked hush descended upon the crowd as Balus' form crumpled and toppled over the edge of the box, landing in the sand with a muffled thud.

The guards quickly recovered from the shock and ran to their captain, who remained motionless. "He's dead," one of them announced, turning Balus' body on its back for further evidence. Murmuring sparked into crackling life across the stands, encircling the arena in a rising verbal blaze as Gilthanius appeared at the box's ledge. His dark green toga was a simple contrast to his gold-trimmed white tunic but complemented the golden diadem resting on his short black hair.

"Take him alive!" Gilthanius shouted.

His time had come. If he didn't act now, he'd never get this close again. As the guards sought to surround him, Dugan focused on Gilthanius' box and the two carts nearby. Breaking into a sprint, he pressed past the guards, aiming for two slaves carrying the corpse of a Telborian gladiator between them. They dropped the body and fell back at Dugan's approach.

Not stopping for anything, Dugan fixed his eyes on the red banner that had always been out of reach as he took to the cart beside the one already piled with a good load of corpses. Empty and unattended, it had tipped itself into the sands, leaving the poles rising into the air. Using it as a ramp, Dugan ran all the way to the cart's end before taking a massive leap as the cart tipped in the other direction under his added weight.

The crowd watched, collectively holding their breath as Dugan sailed through the air, within reach of the silken banner, which he grasped with a growl. The crowd exploded with noise—some favoring, some disapproving.

He could hear the orders from above mingling with the fleeing feet of those who had joined Gilthanius for the day's entertainment. Using all the strength in his arms, Dugan shimmied up the banner to the ledge and then pulled himself up to look over it with a small grunt. He found himself staring into a series of sword points belonging to the guards who'd gathered around him. Behind them were Gilthanius and a few brave guests. He was so close. Just a little bit more, and he could die a satisfied man.

"It's your choice." Gilthanius put on a brave face, but Dugan could see the trembling hand at his side clear enough. "The guards can run you through, or you can surrender."

He made an effort to lift himself over the ledge and received a fast series of jabs from a few of the swords. Somehow he managed to avoid them unharmed. Just as he began to feel a sense of optimism, his right shoulder exploded in pain as a crossbow bolt found its way into his back and brought him to a halt. This was followed by another, and another grunt as he tried keeping himself on the ledge, all the while feeling the strength drain from his back and shoulders.

His right hand slipped, bringing all his weight to bear on his left. Gritting his teeth against the movement that had almost dislocated his shoulder, Dugan dared one more glare over the ledge. The next moment he fell, toppling to the sand a few feet from Balus but facing the opposite direction, toward the emperor's box. The crossbow bolts in his back had broken their shafts in his fall but were still in him, and had worked themselves deeper in the process. A moment later he was surrounded by sneering guards and their accusing sword points.

"What's the verdict?" one of the guards asked another. Dugan knew full well what would be coming next. The emperor would pass judgment on him for his actions, as he did on all who faced one-on-one combat. Sometimes a white flag would be thrust forth, indicating mercy should be extended. But at other times—

"Black flag," the guard said with a satisfied smile. "You know what that means."

"Crucifixion." Another guard glared down at the Telborian. "Better than you deserve." This was followed by a sharp kick to his head, sending him into unconsciousness.

CHAPTER 5

REVENGE IS LIKE SPOILED MEAT SLATHERED
WITH AN INTOXICATING SAUCE.
IT MIGHT TASTE GOOD AT FIRST BUT CAN
WIND UP KILLING YOU IN THE END.

—Bolin Miders, Telborian philosopher
(5340 BV–5231 BV)

Dugan awoke in a room he thought he'd never see again: the cell where Balus had first welcomed him into service. It had aged some, like the rest of the inner workings of the arena, and still reeked of old blood, rust, and sweat, but it was the same cell he'd first been taken to half a decade earlier. The biting shackles bound him to the wall with just enough slack for him to find some rest on the floor—which was where he presently resided—but never enough to allow him to come close to the door. Gods knew how he'd tried, though.

At least this time they hadn't bound him about the ankles. And he could take some comfort in knowing Balus wouldn't be making a return appearance. But it was a small comfort, knowing what awaited him in the morning. As he stood, he was pleased to note they'd let him keep his boots. The bronze greaves attached to the tall leather would help keep his feet warm, but the breechcloth would be scant defense against the damp cell's chill.

The pain in his shoulder was now just a dull ache. He thought he could make out the feeling of stitches lining the holes the bolts had left in him. Strange that they'd taken the time to patch him up, but he wasn't going to complain. They could have left the tips in him until morning. Another small comfort.

Thinking on how he'd got to this point, Dugan's attention turned to the stylized spread eagle seared into his left shoulder. The branding, now just a pink, puckered mark, remained a constant reminder of all he'd lost. The irony that this was his final resting place before his execution wasn't lost on him. He wouldn't be surprised if Gilthanius wanted to remind him one final time who was the master of whom.

A small torch on the opposite wall, near the door, provided the only light. It wasn't much, but there wasn't much to be seen. He was alone with his thoughts and the imaginings of what was soon to come. He could see it quite clearly, having borne witness to it more than once—the horrid display of public execution to which even the most hardened of criminals feared being sentenced.

In the middle of the arena a large hill would be raised up, using the many hidden trapdoors under the sand. Atop this hill would be enough room to display several people as they were hung on the crosses for the crowd's entertainment and admonishment. The naked victims would hang until dead, slowly turning like meat on a spit by means of another clever device built into the hill. All—no matter where they sat—would see the agony and full extent of their pain, while some bet on how long they could hold out for added sport. A hard end to a hard life.

When he was five years old, Dugan's parents had been murdered, and his village had been razed to the ground by invading elven forces. A few weeks later, he found himself in the work yard of a minor noble, dyeing wool at one of his factories. Why the elves attacked, he never knew. He'd lived in a very secluded fishing community on the western coast of Colloni. While predominantly Elyelmic, a good mix of Telborians called it home as well. Because of this racial mix, Dugan had long put away thoughts that the attack was an effort at ridding Colloni of humans. As the years dragged on, he simply gave up trying to figure out what *had* motivated them. There wasn't any benefit in such ponderings, only old wounds to agitate. And he had more than enough to contend with as it was.

When the minor noble was murdered by some rival political faction, the factory was reorganized. A few prominent slaves noted Dugan's strength and size, for he'd grown into a very strong man over the thirteen years he'd been there. It didn't take those interested in him long to acquire him. This took him to Gilthanius, a rich and influential elf who'd come to be one of a handful of men who helped keep the arena stocked with various spectacles and sport. It was a business that constantly required fresh acquisitions to make it both popular and profitable.

Just as he was recalling his first introduction to the elf, the door opened and Gilthanius himself strode inside, surrounded by skittish guards. "You put on quite a show today," he said in Telboros. "I don't think there's been a Founding Day celebration like it. Pity it had to end the way it did but—"

"You'd be with him too if you weren't hiding behind your men."

As one, each guard's hand went for their sword. "Rest easy," Gilthanius assured them. "He's more bark than bite now, aren't you, Dugan?"

"Why don't you come closer and see?"

"It seems you tried that once already. And I don't recall it working as well as you had hoped. However, your antics did help us find some weak spots in our security, which I'll have to pass on to the new captain, since you removed Balus from his post.

"He warned me about you, you know," Gilthanius continued. "Balus said you'd be a hard one to break and pushed for me to have you be one of the rank-and-file warriors. But I thought that extra fire would prove more profitable. And I was right." If Dugan's eyes had been spears, Gilthanius would have been pinned to the wall behind him.

Gilthanius searched over the bruises and scabs that covered Dugan's healing body. "I see you made a satisfactory recovery. Then again, you *are* pretty hardheaded." The elf smiled. "But I could have told the physicians that. I was against it, but they insisted they stitch up your wounds. They said it would make you last longer tomorrow, and I want to get as much gold out of you as I can."

"I got close to you before." Dugan's voice was rough. "I can do it again."

"I don't think so." He called Dugan's bluff. "But I will have a good seat. As will the emperor, who was impressed with my bravery in the situation." Gilthanius again flashed some teeth. "You've actually helped my standing with him. And your crucifixion tomorrow will make me richer still." He sneered. "I thought it only right to thank you in person." The sarcasm was a knife he enjoyed twisting in Dugan's gut. "If not for your actions today, I wouldn't be on my way to even greater riches and glory." He paused, a gleam in his eye.

"I'd wish you a fair slumber, but then I'd be lying. I will say that I've opted for straps with the nails—to help keep you up longer. I'm told they prolong the agony by at least a few hours. I'll be eager to see *how* long exactly. Until then, I have a party to attend. It seems my bravery is being honored." Gilthanius made his way for the door, adding, "So I guess that means you've served your master well. The perfect slave in the end. Maybe Balus was wrong after all."

The guards slammed the door behind Gilthanius, being sure to latch it as loudly as possible. Dugan pressed for the door, straining the chains and his fresh stitches, but to no avail. Relinquishing his rage, he slid down the wall and rested on the cold floor, lost in depressed silence, until a small, masculine voice filled his thoughts.

Dugan.

He looked around in bewilderment. No one had entered his cell or was looking through the small barred window on the door.

Dugan. This time the voice was louder, but still calm and seductive.

"Show yourself." Dugan leapt to his feet. He was well past the point where he'd play the fool for any games the guards or Gilthanius might have invented for his final hours.

Peace. I mean you no harm. The voice seemed clearer now.

"Then show yourself!" The gladiator scanned the empty room. His eyes saw no movement in the flickering light.

Look to the flame.

The torch by the door suddenly changed from a dirty yellow to a copper flame that shot up a good three feet, licking the ceiling.

I've heard your prayer, Dugan, and have decided to aid you . . . personally. The last word of the sentence slithered around his thoughts.

"Who are you?" He stared at the copper fire.

Rheminas. The flame lowered itself only slightly, turning a more brilliant copper, illuminating the entire room in what could have been pure sunlight.

"I've prayed for years and *now* you show up?" Dugan searched the room again in growing frustration. "They're going to crucify me tomorrow. What good can you do me now?"

There's a mighty fire already at work in you. I just need to stoke it to greater heights.

The torch's flame leapt from its roost, landing on the ground like a gelatinous mass. Slithering toward the gladiator, it wound itself around his leg and coiled—twirling up the muscular appendage rapidly. Dugan winced and waited for the flame to singe his skin, but it never did. There wasn't even the sensation of its touch, or a spark across his skin, as it continued its coiled climb. He felt his heart clench as the flame twisted itself around his arm, aiming for the brand on his shoulder. As it did it began taking on a more literal serpentine form.

I'll give you the revenge you seek. The copper serpent peered straight into Dugan's face. *You'll destroy this elven owner of yours—along with anyone else who should cross your path—and win your freedom as you desire.*

"Nothing's free." He stared back unflinching at the fiery snake. Its tiny scales and glowing red eyes made it seem all the more lifelike. "What will your *favor* cost me?"

Your soul.

Dugan kept his face an expressionless mask. "So when I die, what then?"

You'll pass into my realm.

Though he wanted to finish what he'd started with Balus this afternoon more than anything in the world, Dugan actually wanted a better afterlife, too. Something to make up for the sad excuse of a life he was currently enduring. He wasn't a priest or sage; his understanding of the realms beyond was only a mass of fragmented sparks in a great darkness at best. He'd gathered, from a few smatterings of myths and tales he'd heard over his years, that Helii, the realm where Rheminas ruled, was a place where eternal fires blossomed like weeds, scorching all who passed their way. It was far from anything he'd want to call home for the rest of his eternal existence.

"That's not much of a bargain."

You'll have an afterlife befitting any brave warrior, I assure you. Better than anything you've had here . . . and what's awaiting you tomorrow.

Dugan held his tongue.

I don't plan on waiting long for an answer. Your executioners won't show you any more mercy, let me assure you.

When he closed his eyes, he felt the flame slide from his shoulder, encircling his massive chest. The scales were smooth as velvet and as warm as a beam of sunlight upon his skin.

Imagine what you could do if finally let off your leash, Rheminas whispered. *Imagine the delight in seeing that weak elf groveling before you . . . begging for his life, with you the one in power over him—the lord of his life and death.*

Blood began racing through his temples as Dugan envisioned the scene. He'd wanted to run Gilthanius through very slowly, very painfully; he wanted to look into his eyes as he did so, to take in the full effect of his actions upon the elf. It wasn't something most men would hold to but with him, the greater he meditated upon the vision, the more his need for revenge overcame any other thoughts.

Are you really going to toss my gift aside in favor of a crucifixion? The voice was growing impatient.

Dugan's eyes shot open. "Gilthanius *and* my freedom?"

Of course. He could hear the smile behind the voice. *Can't have one without the other, now can we?*

He let out a small sigh of submission.

Good. Now open your mouth.

Dugan's countenance darkened.

Trust me.

As he slowly opened his mouth, the flame-birthed snake coiled around his neck, twisting over his tongue and down his throat in the blink of an eye. He suppressed a gag as Rheminas slid deeper into his chest, intensifying in heat as he did so.

Revenge. Revenge. Revenge. Dugan heard the word spoken in rhythm with his rising heartbeat. He felt a small part of his heart go numb, then screamed in agony as his chest was engulfed in flames. Smoke poured from his mouth and nose. His vision blurred and was tainted with red. Falling on his knees, he coughed up spatters of blood along with his new master, who hit the floor in a shower of sparks—coiling and twisting into a copper inferno before him.

I've given you the power and strength to meet your goal. Now embrace your hatred and do the rest. Break your bindings!

Though his chest throbbed with pain, Dugan strained against his shackles. The chains looked as if they were centuries old, but even as he tugged with all his strength, they held fast.

Release my gift to you.

He grunted as veins pulsed from his head and neck. He fought to lay hold of what Rheminas had planted inside him. A moment later, he connected with it at last, and his heart and mind became alight with incredible power. It was the power to take back control of his life, the strength to rule over his oppressors, and the means to exact his revenge. With a bestial roar, Dugan shattered his chains—the iron links exploding into shards.

Good! There was a deep satisfaction nestled in the tone. *You've taken the first step. Now take the last. Approach me.*

Dugan paused, recalling the pain he'd just been dealt by the god. "How? I'll burn myself if I touch you."

You have already been burnt, Dugan. You can't be wounded any more than you are now.

"What do you mean?"

I thought you wanted revenge? The longer you remain indecisive, the more time your captors have to react to the noise. You'd best be ready for them.

It was too late to turn back now.

Approach me!

Dugan drew near the shaft of flame, which once again illuminated all in a coppery light that was as warm and bright as natural daylight.

Take this weapon. Once it takes the life of the one you seek, I'll owe you nothing more. The flame shrunk to about two and a half feet in length before glowing bright white—like metal in a forge. The heat in the room intensified, rivaling a furnace. Sulfur permeated the air, as did the acrid perfume of burning metals. The heavy smoke clogged Dugan's already sore lungs, causing him to cough up even more blood. The smoke the process produced obscured his vision, causing his eyes to water and lose sight of the manifestation altogether.

Take the weapon. Claim your revenge.

As soon as Rheminas' words faded from Dugan's mind, the smoke cleared, revealing a sword standing where the flame had been. It was crafted from a strange black metal, but looked sturdy enough to do anything he'd require of it. Grasping the hilt, he found it to be a perfect fit. No sooner had he done so than the metal cuffs around his wrists unlocked, falling like rotten fruit to the floor.

As he swung the blade, he noticed it was not only well balanced, but worked as though it was an extension of his arm. Even more peculiar was its ability to connect with—even increase—the burning inside him. The longer he held the weapon, the more enraged he became, and the more he wanted to slaughter anyone who crossed his path.

Go. Take your revenge. The words now whispered from some distant place.

Dugan smiled as he heard the guards approaching from the outer hall, and raised his sword in anticipation. The lust for retribution pumped through his veins like a tidal wave, which he channeled into a great bellowing charge, bringing the black blade down upon the cell door. The wood split in two before bursting into flames, toppling to the floor like kindling.

Dugan heard his own voice, so raw and distorted with rage he barely recognized it. He yelled as he burst out of the cell, blade arcing down with an accuracy honed by countless kills. "Die!" he shrieked as he raised the blade above his head, preparing for the next blow. The weapon sliced into the nearest elf's stomach, spilling his intestines out onto the floor in flaming pools lit by the touch of the fiery sword.

He slashed the second guard across his upper torso. The elf fell to his knees, gripping his wound in horror as blood spilled out of the flaming gash. His hands clenched at the wound in a pathetic attempt to keep his fate at bay, but to no avail. The elf fell face down onto the floor, his final words a wet gurgle.

His path now clear, Dugan ran to find Gilthanius. He followed the smell of spiced meat and sweet breads down another hallway and up a flight of stairs. The scent of privilege wafted from these upper levels of the arena, where the gladiators' owners and lesser nobles kept personal suites for hosting parties and private fights.

As Dugan drew nearer, he heard music, and even the occasional night calls of birds. Once he cleared the top of the stairs, he ducked into some shadows as a patrol crossed his path. He watched them silently, but refrained from striking. He knew if he did, Gilthanius would be warned and could very well find time to escape. As he stood still, he heard Gilthanius sing a merry tune. It seemed he wanted his guests to take note of his other talents—craving ever more honor and praise.

"Oh, the rose is a beautiful flower, but on them many a thorn does roam." Gilthanius' singing increased Dugan's ire, like stoking a raging fire. In short order, the guards passed and Dugan darted up the hallway.

"That's the way, my darling, I feel when you're not at home." Dugan neared the door, preparing to break it in. He wanted to give himself enough distance from the guards who'd just passed so he could work his will without immediate interruption.

"Glades and meadows are charming, but not as charming as you. Like the shiny fairy, I love you . . ." Dugan brought his sword down upon the door, shattering the wood into flaming splinters with one mighty sweep of his arm.

"GILTHANIUS!" Dugan shouted with such a mass of hatred and blood lust the company inside the room—musicians, dancing girls, and other nobles and persons of a lesser rank—paled to a deathly white before seeking the nearest refuge. Many tripped over each other in their haste for an escape from the madman, screaming in hysteria and panic. More than once Dugan heard his name whispered in terror. Each time it sent a thrill down his being. The respect . . . the *fear* of him in so many . . . the power he wielded over them gave him even greater desire to unleash it.

He ran through the scattering crowd, cutting down those who got between him and his target without any thought of innocence or guilt. He would not be denied his prize. All fell before him, gurgling their last breaths and clutching grievous wounds as he headed for Gilthanius, who was cowering behind a purple settee.

THE WIZARD KING TRILOGY

He stopped when he reached the elf. The room grew silent. "Mercy," Gilthanius whimpered, his face dripping with tears.

Dugan raised his sword.

"No!" Gilthanius extended a ring-covered hand toward the gladiator. "For Aero's sake, spare me."

Dugan responded by plunging the tip of his blade into Gilthanius' left eye. Searing smoke and blackened blood ran down the ruined opening as the elf screeched for his life. Dugan ignored the gibbering cries, slowly running the sword in a path from Gilthanius' eye, down his cheek and neck to his chest and stomach. As he cut into the elf, a small flame erupted and chased the line the sword drew while Gilthanius' screams grew louder and less coherent. Dugan picked up the convulsing mass of flesh with one smooth motion.

"Guards . . . Guards!" The wounded elf could barely speak through the pain.

"They won't get here in time." Dugan's delight had become sadistic, but he knew the truth. His window for action wouldn't remain open forever. Reinforcements would be coming soon no matter how much he pretended otherwise. Still, they were nothing but distractions now. He could die content he'd sent Gilthanius to Mortis screaming in agony. He would have wished the same for Balus, but at least both would be dead by his hand.

He grunted as he dragged Gilthanius into a short hallway, toward the elf's box overlooking the arena.

"I'll let you go." Gilthanius was nearly mad with panic. "I'll get the emperor to reverse his decree. I have some rank now, he'll—"

Dugan hoisted the bleeding elf over his shoulder and moved for the edge of the box, staring out over the arena floor two stories below. The arena was empty and dark, with only a gibbous moon shining down upon the sand. He flung the wounded elf off his shoulder. Gilthanius landed on his back with a heavy thud. Dugan leapt over the ledge to join him, landing on his feet. Gilthanius inched backward from the crazed Telborian, but the sand and his injuries slowed his progress.

"I'll give you gold," Gilthanius said, scuttling away from the advancing gladiator. "Gold and your freedom."

"Can you take away my scar?" Dugan thrust forth his left shoulder for Gilthanius to clearly see. "Give me back the life you stole?"

Gilthanius' back now pressed against the arena wall behind him. "Please . . ."

"Can you?" Dugan rushed forward, taking a downward swing with his sword. The elf screamed as his left arm was lopped off with one smooth strike. "Can you?" Dugan hacked off Gilthanius' left leg at the knee. Blood started leaking out in a thick pool, which the thirsty sand worked quickly to absorb. Dugan watched the doomed elf struggle to stay alive. It reminded him of a squashed bug twisting in its death throes.

"Why?" Gilthanius weakly forced through his pale lips.

"*Why?*" Dugan growled and kicked his former owner in the side. "You stole my life and ask me *why?*"

Dugan slowly lowered the blade into Gilthanius' heart. He let it slide in inch by horrible inch so Gilthanius could feel every bit of his life leeching out amid his pain-filled convulsions and anguished screams. Finally, the sword plunged through the other side of the elf's chest, pinning him to the stone wall. Gilthanius jerked wildly, pushing more screams and bubbling blood out of his lips before he lay still.

Before Dugan could let this moment of victory wash over him, his sword began heating up, causing him to jump back. He watched the weapon turn white hot before bursting into copper flame. Retreating a few more steps, he witnessed the sulfur-scented fire scorch Gilthanius' remains into a powdery ash before dying away into its own pile of lifeless ash. When the fire had subsided and the stench of the sulfur descended around him, Dugan finally realized the gravity of what he'd done, and what now awaited him. As the full price of his deed dawned on him, a clamoring of guards echoed from the tunnels and side corridors honeycombing the arena.

They were coming his way. He could already see the bobbing torch light behind the portcullis off to his left. The echoing shouts were in Elonum, the language of the Elyellium, but he could understand their implications well enough. There, in that darkened arena, the sweetness of revenge turned horribly sour as he saw the rest of his life unfolding before him . . . and it frightened him.

CHAPTER 6

DRADIN MAY HAVE GIVEN MAGIC TO THE DRANORS
BUT IT'S BEEN LEFT TO MAGES TO TRULY UNDERSTAND AND MASTER IT.

—Loral the Lovely, Patrician wizard queen
Reigned 220 BV–114 BV

Valan rubbed his tired brown eyes. He'd been searching the timeworn tome for hours. The yellowed pages were scratched with a black script that had once been the common language of the land, before falling into corruption and becoming nearly forgotten. While the ancient dranoric tongue was the entrance into the wondrous world of magic, the tome Valan currently studied carried something just as great, if not greater. He'd become convinced since finding out about the Transducer that the book was the key to properly deciphering the device's long-hidden secrets. With the Transducer fully mastered, he could gain levels of power and ability undreamt of by even the greatest of wizards. It was all just waiting for him.

The scrolls and tomes he'd gathered from the priests hadn't brought him any greater insight. There were some simple observations and a few items here and there they'd found on older scrolls discovered in the rest of the ruins. However, none of that shed any more light on what he'd already learned from his previous research.

One small comfort, he supposed, was that he had a secure area in which to carry out his experiments without any major disruptions. He also had access to a near-endless supply of test subjects. And then there was Hadek, who had proven true to his claims. The goblin had shown himself quite a help in Valan's studies, even informing him of the tribe and its history, not to mention being the mage's translator when needed. It might not have been ideal, but there were always sacrifices if one wanted to master greater power.

The seven bookcases from above had also been added to the chamber as he'd ordered. They were placed between the fence and the mosaic wall in what he'd made his personal study. The lectern from the temple was also there, facing the Transducer. Valan always wanted to have it in his sights. Before the bookcases were a small table and two chairs. He and Hadek used these for their studies. In the far corner of the room stood a simple bed, but the thin layer of wool and hay saw little use. Valan wanted answers, and they wouldn't come while he slept.

"What am I not seeing?" Valan snarled as he paced toward the fence guarding the Transducer. The floating orb of light followed him. He almost always had it in use, even though some torches had been added on the side walls and by the stairs. Hadek made do with a couple of candles in an old candelabrum—just enough light to read the aged texts but little else. Of course, there were also the Transducer's glowing runes, to which each had grown accustomed.

"Tell me again about what the priests did when they found it," he ordered Hadek, stopping just outside the fence.

"They didn't find much." Hadek rose from his seat, making his way to the mage. "They just tried to make sense of the symbols but didn't get that far with them. After a while, they gave up and left it alone."

"No prayers or curses of any kind?"

"No." Hadek had now closed in on the wizard.

"And so they gave up and left this place for storage, like you said." Valan jabbed a finger at the scrolls in Hadek's hands. "What are those?"

"You told me to search for anything in the scrolls that might be of use."

"And?"

"Some of the priests wrote down what they thought some of the symbols might mean." Hadek offered the scrolls to him.

"I thought I read everything they'd written on the Transducer." Valan shot the goblin a curious eye.

"I just found them stuffed in a corner of the old temple," said Hadek.

"Hidden away?" Valan snatched up the scrolls at once, unrolling one at random. "That could be promising." While he was able to speak Goblin fairly well, the written form still wasn't entirely clear. And he'd no strong desire to learn more of the language now. Not when there were more pressing priorities. Besides, there was always Hadek to help translate.

"Chaos . . . Change . . . Death . . . Life . . ." Valan read aloud flatly. "Nothing more than what I've learned already." He rolled up the first scroll in distracted thought. "And this was *all* you found?"

"You have all that was in the temple," Hadek meekly replied. "And now these and anything else that might be discovered."

Valan shifted his gaze back on the Transducer. "But there's still a part that's missing. Something I'm not fully seeing. I know it's there, ready for the taking. I'm so close.

"I think it's time for another experiment," he informed the goblin. "Go tell Boaz we need another volunteer."

"Stay where you are, Hadek," Boaz's voice boomed across the chamber, alerting them of his presence on the stairs. Valan noted Boaz's five subchieftains in tow. There was something unusually determined about Boaz's demeanor as he descended. A flash of defiance not seen since their first encounter.

"Just in time," Valan said in Goblin as he crossed the room. "I'm in need of another volunteer." He added a sarcastic bite to the last word, knowing full well they were far from willing candidates. Once Boaz had run out of goblins to throw his way, the chieftain had constructed a lottery in which anyone's name could be randomly drawn. As fair as it was supposed to be, he found it interesting that neither Boaz nor any of his subchieftains had ever had their names pulled.

Boaz descended the last stair and stood defiantly before the mage. "You've taken enough lives from us."

"I can always take them by force," he reminded Boaz without raising his voice. "At least with the lottery you can pretend you're still in charge."

Boaz locked his jaw. "I want to make a deal."

"A deal?"

"You give the tribe rest from your experiments if we give you another for the column."

"And why would I want to do that?"

Boaz eyed the Transducer with a resolute gaze. "Because I plan to live through it."

"*You?*" Valan was taken aback. "You'd offer up yourself? Why?"

"I'm the chieftain. If I can't protect the tribe from you, at least I can lessen your touch upon it."

A quick study of Boaz's face told Valan he meant what he said. Amazing. It was like the chicken coming to offer the farmer his neck— even laying it down on the chopping block for him. If Boaz died, then Valan would have an even freer hand in taking greater command of the tribe. The subchieftains wouldn't present the same obstacle as their chieftain. And, since none had made it through the process so far, having a chance at getting one or even two favorable results out of this was something he'd be foolish to deny.

"All right." Valan jabbed a bony finger Boaz's way. "*If* you survive I'll have some information I can use to stop the experiments for a time—but not forever. I'll master this column no matter how many lives it takes."

One of the subchieftains spoke up from Boaz's shoulder. "What about your own?"

"Kaden, isn't it?" Valan gave a lingering glance at the other, noting his short black hair and solemn face. "Why don't you help your chieftain into the Transducer." A wave of his hand caused the gate to open.

"I can see to it myself." Boaz boldly strode inside the fence and into the doorway at the column's base. Another gesture from Valan slammed the gate shut behind him, making sure the invisible barrier holding Boaz inside the column was also erected. He didn't want the chieftain getting cold feet at the last minute.

"Thoth ron heen ackleen. Lore ulter-bak ulter-bak . . ." Valan raised his hands as he felt the energy within the blue column spark to life. With that awakening came the now familiar hum that soon would increase in volume, eventually making all present feel like their bones were throbbing in unison. The purple glowing runes burst into a brilliant flash as Valan continued the spell.

• ● •

Boaz's grating bellow carried throughout the torch-lit chamber like a tormented wave. Gritting his teeth did little to ease Kaden's rising wrath at what he and the other hobgoblins were forced to endure. Like the four other subchieftains with him, Kaden wore a chain mail shirt and carried a sword at his side. It was meant to convey a message of strength, but they all knew it was more for show than anything else. No one could successfully stand against the wizard.

This wasn't how it was supposed to be. Not for their tribe and certainly not for their chieftain. Yet, here they stood, in this dank chamber that had yet to bring any good to the tribe since they'd inhabited the ruins above nearly half a year ago. Only a few weeks before they'd been prospering, but now . . . now they were slipping down a muddy hill toward inevitable destruction. All their lives—their very futures—had been tainted with Valan's arrival. Even the chamber he claimed as his own had started taking on the human's scent: a faint, musky tang reminding him of old shoe leather, mingling with the aroma of wood smoke and ash. It only grew more rancid with the increased humidity. Interlaced between this miasma and the musty note of old books and tomes was the subtle hint of death. It prowled the shadowy perimeter and slithered out of the corners, telling the *true* history of the place.

Focusing on his hatred for the mage drew Kaden's attention back toward the brown-haired Telborian at his right. The mage's silver robes had turned an incandescent blue in the purple light, which aided in producing an unsettlingly surreal nature in the chamber. Valan appeared utterly lost in his spell—arms raised with his voice as he continued to bring the full might of the column to bear against Boaz.

Kaden had heard of the mage's habits when the spell was being cast—how he appeared to fall into a strange trance—seeing it firsthand was chilling. He could also tell it wasn't really a trance. There was something unsettling and unnaturally cold behind Valan's blank eyes as he worked his magic: a strange detachment mingled with a hint of madness.

The subchieftains hung their heads as Boaz's screams grew more tortured. It would be over soon, as it had been before with so many others. Kaden drew a short breath when the growls and bellows stopped. The column's purple light faded. The droning hum emanating from the column's very stone was swallowed in silence. The sole light remaining on the cylinder glowed a soft purple and came from the strange runes and symbols carved upon its exterior.

Those gathered held their breath. So far, from what Kaden knew of the process, this had been the pattern of all those who were forced into the column before. The screams and then the silence. Silence which meant the victim had died, and horribly at that.

All eyes watched Valan march for the gate, which opened with a simple gesture from the mage. As he neared, the magical barrier blocking the entrance into the column's base turned opaque purple then faded before vanishing altogether. Kaden barely took note—the real matter of import was what remained *inside* the column.

"Boaz?" Nalis, another of the subchieftains, approached cautiously. Unlike the others, Nalis kept his black hair long, letting it flow to his shoulders in a youthful manner.

Nalis edged nearer the gate, asking once again—this time with more strength. "Boaz?" He gasped at the sight of a dark shape crawling out of the column's interior.

"He's alive!" Kaden rushed for the column, the others fast at his heels. He noticed from the corner of his eye Valan had taken a few steps back, keeping a studious gaze fixed on the emerging form. But Kaden's momentary joy at Boaz's emergence quickly fell into fearful despair when he saw what inched its way out of the column.

"Khuthon's axe!"

Boaz no longer resembled a hobgoblin. His pointed ears, long canine teeth, and clawed hands remained, but his skin, once the color of a ripe pear, had turned a deep red, and his formerly black hair gray. The worst, though, was the set of two white bull's horns jutting from his forehead, curving to an arc above his head. What a price. But at least he still lived. A miracle if there ever was one.

The subchieftains hurried to help Boaz up. His flesh was warm to the touch, but there was still solid bone and muscle underneath it. Nothing else seemed out of place, nor did they find any sort of wound. This, Kaden noted, was not missed by Valan, whom he continued watching out of the corner of his eye.

With the subchieftains' aid, Boaz walked outside the fence. As they passed, Kaden made another quick inspection, noting no signs of blood other than a few sprays here and there around the collar of Boaz's light brown tunic. So there might be internal injuries to deal with, but nothing that looked like it appeared life threatening. Still, he needed some rest and a careful looking over, and a healer to make sure all was well or at least on the mend. Boaz had other plans, facing Valan once he'd cleared the fence.

"I've survived." It wasn't delivered with his voice's normal strength but was strong enough to get his point across.

"So you have," Valan returned in the same tongue while coolly continuing his examination. Kaden noted Valan's eyes trace the blood around Boaz's collar then trail downward to the smeared blood on his inside right wrist and along the cuff of the sleeve—telltale signs of having been wiped away from elsewhere. The smile that followed was far from sincere. "And how do you feel?"

"I'll live."

"I suppose you wouldn't mind me waiting a few days to make sure of that?" The smile remained plastered on the mage's pale face.

Boaz's red eyes narrowed. "Not if you hold to the agreement in the meantime."

"I suppose we can." Valan's tone and expression turned businesslike. "I'll need time to learn from this event, anyway."

"Hadek?" Valan shifted his gaze to the collection of books and scrolls filling up the worn bookshelves to his right.

"Yes?" The bald goblin emerged from the shadows like an obedient dog. Kaden joined the rest of the subchieftains in an ire-filled glare.

"I'll need fresh paper and my inkwell filled."

"I'm holding you to your word, mage," Boaz growled once more.

"I'm sure you are," Valan said, making his way back to the stone lectern.

"You should get some rest," Nalis offered as he took hold of Boaz's right arm. "Let us help you up the steps." Boaz allowed his men to guide him to the stairs. Kaden took Boaz's left arm to assist.

Boaz spoke loudly enough so it reached Valan's ear. "If Khuthon's merciful, I'll have that mage's head on a spike." His fingers found the new horns protruding from his forehead and his expression darkened with anger and loathing. "Maybe I'll even impale him on *these* for added measure."

Ranak, who favored a clean-shaven face and head, spoke from close behind Boaz and Kaden in a low voice, hands ever ready to support his chieftain from his left shoulder and middle back. "You've bought us some time."

"Just not *enough* time." Boaz stopped as he neared the base of the stairs, turning back for another look at the mage writing at his lectern with Hadek at his heels. "I'll have Valan's body dead at my feet. *That's* the only way we're going to be free of this madness." They began the slow procession up the stairs. If Valan heard or noticed the retreating group, he gave no sign.

"How long do you think he'll wait until experimenting again?" Morro, the eldest and heaviest of the subchieftains, asked. He stood opposite Ranak, taking great care in assisting Boaz as they all climbed the steps together.

"I don't know, and I don't intend to find out," said Boaz. "Kaden, I want you to take some men and search for anything we can toss Valan's way. There has to be *something* in this jungle that will keep the wolf at bay—for a little while at least."

"Lizardmen?" Nalis asked.

"Too hard to manage," said Boaz. "And I don't think Valan would be that interested in them. They're more animal than man."

"Celetors then," offered Ranak.

"It wouldn't be that hard to capture a few," said Nalis, "not if what those old scout reports said still holds true."

"If we press too hard we might risk a counterattack," Morro cautioned. "Then we'd have *two* enemies to contend with."

"And nothing really to gain," Ranak added gloomily.

"But we'd be saving hobgoblian lives," Kaden was quick to point out.

"At what cost?" asked Nalis.

"It's a risk I'm willing to take." Boaz's statement brought an end to the debate. "Take some men, but gather only a few—we don't want to cause any great stirring. Hopefully they'll buy us time to think up a better solution."

"Or give Valan time to reach his goal," said Morro.

"I don't think he ever will." Boaz slowed as they neared the place where the stairs turned into the ascending hallway. Elek, the last of the subchieftains who'd taken the steps before them, was opening the hidden door at the hallway's end.

As they neared him, Kaden observed a line about as thick as a hand's width, glowing with a faint white light in the middle of the wall. It always rose from its dormancy as people neared, rising parallel to the stairs and ascending on both of the corridor's walls to where the door and walls met. What it did and why it was there was just one of many things no one—not even Valan—could figure out. At least it created enough light for continuing their climb.

"I'll leave at once," said Kaden. "If we press hard all the way there and back—"

"Just be wise and attack at night," Boaz instructed. "The more you can hide your actions, the better. Enough of the ruins have been rebuilt to withstand an assault, but I'd rather not test them just yet."

Nodding, Kaden helped Boaz onto the last step and through the door that Elek had opened for them. A heartbeat later they'd all finally ascended from the accursed abyss and into the brilliant light of late afternoon. Singing birds and other melodious sounds of jungle life nearly succeeded in helping Kaden forget the last few moments of his life. Nearly, but not quite. Already his thoughts flew around plans and tactics for what lay ahead. Like Boaz had said, a night raid would be the best, but it would take time to assemble the right men for the task. Time that had been secured at a terrible cost and couldn't be wasted.

Leaving Elek to take his place, Kaden hurried toward his duty.

• ● •

Hadek observed Valan feverishly recording the results of his recent experiment from a short distance away, ready to provide anything the wizard might require as quickly as possible. He'd learned the hard way what it meant being tardy in taking up the mage's commands. As he stood at the ready, he noted Valan's brown hair now fell over his shoulders. It hadn't been that long when he'd first arrived, but the mage didn't seem too concerned about cutting it anytime soon. He did manage to bathe and keep himself clean shaven, as Hadek had never known the wizard to get as rank as some of the hobgoblins, who often put off a bath longer than they should.

Valan was also rather thin and pale—at least for what Hadek thought was right for his race in general. He'd only read about Telborians, and before Valan, had never seen one in the flesh. The mage's paleness had grown more pronounced since his arrival; he never left the chamber. Hadek didn't know when he ate, if ever, but supposed he had to at some time, else he'd be dead by now. But these were all just surface thoughts— simple observations that helped him pass the time, to try to make sense of the man he'd come to serve for the promise of his continued life. More and more he found himself wondering if that promise was more curse than reward.

"So why did he survive?" Valan spoke aloud in Telboros. Unsure if he was speaking to himself or wanted a reply, Hadek didn't answer. He'd made that mistake once too often too.

"Is Boaz a full hobgoblin?" Valan sought Hadek for an answer.

His brow furrowed as he replied. "What do you mean?"

"What of his parents—his lineage—are they all hobgoblins? No mixed races in this family line?"

"No." Hadek wasn't even aware it was possible for hobgoblins to sire anything *but* hobgoblins. While there were some more fanciful tales about their origins, the jarthalian races—ogres, hobgoblins, and goblins— had never sired anything but their own races, and then only with others of their same race.

"Then what is it? Random chance? How did he live?" Valan contemplated the mosaic on the far wall of the room opposite the stairs. While it seemed a simple spiral design of azure and violet tiles, he knew it was far more than that. Valan had shared it was the way he'd initially come to the ruins. As to how it worked, Hadek had no idea. In truth, he didn't really desire to know. He was too consumed with the task of staying alive.

"Do you need anything else?" Hadek braved.

"No. I'll summon you when you're needed." Valan kept his eyes on the mosaic, pondering.

Hadek made his departure. He wasn't going to stay any longer than he had to. In the midst of everything else seeking to confine him, he'd found a place he thought a safe-enough retreat. It wasn't much, but it was something, and any bright spot in these dark days was a welcome thing. He hurried to the stairs and started climbing.

So rapid was his climb and his mind so focused on seeking his place of refuge that he rushed headlong into one of the two guards Boaz had assigned to guard the secret door. The guard wasn't pleased with the collision and planted his fist into Hadek's jaw. This punch sent Hadek flying into the statue blocking the hidden doorway with enough force to drive the air out of his lungs.

"You're lucky Boaz is still alive," the guard yelled at Hadek. "When the rest of the tribe hears what happened, you're going to get just as much of the blame."

Hadek gave a huff through his sore teeth and swelling lips, sending out a fine bloody mist over his tunic. Grunting as he forced himself upright, he carefully made his way around the two guards and started down the hallway.

"You and your master are going to pay," the same guard called after him. "You hear me, you little rat? You should've been the first one we tossed into that column!"

Hadek heard him but tried his best to put it out of mind as he entered the former altar room. Now completely empty, only the bloodstains remained to haunt the living. Hadek did his best at ignoring them, focusing on the wall opposite him. He headed straight for the old door standing close to the stone pillar. Though part of the original ruins the door still opened smoothly.

Once through he made his way down a short corridor, proceeding through the dim walkway until he reached another door with light issuing from a thin crack beneath. He flung it wide, letting daylight stream into the dingy hallway as he shielded his squinting eyes.

He entered an open area that had once been a beautiful courtyard. Prior to the tribe's habitation, it'd been left to the jungle's mercy. Now that it had been reinhabited, the tribe had cleaned up much of the old debris and choking growth, restoring the courtyard to at least some of its former glory. Hadek slowly made his way over what had become a well-beaten path. It brought him around a collection of tall, headless statues, which he noted as he spat out more blood. He could feel his jaw throbbing and knew it would begin swelling soon enough.

"So what now?" he asked himself as he slumped onto a broken bottom half of a pillar. In some ways he found himself yearning for how things used to be. While it may not have been ideal, what he'd known before had a certain element of order and structure, not the constant uncertainty these new days wrought. It also had its fair share of challenges, but at least Hadek knew what he was up against. In dealing with Valan he never truly felt secure from one day to the next.

Boaz had survived the Transducer, but what next? Hadek knew the chieftain wasn't going to do it again . . . at least he was pretty sure of that. He was surprised Boaz volunteered in the first place, but to try risking it a second time? He didn't think so. So that put them where? The lottery? Nothing good could come of that, and if he was getting beaten up now what would follow after a few weeks of more hobgoblins getting killed by Valan?

Maybe it was time to finally think about leaving. He'd entertained the thought at various times throughout his life but never taken it up for fear of having a worse existence somewhere else. From what he'd lived through so far, Hadek believed he didn't really have a place in the world. No purpose. No reason for being. At least with the tribe there was somewhere he fit—or rather was wedged into a spot to serve some sort of purpose. But now . . .

now what could come next could very well make a place outside the tribe—no matter how far-fetched—attractive in comparison.

Seeking to clear his thoughts, he took in the headless statues around him. He'd often look up into the forms and wonder who carved them. Certainly not anyone the goblin knew of. They looked like no race he'd ever seen. The priests said they were statues of the dranors, but they couldn't really prove it. From what he'd learned serving Valan, however, it was possible. Valan believed the Transducer was crafted by them, and so it stood to reason the statues had been too.

Without their heads, though, it was impossible to know for sure. Whoever they were made to represent, they were strongly built, crafted from hard stone, and their bodies were well muscled yet slender. This, in effect, made them seem more mythical than real. Hacked off by what looked like sword and axe strikes, the missing heads were nowhere to be found. Hadek had given it a go shortly after he found the place and turned up nothing for his efforts.

Goblins, and hobgoblins for that matter, had never been very interested in tales of the ancient past or how they related to the present—at least the ones Hadek knew. Only stories measured in generations were the stock and trade of their firelight tales—things noble and true to goblinkind about goblinkind. This, of course, meant *hobgoblins*, not goblins. Here again Hadek was the exception. It was through his experiences with the priests he'd come to know of a higher culture and the importance of history as a tool for understanding the world.

From the priests he'd learned that the dranors commanded vast territories under their empire, making a great name for themselves before vanishing. This was the same race Valan so longed to tap into in order to gain their knowledge and power. Hadek had begun learning more about such things, but what he caught were mere snippets here and there—scraps he gobbled up when Valan wasn't looking. It didn't help he wasn't free to pursue such topics, too busy fearing the next tirade he'd have to endure.

And Valan seemed to be unleashing more of them with each failed experiment. One day, the wizard would snap, and he hoped he was far away when it happened. Shivering at the thought of what a truly insane wizard was capable of, Hadek forced his mind onto something more soothing, expelling what stress and worry he could with a sigh. It didn't work as well as he had hoped.

•●•

As night spread over the Abyss, Cadrith leaned back in his throne, taking a break from studying the scrying skull. So Valan had actually gotten the Transducer to work. A strange turn of events, but Cadrith doubted there would be any further successes. He could tell just by what he'd seen and learned since he first came upon the wizard that any effort was a fool's errand. While the success was interesting, it didn't really play into Cadrith's larger picture. Thankfully, the hobgoblin hadn't died. That would have set off more instability, perhaps forcing him to act sooner than he was prepared to. There were still a few loose threads needing some attention. One of them he could feel entering the room now.

Like thickening smoke, a shadowy entity began coalescing behind the throne. Cadrith didn't have to turn around to know it was there—coiling up and around like a snake. Acting quickly, he waved his hand over the scrying skull, extinguishing Valan's image from its surface, while leaving the violet and silver runes to glow amid the bone.

"You've been silent of late. *Too* silent for my liking." Not even the scrying skull's glowing runes could illuminate Sargis' semihumanoid form floating just behind the throne. From the waist up he resembled a sort of dark-skinned giant. From the waist down he was a mass of black cloud and mist. No matter how hard he tried, he just couldn't get a solid body to form below his waist. Even his former wings failed to manifest in this spiritual form.

When they first met Sargis was dying. Seeing an opportunity, Cadrith made a show of saving the greater demon's life. He claimed the shadowy form was the only way he could have kept Sargis' spirit from total annihilation. He also assured him the situation was temporary. He'd be able to find a remedy but it would take some time. And Cadrith would use that time to find a secure environment to complete his plans. In the meantime Sargis was kept dependent on Cadrith.

As long as he pretended to make some progress in finding a cure Sargis was willing—though more and more grudgingly—to acquiesce to the lich's demands. But as the years increased the ploy wore thin, forcing Cadrith to make a new offer. He'd take Sargis to Tralodren with him, where the demon not only would be physically restored, but able to build a new base of power from which to rule. Yet while this new offer was gladly accepted, it couldn't mend the frayed strands of their relationship. Soon enough the final threads would snap and then . . .

"When I have something to tell you, I will." Cadrith's skeletal hands rested on the throne's armrests in a show of quiet resolve and patience. "Didn't Akarin make that clear to you?"

"Unless it's something you don't want me to know." Sargis' glowing red eyes danced with a sinister glee as he floated to the front of the throne. Cadrith put on a show of ignoring the demon, but could only pull off a halfhearted effort.

"I thought you said you'd found a suitable pawn." Gazing at the skull, Sargis continued, "What else do you need?"

"Time and silence," Cadrith said, tilting his head in the demon's direction.

"Ah, but time is something you don't have too much of anymore, is it?"

Cadrith's bony fingers clenched the armrests with a death grip. "Not everything is how it appears."

"Are you referring to yourself or what you said you're bringing about?" Cadrith was less than thrilled with the hard edge to the demon's words. Taking hold of his staff, he jumped up from his throne, calling forth a white burst of light from the skull. Delighting in the demon's small retreat, Cadrith made his way to the window, dimming the skull's brilliant gleam in the process. No need to alert the whole benighted countryside to his presence. One unwanted visitor was enough to contend with.

"Valan should work out well, but I have to make sure everything is in place before I act. It isn't just him we're dealing with. There's also a tribe of hobgoblins and the Transducer, among other things."

"The mighty Cadrith Elanis, afraid of a tribe of hobgoblins?" Sargis mocked. "From what you've shared of them they seem little more than petty annoyances. At least for someone as great and powerful as the last wizard king of Tralodren."

Cadrith kept his focus out the window. "And with all your boasting these past five years, you still haven't gained more than a handful of attendants, and even those are lackluster at best."

"I'd have more if it wasn't for your *help*."

"Which you were glad to take at the time," he said, peering over his shoulder. "Or do you want me to reverse the spell keeping you alive and let you pass into total oblivion instead? I'd be happy to do so."

Sargis hovered closer to the lich. "A world, Cadrith. You told me—"

"I know what I said." He turned round and faced the demon. "But you have to let me finish my work. I've almost reached the end."

"Perhaps the same can be said of my patience." Sargis glared back. "My doubts have also started to increase. Maybe you need to be reminded that if you think you can deceive me—"

"Your threats are more hollow than your frame." Cadrith offered up a dismissive bony hand, careful to use just the right tone to dig his barb in as deep as he could without increasing the demon's ire any further. He still needed Sargis to be cooperative . . . for a little longer. No use in raking all the coals up just yet—no matter how much he wanted to—but it was an old wound he enjoyed picking at from time to time.

"And *you've* lost much of your bargaining power, haven't you?" Sargis' eyes flared a fiercer red than before. "I wonder if there's more dust in you now than magic." His eyes narrowed to bloody slits. "There's an easy way to find out."

"Try me."

The silence that followed crushed anything before it as the two stared at each other for a long moment. At one point Cadrith thought the demon might actually call his bluff. Instead, he backed down.

"I'll summon you when I'm ready." Cadrith returned to the window.

"You've promised me much."

"And you'll have it, and maybe more."

"I'll be waiting to hear of your progress." Sargis retreated a few feet. "And it had better be soon. Don't forget, you've only been able to get as far as you have by my protection. Protection I can withdraw anytime I wish." The demon began fading from sight, melting into the air from which he'd appeared. So, a bluff for a bluff. If Cadrith still had lips, a small smile would have worked its way up the corners of his mouth.

He waited a few moments, scanning the room and the shadows lurking in the corners—shadows that could be hiding more than cobwebs and cracks. Sargis had blended himself into the darkness once before. It was how he'd discovered Cadrith's weakening hold over his magic. The demon had been annoying enough to deal with before, but upon learning of his present state, was ten times worse. He swore he'd never be so foolish again. If his only leverage was waning, he couldn't waste a single moment. He dreaded to think of falling into the tender mercies of the locals—let alone Sargis—without any access to his magic. No, that was something he swore he'd keep himself from at all costs.

But Sargis breathing down his neck was one matter. Valan's growing desire to master the Transducer was another. There was something in Valan's drive that didn't sit right. Something that made Cadrith second-guess if he was the right one to make his key. While no stranger to such dedication, Cadrith still felt something was a bit off with Valan's particular brand of fervor. He just couldn't put a finger on what it was just yet.

Even so, he'd take what time he could afford, seek other possible solutions, and go over the matter from yet another angle, searching for any flaws. He had to be right. He couldn't take too many bold risks. He was working with rationed strength and calculated effort. Even so, there was still a margin he left for any surprises—Sargis chief among them. Returning to his throne, he put aside his staff and the light it provided. Sifting through all he'd learned from the scrying skull, he considered the last of his options, weaving the end of his plot into its final form.

CHAPTER 7

THOUGH WE NOW FACE SOME HARD DAYS BEFORE US,
I STILL HOLD TO AERO'S DREAM. WE SHALL ONCE AGAIN BE A
GREAT EMPIRE, RULING AS ONE RACE TO THE GLORY OF
AERO TRIPTON COLLONUS, THE ETERNAL EMPEROR.

—Marcus Hectoris Septara, second emperor of Colloni
Reigned 2810 BV–2782 BV

The soft breeze tickled Dugan's hair, waking him with a jerk. His movements were swift as he scanned the surrounding forest in which he lay, occasionally tilting an ear to the breeze. Crouched amid the undergrowth, he found no threat nearby. A good sign, but nothing indicative of the reality of his situation.

The muscles on his naked torso tensed when a nearby rustling had him searching out its source amid the birds' songs and crickets' chirps. In short order a squirrel made its presence known on a tree trunk. He sighed and began to relax. Then he heard the screech of a hawk in the distance. He'd learned to both despise and fear the shrill cry; it told him the hunters now knew his location.

At the sound, the squirrel dashed into the thick canopy of leaves. Dugan followed suit and broke into a run. He'd been running from the hunters for five days now, taking what food and rest he could when he could. No matter how far or long he ran, though, he knew they'd never cease their pursuit. As long as an escaped gladiator was on Colloni, it was fair game to hunt and retrieve him for a bounty. Given his recent actions, Dugan was sure he'd fetch a fine sum, not that he looked like so great a catch in his breechcloth and battered boots. But if he could make it to the coast, he had a chance. At least that was what he kept telling himself.

As he ran through the Remolosin Woods with his muscles methodically pumping his famished body forward, he gathered his thoughts. His destination was the coast. But once he emerged from the woods and into the open fields, he wouldn't be able to cloak his movements. Not that he was doing such a great job of it now. Speed had been more his ally than stealth. Leaping over a fallen tree, he heard a hawk's cry and stopped abruptly. His fiery green eyes squinted against the scattering sunlight as he strained his ears.

He heard barking in the distance. One . . . no, *two* dogs. He cringed when he saw movement in the underbrush behind him. They were closer than he'd thought! Dugan ran for about another thirty feet and then jumped as high as he could into a thick collection of branches, getting enough of a boost to reach a high-placed limb of a tall oak.

Not missing a heartbeat, he pulled himself up into the foliage and further cover. Within moments, two sleek brown dogs tore out of the underbrush and halted beneath the tree where he hid. Sniffing around the mossy base, they quickly started pawing the trunk and barking.

Dugan's heart galloped in time to his rapid breaths, but to survive, he had to control the rising stew of fear and rage boiling in his veins. Closing his eyes, he pushed the dogs from his mind so he could bring a plan clearly into focus. It had to be timed just right or his life was forfeit. Straining his hearing beyond the bellowing hounds, he sat as still as a jungle cat and waited for the hunters to arrive.

From his vantage point, he easily caught sight of movement amid the forest growth, moving faster toward him with each passing moment. Soon he could hear voices and running feet pounding the ground with no attempt at stealth. The hunters were so excited that he couldn't understand much of their conversation. All he could glean was something about gaining some coin and enjoying his death. Drawing a breath, Dugan poised himself for the attack. There would be no second chances.

Dugan watched the first hunter move out of the forest's undergrowth. He was tall for an elf—about six and a half feet if he had to guess. He wore the leather armor common to all elves engaged in the hunt, a poetic take on the collecting of bounties from debtors, criminals, deserting soldiers, escaped slaves, and anyone else who might bring in some decent coin.

The leather armor the majority of hunters wore was preferred since it was easier to wear, maintain, repair, and didn't make much noise when worn or carried. Dugan made note of the lead elf's armor. The dull wheat hue wasn't the tree-bark shade that was common. He realized he was dealing with an experienced hunter; the discoloration could only have been caused by constant sun exposure and use. Taking out a skilled hunter would be harder, but Dugan was confident he could.

A second figure emerged right on the heels of the first. He too wore the armor of a hunter, but it looked newer, almost freshly made. Though it was almost impossible for a human to guess an elf's age, he surmised the first figure was the other's superior by the way the second carried himself around the other. So then there was only one real threat.

The hunters reached the tree and drew their gladii. Both blades appeared to have seen action in recent days. As they neared, Dugan could smell the aroma of sage, nutmeg, and pine sap mingling with their sweat and armor. He'd heard it called "the hunter's scent." The fragrance was supposed to aid hunters by better cloaking their own scent in the wild, where most of their prey often ended up. From both present and previous samples, he didn't see how it could mask anyone's scent from detection. If anything it made their victims only too aware of their approaching presence.

As they cleared the remaining distance, Dugan remained as still as stone. The older elf moved forward with an even gait as he called the dogs away from the tree. The younger one stayed behind, wary and observant of his surroundings.

Seeing an opportunity, Dugan leapt from the tree. His large frame crashed onto the older elf like thunder, sending him face first into the earth and unconsciousness. From on top of the fallen elf, Dugan glared at the younger one. The hunter rattled off something in Elonum as he rushed forward and took a swing with his gladius.

Dugan dodged it easily.

Renewing his attack, the hunter yelled an old invocation for protection to Aerotripton. Dugan grappled the other's blade away from him, seizing hold of and then crushing the hunter's wrist with a crackle of tendon and bone. The gladius fell harmlessly at Dugan's feet as curses flowed from the elf's lips.

It was then the dogs bit into Dugan's flesh. The hounds were trained to take down their prey with the least amount of damage. For "the better the prey, the better the pay" went the old hunter adage. Most of the time, this was achieved by attacking the legs, which brought about a fall, ensuring an easy capture. He'd no plans on cooperating with such tactics.

He picked both of the beasts up by the scruff of their necks. Their vicious snarls and saliva-splattering attempts at biting his hands and arms didn't faze him. He'd fought fiercer beasts in the arena.

With a grunt, he hurled the protesting animals into the nearest tree. There was a thick thud upon impact, followed by shrieking barks, small whimpers, then silence. The action left smears of blood trailing down the thick, mossy trunk. Under it rested the dogs' still bodies, their heads bent at awkward angles. Just one more threat remained.

The hunter's wide green eyes darted between Dugan's advancing figure and the unconscious hunter sprawled out a short distance from him. In clear desperation, the young elf charged headlong into Dugan, fists flying. It was the final effort of a cornered animal. Dugan met the elf with trained blows and hardened knuckles. The young hunter was unconscious before hitting the ground.

Dugan caught his breath. For a moment he stood silent amid the fresh carnage, his eyes taking in the scene—his senses in rapt attention. Confident he was alone once more, he bent down and snapped the necks of his would-be captors, cracking them as if they were simple twigs rather than sentient flesh. Better than they deserved, but he didn't have the luxury of doing anything more.

Following this, he quickly looted their belongings. Knowing the leather armor was too small, he picked up the two gladii. They seemed relatively new, despite their recent use, and in good condition. He spun them both in a clockwise motion, creating two circles of steel as he tested their balance. They'd work well enough.

He finished pawing through the elves' backpacks and belt pouches. He made swift work of the dried meat and pieces of stale bread and cheese among their rations, washing it all down with what water remained in their small waterskins. He hastily relieved them of their sheaths, strapping one on each side of his waist. After a quick check of his surroundings, he was off.

Confident of a temporary reprieve, he settled into a comfortable jog. He kept the two swords in hand as he ran, eyes ever cautious of his surroundings. The farther he advanced, the more the towering oaks, maples, elms, sycamores, and pines receded in favor of smaller plants and bushes. He slowed his stride as he took note of the increasing grasses spreading across the landscape.

The Remolosin Woods were really a series of three rings of forests separated by open spaces just like the one he was nearing. He'd heard enough from stories and what he'd now experienced firsthand that he could put two and two together. The forest rings served as a setting in which the great city of Remolos—the only origin city to have survived the Imperial Wars and been inhabited since its foundation—rested like a prize jewel.

The concept was carried over from the Elyelmic mindset of old in which they sought domination—both of nature and of their people—by a culture of order and control. He'd already crossed through three bands of forest, but he wasn't really sure what to expect next. He did know once in the open he was at a greater risk, and if this was truly the end of the last forest, he'd have to start adjusting his bearings. By the placement of the sun, he figured he had close to six more hours of light and then some twilight if needed. That would get him somewhere safe for the night, he supposed. He was about to move onward when a voice from behind spoke a command in Telboros.

"Turn around . . . slowly." There was an accent in the voice.

Dugan obeyed, cursing himself for letting his confidence get the better of him. He hadn't even heard this one's approach. Besides the accent, the voice possessed a strange quality he couldn't place. The speaker was purposefully lowering the tone in order to sound imposing.

The hunter's hood was pulled over his face, fully hiding it from view. But it wasn't the face that concerned him. His gaze rested on the arrow pointed his way. Not too many hunters used arrows—at least not the ones he'd heard of and encountered. But whenever one is pointed at you, it's wise to take precaution. The chance of missing at such a distance if he either stayed or fled was low. Even so, Dugan wouldn't be taken easily, and readied his gladii for a fight.

"Drop the swords," the strangely accented voice ordered again in the same odd timbre. "I said drop them, Dugan." The words were a low growl.

His eyes narrowed.

"I can either shoot your hands and *make* you drop them or you can do it on your own." Dugan reluctantly complied. The swords fell to the ground with a muffled rustle of grass. "That's better," said the hunter. "Now maybe you'll listen to me instead of trying to cut me down."

"If you're stalling for time—"

"I'm not a bounty hunter." The hunter's hood was pulled back, revealing the face of an elven woman.

He was immediately drawn to the shimmering silver hair flowing out and around the woman's face, whose brilliance was enhanced by her sparkling sapphire eyes. Her complexion was the most amazing thing he'd ever seen: a sort of alabaster hue with a soft gray tint that added some warmth to her pallid skin.

"I'm here to save you." The elf lowered her bow. Lithe and graceful, her light frame seemed to float when she moved.

"*Save* me?" Dugan's eyes again narrowed, cold logic taking hold once more. She might have worn a hunter's cloak—complete with the scent—but the sword he could see strapped to her waist and the rest of her garb didn't hold up to what he knew was common among the Elyellium. A dark green tunic flowed over brown pants, which were tucked into black cuffed boots.

"Look," Dugan started, "I don't have time—"

"Would you *listen* to me?" The woman's words were rushed and frustrated. "I'm not a hunter! I'm your only way *off* Colloni."

"Right." Dugan snorted and moved to retrieve his swords. In an eyeblink she'd pulled back her bowstring, pointing the arrow straight at him.

Dugan's jaw clenched. He could strike now, should he wish. Even if she did get a good shot in, he could still survive long enough to do some harm. He didn't need a blade to kill, and his hands could make short work of her thin neck.

"You had your warning," he growled.

"As did you," she returned. The steel in her voice surprised him. "Just let me explain. I'm willing to help you escape Colloni if you'll just stop being so pigheaded!"

"I got this far on my own, and—" He was cut short by shouts of other elves calling out their location. Dugan hissed as he picked up his weapons and sprang into another sprint. But before he could get far he heard the bowstring's release. He felt a sudden pain in his back which quickly flowed into numbness followed by lightheadedness.

The next thing he knew he'd fallen on the ground.

"Why do men always have to be so stubborn?" The question was the last thing he heard as his world was enveloped in darkness.

•●•

Alara glanced again at the slumbering man a short distance from her. She figured he'd wake up soon enough. When he did, she wanted to be ready. In the meantime she finished tending to her bow and kept her falchion within reach. They weren't out of danger just yet—another reason why she opted to not keep a fire, though it might have benefited them on this cooler evening. Even cooler for the Telborian than for her, given his limited attire. She'd already shed her cloak; she was warm enough with her tunic for the time being.

She shifted her attention from the makeshift camp. The only sounds in the starlit darkness were crickets and swaying grass. It'd become a beautiful night. Had she been elsewhere she would have enjoyed it. Still, she found herself gazing up into the heavens. There was a first quarter moon tonight—which helped them remain undetected, but also made the stars all the brighter. She easily found the constellation of the Virgin, which was sitting a bit lower beneath the Dolphin swimming by—two signs that summer was just around the bend.

Returning her focus to the maintenance of her bow, she caught the gleam of starlight on Dugan's sword as it lay beside her. She'd taken both swords when he was knocked unconscious by her enchanted arrow. It had been enchanted with enough strength to knock out a large animal, allowing her to easily put the Telborian to sleep. That had been the easy part. Toting his unconscious frame through the wilderness had taken its toll, but eventually she'd found somewhere safe enough to rest for the night.

Wait. *One* gladius?

Alara went back to the weapon—the *single* weapon. She swept the area around her for the missing blade, but came up empty handed. She'd made sure she kept them close at hand and out of Dugan's reach. And both were there when last she checked, so where was it? It couldn't have just gotten up and walked off by itself. Alara got her answer when the edge of the blade pressed up against the front of her neck, the hand wielding it reaching around from behind.

"I want answers," Dugan whispered in her ear. Alara tensed.

"It might be a bit hard to give them with a sword against my neck," she said, feigning what confidence she could.

"You seem the resourceful type," Dugan growled.

Alara swallowed hard, then tried to relax.

"For starters, where are we?" The gladius' razor-thin lip pressed more intimately against her neck.

"The Grand Fields—the plains outside the Remolosin Woods. They flow all the way to the coast."

"How did I get here?"

"I carried you."

He laughed with a mirth that was too dark for her liking. "You working with someone else?" She noticed Dugan making a rapid survey of the area.

"There's no one here but me."

"And who are you?"

"Alara Airdes."

"A hunter?"

"No, I told you I'm not a bounty hunter. I was sent to find you and take you off Colloni."

"Why?"

"We need your help." She tried getting some more room to breathe, but Dugan's other hand gripped her left shoulder, stopping the effort before it could begin.

"*We?*" The blade came close to biting into the soft skin of her neck. "I thought you said you were alone?"

"I am," Alara rushed, "but I'm working for someone else. They're the one who sent me."

"So who you working with?"

"I'd rather not say at the moment, but I *can* say we're on the same side."

Dugan's chortle made clear Alara wasn't connecting. "You probably haven't heard of my people, but I'm a Patrious—another race of elves who live far to the west." She then quickly added, "And we have little love for the Elyellium, let me assure you."

"Elves sent you to retrieve me from *other* elves?" Dugan wasn't believing any of this. She'd been afraid he wouldn't. She just hadn't expected she'd have to bring him around with a sword at her neck.

"Yes, from the Republic of Rexatoius—my homeland." She measured her words.

"Never heard of it." Dugan drew the blade a little tighter, drawing a thin trickle of blood. "If you're not a hunter, how did you know where to find me, or even *when*?"

Alara grimaced under the pressure. "I wasn't quite sure . . . I only had a vague location where you might be. I had to track you for a day before I found you. But I didn't have to travel far before I heard the news of a large reward for an escaped gladiator who happened to kill the arena's manager. It's caused quite a stir and is calling down bounty hunters on you from all over Colloni."

Following her comment, Dugan fell maddeningly silent, leaving Alara uncertain of anything. All she had been planning—what she'd thought would be needed or worked out through a very different process—had been tossed out the window.

Finally, he spoke.

"It's night. We can part ways without anyone getting hurt. You can always say you lost me in the darkness."

She was losing him and fast. She needed to turn this around.

"*Where* would you go, though?" she asked. "Or better yet, *how*? You think you can just walk into a city and pick up some sort of transport off Colloni with that wonderful scar on your shoulder and all these hunters on your back? Not to mention your lack of proper attire. If it wasn't for me, you'd be back in Remolos right now, getting ready for your cross." Alara's forehead started beading with sweat. She cringed as Dugan yanked her head to the side, forcing her to peer into his cold and mirthless gaze. She felt the small trickle of blood glide farther down her throat. She'd underestimated him, and that miscalculation might now cost her life. She needed to regain control.

"What if I told you I'd help you off Colloni first, *before* you had to decide." Alara made her face match her calm tone. Even her eyes were still ponds, masking like a sheet of ice the seething chaos beneath. "A goodwill gesture to prove my intentions."

Dugan hesitated. "You'd *really* offer me freedom without any strings attached?"

"Yes. It's up to your honor and conscience to decide where your obligation lies after that."

Dugan smirked. "You're assuming a lot about my conscience and honor then."

"Maybe, but it's a risk I'm prepared to take." This time her words were bold as well as true.

"So why attack me instead of telling me all this?"

"I believe I tried to." She did the best she could with hiding her frustration. "But *someone* was too bullheaded and bent on running to listen. Besides, we didn't have time to stand around and talk. The hunters were right on your trail. You left a swath of tracks even a blind boar could follow."

"And your arrow was drugged."

"Enchanted to make whatever it hits sleep."

"You a wizard?"

"No. There's only the arrow. And once you were out I brought you the rest of the way."

"You really expect me to believe that?" He made another quick look about. "Where are the others who helped you?"

"There's just me," she replied. "And you'll find I'm *full* of surprises." Her eyes darted for the gladius at her jugular. "We'll be safe here until morning. Right now, we both need some rest."

The blade didn't move. "Assuming I agree to follow you tomorrow, where are we going?"

"I have a boat waiting for us in Argis, a small town about a day's journey from here. From there we'll head out to sea and you'll be free from Colloni for good." The gladius relaxed a bit. She hoped it meant he was beginning to trust her. At the very least, a return to reason was a blessing.

"I'm risking my life for your safety and freedom. At least put down the gladius." Surprisingly, the weapon departed from her neck. Dugan remained behind her, though, ready to strike at any time.

"Thank you." She carefully wiped the blood from her neck with her fingers. "You can leave anytime you want, but it would be foolish to try. Like I said, there's nowhere on Colloni you'd be safe. As long as you're on elven soil, you'll be tracked down like a dog." Growing bolder, she peered back at the gladiator, adding, "The best chance you have is me, and you know it."

"All right," he said, wiping the gladius on his breechcloth. "I'll go as far as the boat ride from Argis, but then I choose where to go after that."

"That was the deal," said Alara. "If anything, I'll have done some good in helping you escape." She pulled a corner of her cloak to her neck and cleaned up the rest of the blood that had trailed along her collarbone. "But I *do* think you'll consider joining our cause once you understand the nature of the situation."

Dugan studied her closely. "You called me Dugan in the woods. How did you know my name?"

"You mean before I heard it from the hunters?" She returned the cloak to its resting place, satisfied the worst of the bleeding had stopped. "I'd rather not say out here. It'd be best left until all those concerned meet together."

"And why's that?" She could feel Dugan's eyes hard upon her as she unpacked a simple brown cloth from her pack before unrolling it on the ground.

"You'd better get some sleep." She lay on her blanket and covered up with her cloak. Her short bow and sword lay ready at her side, but she didn't make any move toward them nor even seek them out with her eyes. Although there was a reprieve, she knew the smallest gesture could fracture their fragile peace.

"What about the other hunters on my trail? What happened to them?"

"Get some sleep. We have a good ways to travel tomorrow."

Dugan stood for a moment before putting a few feet between them. Seemingly unsatisfied with the distance, he added a few more paces before focusing on the immediate area. Constructing a bed with dirt and grass, he made his rest opposite the elf—his blade never out of reach. Alara decided on one final check of her new companion before finally taking her rest. When she did, she found Dugan's eyes staring right back at her while his hands searched across his lower back.

"If you're looking for a hole, you won't find it," she said. "The arrow was enchanted to cause sleep, not harm." She turned away from the Telborian, focusing solely on sleep.

"Magic." Dugan's hoarse whisper was more like a profanity than anything else.

CHAPTER 8

"You sure this is the safest route?" Dugan stood in a small area secluded by a clump of waist-high, bristling bushes about a quarter mile from Argis. He'd long ago sheathed his gladii, which Alara took as a sign she might have earned some trust.

"Yes, and we made good time too," she said, removing the pack from her shoulders. They'd started their trek westward at first light. Alternating between running and jogging, they had slowed to a walk as they'd moved into their present location about eighty yards from the flagstone road leading up to the gate. They'd more than enough room to run or hide, while also having a clear view for much-needed surveillance.

"My boat is waiting at the docks." Alara rested the backpack by her feet, digging through it as she spoke.

"It doesn't *look* that impressive." Dugan studied the port town with a doubtful gaze. It really was a simple affair. Common stone walls sectioned it off from the plains while leaving it open to the beach and waves. There was some traffic here and there on the road, but it was sparse.

"That's the idea," Alara said, pulling out a common brown cloak from her backpack. "Someplace out of the way to shield us from anyone who still might be after you.

"All we need to do is get to the boat," she said, shoving the cloak at Dugan. "Take this. If you hold it closed tight it should keep you hidden, as long as you don't speak. Slump to hide your build and keep your face in the hood."

Dugan scowled at the garment. "It smells like a hunter."

"I got it off one while I was tracking you. The scent should add to your disguise. I expect you've had enough experience with them to pretend to be one."

"You were right." Dugan donned the cloak. "You *are* full of surprises."

Alara let a small smile trace her lips as she drew up her hood. "Are you ready?"

"Why are *you* cloaked, though?" He raised an eyebrow.

"I'm a Patrious. The Elyellium don't favor us too highly. Right now it's better if I assume the role of a hunter as well."

"Better for who?" Dugan drew up his own hood, adjusting it to conceal as much of his features as possible. "I thought you said I'd be safer with you than on my own."

Alara finished donning her backpack. "As long as you stay with me, you *are* safer than on your own."

Dugan paused before giving a curt nod. "To the docks, then." She made her way for the road, Dugan behind her.

"So why don't the Elyellium like you?"

Alara kept her attention directed on Argis' advancing gray walls. "You'll find out soon enough."

Beyond the town's thick, iron-shod wooden gate, a whole new world appeared. A commercial sector thrived amid stern stone edifices, columns, and walls, and color leapt out at all who regarded the shops and carts and people milling through the streets. Argis' narrow lanes and outer walls didn't make fresh air too common, which allowed for some less-than-pleasing odors alongside the aromas of fresh-baked bread and exotic spices dominating certain sections of the town.

"How much farther?" Dugan rasped from his hood while taking stock of a drunken beggar plying his tin plate for sympathy against a nearby step.

"We're near the docks." Alara's eyes darted small looks here and there as they walked through the thinly populated streets, careful of anything or anyone who might hint at causing them harm. "About another two streets, and we should be there."

Much of the population were elves, but some were Telborian sailors and merchants. None of them appeared curious about their presence. This was good news, for they were reaching the area of Argis where the hunters would be roaming—seeking those who might try an escape by sea, as they were about to do. Get past them and they'd be free.

"Aghh!"

Alara spun around and found Dugan had stopped. He was looking at the sole of his boot.

"What is it?" She kept her voice low. "Are you hurt?"

"No," Dugan muttered in a hoarse whisper. "I stepped in a pile of—"

"May I be of some assistance?" A voice speaking Elonum drew the duo's eyes to a lean elf wearing the garb of a hunter. He appeared an average-looking Elyellium, black haired and blue eyed, but his manner spoke of some training and experience. Alara cursed under her breath as she managed a smile. They were so close.

"Are you hurt?" The elf addressed Dugan, who was still deeply cloaked in the dark hood and now lowering his foot as calmly as he could.

The air seemed to draw itself closely around the pair as the elf continued staring at Dugan. Alara sweated profusely as she tried to think up ideas to get them out of the hunter's grasp without arousing any unwanted attention. As she racked her brain, Dugan saved them both.

"That's all right." An old voice speaking Elonum came out of Dugan's hood. "I just stepped on a bad spot of road, that's all. Thank you for the offer."

Alara couldn't believe what she'd heard.

"Very well. Take care—you too, sister. I'd advise some rest. You look fairly pale. Good hunting." The congenial words were more unnerving than his presence.

"G-good hunting," Alara stammered in Elonum with disbelief.

As the hunter made his way for the harbor, Alara stared at Dugan in astonishment.

"How did you do that?" she whispered in amazement.

"I'm full of surprises too," he replied, scraping the sole of his soiled boot on a nearby wall. "Let's get to the boat."

"That's just the kind of thinking we need on the mission."

"The boat." Dugan's face became like stone.

Alara nodded, her manner all business again. "It's up ahead."

"Good. I'd like to be out of here by nightfall." He made his way forward.

Alara pulled into the lead. Silently, the two continued for the harbor, keeping to the shadows as much as possible.

Argis' harbor was a simple collection of docks constructed from wood and stone that jutted out into the Cerulean Sea. Vessels of varying size, from small fishing boats to massive trading ships, were tied at every pier, while others sought to depart or dock. Men scurried up and down the gangplanks with crates and barrels filled with a multitude of goods. Others hauled thick nets about, fat with fish and other delicacies.

All this was carried out in a self-contained world: a whole clockwork motion of people and things set to its own rhythm. Fishermen and traders worked from shops or directly from the back of their boats, seeking what business they could before day's end. Shouts and creative chants tried to reel folks in for the catch of the day or the latest bolt of cloth, spices, or gems. While Alara and Dugan didn't get distracted by such temptations, their progress was slowed by those who did, making it all the more maddening with their destination just in reach.

Slowing down for the fifth time, she dared a glance over her shoulder. Dugan wasn't behind her. Frantic, she rapidly searched the area until she caught sight of him walking back into Argis.

"Dugan! What are you doing?" she hissed in Elonum, chasing after the bulky human as inconspicuously as she could.

He didn't respond, just continued walking, reaching out his hand into empty air. Then suddenly he stopped and drew his gladii as if facing a fellow combatant. Alara stood in shocked horror as she watched him begin swinging wildly in the air, the motions of his thrashing causing his hood to fall back and scattering the people who quickly turned and stepped back or outright fled from him. The gladiator's erratic behavior also attracted the attention of an elf entering the docks, who, upon seeing his antics, ran back into town shouting excitedly.

"What did you get me into, Gilban?" Alara wondered aloud before running after the Telborian.

• ● •

Dugan had been following behind Alara when he'd heard a whisper.

"This one too?" It sounded like someone right beside him speaking in Telboros. Turning his head, he didn't see anyone. Thinking it was nothing but his imagination, he continued on.

"Yes, him as well." Another faint voice trailed past his ears. Turning around again, he stopped for a moment, looking more carefully than before at the motley scene around him.

Nothing.

As he was about to resume his trek, a shimmering white light appeared a short distance from him. It was faint and subtle, like a cascade of diamond dust, but it drew him toward it nonetheless. Almost as if in a trance, he instinctually stretched out a hand toward the sparkling air. But even as he did so, the same area grew dark and a series of ropy black tentacles began spilling out.

Reflexively, he pulled out his swords and took a few steps back, watching the tentacles shoot out of the now pitch-black section of open air. Each tentacle held a cruel-looking mouth, which snapped ravenously at the empty air—eager for something to catch between its teeth.

Dugan quickly leapt back when a larger tentacle darted for his head. Dodging the attack dropped his hood as he replied with an attack of his own. His sword passed through the tentacle as if it were nothing more than smoke. A haunting laugh followed the failed action, along with a bright white light. When he opened his eyes, he found himself facing an outpouring of hunters coming right at him.

"Are you mad?" he heard Alara shout as he felt her arm on his back. There was no time for explanations as the hunters and a few human sailors closed in on them like sharks smelling blood.

A small gathering of humans stopped their labors on the docks and sat on some chests and casks, eagerly cheering on the approaching fight. Many others dashed off for safer quarters until it was over.

"The slave's mine!" said an Elyelmic male with a husky voice and twisted smile.

Dugan's first sword clanged heavily against the nearest hunter's blade. Swinging his second gladius, he pushed violently against the hunter and used his greater strength to gain access to the middle of their circle, which was quickly enclosing him. He estimated their numbers at half a dozen. He'd faced worse odds before.

He was half aware of Alara engrossed in her own conflict, but focused on his own battle. Human thug joined elven hunter as they encircled their prey, hoping he'd be an easy take. They swung wide for their first attack, giving him the time he needed to ready his stance. He unleashed one deep thrust followed immediately by another, sending two hunters to their graves. As the elves fell, the rest of the hunters attacked with vengeful fury.

Of the three Telborian sailors and thugs who also joined the fight, two were hopelessly drunk and missed Dugan by such a large margin that they nearly managed cutting off their own heads. One of the two remaining hunters jabbed into the fray, making it through an attempted block. This attack pierced Dugan's side. At the same time a blow from behind struck across his back. He felt the blood flow from the wounds. He knew he wouldn't last much longer at this rate. The hunters drew closer, dark mirth dancing in their eyes.

A new surge of rage filled Dugan, flooding his muscles with pulsating strength. Shouting a deep-throated roar, he swung his blades wildly, cutting down the last of the elves. His swords laid waste to much of their flesh, even cleaving to the bone on one strike. He quickly yanked the weapons free, shifting to his next challengers.

Witnessing the carnage, the remaining slack-jawed humans decided no award was as important as their lives and ran off into the streets, merging with the cowering populace. Watching the fleeing thugs, Dugan grinned wickedly before seeking out Alara.

He saw the other hunters had surrounded her. She was holding her own for the moment, but appeared in danger of losing that advantage rather quickly. With fierce determination, he leapt for the circle of brown-cloaked elves.

•●•

Alara lost Dugan in a flowing ring of steel and brown cloaks that rapidly swirled up and around him. Some of the elves had continued forward, advancing on Alara, but their threatening posture faded when they realized she was an elf. Her hood was still drawn, hiding much of her distinguishing features, but she kept her falchion readied in hand.

The hunters hesitated.

"Are you hurt?" a thin elf asked Alara in Elonum.

"Not yet," Alara replied in the same tongue.

"Then come with us," said the same elf. "We can get you to safety and then work out the details of how to split the money when we take the slave in for a reward."

"That could be a problem, since I'm aiding in his escape." In one smooth motion Alara pulled back her hood, birthing a small gasp from all present.

"A Patrious in Colloni?" questioned the thin elf in shock.

"She's a *spy!*" A haggard, scratchy-voiced thug stepped forward with his cutlass firmly in hand.

"She might be worth more than the gladiator." The thin elf had become bold. "Take her alive."

"Don't come any closer." Alara planted her feet. "Stand down, and none of you will be hurt."

"Get her!" A hunter pointed his weapon at Alara.

The hunters formed a tight formation around her, their weapons poised for any resistance. But to Alara's surprise the hunters didn't move. She was unclear as to why until she felt the unmistakable pinch of a dagger point at her kidney. A rough arm then laid hold of her neck in a choking grasp as hot, sour breath slapped her ear.

"Not so tough now, are you?" the voice sneered. "Nothing says we can't have a little fun with you before we turn you over to the emperor either. And I can think of at least *one* way to entertain—" But his bravado was cut short by a sword strike through his neck. His severed head fell at Alara's feet with a hollow echo. The three other hunters rapidly retreated from the spectacle as the headless hunter's grip quickly uncoiled from her neck. From out of the corner of her eye she saw the body drop, joining its head in a growing crimson pool.

In a blur of motion she witnessed Dugan race into the fray. When she dared a look backward, her mouth dropped at the carnage the gladiator had wrought. The clanging of steel pulled her focus back toward the man himself as he swung his swords in a great arc, slicing through all three of the stunned elves. As soon as the final hunter fell, Dugan's eyes found Alara.

"Where to now?" A brief coughing spasm took him, ending with him spitting out some blood.

Taking in a deep, shaking breath, she carefully drew near. "How badly did they—"

"Boat." Dugan snarled through his bloody lips.

"There." She pointed to a clump of boats docked for the day. The dock was deserted following the fight; only a few brave souls still watched while hidden away in shadowy corners or from behind fat barrels they'd recently mounted.

"Where?"

"That one over there." Alara motioned to a single-mast sloop whose white sails were rolled up tight. "Come on." She dashed for the vessel. "I don't want to fight the town guard too."

Once he saw it was safe to follow, Dugan returned his swords to their sheaths. Jogging after Alara, he kept a hand at his right side, grimacing with every step. In the short time they'd been running she noticed the wound had already drenched his hand in blood. As vital as it was to attend to the injury, the only goal right now was making it to the boat. That and nothing more.

The boat and nothing else.

CHAPTER 9

I'VE COME TO SEE THAT HISTORY, INDEED LIFE ITSELF, IS A SERIES
OF CYCLES. IF YOU LEARN THEIR PATTERNS YOU CAN PREDICT YOUR FATE.
PREPARE FOR THEIR TURNINGS AND YOU WILL DO WELL AND PROSPER.
HEED THEM NOT AND YOU SHALL SUFFER.

—Korlin, jarthalian philosopher
(5000 BV–4863 BV)

K aden slowed, commanding the other six hobgoblins with him to do the same. He listened carefully to the jungle. It was early morning and already the birds and other animal life were awake, filling the area with their presence. He'd heard something else amid the jungle's song: the sound of a falling body. Eagerly, the hobgoblin crept closer to a section of damaged brush, motioning his men to be ready.

Pressing beyond the underbrush, the subchieftain found his prey: a lone Celetor lying on the ground. Naked save for a breechcloth, he appeared unconscious. Keeping his gaze fixed on the human, Kaden cautiously drew nearer, short sword at the ready. Upon examination, he saw the Celetor still drew breath but wouldn't be doing so for long. It didn't matter. He'd just be the first tossed down Valan's gullet.

Kaden bent down, needling the Celetor with the point of his sword. The man remained still. He gave the human a kick that flipped the Celetor onto his back. No response. Satisfied, he sheathed his weapon. "Tie him up."

Like vultures, four hobgoblins circled the fallen Celetor and tied his feet and hands together. The other two went to a nearby tree to hack off a limb with their swords.

"Khuthon's shown us some favor." Kaden stepped back and let the hobgoblins finish binding the human. "We didn't have to run far to find him." Once a suitable limb had been acquired, the Celetor was latched onto it with the same bast rope binding the rest of him. The four large hobgoblins lifted the branch between them.

"We'll be out here again soon enough," said one of the unburdened hobgoblins. "The wizard will burn through them like all the rest. And then the lottery—"

"No." Kaden quickly interjected. "Boaz isn't going to bring the lottery back."

"Then what are we going to do?" asked the other. "The wizard can't be killed."

"It will be taken care of." Kaden motioned they'd return the way they came. "Now move! Double time."

The hobgoblins got into line, trudging through the dense undergrowth and moist air until they reached the rebuilt stone gate of the ancient city the Basilisk Tribe had come to inhabit. Carrying their cargo past the restored walls, they took stock of the other Celetors they'd captured. It was from this lot the one they carried had dared his escape before they'd fully made it into the city.

Upon their capture, the Celetors had been herded into the open area of a courtyard, and it was there they remained until Kaden returned with the escaped Celetor. All were bound at the wrists, like their comrade, with another rope looped around their waists connecting one to the other, like livestock on their way to the slaughterhouse. Their herdsmen were armed and armored hobgoblins—dressed in the same chain mail shirts and carrying the same short swords as Kaden and those with him.

"Make sure they see him," Kaden said, referring to the other Celetors. "They need to know they aren't getting out of here alive." The men obeyed the order at once, adjusting their position so the hanging Celetor was clearly visible. The faces of his fellow humans, pale and pained, made it clear they understood the message.

"I give 'em three weeks," said one of the hobgoblins carrying the Celetor.

"Might last four," said the one beside him.

"Two at the most," another ventured.

"As long as they keep Valan occupied, it'll be worth it," said Kaden, as the forty waiting Celetors were pulled away to their cells, where they'd await Valan's good graces.

"Keep it going," Kaden ordered as they made their way toward a massive building named the King's Tower. The building stood one hundred feet tall and appeared to have been a bastion of defense in the once mighty city. The tribe realized the potential of the tower immediately and had turned it into a command center from which Boaz could rule with relative security. Most of it had been repaired, save for a crumbled section of masonry on the southwest corner, which remained open like some festering wound. The corner proved a tricky fix; the materials they'd first used failed to keep, and it'd taken some time to solve the problem. But by the time the answer came, so too had Valan, and all plans for completing any business as usual were put on hold.

Double stone doors with worn and defaced friezes guarded the tower's entrance. Like the friezes on the doors, much of the ruins had eroded into faded memories, which none of the tribe—with the exception of the priests—had ever been interested in studying. These massive doors were pushed aside by two hobgoblian guards as Kaden's band drew near.

Kaden stopped and addressed the six men behind him. "Two of you take the Celetor to Valan while he's still of any use. The rest help settle our new prisoners into their cells." The four still carrying the Celetor shifted their burden, allowing half their number to set about their task as Kaden made his way into the King's Tower.

Behind its doors, Kaden entered a small antechamber with two strange statues standing at attention on either side. Each was devoid of any detail save for their legs; their heads were missing, and their upper bodies were marred to the point of ruin. Kaden strode by them without a second glance, aiming for the stairs at the end of the room.

As he climbed, he noted the small roving bands of guard dogs who, like him, were dressed for battle: a combination of leather and chain mail barding. Bred from wild wolves, the dogs made the largest and most aggressive patrol animals possible. With them were the fearsome basilisk patrols. While the extra patrols were enacted after Valan's arrival, they really wouldn't do much against the wizard if it ever came to an actual confrontation. Everyone knew that on some level, no matter how much they tried saying and acting otherwise.

In short order, Kaden climbed the stairs and worked his way through a handful of hallways before stopping at another set of stone doors. Unlike the ones he'd first entered, these still held their intricate carvings. On the left door was a gleaming spear suspended vertically. On the right, the image of a large, grinning skull. No hobgoblin—whether priest or commoner—could decipher the meaning behind the carvings but many liked the symbols just the same, including Boaz, who felt they were a favorable omen and therefore took the room behind them for his throne room. The hobgoblins guarding these doors promptly opened them for Kaden's passage.

Boaz's throne room wasn't opulent, but was an awesome sight nonetheless. The room could comfortably hold a giant and still have space for a good-sized throng. Around its walls were faded and marred frescoes of blue-skinned beings. All of their heads and faces had been chipped away, like everything else they encountered in the ancient ruins.

In these images the figures were engaged in various everyday tasks, from farming to raising livestock and even metalworking. The images were in the middle portion of the walls, looping around in a continuous band. Whatever else might have been part of the room's decor was long since lost and forgotten. Only a polished granite throne remained fastened to the wall opposite the doors. Here it was that Boaz, with the rest of his subchieftains, had staked his claim.

"How was the hunt?" asked Boaz. A set of braziers crackled in the two corners of the room on either side of the throne. Apart from a set of torches attached to the wall on either side of the door, these were the room's only light sources, and cast a sinister shadow over the winged serpents carved into the throne's armrests.

Kaden was amazed at how strong Boaz appeared. If not for the physical deformities he'd suffered, he would have been back to his old self. It was a good sign; these weren't the days to have a weak chieftain on the throne.

"Good enough," he said, making his way before the throne, joining the other subchieftains gathered there. "We're putting the Celetors in the cells now."

"How many?" asked Boaz.

"Forty."

"A decent number." Ranak, like the rest of the subchieftains, stepped aside so Kaden had full access to Boaz.

"How many losses did you take?" Morro inquired.

"Only two," Kaden reported proudly. "They tried to follow us but we quickly beat the fire out of them."

"I had one of the weakest ones sent to Valan, though." Kaden sought out Boaz's face as he spoke, making sure Boaz knew Kaden didn't act without thinking the matter through. "He wouldn't have made it that much longer anyway. He tried to run too."

"So you made an example of him." Boaz nodded. "Wise."

"Now we have some more time," said Ranak.

"To do what, though?" Elek crossed his arms. "This whole process has just made us more his servants, and you know what the Manual of Might says about that."

"How large was the village?" Morro asked Kaden.

"Modest. It isn't a threat to us. Even if they tried attacking, we could crush them with only half our warriors."

"All right." Nalis now joined the conversation. "But we really don't know how much time we have." He shifted his gaze to Boaz. "Then what? If we start up another lottery—"

"There won't be any more lotteries," Boaz thundered.

A moment of silence followed before Boaz starting speaking with Kaden. "Before you arrived, we were talking about how best to put an end to Valan—permanently." Kaden thought they'd discussed the matter before and come up with no solutions—it was what had led them to Boaz's sacrifice and even the capturing of the Celetors—but he did his best to keep his thoughts hidden.

"There are a lot of matters to consider, but it's been an *intense* discussion." Morro was cautious with his words.

"*Debate* is more like it," Elek retorted.

"What's there to discuss?" Kaden searched for answers from the other subchieftains. "All we have are swords, and if we can't kill him with them there's little more we can do."

"I thought so too . . . at first." Kaden listened to Boaz carefully, intrigued by the dark levity playing about the chieftain's features. "But what if we can use that column against him?"

Kaden's eyes widened. "How?"

"That's what we've been debating," said Elek.

"None of us are wizards." Kaden pointed out the obvious. "Or priests," he added for good measure.

"But some of those Celetors *may* be shamans." Ranak shot Kaden a grin as recognition grew in his eyes. "You see it now too, don't you? These Celetors could be a twofold blessing."

"But *none* of them are shamans," said Kaden. "We made sure of that before we tied them up. How do you—"

"Everything isn't clear just yet," said Nalis, "but it just seems too good to pass up. And these humans will help give us more time to see how best to do it."

"But none of them *are* shamans," Kaden repeated with mild frustration. "Haven't you been listening? We've only more wood for the fire, nothing else. There isn't some dagger hidden in these logs."

"But there could be more out there," Elek returned, "perhaps even looking to find their way to us."

"Are you old men or women?" Kaden's rebuke roused some fire behind the subchieftains' eyes. "Are you so afraid of Valan that you're trying to make strategy from wild dreams and wishes?" Motioning to Boaz, he added, "Is this how you honor our chieftain's sacrifice? With fear and trembling before a human wizard?"

"And what would you have us do?" asked Ranak.

"Be men and be strong," answered Kaden. "As Khuthon made us to be."

"Khuthon helps those who help themselves," Morro said, quoting another truth from the Manual of Might. "And we've done just that."

"Then we need to find the next step." Kaden eyed each subchieftain in turn.

"Which brings us back to the column," said Nalis.

•●•

Valan didn't take much notice of the two hobgoblins who entered the chamber. His face was intently planted in a book resting on his lectern. Above him floated the ever-present glowing globe, whose light aided his reading.

"What do you want?" he asked in Goblin.

"We were told to bring him here." Valan heard a hobgoblin step closer, followed by the sound of something heavy dropping on the floor. Valan peered up from his work with mild interest, then quickly became more focused and alert once he caught sight of what they'd brought.

"A *Celetor*?" He hurried to the hobgoblins. "Where did you find him?"

"In the jungle," said the same hobgoblin. "We captured a good many."

"Finally, a *human* test subject," Valan said to himself in Telboros. This would be a welcome change. The hobgoblins and goblins had been suitable for working on the Transducer's basic functions, but if he was really going to master the finer traits, he needed a human candidate.

He came to stand before the Celetor, searching his crumpled frame with intense interest. He wasn't sure if he liked what he saw. There was a look of weakness about him. "Is he wounded?"

"No." The hobgoblin shook his head.

"Then untie him." Valan carefully watched the hobgoblins hurriedly free the Celetor from his bindings. While there were no wounds, there was still a less-than-animated nature about him.

"You sure he isn't dead?"

"He's not dead," said one, "just ginshaw."

"Ginshaw?" Valan searched his mind for the correlating Telborian word. "Unconscious?"

"Yes." The hobgoblin gave a small nod.

"Then wake him up!"

The hobgoblin slapped the Celetor's face until he made a low groan. Valan took this as a good sign. He'd need the Celetor fully awake if he was going to get the most use out of him.

"Now place him inside." He motioned to the Transducer.

Finally awake and alert, the Celetor started screaming bloody curses at his assailants as they dragged him up to the opening at the column's base with scant care or finesse before throwing him through it. Landing on his back, the Celetor quickly righted himself and attempted to maneuver out of the column, finding the exit blocked by an invisible barrier.

"Don't waste your strength trying to escape," Valan informed the Celetor in Telboros, though it was doubtful he could understand him. "It's quite secure. And you'll need your strength in any case." The mage hurried to his lectern, ignoring the shouts accompanying the frenzied pounding on the invisible barrier.

Once they realized Valan was about to work his spell, the hobgoblins quickly cleared out, shivering as they heard the wrought iron gate close behind them. Both stood transfixed with anxious eyes as Valan raised his arms and recited the words to the ancient spell he'd said scores of times before.

"Thoth ron heen ackleen. Lore ulter-bak ulter-bak . . ." His voice was drowned out by the Transducer's rising hum. As he continued, the runes on the column flared into new life. Blazing-hot purple light singed the chamber walls, forcing the hobgoblins to squint. The Celetor let out a few cries, but they were muted and muffled, as if he was willing himself to remain silent.

The humming grew stronger, as did the light, until the room was completely swallowed in the eerie illumination, totally obscuring the view of the column's interior. Valan escalated the incantation, taking it to the next level of power—higher than he'd dared so far. It was time to push himself to the limit—and then beyond—in order to find the missing answers. He pressed as far as he could before finally letting the spell complete its course.

The purple light grew dimmer and dimmer, until only the glow of the runes scrawled across the column remained. The opening in the column finally stopped glowing. Valan took a deep breath before making his way through the gate. As he ventured near the column's opening, he strained his ears in the overpowering silence, focusing on what might lay inside.

"No!" His voice became a low growl upon seeing the smooth, curved walls of the Transducer's interior splattered with blood and innards. Small chunks of anatomy hung on the walls in sticky globs, while a great pile of ruined mess congealed in its center. This molten mound of flesh lay like a pile of butcher's refuse, sinew and bone crossed in a macabre sculpture.

"I was so close." He took special note of the skull crowning the cooling flesh. There was something very awkward about its appearance, as though it were looking inside itself. It was then he realized with growing rage that the skull, and the rest of what had been the Celetor, had been turned completely inside out.

"So close. How could this happen?" He departed the cooling remains and ran to his tome, wildly tearing through it like a man possessed. After a few frantic pages, he fell silent, raising his gaze to the hobgoblins, who continued staring stupidly at the column.

Taking a calming breath, he asked, "How many more do you have?"

"About two score."

He slowly nodded. "Clean up that mess," he said, pointing at the column. "I want it ready for another test in an hour."

Timidly, the hobgoblins obeyed. Valan focused again on his tome, muttering to himself as he searched for answers. "I *will* master you!"

CHAPTER 10

AEROTRIPTON HAS GIVEN ME A VISION: ONE ELVEN NATION
UNDER UNIFIED RULE. AND IT ALL STARTS WITH THE INFORMATION
WE'LL FIND HIDDEN IN SOME RUINS ON TALATHEAL.

—**Barius Leonicus Marro, current emperor of the Republic of Colloni**
Reign: 714 PV–present

Alara manned the rudder, wiping fresh sweat from her brow. The warm sun would wring out more soon enough. The sloop she steered was a simple affair: large enough to allow some comfort while they traveled, but small enough to keep from being seen as a threat or of interest to anyone they might meet. It flew no flag and bore no markings, a nondescript vessel hopefully keeping under the notice of all it passed. And so far it had worked. She prayed it would continue working until the mission was over. She didn't want any more surprises.

Thinking of surprises had her checking on Dugan. She'd placed him across from her, having him rest perpendicular to her present location. Close enough to keep an eye on but still far enough out of the way. She'd washed the minor wounds, content they'd eventually heal into new scars, and bound the one at his side with light cloth torn from her blanket. The simple bindings were stained a deep red but held firm.

She also made sure his swords were free of his person. She'd taken the sheaths along with the blades, keeping them to her right. She could have hid them from him but wanted to display a sign of trust—measured trust, anyway. She wasn't disarming him outright, as in theory the swords were still in reach, while he'd proved he didn't need them on hand for the voyage. While there was a logic to this, she didn't know how well he'd take it, and she wouldn't know until he finally woke. And given the last few hours, that didn't seem a likely event anytime soon. Confident she'd continue enjoying some more peace and quiet, she was startled when Dugan suddenly jerked against the deck.

"Sit back," she ordered. "You'll break the bandages."

Dugan eyed her with a groggy expression. "Where are we?" His voice was hoarse.

"On the boat. You passed out shortly after getting onboard. I thought you'd be out for days."

Dugan tried pushing himself upward but fell back onto the deck with a thud and a groan. "How long have I been asleep?"

"We've been at sea for half a day." She set her eyes on the full sails billowing out from the single mast toward the sloop's bow. "I'd wager we'll dock on Altorbia by evening tomorrow if the wind continues favoring us." Once more she brought her gaze his way. "Then we'll be off to our final destination."

"Which is?" Dugan half whispered, closing his eyes.

"Talatheal. You should be safe there." She observed Dugan's eyelids flutter as he tried staying conscious.

"This isn't a normal wound."

"I was told some hunters use a drug on their swords to keep the wounds bleeding and make their victims dizzy."

"Told by who?" Dugan turned his head as he cracked one eye partially open.

"The drug will run its course, but only if you remain still and asleep. Get some more rest and you'll feel better when we make landfall. Of course," she couldn't resist adding, "we wouldn't *be* in such a mess if you hadn't been so stupid back on the docks."

"What do you mean?" Both his eyelids shot open.

"You know full well what I mean. Why, in the name of the Abyss, did you start swinging your swords about and making a spectacle of yourself? You gave away our cover just when we were within sight of the boat."

He hesitated before answering. "I saw something."

"What?"

"I don't know, but it started to attack me." From what she could tell, Dugan really believed what he was saying. "You didn't see it?"

"No. Just the hunters and others you brought down on us."

"You bound the wound well enough." He inspected his stomach with modest satisfaction.

"I've had plenty of practice," she replied.

"You a healer too?"

"No, but I've had my fair share of cuts and bruises." She stared ahead at the modest cabin in the middle of the sloop. Part of her longed for the simple cot inside. Getting out of this constant sun would be nice too, but she needed to keep the ship on course until they reached the others. Until then, she needed to press on, and hoped Dugan would remain cooperative. There weren't a lot of alternatives available in the open water.

"Your father was a warrior?" Dugan reeled Alara's thoughts back into the conversation.

"He's an artist, actually—a sculptor. I've seen him craft some amazing things out of simple stone and wood. My brothers were the ones who joined the army." Speaking of her family had her imagining their shock at the sight of her sailing alone on a boat in the middle of the Cerulean Sea with an escaped gladiator. Of course, they wouldn't know this wasn't the first adventure she'd undertaken.

"Still full of surprises." Dugan offered a weak smile.

"When my brothers spent time in the yard training, I'd watch them while tending the goats and sheep. Then, when I was alone, I mimicked their movements and learned how to fight on my own."

"It's quite a jump from simple practice to doing it for real." Dugan winced again as he shifted his back.

"I did more than just mimic their moves," said Alara. "I found ways to put what I learned into practice. And there were plenty of thieves and brigands to help."

Dugan let loose a rough laugh that made her fear he might actually harm himself. This was especially true when his mirth quickly ended with another wince and tightly scrunched eyes. "Must have surprised your family." When Alara didn't respond, Dugan smirked. "They don't know, do they?"

"I wasn't going to be content keeping sheep and goats all my life."

"And why's that?"

"You should get some rest. You'll need your strength if—"

"If I decide to join you," Dugan interrupted. "I haven't yet."

"No." Alara gave a small sigh. "You haven't yet." She was hoping they could avoid that part until after they were back on land—open water and fewer options and all that.

"And you still think I will." There was only a hint of mockery in the Telborian's voice.

"I wouldn't have gone to all the trouble of finding you if I didn't."

Dugan started saying something but instead began to shudder, holding back a muffled groan through clenched teeth.

"Rest now." Alara took on a maternal tone. "All that matters right now is that we got out alive."

"You . . . never told me," he grunted through a stiff jaw, "how you knew my name."

"Later. Just rest." And though Dugan fought it for a time, slumber came over him once more. She leaned back and let her mind drift as her hands aptly worked the rudder.

The next day found her still stationed at her post, watching the setting sun sinking into a bank of red clouds. A lone seagull circled above them, having done so for the past hour. It was a good sign they were getting closer to land. Dugan still rested where she'd placed him. She didn't dare move him, just gave him some water from time to time and made sure he was as covered from the sun as possible.

It appeared he'd made it through the worst of it, which was a relief given all she'd gone through to get him onboard. The hardest part was learning to take short naps while also being ready for instant action upon waking. There was a latch to help keep the rudder fixed in place, but adjustments still had to be made if they wanted to stay on course. It might not have been ideal, but the momentary breaks helped keep her strength up and sped their journey.

As the day aged, she noticed a faint haze outlined on the multicolored horizon. It was small and fleeting at first, the waves blocking it from view with their crests only to reveal it once more, but it was there nonetheless. Altorbia. They'd nearly made it. She speculated they'd reach the island well under the cover of darkness, which would help her disembark and reach the others without any undue attention.

Elyellium populated more than half of the tiny isle, while the rest of the inhabitants were Telborian merchants getting fat off the rich commerce passing through the ports every day. Although Altorbia was somewhat diverse in terms of its racial makeup, it was still considered part of the Republic of Colloni. This meant there could still be some hunters, especially given how many seemed to have been stirred up like a hornet's nest back on Colloni. Their visit would need to be brief and their departure well before dawn. The harbors and docks were watched very closely on Altorbia. If she was going to run into any trouble, this is where it would happen. And given the unexpected encounter back in Argis, she wanted to be extra careful.

Night fell as the boat silently coasted into Altorbia's sleepy western harbor. The cobblestone wharfs were dimly washed in the orange glow flowing from lampposts lining the docks. These lampposts were a unique feature of the island, having thick, square bases jutting out about five feet from the ground and capped in fat glass domes overlaid with metal netting. Their wicks went all the way down the interior of the posts, into the bases where the oil was stored. The posts had been crafted to withstand heavy wind, storms, and turbulent waves. The tiny fire behind their globes emitted just enough light to outline the docks, preventing ships from ramming into the wharfs—though the docks were supposed to be closed to night traffic—and keeping guards from losing their footing in the darkness.

Most of the docks rested on a beach stretching for some twenty feet inland before transforming into rocky earth. Dark trees a short distance from this stony ground swayed in the moonlit wind, carrying the off-key notes and banter of sailors spending their evening in the taverns beyond. Alara noted the sounds and terrain as she quietly maneuvered her sloop to a secluded section of dock about fifty feet from the island's end. She'd made arrangements for this portion of the dock to be empty and ready for her arrival. Once she got close, she moored the boat to a slab of granite jutting out of the platform. Apart from the sounds of the drunken sailors, all was silent. Not a guard in sight. Even so, it was best to remain cautious.

Taking stock of Dugan, she weighed her options. She'd put a fresh dressing on the wound a few hours ago, and was pleased to note it was still clean, but worried he'd be too weak from the blood loss to undertake any activity. Even so, she wasn't going to just leave him to wake up in a strange harbor in the middle of the night, either. It could easily cause more problems she'd rather not have.

She crouched at his side and softly slapped Dugan's cheek.

"Wh—"

"Shhh," she whispered. "Be still. The poison's gone, but you're still weak. We made it to Altorbia, but I don't want us to be discovered. How are you feeling?"

Dugan struggled to sit up. "Fine. Just tell me where we're going."

"I'm going to a tavern to get the others, then—"

"*We're* going." Dugan managed to remain sitting and clutched his bandaged side. "I won't stay here."

"You're in no condition to come with me. You need rest and food. I'll bring you back some meat from the tavern when I return with the others."

"I need the food, but I've had enough sleep." Alara noted his eyes gaining an inner flame. "If I slept any more, I'd be dead."

"You almost *were*, so don't go risking your life doubting my integrity." She nervously shifted her eyes back to the harbor before circling back on Dugan. It was still empty. "Gilban was right about you. You *are* stubborn beyond all reasoning."

"*Gilban?*" Dugan demanded. "Who's he?"

"The one who told me where I'd be able to find you."

"Another elf?"

"Yes. He's Patrious, like me."

"What does he want from me?" Dugan struggled to stand, failing in his attempt with a groan.

"We're wasting time. Gilban can tell you himself once I return with him and the others. Please understand, you have nothing to fear." Alara turned to leave, but was stopped short by Dugan's firm grip around her ankle.

"Let go, you big ox!" she whispered, trying to shake her leg free. "We've wasted too much time already."

"Both of us go," Dugan grunted.

"Let go, or you'll ruin my timing!" Alara kicked at him more brutally.

Dugan abruptly released her ankle and quickly rose to his full height. She was about to rebuke the thoughtless gladiator, but he stood defiant, eyes blazing fiercely in the dim lamplight. She also noticed he'd regained a sword, holding it firmly in his clenched fist.

"Haven't I gained *any* trust from you?"

The two stared at each other for a few heartbeats before Dugan broke the silence. "I'm going with you."

"Fine." Alara reached down onto the deck where she'd placed her bow and quiver, and pulled a second hunter's cloak from a sack of supplies. "Take this—the one you have on soaked up too much blood."

"Three then, huh?" Dugan said as he swapped the bloodstained cloak for the newer one, letting the soiled garment fall in a clump at his feet.

"What?" Alara slipped her quiver over her shoulder, followed by her bow.

"This cloak's newer than the last one." Somehow he managed retrieving the two sheaths and other sword when she wasn't looking, strapping both across his waist as they'd been before. "You must have killed more than one hunter. The cloak back at Argis, this one, and another for *your* new cloak . . ." Dugan grinned. "Unless you washed it on the way."

Alara gestured for him to follow then jumped nimbly onto the dock. After making sure the sword belts were firmly in place, he did the same.

"If you fall over from your wounds, I'm not stopping to pick you up!" She drew her hood as she started on her way through the night. Wrapping the scented cloth tightly around his body, Dugan followed her onto the sandy streets.

"Even after you dragged me through the forest and bound my wound?" The question was more tweaking barb than simple inquiry. But he did have a point—it *was* a pretty foolish threat.

She cocked her head to one side, whispering, "So what more have I got to do to prove to you you're safe?"

"Show me this Gilban for a start." Dugan brought up his hood.

"You won't have to wait long."

The two of them reached the Musky Otter without incident. From the noise emanating from the tavern, it seemed as if the entire island's population had migrated into the alehouse. The simple structure was of aged timber with a few open windows here and there and a nondescript door a few steps from the main street. Above the door a placard sporting a comical image of an otter holding a mug of foamy ale told all who couldn't read the Telboros and Elonum beneath that this was indeed the Musky Otter.

"Are you *sure* you want to go inside?" she whispered, watching Dugan draw up behind her. "There's still time to go back to the boat."

"I need some ale." He clenched his jaw and closed his eyes. When he next spoke, his voice was a hoarse whisper. "Mutton and ale."

"Just don't talk if you don't have to, and if you do, speak in Elonum. We can't afford another fight if anyone notices us here."

He made for the tavern door. "My stomach may be sliced, but I'm still hungry."

Alara couldn't blame him. After two days at sea her own stomach leapt at the prospect of getting filled, even groaning a bit at the smells of roasted meat wafting her way.

Looking hesitantly about before advancing farther into the light leaking out the tavern's windows, she waited for Dugan to reach the doorway, then followed. A curtain of smoke and grease greeted their entrance. Once through, Alara studied the patrons seated at the large barrel tables and shabby stools. Benches lined the walls and key traffic locations, allowing those who simply wanted a tankard of ale a place to rest their feet. It was a good-sized tavern and the ideal setting for those wishing to stay hidden from prying eyes, and so suited their needs perfectly.

Drunken elven and human sailors filled the establishment, laughing at bawdy jokes or trying to grab the serving women who maneuvered in and around benches and stools with the ease of practiced dancers. A few patrons glanced at the newcomers, assumed they were two hunters, and simply continued on with their business. In short order, a new round of obnoxious singing began from the distant corners of the room. In time, more vocal drunks joined in, swinging their ale-filled mugs in an off-key salute to these maritime ballads, spilling their ale in amber cascades as they sang.

"Follow me," she told Dugan, who shadowed her as they made their way to the opposite side of the room and a small counter. It was a fine spot to watch the set of stairs leading to the guest rooms on the second story. Upon taking their seat, a tall and well-muscled Telborian appeared behind the mahogany countertop. He'd the rugged looks of a local tough, but these were softened by his aging face, gray hair, and laugh lines.

"What you having?" he asked in Elonum.

"Ale and mutton," Dugan replied in the same language.

The innkeeper turned to Alara. "How about you?"

"Wine, and some bread," she replied coolly.

The innkeeper left the duo for a kitchen through a door a few feet away. As he did, the odors of flaming grease and soured milk wafted into the dining area.

"I don't see anyone yet," Alara informed Dugan, "but I think we're a bit early." She kept her voice low as she spoke in Telboros.

"Who're we looking for?" Dugan whispered.

"You'll know him when you see him. Actually"—Alara's eye caught the movement of a familiar shape—"there he is now."

An elf, dressed in coarse brown robes tied with a simple hemp rope, made his way slowly down the stairs. He wore black high-necked sandals and carried an oak staff in his left hand, thumping in succession from stair to stair as he made his descent. A silver necklace of ornate design hung around his neck. His eyes were white—devoid of sight—but there was a look of calm wisdom in his features. Like Alara, he was a Patrician elf, although signs of aging showed across his face. The biggest difference was his clean-shaven head.

"You mean *he's* your leader? That *blind* old elf?"

Alara glared at Dugan through her hood like a cobra ready to strike. "That blind old elf told me where to find you *and* your name—*before* it was being blabbed around by all the hunters."

"So he's a wizard?"

"He's a priest of Saredhel. We can trust him."

"Saredhel?"

"She's a goddess who enlightens chosen servants with visions and other prophetic gifts. Gilban was one who received a special vision—but I'll let him tell you of it when he reaches us."

"*If* he reaches us. And he probably won't without being lifted of coin and balance along the way."

"Then you don't know the power of Saredhel, Dugan," a rather low and aged voice, speaking the same strangely accented Telboros as Alara, calmly replied near Dugan's ear.

Dugan spun and faced the wizened elf, nearly knocking his hood off in the process. "How did you get here so quickly?" he whispered, forgetting to use Elonum and reverting to Telboros.

"I walked," he said before turning to Alara with a blind stare. "He's wounded, is he not?"

"It happened before we reached the boat."

"How'd you know that?" Dugan studied Gilban's sightless face. "You haven't even touched me."

Gilban simply smiled and accepted a stool beside Alara. After adjusting it, he sat down, then placed his staff at his side, letting it rest against the counter.

"Why aren't you cloaked like she is?" Dugan motioned to Alara. This time he remembered to use Elonum.

"Altorbia has no care about my presence," said Gilban in Telboros. "If I were a buxom young maiden rather than a wrinkled, blind priest, things might be different. I pose no danger, and most would just as soon ignore me. It is therefore unnecessary for me to be cloaked. I have nothing from which to hide." The blind priest shared a small smile, adding, "Saredhel sees to the rest."

Dugan grew silent.

"I trust you found him as I instructed?" Gilban asked Alara.

"Yes, he was just where you said he'd be."

"Good." Gilban's pure-white eyes seemed to almost look right into Alara's own. It was something that used to unsettle her, but she'd gotten used to a blind priest who behaved at times as if he still had sight. "Where are the others?"

She scanned the tavern once more. "I haven't seen them yet. They may have encountered some trouble."

Gilban closed his eyes. "No, they're fine, though the dwarf seems to be moving rather sluggishly at the moment." They proceeded to talk in hushed tones, stopping only briefly when the innkeeper brought Alara and Dugan their meals. Alara filled Gilban in on everything that had happened since last they parted ways, making sure she didn't leave anything out when it came to Dugan.

● ● ●

As Dugan ate, he studied the priest. There was something odd about him. He matched the general traits of the elves, at least as far as he knew, but Gilban was different. He was older, similar to a human male of sixty, maybe seventy—though he knew that wasn't the case. He was probably far older than most humans could live to even in their ripe old age. But his age wasn't the most unusual thing about him.

He was taken by an otherworldly essence which made the elf seem very wise and observant of all around him. And this even though he lacked sight. Additionally, Dugan found himself drawn to the priest's necklace. Crafted of silver, it was inlaid with a clear crystal resting at its center, reflecting the light. The crystal was surrounded by a coronet of mother-of-pearl from which radiated a multitude of gold lines. This left an impression of the center of the crystal swimming in a sea of milk and gold.

The longer he stared at the pendant, the more he was convinced it looked like an eye. The crystal was the pupil, the mother-of-pearl the whites, and the gold lines the iris. Truly, it was a wondrous, if strange, symbol. What it could mean, however, was beyond him. Seeing he wasn't going to get any more answers just yet, given their rapid babbling he couldn't decipher even if he tried, he decided to focus on his food.

He sipped his ale as he scanned the tavern, instinctively looking for signs of trouble, especially hunter trouble. He'd never known a lifestyle like that around him. All he could see was decadence and debauchery. Up until now, his world had been a stone cell where he was chained to the wall, his bed cold dirt and straw-covered stone. His food had been nourishing gruel served lukewarm. He was in a new world now and determined to make the best of it as long as he could. Should he find his way off this island, he was looking forward to delving more into what this new world could offer a free man.

His mind was ripe with such thoughts as he devoured his meal. Even though it made him sick with its richness, he continued gorging. His greasy hands grabbed the common goblet and drained what was left of its contents into his stuffed stomach. He'd never known the feeling of satisfaction until he awoke from his trance-like gluttony and found his plate empty and goblet bone dry. He had to admit it was an addicting and pleasant sensation. He was licking his greasy fingers when he noticed Alara watching.

"What are you doing?"

"Eating. This is the best food I've ever had."

"It could be your last. Did you ever think to use the fork or knife?"

For the first time he noticed the unused utensils beside his empty plate. "No."

"Well," Alara said as she looked around the room, "elves and other civilized folk use them, so you'd better hope nobody saw you eating."

The tavern quieted as a cloaked figure fluttered through the open door. He was of a taller, thinner build than most of the sailors in the establishment, and at first glance it was hard to tell if the new arrival was friend or foe. The matter was quickly resolved, though, when the smell of pine sap, nutmeg, sage, and leather made itself known.

"Who is it?" Gilban asked.

"Hunter," Dugan whispered in Telboros.

Gilban rose from his seat. "We have to get out of here before we're seen."

"Too late!" Alara whispered. "Try not to talk," she told Dugan. "Let *us* handle this."

The gladiator wiped his hands on his cloak before pulling it shut. He sat motionless, resisting with every ounce of will the instinct to attack the advancing threat.

"Hello, friend!" The hunter addressed Dugan in Elonum as he approached. "Might I join you for a bit?" He indicated the open seat on Dugan's left.

Dugan gave an anemic nod.

"It's nice to have somebody to talk to who enjoys the same profession." The hunter took a seat. "I don't often see too many hunters this far out these days. Least not with all the news of the ruckus in Colloni. Now *there's* a catch if there ever was one, eh?"

Dugan pretended he was searching for something inside his cloak. In reality, he'd turned to Alara, signaling frantically at her with his eyes about the growing danger. Alara indicated with her own to remain calm. He also noticed Gilban had vanished and gave Alara a questioning look. She shook her head slightly, warning him to concentrate solely on the hunter.

Seeing there wasn't much he could do at the moment, Dugan returned to his hunter "friend." He wondered what Gilban was up to. He never did like priests much, nor the gods they served. He just hoped he could last with the hunter long enough to think of a way to escape.

"I haven't claimed one bounty this year," the hunter continued. "The way I figure it, one has to cross my path soon enough. And when it does, I'll be living well for the rest of the year. How about you, friend—gain any coin yet?"

"No," Dugan said in a rough voice hidden by the Elyelmic tongue.

"That's just the way things go, I guess. The gods just hand out blessings differently to different people. I figure with so many out in Colloni looking for that escaped gladiator, the practical thing is to stay behind and pick up the slack they dropped. Course, if I happen to run into him, I wouldn't turn him down either." The hunter laughed. "Though he wouldn't stand much chance against you, I'd wager."

The hunter's eyes narrowed as they loosely searched Dugan's body before relaxing their gaze. "What's your secret to getting so large? If I was as sturdy as you, no slave would stand a chance!" The hunter reached over and grabbed the upper portion of Dugan's left arm. Dugan wasn't able to move fast enough, and the hunter's hands quickly encircled it.

Out of the corner of his eye, Dugan saw Alara cringe.

"Tripton's bow!" the hunter exclaimed, squeezing Dugan's bicep. "It's like iron!" Unfortunately, when the hunter had grabbed Dugan's arm, the front of his cloak shifted, exposing part of his bare chest. At first, the hunter didn't notice the gap, continuing to admire Dugan's strength. But after a few seconds, his eyes found Dugan's exposed skin and the branding mark that must have shone like a beacon on his shoulder.

A smile traced its way around the hunter's lips. "You're mine, sla—"

Dugan's fist rammed into the hunter's mouth. The blow shattered some of the elf's teeth and sent a shower of misty blood into the air. In spite of this, the hunter desperately struggled to hold on to Dugan's arm as he tried drawing his sword.

It was then that Alara struck, jabbing a dagger into the hunter's neck with lightning speed. An eruption of crimson spurts and spasms followed. The hunter struggled for a final moment, trying frantically to remove the deadly weapon from his jugular, but to no avail. A handful of heartbeats later he slumped to the floor, his life leaking away with each spasm.

"Come on!" Alara shouted over the tavern's growing commotion.

Dugan didn't linger. He took one big stride past Alara and then burst into a sprint from the inn, feeling like a hunted beast once more. Cries of outrage and disorder erupted from the door as they hurried onto the street. Filtered throughout the chaos were shouts for the guards.

The streets were a blur as they ran through the night. "Go to the right!" Alara ordered. Dugan obeyed without hesitation, even though the strenuous action of running made his wound leak and burn. He ignored the tiny streams of warm blood trickling down his waist, continuing forward with all his might.

The sliver of a moon was the only source of light in the alleyways they now traveled. The moonlight barely illuminated the path ahead, but he thought he spotted movement in the gloom of the alley on their right. He stopped suddenly, causing Alara to barrel straight into him.

Dugan drew his swords.

"What are you doing?"

"Someone's in that alley." He shook his head to clear his blurring vision.

"Are you sure?" Alara's breathing was shallow as she spoke. "I can't see anything! We don't have time for you to start fighting air again."

"Someone's there." He continued pushing off the fuzziness of his peripheral vision.

"Just keep going. The guards will be upon us if we wait any longer."

Dugan remained motionless. "Who's there?" he shouted in Telboros.

The only sound filling his ears was the footfalls of the advancing guard.

"Come on! The guards are almost on top of us!" Just as Alara took hold of Dugan's arm, the figure in the alleyway moved into the moonlight. The slender form leaned on the staff in its left hand and wore a brown robe tied with a hemp rope belt.

"It's Gilban!" Dugan hissed. "How'd you get all the way out here?"

"I walked."

"He set us up to be captured by that hunter! Now he wants to finish the job!"

"That's nonsense. I already told you—" Alara's features were suddenly awash with fresh concern. "Are you feeling all right?"

"I—" Dugan staggered. He felt his mind going black and his legs growing numb.

"Gods above, you're bleeding to death!" Alara hurriedly tried propping him upright.

"It's nothing." Even without looking he could feel himself bleeding a good amount now. Not as bad as before in Argis but enough to do him harm the longer it continued.

"We have to get off the street." She tried helping him get to the alleyway.

"I . . . won't trust . . . that devil."

"Don't be stupid!" Alara persisted in assisting him to stagger forward. Behind them, the boots of the local guard grew ever nearer.

"I don't . . . need help . . ."

He collapsed with a thud.

• ● •

"Bring him, Alara, and hurry!" Gilban spoke from the darkness. "There isn't much time."

She struggled with dragging Dugan's dead weight by his ankles, managing to only move him a foot before stopping to catch her breath. She was still sore from moving him the other night on Colloni, but approaching torches forced her to find new strength. In short order she'd lugged him into the alleyway before hunching over on her knees with a heavy sigh.

Gilban's empty stare fell upon Dugan's bloodied torso as Alara dared a quick look the way she'd come. She didn't want to leave anything behind for the guards to discover. Confident she hadn't, she returned to Dugan. The wound had grown deeper with their run from the tavern and was bleeding profusely through his bandages. Shouts in Elonum and heavy footfalls brought her into a squat beside Dugan. She held her breath and watched a group of torch-carrying elven guards run past the alleyway.

"Remove the bandage," Gilban said after they'd passed. Without questioning, she unwrapped the wet dressings, exposing the hideous gash. "Place my hands on the center of the wound."

Gingerly, she gripped Gilban's hands, helped him get down into a kneeling position, then gently placed them on top of the red mess. Muttering, Gilban caressed the wound as Dugan grunted his displeasure. Gilban began speaking in Pacolees, the tongue of the Patrious, to a goddess few knew.

"Saredhel, Mother of Prophets, Seer of All, I ask from you a favor. I ask that you wrestle the life of this man from the gates of Mortis. You can see the end of all things and know the tasks this man is yet to perform.

"Save him from this fate, for you alone know his true fate and how he shall tie his life in with those who have been called for this holy task. Please, Spawn of Dreams, hear me and grant my request." Gilban's hand began to glow with faint lavender light as the wound beneath it slowly closed—folding together like wax and melting back into healthy flesh until it was completely restored. Not even a scar or blemish remained.

Dugan's eyes fluttered, then opened.

Gilban smiled calmly as he completed his prayer. "Thank you."

CHAPTER 11

IT'S OFTEN THIN THREADS THAT CONNECT ONE TO ANOTHER,
BUT IF YOU WEAVE THEM TOGETHER YOU'LL HAVE A STRONG ROPE.

—Old Tralodroen proverb

D ugan couldn't help noticing Alara and Gilban's faces peering down at him. He remembered falling and could feel the rough stone beneath him. Then he saw the dimming lavender light around the seer's hands.

"What did you do?"

"Kept you on Tralodren a while longer, apparently," said Gilban. "It seems your destiny is yet to be fulfilled."

Dugan sat up and rubbed at his side where his wound had been; his flesh was now completely healed. There wasn't even a hint of discomfort, let alone pain. Even the other wounds from the fight in Argis were gone—*and* the previous wounds in his shoulder from the arena.

"How—"

"There are higher levels of existence than this material life, and higher matters of importance than the daily routines in it," said Gilban. "We all have a part to play—and an important one at that."

"I thought only Asora healed." Dugan ignored the elf's comment as religious mumblings. He needed to know what had happened. He needed to know just what sort of goddess Gilban *really* served. Maybe one strong enough to—

"She does . . . for the most part."

"But then—"

"I suggest being wiser next time you get into a fight," Gilban continued. "Saredhel might not be so willing the second time around."

"It's still nothing short of miraculous!" Alara exclaimed. Clearly, this sort of thing was just as uncommon for her as it was for him. It made him wonder how much she knew about this blind priest she was following.

"So what do we do now?" He cautiously stood, making sure everything else was as it should be. It was. In fact, he felt better than he had in days.

"*We?*" Alara raised an eyebrow. "You've decided to come with us?"

"I think I've been convinced to stay." He motioned to his healed side.

"Then as soon as you're ready, we'll find the others and get off this island."

"What then? What's this mission about?"

Alara paused as if sizing him up one last time. "You're to aid Gilban and me on a matter of dire importance to the Republic of Rexatoius. You already know Gilban and I aren't the same type of elves you've come to know. It's the Elyellium who have sought to build a vast empire in ages past, and it's the Elyellium who took you as a slave. We Patrious departed from their fold thousands of years ago and look to keep them from repeating the mistakes of the past.

"Recently, Gilban received a vision from Saredhel. It told of the Elyellium calling for the rebuilding of their empire through some knowledge hidden away in ancient ruins in the jungle of Taka Lu Lama on Talatheal. If they get their hands on this knowledge, they'll use it to expand their power and influence, and the Republic of Colloni will become an empire once more."

"And you're sure about all this?" Dugan went from Alara to Gilban.

"I have foreseen it," came the priest's reply. "We must make sure the Elyellium don't gain what they seek."

"So what *is* this knowledge?" Dugan pressed Gilban. "And what are *you* planning to do with it once you get it?"

"We Patrious have long known that before mortalkind first emerged, there was a single race, called dranors," said Gilban. "They were powerful beings blessed by the gods, able to do things we mortals can only dream of, but they fell into disgrace." The elf's unseeing eyes seemingly locked on to some far-off vision as he spoke.

"They became self-righteous, self-worshiping, and in their arrogance, they attempted to control the world. Some even claimed themselves to be gods, until the *true* gods punished them for their sins and sent them to their doom. However, before eradicating the dranors, the gods used them as the seedbed of mortalkind. That is the true history of the world, and very few know, save the Patrious and those who take the time to seek it out.

"The ruins hidden away inside Taka Lu Lama are what remains of a once-powerful dranoric stronghold. They contain information on how to build and maintain a strong empire for countless millennia, if not an eternity. We need to stop this information from passing into the hands of the Elyellium, for it was fragments of this knowledge that enabled them to establish their empire in the first place. To gain greater insight into such information would be to assure the new empire they'd build would be mightier than the current races have ever seen." Gilban sighed, shaking his head. "I've foreseen the time when all I have told you will come to pass, and it is fast approaching."

"You believe all this?" Dugan asked Alara.

"The priests of Saredhel don't lie, and Gilban is one of the strongest among them. I trust him with my life, as do those who sent us and chose him as their representative on this mission."

"But what happens to this information once *you* get it?" Dugan kept an eye on Alara.

"The Patrious have always been lovers of knowledge and history," she replied with a small degree of pride. "Since the days of Cleseth, our nation's founder, we've sought to record what has transpired in the world, both incredible and mundane. Through our efforts, we've managed to restore lost insight from ages past, after the various dark ages that covered the world. We also look to keep potentially harmful knowledge—like what the Elyellium seek—hidden from those who would abuse it or use it for great evil. We respect peace and don't want to see another war for domination of Tralodren."

"Their story checks out if you're having second thoughts," a gruff voice speaking Telboros said from the darkness. "At least as far as I've come to understand it."

Dugan instinctively spun around, brought up his swords, and planted his feet. All he found were shadows in the street outside the alleyway.

"Show yourself."

A figure slowly materialized out of the darkness. Dugan was amazed to see a dwarf stepping forward. Dwarves normally didn't frequent the arena. He'd only learned about them through exaggerated tales from the other gladiators. Such stories gave them mythical qualities this dwarf apparently didn't possess, like fiery eyes and a frosty breath capable of freezing a man solid.

The dwarf stood four and a half feet tall, stout and strong with thick muscles bulging from his arms and legs. His leathery skin was tinted a charcoal gray—darker than the two Patrious' lighter gray complexions. His stern mouth was enshrined in a salt-and-pepper beard braided in two distinct strands cascading over his copper-studded brigandine leather armor, with the tips of each braid dyed a deep crimson.

His double-bladed axe swung from a holster on his belt. It was decorated with a collection of runes carved deep into the metal's surface, twisting down the handle before ending at the dwarf's ankle. He walked with a shortened gait and slight limp, which Dugan suspected was the result of him counterbalancing the axe's weight. Not until he looked straight into the dwarf's face did he see that his left eye was covered by a black leather patch decorated with golden runes similar to those on the axe.

Alara gestured to the new arrival. "Dugan, this is Vinder, one of the others we've gathered for this mission."

"And what have we here?" The dwarf tugged at his braids. "This wouldn't be the fellow who raised all the ruckus with the guards I saw a few blocks back now, would it?"

"Maybe." Dugan lowered his weapons.

Vinder closed the remaining gap between them, narrowing his ice-blue eye as he neared. "Don't tell me I have to work with an escaped *slave!*"

He motioned at the mark on Dugan's shoulder. "And a gladiator no less. I won't join this mission if *he's* along."

Dugan saw Alara direct a concerned glance at Gilban, who simply stared blankly into space, a thin smile piercing his lips. "Why?" Alara calmly approached the dwarf. "I told you I was getting another sword arm. You knew he was coming. Why back out now?"

"We have enough to worry about without having to keep watch for bounty hunters. Trouble follows this one. I know his type. We don't need trouble. *I* don't need trouble."

"But he's a good fighter," Alara rebutted.

"Most gladiators are. I just don't want to be watching my back more than I have to. I have enough to worry about as it is." Vinder crossed his arms. "You've seen what happened with the guards here. I'm not looking forward to a repeat of that wherever we go."

"Once we get out of the Elyelmic lands, we'll be less likely to run into any bounty hunters," Alara continued. "We'll be safer once we leave Altorbia. Trust me."

Vinder lowered his head and closed his eye. After a moment he looked up again with a sigh. "You haven't dealt falsely with me yet. I suppose I can afford you some more trust. But if we start getting more than our fair share of unwelcome guests, I might have to reconsider."

"Your trust isn't misplaced." Alara's faint smile helped smooth whatever rough patches remained.

"I wouldn't worry about it too much," Gilban added. "You, as well as Dugan, are twined in this thread of fate. As are we."

"He makes those flowery speeches a lot," Vinder told Dugan.

"I noticed."

"Well, I suppose you want the armor now, too, huh?" Vinder disappeared into the shadows once again. "Probably need it sooner rather than later."

"Armor?" Dugan asked Gilban.

"You need to be properly outfitted if you're to be effective," explained the priest. "I sent Vinder to fetch some for you, along with a few other supplies."

"We already spoke about this." Alara's face echoed the slight frustration in her voice as she cast Gilban a sideways glance. "I thought once we reached Talatheal we'd outfit him with armor there."

"I have foreseen—"

"You told me confrontation could be avoided if we moved in haste."

"The future is always in motion, Alara. You should know that. When I told you of potential conflicts, they could have been avoided. But the future is always changing its course. It's still possible we can move ahead unmolested, but it's wise to have him outfitted for further travel. That's why I sent Vinder to retrieve some suitable armor before you arrived."

Dugan raised an eyebrow when the dwarf returned toting a large sack, which he dragged across the cobblestone street to the mouth of the alley. "It took me a while, but I found it," he huffed.

"I trust the funds were sufficient," said Gilban.

"To the last copper piece. I'm just surprised they even had the suit for sale." Dugan watched Vinder pull the armor out of the sack. "I hope it fits."

"Your armor, Dugan." Gilban gestured to Vinder and his sack. "Go ahead and try it on. You'll need it in the time to come."

Dugan sheathed his swords before picking it up and holding it to his shoulders. The armor, chiefly a scale mail shirt, appeared newly forged. It shimmered in the moonlight with a rainbow incandescence and, at first glance anyway, appeared to match his frame perfectly. The studded brigandine leather sleeves reached his wrists, and the shirt completely covered his torso.

"Oh." Vinder dug out a gray tunic from the sack. "You might need this too."

"Haven't worn one of these in a while." Dugan placed the armor at his feet and shed his cloak before donning the tunic. He stretched his arms across his chest, testing the garment. It was of good quality—far above anything he could ever have expected in the arena.

"It's a perfect fit."

"Gilban thought you might like some pants too." Vinder rummaged through the sack once again. "I don't blame him. I wouldn't want to be looking at that breechcloth any longer than I have to either." The dwarf thrust a wide leather belt and a pair of black trousers into Dugan's grasp.

He kicked off his boots and undid his sword belts. "So Gilban had you *shopping* for me?"

"Just be thankful I did it," the dwarf growled. "If you had that wizardess doing it, you might still be waiting. The lass keeps her head in the clouds more than her feet on the ground."

"You have a wizard too?" Dugan slid the pants up under his breechcloth and belted them to his midriff. The pants, like the tunic, were a perfect fit. He pulled the mail shirt over his head. Having become accustomed to wearing all sorts of armor, he found it easy enough to don.

"We needed two strong sword arms and an extra hand in the matters of magic," Alara replied, watching him drape the cloak over his shoulders. "And we have reason to believe the knowledge we seek might be protected by magical forces of some kind.

"Speaking of which"—Alara focused on Vinder—"have you heard anything about Cadrissa?"

"I'm here." A sable-haired woman of Telborian descent entered the alley.

Dugan glanced up from putting on his final boot just as the moon returned from behind a cloud, allowing clear sight of the young woman. She was clothed in golden robes which flowed gracefully around her slender body. Silver runes embroidered the collar, hem, and cuffs, glistening where the moonlight hit. He also noted the handful of pouches hanging from her belt and the simple pack resting on her back. As with dwarves, the tales he'd heard in the arena about mages were fairly wild. And just as he'd learned when he first saw Vinder, it seemed not even a quarter of them were true.

"So *this* is the mighty warrior you went through all that trouble to acquire?" Cadrissa eyed him as if sizing up a prize bull. He noticed a slight turn at the corner of her lips as she did so.

"Cadrissa, this is Dugan," Alara said, introducing them.

"I'm impressed." Her manner was womanly, but her face and soft green eyes spoke of a naive nature, mingling with a strange aura he couldn't quite identify. Dugan guessed she was fresh into the bloom of womanhood by no more than a few years. Her smooth, pale skin, delicate hands, and slim waist attested as much.

"A bit young to be a mercenary." He busied himself with retrieving his sword belts, realizing just how naked he felt without them.

"*Mercenary?*" She was taken aback at his appraisal. "I prefer to think of myself as an explorer—an adventurer. You can only get so much knowledge from books. The rest you have to glean from experiencing the world around you."

"Great," Dugan moaned while strapping on his swords. "Another philosopher."

Vinder chuckled beneath his breath. "She's not too bad. If you can keep her from daydreaming. Haven't had a chance to see her in a fight, but maybe she'll be able to help as a distraction." Vinder shot Dugan a mischievous wink. "The pretty face and all."

"Just because I don't rush headlong into every situation brandishing an axe like some drunken ogre doesn't mean I'm useless," Cadrissa retorted.

"Nobody said you were." Alara came to stand between Cadrissa and Vinder. "And in time each of you will help fill your place in this mission."

"Indeed," Gilban added. "Now, we haven't much time, so listen carefully." He motioned for everyone to draw near. "You have all been told the reason for your selection for this journey. You've also been promised certain rewards, but only upon the mission's completion."

"Rewards?" Dugan shot Alara an ocular jab.

"Don't tell me they didn't tell you about the reward?" Vinder was surprised at Dugan's ignorance.

"Not yet." He noticed Alara seemed rushed to move on.

"You wouldn't see me here without it," said the dwarf.

"Once we get to the ruins and finish our objective, you'll be free to take whatever you like back with you as payment," Alara informed Dugan.

"Anything?" he asked.

"The ruins hold more than just knowledge," said Gilban. "Riches of all sorts are hidden there too." Dugan's mind was suddenly alight with a whole new world of possibilities.

"Be patient and you'll know everything." Alara pulled Dugan's attention back into the conversation, and to Gilban, whom he now watched with even greater interest than before.

"We are to leave this island tonight," Gilban continued, "on the same boat that brought Alara and Dugan here. We head to Elandor. There, we'll purchase supplies and provisions before setting out for Taka Lu Lama. Once we have retrieved the information from the ruins, Alara and I will return to the Republic of Rexatoius, and you three will be free to go anywhere you like, with any treasure you can secure."

"So we'll *truly* be free?" asked Dugan.

"The Patrious are masters of no one," Alara reassured him. "As we've told you before. Once your task is complete, you can go anywhere and do anything you like."

He nodded with satisfaction. The more he heard the more he liked. Working his fingers under his armor, he took hold of the breechcloth's waistband and ripped it in two.

"You aren't thinking of taking that with you, are you?" Vinder eyed the flaps of cloth dangling from Dugan's hand as if they were something infected. And he wasn't the only one—both Alara and Cadrissa clearly had some reservations. The splotches of blood added from his recent wound no doubt increased the unease.

"No," he replied, casting the garment into the nearby alleyway. "And I'm never going to wear another one ever again." It felt good not only saying the words but also having it free from his waist. He was cutting some of the last strings tying him to his old life, and once he'd made it to Talatheal he'd make swift work of the rest. "Now, let's get to that boat."

• ● •

"There it is," Alara pointed as they neared the lamplit dock. Only the slapping of the waves broke the still quiet of the area. "Looks like we're going to have a calm evening after all." She was wearing her hood again, while the others did their best at maintaining a low profile.

"We haven't made it into the boat just yet." Gilban's commentary didn't dampen Alara's hopes but didn't fill her with peace, either.

"That's right." Vinder charged ahead. "Keep thinking positive now."

"Once we're on board, we—"

She was interrupted by twenty elven guards emerging from a small cluster of simple storage buildings on their right. With gladii drawn, brigandine vests, and nose guard–equipped helmets, they quickly lined up and formed a wall between the group and the sloop. Alara's heart sank as she tried to decide what to do next, though the guards' expressions made it quite clear her options were limited.

"What did I tell you about him causing trouble?" The frustration was clear in Vinder's voice. And while she *was* tempted to blame this all on Dugan, she knew her own actions had caused an uproar as well. She was the one who'd actually killed the hunter, after all. For better or for worse, they were in this together now.

"I count twenty guards ahead of us, Gilban." Alara tried keeping as much concern out of her voice as possible. "And they're not going to let us pass."

"Have you tried asking them to?"

"You're going to have to come with us." One of the guards stepped forward, speaking Telboros plainly while keeping a steady eye on everyone.

"And why is that?" Cadrissa calmly inquired.

"Murder. There's a dead man in the Musky Otter and we're going to need some answers before you leave Altorbia." Alara didn't have the time, nor the desire, to give any answers. It wasn't that she relished the idea of becoming a leader of some lawless band, but these were Elyellium. Harboring an escaped slave was one thing, but being a Patrious at this particular moment was quite another. Better to get through this as quickly and with as little trouble as possible.

"Well, *I* was never in the Musky Otter." Vinder stared the lead guard down.

"And yet you're keeping company with the ones reported to have committed the murder. Like the priests of Ganatar say: guilt by association."

Alara found it odd the elf was quoting Gartarians, who worshiped the god of order, justice, and light, when they engaged in practices the exact opposite of such purposes.

Vinder pivoted toward Dugan. "I *have* told you how much I didn't want any more trouble, right?"

"I think there might be some misunderstanding," said Gilban, stepping forward. "What was done was an act of self-defense."

"Not how we hear it," said the lead guard. "And it seems there's a few things more you'll need to answer for." The guard raised his sword at the priest. "Like what a Patrious is doing here so far from home. But you'll have plenty of time to try to fill us in once you've been locked up for the night."

"I'm not going back to a cell." Dugan pulled his gladii free before anyone knew what was happening.

"Now wait a moment." Alara moved to Vinder's side, seeking cooler heads. In spite of her hood, she knew the nearby lamplight would make it clear to all who cared for a look that she wasn't your average Elyellium. "We don't want to cause any more trouble. We'll just be on our way."

"Not until you've answered some questions first." The guard's resolve was as solid as stone.

"We only acted in self-defense." Alara was running out of diplomatic options to explore.

"You'll have your chance to state your case at the trial."

"*Trial?*" Cadrissa almost shouted. "I'm not going to any trial. I didn't do anything wrong."

"We've been over that already." The lead guard captured some new ground, leading the others behind him forward. "Now, are you going to drop your weapons and surrender peacefully?"

Alara knew the situation had unraveled past the point of being salvaged. Then, out of the corner of her eye, she saw Vinder pull his axe free, and any lingering doubts vanished.

The guards rushed forward in an attempt to overwhelm them. Running to Gilban as she removed her bow from around her shoulder, Alara took a defensive position in front of him. "Try to keep behind me," she said, pulling an arrow from her quiver. She didn't want to kill these men—they were only doing their duty—but would defend herself and the others as best as she was able.

"We just need a path to the sloop," she told the others. "There's no need for a slaughter." She let loose two arrows in rapid succession. Both plunged directly into a guard's leg, causing him to collapse to the cobblestones with a collection of curses as she notched another arrow.

"I'm not making any promises," said Vinder as the battle quickly engulfed them. From her defensive position, she watched the melee unfold.

Two guards rushed into Dugan's path, and with two swift swings, his blades found some soft fields to plow, bringing each man to the ground though not taking their lives. At the same time, five guards faced off with Vinder. At first, he sought to bludgeon them with the flat of his axe, but after knocking the first to the street, he changed his grip and tactic. The next two he struck bellowed their pain and slumped to the ground, each clutching a bloody leg nearly hacked off at the thigh. Three more guards found their sword hands pierced by one of Alara's arrows as Cadrissa finally settled upon a spell.

"Aston laree!" At the wizardess' command a violent blast of wind tossed five more guards into a nearby lamppost, which toppled on them on impact.

"Get Gilban to the boat," Alara ordered Cadrissa before letting loose another arrow, this one pegging an advancing guard in the shoulder and creating an opening for their escape.

"Come on." Cadrissa was more than happy to comply. She took hold of Gilban's hand and began darting through the chaos en route to the sloop. Gilban made an exceptional effort to keep up with Cadrissa's running while she pulled him along like a wayward pup on a leash.

Alara's eyes lost sight of them as she took stock of the remaining struggles. Vinder felled three more guards with a bloody slashing of steel. Dugan dealt death to two more who'd gotten close enough—one sword for each man. So much for not being a slaughter.

"Withdraw!" The lead guard's command sounded like a curse. Each guard made their way back to town.

Alara slid the bow over her shoulder. "Come on," she called to Dugan and Vinder, gesturing for them to make for the docks.

"You go on ahead," said Vinder before hurrying back to the fallen guards. "I'll be right there."

"We need to leave, Vinder." At the words, the dwarf froze.

"I'll just be a moment." His eye wouldn't leave the clump of dead men. "*Now!*"

The dwarf gave a small huff before surrendering his efforts, leaving the dead where they lay.

CHAPTER 12

BLESSED BE THE HUMAN WHO SEEKS PANTHORA WITH A WHOLE HEART.
BLESSED BE THE HUMAN WHO KEEPS TO HER WAYS.
BLESSED BE THE HUMAN WHO HONORS HER,
FOR IN HIS DOING HE TOO SHALL BE HONORED.

—A Paninian blessing

It'd been a few days since the encounter with the Midgard, but nobody had forgotten the horror it'd wrought upon the ship. Every so often, Rowan noticed the odd sailor nervously pondering the water. Whenever someone got close to the damaged sections, they kissed the pendant around their neck in hopes of staving off another ordeal. The dead from the battle had been dumped into the sea, a quick funeral wherein the captain and crew sang a hymn to Perlosa and Asorlok to care for the departed souls, guiding the sailors to their eternal reward. With no priest on board it was the best they could do, and none thought any less of it.

The crew had offered up a sacrifice of a precious ring and necklace before they left port, committing the items to the sea as a gift to the Mistress of the Waves, hoping for safe passage. They added a silver bracelet with the funeral rites, hoping to remain in the goddess' good graces. Rowan didn't hinder the ceremony, but he wouldn't take part in it either. No one spoke about it one way or the other—some might have thought it an ill omen or a lack of respect, but Rowan had to be true to what he knew. If Panthora was his goddess, he couldn't honor anyone outside of her.

Few repairs had been made to the damaged deck and rigging. As the ship was a merchant vessel, it carried more trade goods than materials for repair. Even so, the crew salvaged enough resources from boxes, chests, and barrels to patch the most ruined areas. There were still weaknesses in the pitted wood, and the sailors needed to mind their steps or risk finding themselves in the cargo hold with half the deck on top of them, but it would be serviceable until they made port.

Rowan had completed his prayers for the morning and was finishing off a stale biscuit as he studied the sunrise on the distant horizon. He was happier than he'd been in a while. It had taken a couple of days before he'd rid himself of the troubling thoughts and fears that had surfaced with the Midgard attack. His solution was to find some vault in the back of his mind, shove them inside, and fasten the door tight. With the incident now passed the self-doubt was behind him . . . and he'd keep it under lock and key until his mission was finished. And so far the decision had served him well.

Within a few more days he'd be in port and free to stretch his legs on Talatheal, which was poetically called "The Island of the Masses." From his studies, he'd learned all manner of races lived there, selling their wares and practicing their diverse cultures and religions in a large melting pot. What knowledge he'd gained from his training was augmented by the stories he'd heard growing up. Many of these tales he'd learned with the other children of the Panther Tribe as they gathered around the feet of a gregarious adventurer named Erland Sorenson. He'd often go late into the night telling tales from chance encounters with those from the south. And most of those encounters involved elves.

Erland was a testament to the sturdiness of the Nordic race. Or perhaps he was just incredibly lucky to be alive—if you could believe the pedigree of his wounds. When he grew older, Rowan dismissed many of the tales as yarns created more from warm wine than actual experience. Now he was about to find out if Erland was truthful in at least some of his more grounded accounts.

A few days later, Rowan watched with anticipation as the *Frost Giant* finally maneuvered itself into the Talathealin port of Elandor. The boat would make repairs and then rest for about a month as its crew waited for the merchants to arrive, filling their holds to the brim while selling their current cargo in the process. He figured his journey into Taka Lu Lama should take him about the same amount of time, if not less. He planned for a successful return to a fully restored vessel, ready to head back to Valkoria. There really wasn't anything that could go wrong. Not from what he'd constantly rehearsed over these last few weeks.

As the crew dropped anchor and prepared for unloading, Rowan paced. He watched the gangplank resting near the starboard side of the vessel, ready to be lowered once the ship had been properly secured. Almost immediately upon its descent, Rowan leapt off the boat and onto the docks. As soon as his feet touched the wooden planks, he moved briskly for Elandor's interior. He was dressed in full leather armor, sword strapped to his side. He'd managed to stuff most of his belongings in a pack he'd swung over his back, leaving the chest with the rest of his items in his cabin. As he walked, he made a careful study of his surroundings.

Fishermen cleaned and gutted their catches, dumping the waste into the water as a motley collection of people happened by. Men and women—rich and poor—made their way through the narrow paths toward the inner gates of the city. Spices and perfumes were unloaded from far-off Belda-thal and elsewhere. As always, there were weapons, cooking utensils, bolts of fabrics, and buckets of fresh produce making their way to the central square for trade and purchase. There was also a mix of people about: elves and humans the most dominant amid the collage of flesh and fabric. But some shorter folks did catch his eye from time to time. They easily stood out among the taller people, and their pointed ears further defined them among the masses. From what he'd read and learned in his training, he thought they were halflings. And from what he understood, it was best if he just ignored them like everyone else was doing.

Elandor was the capital city of a powerful Telborian kingdom sharing the same name. It wrestled for primacy with its sister kingdom, Romain, to the south. Both claimed to be founded by the Telborians who had emerged from the ancient city of Gondad, which lay in ruins many miles to their west . . . or so the legends said. For centuries, Elandor and

Romain had disputed each other's claims of being descended from the ancient origin city, each setting up its own doctrine as to why it was right, which had led to more than a few wars and minor skirmishes. But in more recent generations, these conflicts had taken the form of healthy competition in seasonal tournaments between the kingdoms.

Rowan slowed his pace as he neared the gate, the wheel-rutted road now congested with merchant traffic. The people up ahead were held at the gates while guards checked for official documents, illegal merchandise, and other matters of pressing concern. Rowan stood in the line for what seemed like an eternity while exotic smells of sweet perfume and tangy spices tickled his nose. Once the guards looked him over and deemed him permissible, he was allowed through the gate. If he thought what he'd seen so far was amazing, he was astounded by what greeted him.

The streets were mazes of shops and stalls. Vegetables, meats, brilliantly colored cloth, weapons, and furniture crowded tables and windows. Everywhere he saw people hurrying about with their purchases—arms overflowing with produce and merchandise of all kinds. Commerce surrounded him on all sides, not unlike the ocean he'd just traveled.

As he wandered the streets, he took in all the strange merchants selling their wares. One was tall and slightly gaunt with a slender, frail look about him. It wasn't until the merchant threw back his head in laughter that Rowan realized he was an elf. The pointed ears, previously hidden by straight black hair, protruded from his dark tresses.

Erland's stories had depicted them as cold and vindictive, "a gaggle of weak-armed sissies who threw a good punch when you weren't looking." Yet Rowan couldn't help but feel slightly entranced by the figure. The elf seemed ageless, almost eternal or immortal in his being. But even as words of praise for the elven merchant sounded in Rowan's mind, another voice spoke inside him. It whispered that elves were weaker and less skilled in weapons than he was, that the merchant was probably a cheat in his dealings, and he wanted nothing more than to raid the world and make Rowan his slave.

The words were heavy and hard, scraping his heart and mind like a strong plowshare. He'd no idea where these feelings and ideas came from, but from someplace within they bubbled forth. He soon found himself looking at the elf not as a thing of beauty, but as a flawed gem in need of recutting.

As he continued staring at the elf, Rowan felt a nudge on his leg. Peering down he saw a dirty Telborian child dressed in rags with her hand around his coin purse. She looked no more than ten winters old, but the rough life she lived had aged her prematurely. Her eyes were ringed with thick black and purple circles, her skin sallow.

"And what do you think *you're* doing?" he asked the young girl in her native tongue. His training had included the comprehension of all human dialects, both past and present.

Without speaking, the child bolted off into an alley. Rowan shook his head in sorrow as he watched her go. He wished he had time to help all the poor humans in Elandor, but he knew it would only detract from his mission. He reached for his coin purse to shift it to a safer location—away from prying fingers—and was shocked when he found there was nothing to move.

"Hey!" Rowan broke into a run. "Come back here!"

The girl, whether she heard him or not, continued darting through the maze of alleyways and tight streets. Although he easily gained on her retreating back, she somehow managed avoiding his grasping arms. As they ran deeper into the city, the condition of the buildings grew steadily worse until the housing was nothing more than rough wooden planks held together by crude nails and cracking plaster. Dead animals and nearly dead people huddled in corners and other areas where their pathetic and soiled frames wasted away.

The girl finally stopped at a dead end, her back shaking as she faced the stone wall. This allowed Rowan to catch up and put a hand over her shoulder, turning her to face him. Her cheeks were wet with tears. "I just need the money to eat," she sobbed. "Why can't you just leave me alone? I'm sure you have plenty more where this came from."

Rowan stooped to his knee to wipe the tears away from her soiled face, cutting some clear stripes of flesh to shine through the grime in the process. "I'm not looking to harm you." He adopted a mild tone. "But that's all the money I have. It's not even mine. It belongs to my order. I'm on an assignment, and I need it to complete my duties. If you return it to me, I'd be very grateful and give you what I can."

He noticed as he spoke the girl gave him a strange look. It felt like she was looking through him, not at him. Suspicion took him further as her eyes darted over his left shoulder. He spun around, his blade in hand, prepared to defend against an attack. The block stopped the descending club of a heavily muscled Telborian.

"Good work, Sally. Now go run off while I finish this up."

Rowan faced the cutthroat at his full height while Sally dashed off. He was a large man, a head taller than Rowan and covered in a layer of street grime. His long hair was unkempt and greasy, and the bristly briar of his beard still housed particles of his last meal.

"You're going to be a tough one, eh?" He grinned, revealing a number of missing teeth. "Well, I like to have fun once in a while." He swung the heavy club again.

Rowan easily blocked the cumbersome attack by sidestepping to his left. With every downswing, the man exposed his left side, a weakness Rowan was more than happy to exploit. With a quick thrust, his sword slid into the man's chest and skewered his heart on Nordic steel.

The man's piggish face went placid and wide eyed in disbelief. Like a broken child's toy, he tried raising his club for a final defiant swing. Instead, the oaken log fell out of his lifeless fingers. Rowan jerked his sword free, and the dead man fell to the muck-covered street.

"May you find rest in Panthora's arms." Rowan blessed the corpse before wiping his blade clean. He then began looking for a way out of the crumbling area of the city. He didn't want to be around when the dead man's friends came looking for him, and this sort always traveled in packs. He had no idea where the girl had run off to, dashing any hopes at recovering what was stolen. This wasn't good. Not good at all.

While what the knighthood had given him might have been stolen, he did still possess a small pouch of personal monies in his backpack. The coin was intended for minor purchases or emergencies. He supposed having his funds stolen from him would count as an emergency, but the personal coin wasn't anywhere near the amount that had been stolen. How could he hope to accomplish his mission with so little coin?

As he wandered the twisted back ways of the city, he assessed his situation. His shoulders sagged with the weight of increased understanding. He hadn't even managed to be in Talatheal for one day—not even for one hour—before he failed in his mission. Without supplies and a guide, not to mention mounts, he would never find the ruins in the time allowed . . . unless Panthora provided a miracle.

As he found his way into the more refined parts of Elandor, Rowan asked Panthora for forgiveness. By the time he reached the area where the girl had lifted his coin purse, he was so laden with sorrow and regret he scarcely noticed a drunken sailor staggering out of a tavern and into the sun, shielding his eyes from the burning light. The sailor almost collapsed into Rowan as the knight wandered through the street, but with a stumble to one side and a small spin on a lone leg, he staggered out of the way before falling face first into the muck on the side of the road. Had Rowan been in higher spirits, he might have laughed.

The drunken intermission pulled his attention to an inn called the Broken Oar. It resided across the street, exactly opposite the tavern. The placard hanging over the door was painted in Telboros, with Elonum script underneath it. The picture on the sign was plain enough: a simple bed with a broken oar above it. Since he'd nowhere else to go for the rest of the day, and the ship wouldn't be ready to sail again for weeks, he decided to use his meager personal funds and get a place to stay, at least while he decided on a plan of action.

Rowan's entrance into the inn's hazy main room was acknowledged by a few wandering eyes from the modest crowd. It was hard to say who was the more shocked, the patrons of the inn or Rowan himself. Not many Nordicans made it as far south as Talatheal, and even fewer from the south chose to venture up to the Northlands.

The common room was more ample than most taverns had, with a staircase leading up to the rooms for rent. The tavern itself wasn't much different from those of his homeland, consisting of simple wooden chairs circled around reinforced tables and tall stools surrounding the bar. But as he approached the bar, the heavy aroma of perfume descended upon him, strangling his throat and making his eyes water. He barely managed to suppress a gag as he motioned for the scruffy Telborian innkeeper.

"I need a room."

"Two gold pieces for one week," the innkeeper grumbled, watching Rowan dig into his pack and pull out the required amount. The innkeeper tossed Rowan a key. "You can have the first one on the right." He dismissively motioned at a general location at the top of the stairs once he'd pocketed the money. "You'll have it for one week at the most. If you ain't got any money after that or cause me any trouble, then you're out on your ear."

He was taken aback by the innkeeper's uncouth manner, but let it pass. Obviously, not everyone was going to be as hospitable as he would have liked. That didn't stop him from needing a place to rest and getting a simple meal. As he turned for the stairs, the curtain of perfume grew stronger and a feminine arm encircled his waist, drawing him against a pair of slender hips. Rowan suddenly found himself looking down into the eyes of a raven-haired Telborian.

The woman wore her hair braided with golden beads. A bronze brassiere was all that covered her chest while a skirt of some sort of gauzy material dangled to her knees and was slit up the sides to her waist, exposing her entire right leg. A red silken scarf draped across her otherwise bare shoulders. Her green eyes were penetrating, but seemingly clouded to some degree. Her intentions, however, were quite clear.

"Those rooms can get very cold at night," the woman said, twining a strand of hair around a finger. "Perhaps you need someone to help warm your bed." She licked her red-stained lips.

"I prefer the cold."

The woman put her hands on her hips, still smiling. "You don't know what you'll be missing, boy."

"I'll survive." Rowan turned and made his way again for the stairs. The innkeeper, who'd obviously been watching, laughed at the exchange. Rowan just kept walking. He heard a barstool scrape against the floor as the woman no doubt plopped herself beside the counter.

"You'll be back," she shouted over the din of the room.

Rowan climbed the stairs and released a relieved sigh when he found his room. He slammed the door behind him, leaning against it in relief at the solitude and privacy. He rested there for a few moments before taking interest in his surroundings. The accommodations were spacious compared to the size of his cabin on the *Frost Giant*.

It had all of the necessities: a bed and chest with a lock and key for valuables. There was also a small window, which Rowan discovered was nailed shut—perhaps to prevent nonpaying customers from escaping. If that was indeed the intent it didn't speak too well of the clientele, but it was better than sleeping on the streets or returning to the ship like a dog with his tail between his legs.

Once he'd had a look around, he started putting his meager belongings away. This done, he opened his purse on the bed and fingered through his money, counting thirteen gold and ten silver coins. Hardly enough to buy supplies and hire a guide, let alone keep him fed and supplied for the weeks to come—but it was all he had and better than nothing. He sat on the bed, contemplating his coins in deep thought, until sleep snuck up on him and ensnared him in its net.

• ● •

Rowan found himself in the midst of a strange jungle. A fat sun hung low above him, adding to the already oppressive heat and greasy hue of daylight. Tall, thick trees and vein-like roots clustered around him. Insects buzzed about his head, nipping at his sweaty flesh. Swatting at his forearm, he realized he was wearing his dedication robes. He could feel rivulets of sweat running down his back and neck beneath the heavy garments as he hunted for a way out of the strange terrain.

As he began to move, a faint whisper floated his way. At first it was weak, like the brushing of leaves by a gentle wind. But then it grew in volume.

Come . . . come . . . come this way. The voice seemed to emanate from the jungle's interior, but Rowan heard it clearest in his head.

Come . . . come . . .

Though he didn't want to go deeper into the jungle, he found himself drawn to it—as if another had taken over his body, moving it like a puppet into the mysterious, humid vegetation.

With the logic of dreams, he had the distinct impression of time passing while he journeyed on. Just how long it was he didn't know. All he did know was the unrelenting voice ushering him onward. Several times during his trek he tried pulling himself away, but to no avail.

Eventually, he reached a small clearing amid some giant leaning trees. He saw what appeared to be a large stone formation. It shone through the dense green growth like jagged bones. Half the size of the knights' keep, it was fashioned of white marble and carved with a collection of strange symbols and designs that Rowan couldn't quite place. It spoke of an older age—maybe even before the birth of mortalkind. How he knew this, he wasn't quite sure. The knowledge simply increased his understanding, like air swells the lungs.

As he drew nearer the structure, he heard another sound—this one emanating from the marble building itself. It was a bestial growl, and yet it also sounded like a warrior's scream.

His apprehension grew as the faint daylight filtering through the trees dimmed to darkness. It was now a starlit night.

Stairs stretched from the green carpet of jungle, leading to an empty shell of a doorway—long since fallen to ruin and decay. The growling grew stronger as he crossed the threshold. The faint smell of musk marked the entrance as an opening to some type of animal lair.

Suddenly, a force stronger than a hurricane blew him from the lair onto the stairs outside. Rowan gasped as flashes of pain flared across his chest. Too shocked to move, he found himself staring into the fierce black eyes of a giant gray panther. Its height at the shoulders was at least six feet; its width seemed twice that. Its muzzle was pulled to a drooling snarl filled with malice, and its claws dug firmly into his flesh.

The weight of the creature was immense, like a huge boulder pressing on his chest. He could do little more than struggle for breath. The searing pain of another claw scraping across his chest increased the urgency of finding an escape. His options were limited, as the panther had both arms and legs pinned. As his thoughts raced, the panther's jaws snapped, narrowly missing his face.

Desperate, Rowan frantically searched the ground for anything that might prove useful. His hands were all he could move. Fishing around the hard surface of the marble slab, he grabbed a loose chunk. It wasn't much, but without sword or fist the pointed rock would have to do.

Turning the stone so the sharp tip faced upward, Rowan focused all his energy into what could possibly be his last action. Concentrating, he thrust the jagged rock at the panther's underside. The sharp point bit into its soft stomach and dug deep into its flesh. The panther reared in shock, howling in pain and anger. It snarled one final time before turning into gray vapor that first trailed into the air before finally becoming nothingness.

Rowan stared in amazement at the vanishing mist, then took a quick inventory of his person. He wasn't hurt too badly: just a few red stripes across his chest that traced the tears in his robes. As he tried collecting himself, his hand found a foreign object. Through the torn fabric he saw a small paw attached to a leather strap hanging from his neck. The paw reminded him of a cat's paw, but it was dried and shriveled, with a handful of what appeared to be red and black beads laced through the leather strap where it connected with the paw.

Before he could give the object closer examination, he was yanked to his feet by the familiar unseen force and compelled deeper inside the ruin. As he was forced farther into the building, the animal scent grew fainter, replaced with a dusty, timeworn odor. As he entered, a torch on the wall to his right flared into life, lighting what seemed a rather old room. The torch light wasn't enough to reveal everything, but from what he could discern, the square interior had lain empty for some time.

Dust covered the marble floor in a thin, undisturbed blanket, and cracked walls struggled against decay to valiantly hold the ceiling and floor apart. Darkness beyond the torch's reach swam around him, churning in the corners. He also had the sense that something was in that darkness, lurking just out of sight, watching him with a careful eye.

"Choose your weapon." A strong voice spoke out of the shadows.

With those words, a handful of weapons emerged from the shadows on the wall. A broadsword, dagger, mace, and pike were laid out like a merchant's wares, each in pristine condition. Again, under compulsion, Rowan approached the weapons, seeking out the voice's owner as he did so, but finding no one.

As he stood before the weapons, he studied each one closely before taking up the sword. Once in hand it reminded him of his own sword—something he put in the back of his mind as a humanoid shape emerged from the swaying darkness outside the torch's reach. The rag-cloaked figure stepped forth like a man walking out of fog. As he advanced, stubborn black tentacles clung to him as long as they could, before snapping back into the shadows.

Rowan tightened his grip as the figure drew nearer: a skeleton, draped in tattered, dirty rags. Small tongues of azure flame lapped at the insides of its dry, empty sockets. Certain this figure didn't wish him any good, Rowan moved into action. But before he could take even two steps, the skeletal figure raised a warding hand, making Rowan's head swim and mind drift.

•●•

He woke to discover he'd fallen asleep on the bed not far from his small pile of coins. Rising, he observed the moonlight filtering through the murky window. A hand to his chest assured him he was free from any wounds and wasn't wearing a necklace. He also wasn't wearing his dedication robes, just the same clothes he'd been wearing all these weeks. As the waking world grew stronger, so too did the understanding there was still a very large task ahead of him and less time now to deal with it.

He grabbed some of his coin and locked up the rest, then followed his Nordic logic to the lower level of the inn, hoping to find some good leads on a cheap guide or, failing that, at least a map to his destination. He'd scant experience with such tasks but didn't see any other options.

In the dining hall, he purchased a flagon of ale and a meat pie, and found a solitary seat in a quiet section of the room to plan his next move. Thankfully, while still filled with a good many patrons, it wasn't rowdy, allowing him a measure of peace. And it was in that peace the young knight began pondering his strange dream. There were still people in his tribe—shamans chief among them—who held dreams often spoke of important truths to be heeded, or even provided insight into things to come. These were superstitions, of course, but ones that many of his tribe—and all the Nordic tribes for that matter—still held to in varying degrees. Even those who swore they were faithful Panians at times gave heed to the old ways.

It could also have been nothing more than a dream. He'd had a few vivid yet ultimately meaningless ones throughout his life. Then again, the Sacred Scrolls told of Panthora speaking through dreams. The order might not have been open to the notion—claiming that the high father was now the truest voice of Panthora and the more spectacular things of the past had passed away—but Rowan didn't want to push it aside either.

It had been so real. The panther, the ruins, and that skeletal creature . . . Did it tie into what he might face in the days ahead? If so, what was Panthora trying to tell him? Or were the high father and the knighthood right? Was it nothing but overactive anxiety causing him to fret over his present predicament even while he slept? In the end, he wasn't able to settle on any distinct explanation. Tired of shifting through the increasing number of questions, he focused on what he needed to do to get to Taka Lu Lama. That was the real focus. That was his mission. And no matter what else might have happened or would happen, he was going to fulfill it.

CHAPTER 13

Do what destiny tells you to do,
no matter what you feel otherwise.
Keep the temple, the word of divined truth,
and yourself true until death.

—The Sarellian Tenets

Gray mists danced and twirled before Gilban as he slumbered, eventually parting and revealing a strange vision. It was night. There was a cool breeze and the sound of rollicking laughter, like one would hear at a brothel or lower-class tavern. Before he could make sense of what he was seeing, a massive panther bound into his line of sight. The panther was gray and larger than any cat he'd ever seen or heard of. It had to be as wide as a man was tall, and twice that in length.

Gilban twitched in his sleep as the great cat leapt straight for him, only to fade into a cloud of vapor before it reached him. His heart raced and his breathing came in short rasps as he tried recovering his composure. As his heart rate slowed, the mists parted and out strode a Nordican. Though he'd never seen one in the flesh, Gilban had heard enough about them to recognize them at first sight. This Nordican was quite young—at the beginning of manhood if he had to guess—and dressed in leather armor covered in an interesting panther motif.

As he emerged, the Nordican spoke. "Through me is the path to victory."

Even as Gilban tried studying the matter further, he felt the warm, soothing tendrils of the waking world dragging him away. A moment later, he shuddered awake with a name teetering on his lips.

"Rowan."

A heartbeat later Gilban was inhaling the dry, musky odor of the cabin. As he registered the swaying motions and sounds of the waves, he became firmly anchored in the waking world. Rising from his cot, he considered the vision carefully. If he was interpreting it correctly, it seemed another with a similar goal would soon cross their path. Someone who might aid them in their mission. That could be only part of the meaning, however. He knew enough not to jump to unfounded conclusions with visions. He'd known many other amateur diviners of fate who'd fallen into that trap. Once someone overread—or worse, underread—a vision, then it was destined to become false or unfulfilled.

Taking his staff from alongside the cot, Gilban made his way from the cabin with slow, steady steps. He was curious to know what had happened since they'd left Altorbia, as well as eager for Alara's take on their fellow travelers since making their departure. Such things might afford further insight into the vision.

• ● •

The sun was still rising over the horizon as Alara once again found herself manning the rudder. She'd been stationed there for about half an hour now, ever since Vinder had given up the position in exchange for food and rest. She couldn't blame him. It had been a long evening. But at least they'd finally entered the Yoan Ocean, which brought them ever closer to Talatheal.

Once they'd gotten past the guards, they'd quickly boarded the boat. After the sails had been unfurled, Cadrissa had conjured a strong wind, sending the sloop speeding into the anonymity of night—vanishing before any pursuit could be organized. As the lights of Altorbia disappeared, exhaustion overtook them. The lapping waves on the boat's hull lulled most of them into sleep. Even Alara had managed some rest—not as much as she would have preferred, but enough to keep her going until things had settled a bit. And with the coming dawn, that time seemed close at hand.

She cast her gaze along the sloop, finding where the others had set themselves up on the deck. Partially masked by the bulge of the cabin, Vinder was at the bow, letting his meager breakfast settle. Cadrissa was on the starboard deck. She sat cross-legged, resting her back against the cabin, a small collection of books and scrolls laid about her. Alara hadn't seen the mage go for more than a couple of hours without putting her nose into some book or scroll. She hoped all that studying was going to pay off once they reached the ruins.

On the port side of the sloop stood Dugan. He'd removed his armor and tunic shortly after their taking to the waves, and was now stretching after what Alara hoped was a restful slumber. She knew he was in need of it; he'd endured a great deal these last few days. Even with the distance between them she could clearly see the sword strikes, claw marks, and other injuries he'd sustained over the years. A twinge of sadness overtook her. Dugan had suffered much . . . and by elven hands. Elyellium hands, yes—but still elven—and the sight of it pained her.

Done stretching, he noticed Alara and made his way toward her.

"You slept well, I hope."

"Well enough," he replied, stopping before her. "It's still hard to believe I'm finally a free man."

"Well, you are. As it should be."

"Yet some are destined to be slaves." Gilban finished making his way onto the deck. "Their very actions and spirits declare it."

"It's not in *my* destiny." Dugan's good mood quickly soured.

"You may be right." Gilban made his way to Alara, who rose to meet him. "Destiny is never certain for those who have the strength to shape its path. But few have that ability, and fewer still choose to use it . . . or even know *how* to."

"You should be sleeping." Alara's tone turned maternal.

"I could say the same of you," returned the priest. "Though I think the advice would receive just as much attention. Besides, I've been awakened with new things to ponder."

"Another vision?" She heard the concern and excitement mingling in her voice.

"Nothing taxing, but my mind needs to think on things before we get much farther."

"What was it about?" Dugan's interest was clearly piqued.

"When I became a priest I swore a sacred oath to keep secret the things Saredhel shows me until the proper time . . . if at all. To the untrained mind, the images we'd relate would cause confusion and misinterpretation. Only when the timing is right do we reveal what we've learned."

"But what if the vision could help someone?" Dugan cautiously inquired. "Wouldn't it be better to tell them right away?"

"And if the vision is catastrophic to that person?" Gilban countered. "Let us say, his death. What if I, or one of my brothers or sisters, told someone of their approaching demise—how and when it would occur. How could that person prepare to face it?"

Dugan struggled for a response.

"Throughout my service to Saredhel, nearly everyone I have come into contact with has asked the same question at some time or another. I find it amazing so many wish to leap into things for which they're not ready." Gilban adopted a more scholarly tone. "Would you plant a field without first plowing it?"

"No, I guess not."

"Exactly." Gilban nodded. "You wouldn't get a crop. So it is with these matters. You have to let life make ready the field by plowing it with experience. Then the vision can be planted, the words shared and allowed to grow through time and understanding. If you didn't follow this method, you would do more harm to both the seed and the soil rather than produce a bounty of richness for life.

"However"—Gilban raised a warning finger—"you must learn what to plant in a field and what will grow." His pure-white eyes fixed upon Dugan's face. "One could not escape death if he were destined to die, as all things are. Some as blackened cinders."

Dugan squinted for a long moment before departing with pounding steps.

"What was that all about?" Alara asked, watching Dugan quicken his step for the bow of the boat.

"There are great wars being fought inside him. Battles which would put the Imperial Wars to shame," he confided. "But I said what was necessary."

"Will he be okay?" Alara took another worried glance at the retreating gladiator.

"It's difficult to say. Even a brick wall crumbles when enough pressure is applied."

"Don't you ever get tired of speaking in metaphors?"

"Not when they answer so potently," he replied, taking a seat near the rudder.

•●•

While Dugan, Gilban, and Alara were talking, Cadrissa was lost in a world of her own. Scattered around her in a neat semicircle lay a collection of scrolls and tomes of varying sizes. The majority she kept in the open chest beside her, with a few more in her backpack. She'd first purchased the chest after she started her instruction at the academy in Haven. Lined with cedar, it supposedly kept safe from vermin any parchment or paper placed within. It also had the added benefit of making everything smell like cedar.

About thigh length and half that in width, it couldn't hold much, but she had enough for her trip. While she would have enjoyed traveling with more of a library, she hadn't amassed a sizable one of her own yet. And then there was the whole matter of needing to carry and transport everything. That could get tiring and expensive fairly fast. And they really had only just started their journey. So what she'd taken were the bare essentials, and so far it was serving her well.

She made every effort to take in as much information as possible in the time she had. These respites were golden opportunities, and the others were counting on her to help decipher and maybe even verify whatever they find. She needed to be ready for just about anything, and that meant keeping her mind sharp.

She took another bite of a dry biscuit—the entirety of her breakfast—washing it down with fresh water from a tin cup beside her. She thought again of how fortunate she was to be able to do what she was doing. Only a few hundred years ago she would have been hounded by fearful people seeking to put an end to her life, or would have had to hide away to learn more about—let alone engage in—magic. And now, here she was seeking more knowledge and using what she'd learned openly. Truly, as was often repeated in the Haven Academy, these were good days to be a wizard. And the thought of getting to see some dranoric ruins? Well, that was a once-in-a-lifetime event. And who was to say what she might find there? Such knowledge just waiting for her to lay hold of it . . . The thought brought a broad grin to her face.

"And what are *you* so happy about?"

"What?" Cadrissa awoke from her daydream to find Vinder's bearded face peering down at her. She didn't think she'd ever seen him smiling or not wearing his armor. She'd met up with the dwarf in Altorbia after being recruited in Haven near the academy. Neither talked to the other much, tending to keep to themselves and their own interests, which suited Cadrissa just fine. More time to study.

"You haven't strayed too far from your pile since we've met. I thought it was time to see what's got you by the nose."

"Plenty."

"Something useful for the mission?" He scanned the assortment of works cluttering the deck.

"Yes and no."

Vinder snorted. "What's *that* supposed to mean?"

"That some matters are still a bit inconclusive."

"Inconclusive? All that time reading this drivel and you haven't found anything useful?"

"I wouldn't call it drivel." A defensive streak arose in her.

"If it isn't going to help us, then that's what it is to me. I thought you were brought along for a purpose. Dugan can at least swing a sword but all you got is books, which apparently have no answers."

"Were you even awake last night in that fight?" She braved raising her voice.

"Okay," Vinder weakly admitted, "you have some magical talent, but that isn't enough where we're going."

"It isn't." It was more a statement than a question.

"No. We need to know what we're up against." Vinder again studied the volumes and scrolls as he spoke. "That's why Alara and Gilban brought you on."

"*And* to help protect you from it. Or have you forgotten we'll be entering a potentially magically influenced area?" Cadrissa didn't like the dwarf eyeing her things. It felt like a strange man ogling her baby. "Having someone who knows about magic is a wise precaution."

"Maybe you just need someone else looking things over." Vinder reached down and retrieved a fairly slender tome near his right foot. "I can read other languages too, you know."

"Be careful with that." She reached for the book, but Vinder pulled it away as he turned a page. "Well, here's your problem. You're not even reading about the right subject."

"And how would you know?" She tried another grab for the tome but was denied. "These books are rare treasures." She hoped Vinder heard more of the rebuke in her tone and less of the pleading. "I got many of them from my schooling. I even had to copy some myself because of the age of the master texts."

Paying her little mind, he began reading aloud a section of text that had caught his eye. "And so it was that in the Third Age of the Wizard Kings, there arose the two paths to higher arcane pursuits: the path of knowledge and the path of power. It was from these paths that new evils and greater goods erupted in a celebrated dispersal of magical delight." The dwarf's lone eye pierced Cadrissa with a hard glare. "Now I wonder what you might be so interested in reading about wizard kings for."

"Don't you have something *else* you need to do?"

"Yeah, watching my back." Vinder closed the book with a snap. "You and I both know the wizard kings were a blight on Tralodren. Even the dwarven histories say it was decreed by the gods that the world be rid of them."

"You're wrong," Cadrissa weakly rebutted.

"I thought so." He flashed a crooked smile. "Why would a wizardess as young as you come along on this journey unless they were foolish *or* ambitious?"

"What are you getting at?"

"I didn't know which at first, but now I see you're foolishly ambitious." He grimly nodded. "What better place to go than to the heart of a ruin said to hold ancient knowledge? Knowledge that just might aid you on the same path of the very people you've been reading up on."

Cadrissa lifted her chin and glared through Vinder's accusations and innuendoes. "You barely know me. How can you judge me?"

"Apparently with an open book," he replied.

"First of all, you're talking about things hundreds of years ago, back when fear and misunderstanding filled people's minds about magic and those who practiced it. I just want a chance to be enlightened, helping those I can along the way."

Vinder held his stare, but she wasn't going to let herself wilt under it. "And you'll need me soon enough once we find those ruins."

"Bah!" Vinder shoved the book back to Cadrissa, who cradled it to her chest. "Just keep your motives from hindering this mission. What you do after it is on your own head. But I want to live through this, if you don't mind. And that gladiator has already raised the stakes high enough. I don't need you adding any more headaches." Vinder stomped off toward the stern. Cadrissa glared after him, letting his final words needle her a little longer. She was so engrossed in the matter she didn't hear Dugan's approach.

"This a bad time?"

Before she knew what she was doing, she was greeted with Dugan's naked torso. "N-no." She slowly worked her gaze up the hills of muscle undulating across his frame. "I'm fine, really." She tried making a conscious effort to close her mouth after speaking. "How about you?" She bit her lip upon realizing how foolish she sounded.

Dugan didn't seem to notice. "I heard some of what you said."

"Oh." Her countenance faded. "Come to lecture me too, have you?"

"No, just thought you might be able to answer a question." He paused, studying her features. She felt her heart skip a beat and straightened her back, feigning a confidence she didn't possess. Drawn to the stylized eagle branding mark on Dugan's shoulder, it took a moment before she realized he was waiting for a response.

"Of—of course." She placed the tome she'd been cradling in her lap at her side and fixed some strands of hair behind her ear. "I'd be happy to help if I can." There was an inner fire that radiated out of him, a confidence and strength that was lacking in many of the other men she'd come across. Of course, none of those at the academy had lived the same life as Dugan, either. She didn't know if that was a bad thing or a good thing just yet, but she was enjoying the learning process.

"What do you know about the gods?" He squatted level with her.

"I didn't picture you as someone interested in theology."

"I'm not. I just need some information, and you don't speak in riddles."

"Had your fill of Gilban already?" Cadrissa teased.

"You heard of Rheminas?"

She nodded. "Some call him the Burning God."

"How powerful is he?"

"You mean in the pantheon? Well, there are gods more powerful than Rheminas, and there are many who oppose his will and actions. It depends on whom you believe on the topic, as all priests will tell you their god is the strongest." When Dugan's attention held fast, Cadrissa elaborated. "However, even gods of lesser power don't hold him in the highest of favor. Drued, Aerotripton, and Panthora all hate him—but they're weaker than him. Ganatar, Asora, Dradin, Olthon, Causilla, and Perlosa care little for him also.

"From what I gather, he's not that well received in many lands, but where he is, he's held up for his more *peaceful* boons—the sun and fire and such. It's only a few individuals who worship him for his darker, destructive aspects." Dugan looked as if weighing every word with careful deliberation. It was hardly the sort of thing she would have expected, given their brief time together. Truly the man was worth some further study.

"Does that help?"

"It'll do for now." He stood.

"Are you looking for a new religion to follow?" Cadrissa blurted.

"Something like that." He made his way to the bow of the ship, leaving Cadrissa to appreciate the breadth of his massive shoulders and certain other aspects of his anatomy made more evident by his departure.

"If you need anything else, I'm more than willing to help," she called after him.

"I'll remember that." He responded with a backward glance which made her hope he'd be quick in honoring his word.

•●•

A few days later, thanks to favorable weather, Cadrissa's magic, and some prayers from Gilban, the ragtag company began packing their belongings as they sailed into port. The day was half over when the group finally managed to get ashore. As they strode through the streets into Elandor, the smells and sounds of the lively locale filled Dugan with excitement. The rich, salty aromas of the sea mixed with the scent of freshly cooked meats and spices from the far south. These engrossing odors mingled with soft music and a chorus of voices around the docks.

He saw Telborians mingling with Elyellium and handfuls of Celetors here and there. A few halflings even milled about the pools of people. He'd heard stories about them too, and had actually seen a few when he was young. He'd forgotten how short they were, almost like children who refused to grow any older. And then there were the odd dwarf and gnome appearing amid the brightly colored sails and screeching gulls. The gnomes were another race he'd heard of more than seen, only spotting one in passing when he was first taken to the arena. They fell about equal to a dwarf in height, resembling smaller versions of Telborians, he supposed, in many ways.

He smiled to himself as he tried to take everything in. He no longer donned a hood. Here he was free. No more elven masters, no more of the torture and killings. No more worrying about bleeding his life away on the arena's sand. Dressed in his new attire he felt like a human being, and not some animal kept for sport. A human being in a new world that was ripe for his exploration and enjoyment. And it all came from an elf saving a slave.

He laughed inside at the thought of this freedom. Once he completed this mission, he could live in any Telborian land as a free member of society, reclaiming his life and making it anew. He'd never really experienced life in a human city before; it almost seemed foreign to him. But in many ways it resembled civic life in the elven communities from which he came. And the longer he walked Elandor's streets, the more familiar and right it felt.

"You can rest and look around, if you wish, before we meet up again." Alara addressed the others as they traveled in a group. "Gilban and I will make sure the inn's ready to receive us, but aside from that, we don't have any pressing business until later this evening."

"Where we meeting?" Dugan asked as they moved through the wide and crowded streets of the market district, just east of the docks.

"We've made arrangements at the Mangy Griffin. It's off to the north of the docks, just past the temple of Ganatar and before the granary." Alara helped Gilban over an uneven patch of flagstone. "Feel free to explore the city, like I said, and keep an ear open for any rumors about ancient cities or recent elven activity in the area. We'll meet back at the Mangy Griffin before dusk."

"You do know it's the summer solstice, right?" Cadrissa inquired.

"Yes. Is there a problem?"

"No," she returned. "You've just given us quite a bit of time before dusk, is all."

"Then use it wisely. We'll see you back at the inn." At this, Vinder and Cadrissa stepped away from the group in opposite directions. Alara continued helping Gilban, leading him, presumably, toward the inn. Dugan followed.

Gilban freed himself from the constant crowds by heading to a large plaza and taking some rest on a wooden bench a few feet from a delicately crafted blue quartz fountain. Dugan noticed the fountain resembled a dolphin carrying a Telborian boy on its back. The dolphin appeared to be leaping from the fountain with the spray of water around it, the laughing child hugging the dolphin's dorsal fin with simple joy. He caught himself smiling at the child and his carefree sense of freedom. He waited until Alara left Gilban and entered a local shop before starting for the bench.

"Yes, Dugan?" Before he was less than seven feet from him, Gilban had cast his face in his direction. "I wondered how long you could hold out. You've done well so far. A mark of true inner strength and dedication."

"What do you mean?" He hesitated.

"Don't be so ill at ease." Gilban beckoned him with an open palm. "Come sit beside me and we'll talk." After Dugan cautiously took his seat, Gilban continued. "I know of the battle inside you."

"How? You don't even *know* me."

"Oh, but I do." Gilban's eyes narrowed slightly as he appeared to take in the full figure of the man beside him. Dugan had to shake off the feeling of needles being jammed into his flesh as he did so. It just wasn't natural to see a blind man acting like Gilban. "And I can tell you, there's only one remedy."

"And what is it?" Immediately, Dugan's interest was piqued.

"In this city there's a temple dedicated to the god you serve," he replied. "Hidden away in the shell of a forest east of here, others of like mind have established a place of worship. Like you, they discovered the price of such worship is often higher than they thought they'd have to pay.

"Go there. Confront the god through his servants and face his will." Gilban motioned Dugan away as Alara approached from across the plaza. "It's a sorrowful thing to witness a man destroy himself in the searing flames of revenge. Go quickly, for I fear there will be much to discuss, and the day continues to age."

Dugan didn't know what to say or feel about the matter— momentarily frozen between hoping for answers and wondering if what Gilban said wasn't perhaps too good to be true.

"I thought you said you trust me now," said Gilban, apparently sensing Dugan's hesitation. "Or have you changed your mind already?"

Dugan silently rose, growing uneasy with how Alara eyed him as she neared.

"Go." The blind elf waved him on. "Get your answers while you can."

He shook himself from inaction, traveling eastward with a quickened pace. If he really could get some answers then he might as well go after them. It wasn't like he was going to find any more waiting for him en route to those ruins. And if it *was* too good to be true he'd find out soon enough.

• ● •

"Is everything okay?" Alara returned to Gilban's side.

"Yes." He smiled. "Why do you ask?"

"I just noticed you with Dugan. Is there anything I should know?" She watched the gladiator hurrying from the plaza. "He wasn't causing you any trouble, was he?"

"No. And there's no reason to fear. Even now he's gone to clear his mind and deal with the troubles burdening him. Now, let's get to that inn," said Gilban, rising. "I have to quench my thirst, and I think something will soon unfold there that will prove rather favorable to our cause."

"What now?" Alara asked with mild trepidation. "Hopefully, a less violent surprise than what we've been finding of late."

"Events are yet to unfurl," Gilban said, steadying himself with his staff.

"This have anything to do with that vision you had on the boat?"

"I told you all I could at the time."

"Which wasn't much."

"And you're worried I'm holding something back from you?"

Alara studied Gilban's pendant for a moment, pondering all the things it symbolized. "The thought *has* crossed my mind."

"Then it's done so recently." Gilban wasn't the least bit offended by the comment, adding, "You never doubted my calling you for this mission. Nor any other part of what Saredhel's shared with me. She made it quite clear you were to accompany me and—"

"Lead the others," she said, watching the rushing crowd again. "I know." She took Gilban's arm, helping ease his steps. She'd been aiding him for so long now, her moves were automatic.

"You knew what would be required at the beginning, Alara." The statement birthed a flash of memory. She'd never forget when the men sent to seek out a silver-haired young woman for a mission called for by Saredhel and the republic itself came literally knocking on her parents' door. Nor would she forget her parents' reaction when Gilban declared to them that Alara was the one for whom he'd been searching.

"I thought I did, but now it just seems like too much."

"When the light shines upon an ant, its shadow can grow to the size of a giant. Perhaps it's time to adjust your vision and see things as they really are. Saredhel would not have chosen you if you weren't able to do what was required." He paused. "Don't forget the battle on the docks."

"Which was pretty chaotic," she admitted as they passed a fishmonger hawking his wares.

"Life is seldom as orderly as we'd like."

"No—it isn't, is it?" She now caught sight of a Telborian woman pulling a cart piled with bolts of brightly colored cloth. For a moment she had a flash of the port cities of Rexatoius, realizing even more than before how much she missed her homeland.

"But they followed you."

"But will they in the times ahead, when it *really* matters?" she asked, hoping perhaps he'd let his guard down and share at least some small hint of the direction she needed to take.

"That's not for me to decide."

With an inward sigh she let the matter drop, resting in the silence overshadowing the rest of their journey.

CHAPTER 14

FORSAKING ONE'S HERITAGE IS LIKE BUILDING A HOUSE UPON SAND:
ONLY WITH A STRONG FOUNDATION DO YOU HAVE HOPE FOR THE FUTURE.

—Old dwarven saying

Vinder found himself treading a well-worn street in a forgotten part of Elandor. He had no clear idea of where he wanted to go after adding to the money already on deposit with the temple of Olthon, deciding he'd just wander for a while. It was better than sitting at the Mangy Griffin twiddling his thumbs, and it allowed him some personal time before he'd be joined at the hip with the others for who knew how long.

While he'd meant for the walk to be something of a mindless venture, the more walking he did, the more thinking he found himself doing. He kept wondering if he was doing the right thing by taking this job and if he'd get enough money from it to finally put this life behind him. And then there was the occasional thought that he might not make it back from the jungle at all. Why he even thought this to begin with, he wasn't sure, as he wasn't one to entertain such fears. Nevertheless, the concern was persistent, much to his displeasure.

Lost in thought, and oblivious to where he was going, he eventually found himself trailing a loose fold of men and women who, while not quite beggars, were close. The cobblestone road they traveled had long ceased to be level; it was full of small hills and valleys and puddles of brackish and sometimes putrid water, which he did his best to avoid. This was to say nothing of the scattered patches of grass, weeds, and even wildflowers sprouting out of and further destroying the road. This wasn't the worst place he'd ever found himself in, but he had no intention of overstaying his welcome.

Observing the buildings lining the street, his trained eye found the telltale sign of dwarven design here and there amid some of the structures. Though the shapes were almost faded now, like the rest of the memories the buildings once housed, he could still make out some small clues if he studied long enough. It was strange seeing the sign of dwarven craftsmanship so far from any clan, but Elandor *was* old—one of the first cities to be built after the Imperial Wars—and things were different then.

Those who made their way down the street—humans mostly—did their best to avoid the armored and armed dwarf, giving him a wide berth as they passed. What once were larger stone homes, shops, and even what looked like a temple, had been converted to simple apartments. Not the more common wood, plaster, and stone buildings found in the newer sections of Elandor, but no longer the gloriously refined edifices they'd once been. Now crumbling, weatherworn pieces of once-grand adornments desperately clung to the façades of rows of small dwellings fit for little more than keeping out the elements. Again, he'd seen worse—*been* in worse—over the years and was thankful he'd soon be putting such things far from him.

Oddly enough, Alara and Gilban had found him in an alleyway much like this before he'd agreed to their offer. It'd been in a small town in Altorbia, where he landed after his last job. A well-connected family in that area had wanted help waging a private war against bitter rivals, a family that had been gaining power. The pay was good, and Vinder didn't know nor care about the elven families involved, so he'd taken the job.

The war was short but effective. The rival house was shattered, their climb to power halted in its tracks. Vinder had just healed up from the slight wounds he'd suffered and had been growing restless when Alara and Gilban appeared. If he'd been inclined to Gilban's mindset, he would have thought the meeting fated, but instead he took the path of luck.

Though, if he was back with his clan, he might have credited the deed to Drued instead. Either way it was a welcome thing that brought him closer to his final goal.

He decided to make his way into what he thought might have been a temple centuries before. If that was its origin, it was more squat and utilitarian than any temple he'd seen. Two stories in height, it wasn't grand from the outside, but he felt drawn to it nonetheless. Placing his hands upon the old stone, the smooth surface somehow remained refined and polished even after centuries of abuse from the relentless weather that had so clearly marred other buildings sharing the street.

An open doorway stood to his left. Looking above the sill, Vinder caught sight of a design he thought strange for a Telborian city: two war hammers crossing over a double-bladed axe. The Holy Standard. The relief was clearly discernible, even after all these years. A miracle in and of itself, but what the crest denoted was something even more amazing and drew him through the darkened opening like a moth to the flame.

He took a moment for his vision to adjust in the darkness, before cautiously making his way forward, ignoring the odd rat and puddle along with the dank, musty smell that seemed to be steeped in the stone itself. He found himself in a large room that once had been polished granite but now was covered with small bits of rock, rotting leaves, and a thick layer of grime. What had been in the room during its better days he hadn't a clue, but it seemed able to house a hundred people without crowding. As his eye continued to adjust, he thought he saw the outline of another person farther ahead.

"Hello?" The room swallowed the sound as soon as it left his lips.

The figure didn't move.

Growing closer, he could clearly see the shape seemed to resemble a dwarf. He called out again, this time in his native tongue rather than Telboros.

"Hello there."

The figure remained still.

Finally, he drew near enough to realize he'd been calling out to a statue. Placing his hands upon the stone figure, he wiped away some grime caked into the folds of its clothing and armor with his calloused fingers. As he worked, he imagined who the statue might represent. Even this close, the darkness made it difficult to discern the figure's features. All he could see was a statue of a male dwarf, dressed in a long sleeveless shirt of brigandine armor draped over a robe.

Removing his pack from his back, Vinder went to a small pocket and pulled out a stubby candle along with his sparker. Like most sparkers, his resembled a small annular brooch. It was also utilitarian and well used. The flint ring was heavily worn and the steel needle was covered in scratches. Working it with a practiced hand, he birthed a tongue of flame to light the candle and proceeded to examine the mysterious statue. A thick patriarchal beard flowed from its strong face, upon which twelve adorned braids fell in perfect form.

"Merciful Drued!" Vinder fell to his knees. His heart raced in his chest. This was an omen for sure. It had to be. Before him was a statue of Drued, god of the dwarves. Even in the midst of the shock of his discovery, a sense of shame rose as well. He'd been so long from his clan that he'd lapsed in his reverence to his deity. To find this statue here, and still intact . . . could Drued be showing him he was close to the forgiveness he sought? Telling him there was still hope for reconciliation?

"Forgive me, Drued," Vinder prayed. "I've learned from my mistakes and past sins. I beseech you to forgive me and lead me back to Diamant. I've gathered a tribute worthy enough to honor those whom I've offended. Please bless me on my journey so I meet with favor."

"Now *this* is a good sign." A voice speaking Dwarfish brought Vinder to his feet. Another dwarf, dressed in muted browns and grays, had entered the temple. As he drew closer, Vinder's recollection brightened.

"Heinrick?"

The dwarf was twenty years Vinder's senior, but looked half that. He kept his graying hair in a ponytail that trailed down his upper back. And then, of course, there were the braids in his beard. Every dwarven male earned his first braid upon reaching his twenty-fifth year with an additional one added for every twenty-five years lived after that. The two strands, dyed a dark blue at the tips, flowed over a frayed gray beard, striped with flashes of silver and white.

"What are *you* doing here?"

"You've been away so long you forgot already?" Heinrick greeted Vinder with a sarcastic grin. "I'm picking up a few supplies before winter sets in. Mostly a few trivial items that only come in through the sea trade."

"And I thought Diamants always strove for self-sufficiency," said Vinder. He and every other dwarf in the clan had the ideal instilled in them as soon as they could walk.

"And in time we'll meet that goal," said a clearly confident Heinrick.

"If I recall, we've been seeking to attain it for a few millennia now," Vinder replied, gently ribbing his old friend, who clearly took no offense on the topic.

"We'll get there in the end," said Heinrick. "We're dedicated, if nothing else."

"I think you meant stubborn."

Heinrick gave a small nod. "There's still plenty of that going around too . . . as I'm sure you know."

"Only too well." Vinder's levity faded.

"Believe it or not, I tend to come here when I first arrive in the city, and again before I head back to the clan," Heinrick continued. "After all, it's not every day you come across a shrine to Drued in a Telborian city."

Vinder again found the statue. "I'm surprised it's so well preserved."

"I was, too, considering the rest of the place has just about been stripped bare. But that doesn't tell me what *you're* doing here."

"Looking for some hope," he confessed. "I'm getting ready to go back to the clan—seek to make amends."

"I'm glad to hear it." Heinrick's smile widened, a bit of mischief lurking just beneath his ever-serious face.

"And I'm surprised you're even talking to me. I thought that was forbidden."

"You know I am, and always will be, a true supporter of the clan. However"—Heinrick stepped forward and rested a hand upon Vinder's shoulder—"it's good to see you again, Vinder. It's been a long time."

"Too long," he mused.

"It sounds like you've finally come to your senses, if what I've just seen is any indication."

"You warned me not to go."

"But I respected your decision." Heinrick gave his shoulder a strong squeeze. "Just like I do now." The sincerity of the comment washed over him in refreshing waves, cleansing away the years of fear, regret, and doubt. And for a brief span of breaths he actually felt like his old self again. But such relief wasn't lasting—it wouldn't be until he returned and finished making amends. But maybe everything wasn't as hopeless as he was tempted to imagine.

"And what news of the clan?" he asked.

"The same as always."

"I was afraid of that. But I'm willing to come back, if they'd have me." He extended his hand. Heinrick viewed it hesitantly. "Come, forgive me. I must have at least *some* hope I can return."

"I've heard from your own lips what I need to hear." Heinrick clasped Vinder's hand with a hearty grip. "You've learned from your mistakes. But while I can forgive you, it'll be another matter altogether for the king and the elders to be so merciful."

"Whatever they decide"—Vinder released his friend's hand—"I'm ready to receive it."

"I'm starting my journey to the mountains tonight." Heinrick attempted to lighten the mood. "Will you join me? It would be nice to have some company."

He slowly shook his head. "Not yet. I've given my oath to take care of one last matter. But once it's done, I'll take my tribute and join you and the clan."

Heinrick nodded stoically. "A man must be true to his word."

When Vinder sighed it felt like he'd just lightened a load from his shoulders. The pressing weight had been there for so long its absence now seemed foreign. "Seeing you, this shrine, even the statue of Drued—I can only think it bodes well for the future."

"If not . . . you might be walking into a death sentence."

"That's a chance I'm willing to take. Not unlike the chance you took with me. Standing by my side even to the last moment when I was banished."

"I did what I thought was right," said Heinrick. "Just like I'm doing now."

"If only more dwarves were like you."

"Who says they aren't?" Heinrick grinned. "You might find yourself surprised upon your return. And when that happens, I'd love to hear what's happened since you left." He pointed out Vinder's patch.

"A cautionary tale if there ever was one," he soberly replied while he momentarily contemplated the floor.

"No doubt. Still, it couldn't hurt to pray some more to Drued for protection and guidance until you arrive." Heinrick reached under his beard and removed a necklace he'd hidden there, passing it to Vinder. "May you find favor in his sight."

Vinder studied the necklace in his open palm, noticing it was of excellent workmanship. The pendant was a carved quartz figure on a golden loop, dangling from the leather strap. Taking closer note of the figure, he saw the form was of Drued, dressed in a full suit of armor and sporting twelve braids—each lovingly detailed in the semiopaque stone.

"Thank you," he said, feeling the prick of tears.

"I look forward to seeing you soon, Vinder." Heinrick turned to make his departure.

"Aren't you going to stay? You only just arrived."

"And I've already seen a miracle." Heinrick kept walking for the exit. "And I'll be looking forward to seeing another one back in Diamant."

"You and me both." Vinder watched his friend disappear through the doorway, listening to his footsteps grow fainter, until he was alone once again.

"Thank you, Drued," he reverently whispered, focusing back on the old statue. The tears were already soaking his beard before he was even aware of them. He let them flow while he engaged in a silent prayer to the god he'd let fade from his life decades ago with the rest of his past. And it was in that moment he welcomed and latched on to something else he hadn't known in a long while: hope.

CHAPTER 15

The sun was kissing the horizon when Dugan made his way to the edge of what had been a park a few centuries earlier. Now the sickly saplings, scraggy bushes, and large tracts of dry, open ground were surrounded on all sides by Elandor's older districts and the outer wall of the great city. In the center of the park stood a temple. He guessed it was forty feet at most—tall, yes, but not as towering as he'd first imagined.

The temple was also old and constructed of volcanic rock, giving it a rough and slightly menacing appearance. Four pillars supported the corners of its flat roof that covered the stone walkway around the temple proper, resting about ten feet from the top of the smooth black steps leading up to it. Each column was inlaid with pieces of colored glass, making the pillars appear to be engulfed in flames whenever the sun shone upon them, as it did now at his approach.

Ignoring the extravagant display, Dugan raised his eyes to the temple's crowning achievement: a bronze dome sitting above the black roof, crafted to appear as if it, too, was on fire. Its metallic, flame-shaped tendrils wrapped around its center, as if straining to grasp the fading sunlight.

The acrid tang of heavy smoke became more prominent as he ascended the steps, the air growing warmer until he stood on the last stair, forehead beaded with sweat. The atmosphere became so heavy as he neared the temple's tall iron doors that he found it hard to breathe. Stopping to catch his breath, he slouched against the door frame. Who was he fooling? He'd never be free. Not from a pact with a god. For a moment, he thought about heading back and putting this whole foolish exercise behind him, when a small voice inside him encouraged him to continue. He didn't know if the voice was real or imagined, but he knew that if he gave up now, he'd be tormented until his death with what could have been.

Fresh resolution rising from within, he gritted his teeth and forced his legs onward. Admiring the door's metal, he found certain areas had been polished to reflect the sunlight, giving the illusion of white-hot iron fresh from the forge. He watched the sun dance off the rest of the metal, casting a scintillating patch of light a few steps from him. For a moment, it reminded him of what happened in Argis—the diamond-dust sparkle that had preceded the strange and haunting mass of tentacles that had gotten him into so much trouble. He still had no idea what had happened, sometimes wondering if he'd momentarily gone mad.

He tentatively rested his hand on the door, took a deep breath, and then made his way inside. The temple was hot and dark, dimly lit by torches and small braziers of glowing ash fixed to the walls at random intervals. He found no one in sight, only an intense heat radiating from all around. The walls and floors were made of fieldstone, years of soot and ash dulling the surfaces into a charcoal-gray grime.

The passage he'd entered branched off to the north of the entrance and stretched a few yards beyond before turning a sharp corner. The hallway opposite it held a few darkened archways and doors. The low ceiling trapped the room's heat and made the atmosphere suffocating, increasing Dugan's discomfort.

"Hello?" His voice bounced off the walls and ceiling.

Nobody replied.

He pressed on, examining the walls as he passed. Many were adorned with murals and frescoes whose bright paint had faded long ago. Now, layers of soot hid their exquisite detail. One of the scenes depicted worshipers prostrating themselves before a large bonfire. Another showed them pointing at a sun lovingly cupped by two great flaming hands. Farther down the hallway, a crudely drawn image illustrated people dancing around an erupting volcano.

The final picture was the most vivid and striking. In the center of a field were two figures. One stood with a bloodstained sword gloating over the other, who had fallen, clutching at his chest. The victorious figure was a massive Telborian male with flowing blond hair. The victim was an elf wearing rich clothing and many golden chains. He felt goose flesh rise over his body. He wondered if the heat was making him delirious. Surely the picture was pure coincidence, nothing more.

"You can't see too much of them these days from all the soot, but there's still enough to convey their meaning." Dugan jumped at the husky voice, his hand instantly going to one of the gladii. Turning, he saw the speaker: an older, deeply tanned Telborian whose blue eyes smoldered beneath a stoic brow. He wore an outer orange robe open over an inner robe of red. Both were embroidered in yellow and gold thread that resembled tongues of fire.

"May I help you with anything?" The priest's demeanor was disarming.

"I want to talk to Rheminas." He kept his hand on the pommel of his sword, which wasn't lost on the priest. But if the action troubled him he never showed it.

"It will cost you."

"I don't have any money."

"In that case, one of your swords will do." The priest pointed at the gladius Dugan's hand was resting upon. When he did so, Dugan noticed the priest's fingertips were dyed yellow and glowed dimly in the flickering light.

"All right," he said, and relinquished a gladius—sheath and all—as he looked once more at the unsettling mural with the dying elf.

"Not the best image, perhaps," said the priest, "but it serves to tell its message."

"Which is?"

"Like all the murals, it depicts one of Rheminas' aspects. That particular image portrays him as the god of revenge. It's not how he's widely worshiped, mind you, but still one part of an impressive portfolio." He paused, gazing on the image.

"It's even said Rheminas aided Colloni's first emperor with his rage, forging it into a mighty weapon." He spoke with a smugness Dugan found unsettling. "But I'm sure you know enough about revenge already, don't you?"

"What do you mean?" His hand found the hilt of his remaining gladius.

"I saw it on your face the moment you stepped inside. My lord has chosen you—laid claim to you already. What could you possibly want answers to when your future is already so clear?"

"Get me to him and you'll see."

"Fine." The priest nodded. "Follow me." He began shuffling down the hallway, heading into an even more intense heat, pulling free Dugan's sword for a closer inspection as they walked. "You obviously don't understand what you've done and where you now stand. It'll be my duty then to explain what a life with Rheminas means."

"Like the priests of Saredhel?"

The priest whirled around, a deep scowl lining his face. "Never speak of another god in the temple of Rheminas."

"Why? What's he afraid of?"

"It's about respect"—the priest rapidly resumed his pace—"and knowing when to show it. Something to keep in mind if you want to get your answers. And for another, we don't divine fate like those soothsayers."

"But you just said—"

"I said I'll get you answers, not dig them out from scrying pools and entrails."

Dugan noticed the light had increased as they walked. So too did the heat. He began feeling faint, yet he observed his guide hadn't even broken a sweat.

"Why is it so warm in here?"

"All will be revealed in time."

"Where are the other priests?" Dugan wheezed.

"It's the summer solstice and also one of our most sacred days, the Feast of Flames. The others have gone to celebrate it."

"Why aren't you with them?"

"Someone needs to mind the temple. And it's a good thing I have, for your sake." He led Dugan to a set of massive stone doors carved with an image of a great brazier holding a mighty flame at its center. Blackness began clouding his peripheral vision.

The priest's smile seemed serpentine as he motioned to the large doors. "All your answers are behind these doors. However, if you continue being so stubborn, you'll never get them. You have no need of your armor here, but if you feel the desire to cling to it, I'll humor you this once." He placed his hand upon the swooning Dugan, whispering a prayer over him. Instantly, he felt cooler. His body began to shiver as all the sweat that had been pooling under his mail dried in the warm winds wafting around him, the same winds that had only a moment before felt as if they'd suffocate him.

"Are you ready, Dugan?" A knowing smile crossed the priest's face.

"How—"

"All will be revealed, remember?" The priest waved the thought away as he motioned him forward.

Dugan sighed in exasperation, and leaned his weight into the large stone doors. To his surprise, they swung open with ease. Beyond them he found a huge chamber out of which radiated intense light—as brilliant as sunshine. And there was also a pungent aroma of ash and wood smoke, mingling with some spices he couldn't quite place.

"Come." The priest beckoned him to follow.

The roof of the grand chamber towered above them. He noticed the brilliant light radiated from an oculus in its center, which also allowed the smoke from the twenty-foot brazier below it to escape. The brazier was solid bronze, stood on three man-sized legs, and was covered with swirling designs and images. He assumed these were the heroes of their religion. It was the room's sole decoration. The ceiling and walls had been blackened by the giant flame, cloaking any past adornment.

"Sit." The priest motioned to a plain bronze high-backed chair stationed against one of the brazier's legs.

Dugan sat as the priest moved for a small bronze stand a few feet away. He placed Dugan's sword against the base, and then focused on the small bronze basin the stand supported. The priest lifted the basin overhead and chanted a few inaudible words. A tongue of flame shot out from the great brazier and into the basin, igniting a fire all its own.

"Let us begin," said the priest, approaching Dugan.

"Oh Flame Lord, great Mover of the Sun, hear your servant!" he prayed. "One of your own has come seeking you. Though he has your mark upon him and should already know what awaits him, he yet wishes to petition you. Enlighten me so I may be able to share with him your decrees."

He fixed his eyes firmly on Dugan. "What do you wish to know?"

"How can I get out of this pact?"

"You can't. You're Rheminas' forever." The words hit Dugan in the gut, souring his stomach. Gilban had said he should go here for a reason. If it wasn't about the pact, what else could it be?

"Is there anything else?"

"What about my future?"

"I told you, we're not diviners. We can't discern your fate."

"But you just prayed for answers."

"Yes, answers. Not glimpses of the future."

"Humor me." His comment produced a small scowl from the priest. "I gave you my sword. Might as well get *something* for it."

"Very well," said the priest, sighing, and he stared back into the basin's contents. "You want to know about your future. What about it exactly?"

Before he could respond, the same shimmering diamond dust that appeared to him in Argis materialized between him and the priest like some gossamer curtain. At the same time he noted the smoke floating from the basin twisted and swayed into black tentacles—also like he'd seen in Argis. All of this was lost on the pondering priest, who kept his eyes fixed on the flames.

"What's *this*?"

"What?"

"I-I can see your fate." The priest's face was ashen with fear when next Dugan saw it. The moment he did so, the white shimmer and black tentacles vanished, leaving him wondering once more if he'd really seen them at all.

"That's bad?"

"Yes . . ." He ventured again into the flames with a vexed frown. "I shouldn't be able to . . ." After moments of tense silence in which the priest seemed hypnotized by the dancing fire, Dugan spoke.

"So what do you see?"

"I don't know." His voice was a low whisper. "I—this isn't right."

"What isn't?" He hunched forward, growing ever more curious for news. The priest again became lost in the basin's flames. "Can you see my fate or not?" Dugan growled.

"Yes . . . but I shouldn't be—"

"Then tell me." He didn't shout but came close enough to draw the other's concern. The two exchanged a tense moment before the priest relented.

"You shall live a life filled with passions and dangers—a warrior's life, indeed." Though his voice had gained some strength, it was still shaken.

"A long life?"

The priest shook his head. "I can't see that."

"What will happen to me?" Dugan slid to the edge of his seat.

"I see you living as a free man. The mission you are on now . . . you shall survive. I see a powerful figure as well. One who casts a long, hungry shadow. You and he are destined to meet twice before your end. Ah . . . Rheminas preserve me! How is it possible I can be seeing all this?" The priest gazed into the basin, the flames harshly outlining his troubled features.

"I sense another presence here with us—Rheminas, preserve your servant!" He closed his eyes for a brief moment before opening them, more at peace than before. "I see your last moments. No matter the road you choose, they all lead to the same spot. Only the dates change their form. You shall know suffering and sorrow and feel the lash of indignity upon you once more, like splinters in your back."

"But where do I go when I die?"

"To Rheminas' hand." The priest locked on to Dugan's troubled eyes, sweat trickling down his brow. "Like I've already said."

Dugan's heart sank. "That's it? You don't see anything else?"

"You've made a pact with a god. It cannot be broken." The priest hurriedly returned the basin to its stand.

"Not even by another god?" He did his best to keep disappointment from creeping into his voice. He saw the offense his question had caused but didn't care. He needed to know what his options were—if he had *any* hope left to him.

"Few, if any, would touch the property of another god." The priest gave Dugan a hard glare, reminding him of the look his former masters held when calculating his worth in gold. "But you're a special case, aren't you? I didn't sense it at first but you're carrying something with you. Something that showed me your fate, and now contaminates this sacred space." The priest's eyes shrunk to slivers. "What sort of game are you playing?"

"Game?"

"This whole matter is very vexing. As are you." The priest abruptly returned to the stand. "And the presence I feel is still here polluting this temple." A motion over the basin extinguished the fire. "We've finished with your concerns," he continued, again finding Dugan's face. "I have a deep need to ponder what just happened in prayerful meditation."

"How did you know me?" Dugan asked, slowly rising. "You can at least tell me that."

"Rheminas told me both your name and of your arrival. Even though you reject him, he holds out his hand to you. Truly you're destined to do great things in his service. I wish I could be as blessed as you.

"If you want peace, look to his hand. Fear not its warm embrace. Relish it. Use it to nurture yourself until you see him face to face."

Dugan wearily contemplated the massive brazier, realizing how much it reminded him of some kind of grand pyre. "If this is being blessed, then I'm living in the Abyss."

"Our time really is now passed," the priest pressed. "I've borne this intolerable presence long enough. I can tell you no more." He indicated the open door and Dugan's need to introduce himself to it. "Please leave the same way you came."

Dugan sullenly withdrew from the inner chamber. He'd come here looking for hope and hadn't found it. If anything what hope he had clung to before entering had been burned to ash. And then he saw the answer. The priest never said the gods would *not* listen to his plea for release from his pact. He could still approach them. And if he could still approach them there was still hope he'd find his release.

Cadrissa had given him a brief introduction to the Tralodroen pantheon. Maybe one of them might have sympathy for his case. It looked like Gilban was right after all. He'd found his answer. There was still hope for his future.

As to the strange manifestations of darkness and light—that was another matter. But as long as they weren't a common occurrence and made Rheminas and his priests uncomfortable he could set them aside for now. If he needed to, after this venture with Alara, he could look at things more closely. For now, he'd found a possible key for his last remaining shackles and discovered something that rankled his jailer as well. All in all, he considered his visit a small victory.

Content, he made his way back into the city, using what light remained to take a brief inventory of the various temples and shrines en route to the inn.

CHAPTER 16

ELANDOR SHALL THRIVE AND INSTILL ITS NAME IN GENERATIONS.
WE SHALL PROVE OURSELVES WORTHY OF GONDAD'S MANTLE.

—Marlin Janink, first king of Elandor
Reigned 2968 BV–2774 BV

C adrissa traveled the swarming streets of Elandor at a rushed pace. She truly wished she had more time for exploring. The city seemed full of wonderful ways one could spend a day. But by the time she found what she was searching for, worked out the arrangements, and finished augmenting her supplies, she'd be due at the Mangy Griffin.

She'd left her chest back on the boat, hidden under the simple cot in the cabin. Gilban had said it'd be safe there until nightfall. And because she didn't really enjoy the idea of lugging the chest along with her backpack all over the city—potentially drawing unwanted attention—and perhaps because she trusted Gilban's insights, she'd left it on the boat. She could get it later after everything was settled at the inn.

While there were great sights and things to enjoy in passing, she was searching for something hidden from common sight. From her schooling, she'd learned of shops hidden in the cities across Talatheal and elsewhere that served mages, just like there were shops which helped workers in other trades. Given magic's reception could be questionable in places, such shops were often off the beaten path and hidden from plain sight, better protecting both shopkeep and patrons. But if one knew what signs to look for, they could be found easily enough.

And one of the first things she'd learned at the Haven Academy was the sign of the Tarsu, an ancient order dedicated to the advancement and protection of magic. She'd learned it was a universal marker of sorts pertaining to all things magical. It was commonly used in cities for guiding mages to safer locales where one could purchase wares, secure certain services, or connect with other mages. While she had made use of some shops in Haven for supplies, that had been the extent of her interaction with other mages or their supporters outside the academy. Today would be a new experience; the prospect had been stirring butterflies in her stomach since they'd left the boat.

Soon enough she found what she sought: a series of sixteen-pointed stars over which were laid a slightly smaller eight-pointed star. The faint carvings were subtle in their placement and nature, scratched onto odd bricks here and there, but she still found them. With a growing sense of confidence, she followed these markings like a bee going from flower to flower until a sharp turn suddenly introduced her to the mouth of a squalid alleyway.

A stale and pungent breeze stung her nostrils, reminding her of unwashed feet, urine, vomit, and decay. As she ventured into this rundown part of the city, she noted the population had dwindled from a swarming mass to sparse smatterings of vagrants and lower-class citizens. It was just the sort of place criminals inhabited. And given the looks she received from passersby, her clean golden robes were going to make sure she stood out.

"Just keep going." She ignored the increasing flutter in her stomach and forced herself down the alleyway. "You're almost there." The formerly solid cobblestone gave way to a worn path where tired stones crumbled amid patches of hard-packed earth and seeping puddles. As she continued her cautious advance, she was watchful for the next and hopefully last marker.

She brushed back her hair with a nervous hand, watching another seemingly drunken man pass by with a leering grin. She pretended she didn't feel as sick as she did with his lingering gaze traveling up and down her frame, and breathed a sigh of relief with his passing. Proceeding with measured steps, she made a wide pass around another drunken Telborian, this one seated against a wall mumbling to himself and staring at the spot of earth between his raised knees.

A little farther, nestled between a set of weathered wooden doors, another man lay face down on the ground. She hoped he'd just had too much to drink; the alternative was far from uplifting. As she neared, she watched a small, dirty pup trot over to the man, lift his leg, and mark his territory. This done, the dog hurried toward Cadrissa, gave a few curious sniffs along the cuff of her robes and toes of her boots, then moved on.

Beyond that, the rest of the alley was empty, and her confidence swelled as she made another search of the area. Slowly, she studied the walls and the few doors she could see for any markings. While she didn't think this the best of locations for a shop, it was better than what she might have found a few centuries before. Magic and mages in general had made some great strides since then, for which she was thankful. Even a mage with the most basic of training would have been something of a wonder back then.

Suddenly, she noticed a small marking carved into the gray wood of a door to her left. It wasn't easy to see at first—it probably wasn't supposed to be—but as she neared, she spotted the same mark etched into the lower right section of the door. Looking around one last time, she put her hand to the wrought iron handle and gave it a tug.

Immediately, there was a noticeable change of atmosphere. The smell of decay and urine was replaced with the sweet and soothing aromas of balms, flowers, spices, and rare plants. There were no windows in the shop, yet the interior was as bright as day. Light radiated from a globe in the center of the establishment, resting on top of a bronze holder sculpted like two large hands holding aloft a miniature sun.

"May I help you?" a young male voice asked from behind a wooden counter off to the side of the room. He was dressed in a long, flowing gray hooded robe. Though she couldn't see too clearly under the hood, she thought she discerned his eyes looking her over from head to foot.

This wasn't like the leering stare of the man in the alley, but rather an assessment of any risk she might pose.

"I'm looking for a place to store some spell books and other tomes." Cadrissa stepped inside, closing the door behind her.

"Then I think you've come to the right place," said the other. "How long do you need them stored?"

She paused, mentally counting the days. "I'm guessing a month, maybe two." While she had a rough idea of how long things might take, she knew enough to plan ahead and always round on the fat side when making such estimations. She didn't want to have her tomes and scrolls getting taken out of storage and left to who knows what before she returned. It had taken her a great deal of time and money to amass them, and she wasn't about to lose them with any foolish planning.

The other nodded. "And how much material would this be?"

"Enough to fill a small chest," she replied, again making sure her previous calculations were correct. She'd be taking some additional material in her pack, but the bulk of it would remain behind.

"And you're the only person who will be dealing with it?"

"Yes."

"All right," said the man, pulling back his hood and revealing his handsome features. Cadrissa momentarily found herself lost in his pale green eyes before he brought her back to the matter at hand. "Let's talk terms and payment."

• ● •

Three days after Rowan had made landfall in Elandor, he was no better off than when he'd first arrived. He hadn't had any more dreams, but still pondered what he'd experienced. He ruminated over the memories, hoping and praying for further guidance and answers. Because outside of some divine intervention, the rest of his efforts were not only tiring but getting him nowhere. Finding a bench, he rested his tired feet and searched the square he'd wandered into, observing the press of people coming and going as evening grew. Having walked just about the entire breadth of the city, he was convinced he was on a fruitless quest.

Nordic instinct told him the best deals were made in taverns and inns, and so this was where he'd first scoured for answers. He started in the Broken Oar, and then moved from tavern to tavern, inn to inn. No matter how many people he asked, none of those with whom he spoke seemed a suitable guide for Taka Lu Lama. He didn't have money to waste on another week's stay, putting him under pressure to get something resembling progress. The elves and dwarves who occasionally passed were of particular interest to him. He was somewhat familiar with dwarves; they lived in the mountains and hills of Valkoria. From what he'd heard from others and in his training, they could be trustworthy people, but seldom sought out or worked with others outside their race. It was the elves, however, who were more of an enigma.

Rowan's eyes found an older dwarf leaning against a nearby wall, smoking a pipe. His white, chest-long beard was braided into twin coils, and his almost black eyes scanned the crowds. He'd seen barely a handful since he'd arrived. That wasn't too surprising, since the dwarves he knew about back on Valkoria had been known to keep to themselves. He supposed the same was the case elsewhere. This one possessed a definitely seasoned look about him. The normal charcoal-gray skin of his race was deeper than he'd seen among others that day. He assumed it to be from constant sun exposure. Rowan guessed he was middle-aged, though he wasn't very skilled in telling the ages of other races, and longer-lived races—he was finding—were more challenging to judge than most.

As he continued his observation, it dawned on him that all this time he'd been searching diligently for a *human* guide. He hadn't even thought of asking for aid from any other race. He found it odd that he hadn't allowed himself to consider hiring anyone *but* a human. The more he dug into the matter, the clearer it became that this was one of the parameters he'd unconsciously set for himself. Why? He couldn't find the answer. He'd never had this outlook before. Then again, he'd never been surrounded by so many different races in such abundance before, either.

But even as he started off the bench to talk with the dwarf, an internal voice tried persuading him to leave the dwarf alone and look for a trustworthy human instead. Rowan caught himself before his mind wandered too deep into those waters. The dwarf wasn't his enemy. He hadn't acted against him in any way. So why were his feelings turning him against dwarves? He knew from his training and upbringing he should never be judgmental of someone he'd no knowledge of personally, and yet his mind insisted on pitting him against nonhumans with a will of its own.

A ruckus erupting from a nearby side street yanked him from his thoughts. He wasn't alone; a few others had stopped to take note of what was going on. Curious, he made his way toward the area, where he found a dwarf, two elves, and two humans under attack by a band of brigands. They'd encircled their prey, cutlasses drawn, ready to slice into anything. As he watched, a fire took hold of his brain.

Though he knew the brigands were facing off against more than just humans, all but the two Telborians vanished from his sight. The man was obviously a warrior, given how he fought, but he was outnumbered. The female appeared frail and unable to defend herself effectively. These were two humans who needed his help. And here was a Knight of Valkoria to lend them aid. He raised his sword and charged the gathering, a war cry on his lips.

CHAPTER 17

AND THE FISTS ARE ALL A-FLAILING AND SO TOO IS THE BLOOD,
WHILE A BROKEN STAIRWAY'S RAILING NOW'S FALLEN IN THE MUD,
AND THE COINS AND CUPS ARE A-HAILING, A-HAILING ALL BELOW.
BUT YET STAY WE AND DRINK—BY THE GODS, WHAT A SHOW.

—Old drinking song

The Mangy Griffin was a large tavern and inn with a wide selection of clientele, most of them lower-class citizens who gathered there for the more affordable fare. It also had a reputation as being a port of landing for many nautical knaves. And as evening came, the common room was inhabited by a good many of them—the atmosphere suffering for it. Some of these men lustfully eyed Alara while she stood at the bar. She felt their eyes move over her body like greasy palms. While she'd kept to her previous attire, sans the cloak, she would have thought their eyes would have delighted in the barmaids instead, their cleavage-hefting tops and tight skirts being more enticing.

She was beginning to think Gilban maliciously enjoyed sending her and the others into such colorful places. He leaned against the counter beside her. His face was haggard from their travels, but his countenance was fierce and determined. She knew it would take a lot to push him into exhaustion, but she also knew he was nearing its borders. They all were. It would be good to get a nice rest before they headed out in the morning.

She and Gilban had settled into the tavern after taking the long way to it. This allowed them a brief walk around the city, wandering the busy areas of commerce and the bustling docks. When the sky started darkening, they headed for the inn. But the others didn't arrive as quickly as she thought they should, stretching their wait into something that had begun to try her patience and stoke fresh fears.

"How much longer are we going to wait?" She searched the room, catching glimpses of some of the men sucking in their ale guts as she did so. One obese mongrel with an inch of sea grit in his hair ran his tongue across his cracked lips. Alara gagged and turned away.

"Patience," Gilban replied.

Still feeling the press of less-than-pleasant stares, Alara rose. "I think I'll get some air. Are you going to be okay?"

"Save your concern. I—" Suddenly, Gilban's head twitched, his eyes tightening while his face scrunched into a maze of wrinkles.

"What is it?"

"Perhaps I will go with you after all," he said, in a lower tone than before.

She didn't like the sudden change. "Is everything okay?"

"I believe so." He started to rise.

"Here, take my arm, it'll be faster."

"That it will," Gilban muttered to himself.

"Do you see them yet?" Gilban asked Alara as they exited the inn and merged with the cool night air. They walked to the main thoroughfare from the inn's side street. There they found a bench on which to rest while Alara kept an eye out for the others. It was well into evening, the stars and moon highlighting everything in soft, silvery light.

"No, but they'd better get here soon." She watched over the thin trickle of people passing before them with mild interest. "We have a lot to discuss tonight."

"They'll come back. Have faith. I thought you were a better judge of character than that."

"I used to be fairly good, but these are different people from different races and lands. It's one thing to judge a Patrious from a different region of Rexatoius and another trying to understand the mind of a human or dwarf from as far east as the world permits."

"Are the stars out yet?" Gilban leaned against the backrest, his peaceful manner unfaltering.

"Yes." Alara kept her gaze on the street.

"Then they'll be here soon." He grew more comfortable. "You'll have to learn patience and faith to weather the times ahead."

"What do you see now?"

"Nothing. These are things we *all* must learn if we wish to succeed in life. If you wish to lead—ah, I hear someone now." He turned his gaze toward the sound of the approaching foot traffic.

Alara joined him, ready to reprimand the tardy mercenaries, only to find some of the leering patrons from earlier making their way past Gilban and herself. They were a mix of Telborians and Celetors—about seven in all. They were also clearly drunk with cutlasses and daggers within reach on their belts. Not the best of combinations.

"Not them," she said, continuing to watch the men. Though they were a fair enough distance from each other to leave each to his own concern, Alara couldn't help but notice them crossing paths with an attractive, slightly frightened-looking Telborian woman.

"They'll be here." She was only half paying attention to Gilban. She was fixated on the gang of men. They'd stepped into the woman's path, who searched with visible panic for a way around them.

"They better be." Alara watched the men start joking among themselves as they continued hindering the woman's progress, making it a game. When she tried for a quick dash through a narrow opening they allowed between them, one of the men yanked her back by her long brown hair.

Alara leapt to her feet. "I'll be right back."

Gilban's brow wrinkled. "Is everything all right?"

"It will be." She strode toward the men, hand resting on the pommel of her sword.

"Don't be too long," Gilban called after her. "They should be here any moment now."

Alara only half heard Gilban's reply as she closed the distance between her and the laughing pack of drunkards. The woman between them resembled a snagged fish desperately trying to free itself from its captor's snare.

"Casting lots sounds fair enough, I suppose," she overhead the most cruel-looking and plumpest of the men say before another hit him in the shoulder, alerting him to Alara's arrival. Almost instantly, a nearby Celetor's hand clenched the woman's wrist. Her panicked, pleading eyes found Alara's—uncertain of what was going to happen next.

"Well, well," said one of the Telborians, pawing Alara with his wandering eyes. "Looks like we got *two* for the night. Must be using some pretty good bait." The others laughed.

"Let her go." Alara made sure she kept light on her feet. Now closer, she counted nine total. It was far from an ideal ratio, and in hindsight rather foolish for her to have jumped right into things as she had, but she couldn't change that now. She needed to be smart, careful.

"You should really mind your own business." The Celetor holding the woman gave her a hard tug, bringing her solidly against his person. "Unless you want to make *us* your business."

"And what if I do?" The men began spreading out, leaving the woman and her captor behind them. Among their number was a larger Telborian with a thick black mustache. He stepped forward like the lead wolf in the pack, staring Alara down.

"Then you'd be in for a bit of a rough night." Alara did her best to ignore his lusty gaze, keeping focused on the other woman and her captor's free hand as he groped wildly at his prey.

"I don't know, Jake," said one of the others behind him. "She looks pretty pale. She might be sick—have one of them diseases or something."

"Then I'll let you go first." Jake, the lead man, shot a mocking grin over his shoulder. "You can test the waters for the rest of us."

Seizing the opportunity, Alara jabbed her knee as hard as she could into Jake's groin. He collapsed on his knees, groaning in deep-rooted agony. As he wallowed on the ground, the others yanked out their cutlasses.

Alara drew her falchion. She was glad she'd kept it at her side instead of leaving it in her room with her bow and cloak. It was probably a good policy to adopt for the rest of the trip, given how things seemed to be going. But just because she had a weapon in hand, that didn't mean she knew exactly what to do.

She cursed herself at being so headstrong as to invite trouble in, but upon hearing the woman's whimper as she struggled against her captor's rough kisses, any regret melted away like ice in fire. Instantly she took courage in their drunken swaying and unsteady gazes. Apparently she wasn't as outnumbered as she'd first thought. It still wasn't going to be an easy fight, but her first priority remained clear. Smart and careful.

Moving in one smooth, rapid motion, Alara bent and snatched a dagger sheathed at the groaning Jake's side and lobbed it at the Celetor holding the woman. The blade sank deep into the Celetor's left shoulder near his neck, birthing a stream of curses. As expected, he released the woman in favor of attending to the dagger.

"Run!" The woman wasted no time in complying. Alara didn't have time to do anything other than watch the first attacker rush her. She easily dodged his cutlass' clumsy swings.

"I'm going to teach you some respect!" the scrawny Telborian growled, waving his weapon wildly overhead.

"She's mine!" The Celetor she'd wounded yanked the other back and to the ground. The bloody dagger he'd pulled from his shoulder was in his left hand, his cutlass in his right. His eyes were full of hate.

Alara blocked his first swing with her falchion and was barely able to duck in time to miss the following dagger jab. The Celetor was strong. Perhaps a bit too strong. Gritting her teeth and grunting as she worked her blade, she found herself unable to break his defenses. Ducking again from another powerful swipe that could have easily taken off her head, she heard a loud crack, followed by a splash of warmth across her shoulders.

She remained crouched on the stone pavement, ready to leap out of harm's way and make her own swing when the opportunity arose. Instead, her opponent stood stiff as a pole, his face a mask of surprise, shock, and horror. Alara noticed the sword sticking through his chest, the point exiting his heart. This same sword was quickly withdrawn, and the impaled sailor toppled like a felled tree.

Behind him stood Dugan, bloody gladius in hand. Wasting no time, he charged into the fray, his powerful body raging against the others. A bolt of white energy followed him, slaying two more in the blink of an eye. Alara turned from Dugan and found Cadrissa. Her golden robes trailed behind her as she ran down the street, thin strands of white lightning dancing between her fingers.

Seeing these new arrivals, the pack of sailors broke into smaller groups. Splintered, the thugs stood no chance against Dugan's heavy fists and deadly sword thrusts, nor did they fare well against Alara's kicks, jabs, and slashing steel. But Cadrissa was in need of aid.

The others had massed upon her like a pack of hyenas. Seeing another woman who met their fancy—especially an *unarmed* one—they took to her instantly, grabbing her legs and arms in tight grips.

"This one ain't half bad," one commented.

"Quit your pushing," a second snarled.

"I ain't pushing," another grumbled.

"Well, someone was kicking my leg!"

As Alara tried reaching Cadrissa, a scream rose from one of the men who held her. The wounded man released Cadrissa's wrist, hunching over and covering his bloodied knee. In doing so, he found his attacker: a one-eyed dwarf with a gleaming axe, dripping with a faint hint of red.

"Get him!" As one, the men dropped Cadrissa like a sack of wheat.

Vinder didn't slow for anything. Two swift swings downed the first who drew near. One of the men tried slicing the dwarf's face in half, but he brought up his axe, severing the other's cutlass in the process.

The now weaponless sailor sprinted for the docks. So intent was he on escaping he ran unaware into another blade waiting for him. Alara watched the Nordican pull his sword out of the other man's collapsing corpse. But she didn't have time for pondering, only focusing on clearing a path while fighting tooth and nail with the men who surrounded her.

And yet, as focused as she was, she still kept an eye on Jake. Every time he was close to getting up, she'd reintroduce him to the cobblestone with another swift kick to the groin.

Gracefully moving through the hole she crafted, Alara chanced a glance Gilban's way. Amazingly, he still sat serenely upon the bench where she'd left him, showing no sign of having any idea what was happening just a stone's throw from him. She'd never understood how his life was so favored by Saredhel. At least he was safe. That was one less thing to worry about.

In the process of backing away from the melee, Alara bumped right into the Nordican she'd glimpsed moments before. Valiantly, he parried the impaired swings of another Telborian. Upon catching sight of her he quickly shook his head like he was waking from some daydream, then returned full force into the fight.

Growing up, she'd been told tales of the inhabitants of the Northlands, but never had she seen one in person. It had been said they lived off snow and ice and fought for many strange causes, or even for just the simple outpouring of blood. This Nordican was just a hair or so shorter than Dugan and wore new-looking leather armor decorated with a panther motif. As to what he was doing there and why he'd helped them, she had no clue. For the moment, though, she'd welcome what help was offered.

"Surrender or be slain." The Nordican addressed his opponent in Telboros. The Telborian made an assessment of the situation. Most of his comrades had been killed; only three of the original band, including Jake, remained breathing. Dropping his sword, he sprinted in the direction of the main street, the second remnant of their band following on his heels. Jake finally made himself stand upright and stumbled after the others, clearly still in pain. After a long moment, Dugan, Alara, Vinder, and the Nordican lowered their weapons.

"What was all *that* about?" Vinder asked with more than a little concern. It was then Alara finally realized the extent of what they'd just done. So much for smart and careful.

"I was helping someone out," she explained, not liking how weak the explanation sounded. Apparently neither did Vinder.

"Not from what I saw. First Dugan and now you." The dwarf made another sweep of the area before adding, "And if we didn't show up when we did—"

"But you did." Gilban's voice drew all eyes on his slow approach.

"You could have helped us." Alara attempted to scold him, doubtful it would do any good.

"You seemed capable of handling the situation," Gilban continued, fully joining them. "Considering you created it."

Alara felt the blush in her cheeks. "If someone didn't step in, things could have gotten much worse." She was surprised at how much bite there was in her reply. No one said anything, letting her words and reasoning hover in the air.

"And yet you did, drawing the attention we needed in the process," Gilban continued in the same measured tone he often used.

"What are you—"

"The others have returned, I take it." He sidestepped the attempt for answers, making clear they'd all have to live with his cryptic responses for a little longer.

"Yes."

"*All* of them?" Alara wasn't sure what he was implying. She thought she'd seen all of them during the fight, but could have missed someone, she supposed. A quick summary of the situation confirmed Dugan, Vinder, and Cadrissa were all present and unharmed.

"They're all here," she informed Gilban.

"You sure we haven't picked up another?" Alara and the others followed Gilban's line of sight, taking in the sandy-haired newcomer in their midst. She'd totally forgotten about him once Jake had fled.

"So who are you?" Dugan made his way to the Nordican's side.

"Rowan Cortak, Knight of Valkoria," he responded proudly in Telboros.

"Knight of *what*?" Dugan was clearly unfamiliar with the concept.

"So why's a *knight* helping *us*?" Vinder interjected before Dugan could get his answer.

"It looked as if you needed it, and I've sworn by Panthora to aid humans where I can."

"Panthora," said Dugan. "Never heard of him."

"I have—and he's a *she*," Alara explained. "A goddess for humans, if I'm not mistaken."

"Really?" A sudden sense of renewed interest flowed across Dugan's features.

"Yes." Rowan was now more measured in his reply, watching Alara out of the corner of his eye. "Panthora's a goddess of *all* humanity—powerful and generous to all who'd call upon her. Without her, humanity would be devoured by its enemies."

"Thank you for your help," said Alara, noticing how he retreated a step as she neared. "It was much appreciated."

"We'd have had them in a moment or two," Vinder said from the remains of a fallen victim he was picking over with all the delicacy of a starving vulture. He'd already amassed a good handful of coins and other odd trinkets, which he was busy stuffing into his pockets and pouches.

"Not from what I saw," said Rowan.

"Then you weren't looking close enough." Vinder continued rummaging through the slain men.

Rowan appeared as if he was about to say something more when Gilban moved into his line of sight. How he could do such things so perfectly always amazed her. "Well, it's good to see you found your way to us," he said. "I didn't know how long we were going to have to wait."

"Wait for who?" asked Cadrissa. "*Him?*" She pointed at Rowan, raising her eyebrow in her confusion. Alara could relate.

"Yes," said Gilban.

"And who are you?" Rowan's eyes went up and down Gilban's frame, making careful note of the seer's pendant. Alara wasn't sure if he was confused or just put off by it.

"My name is Gilban. I'm a priest of Saredhel. You've probably never heard of her, as her influence reaches only as far as the Western Lands, with a few temples to the east and south . . . but no matter. You, Rowan, are the last person needed to complete our task."

"I thought *I* was the last one you needed?" Now it was Dugan's turn to share his confusion with Alara.

"So did I," she returned, even more eager for answers.

"I've had a vision in which the Republic of Colloni shall once again become a vast empire," Gilban continued with an authoritative timbre. "They shall come to power when they take possession of some information long hidden in a forgotten city. You"—Gilban pointed directly at Rowan, a move which clearly unsettled the knight—"and the others gathered here are destined to work together to thwart the elves by getting to that information first."

"The vision from the boat." Alara spoke more to herself than anyone else.

"Yes." Gilban nodded.

"I was happy to help those in need." Rowan gave a nod to Dugan and Cadrissa. "But I'm already committed to a mission of my own," he told Gilban, attempting to make sense of his solid white eyes, clearly unsure of just what to do with or about them. "I've been sent to discover an ancient city jus—" He stopped, and found Alara, realization blazing across his face. "You're on the same mission? How can that be? Are you enemies of humanity? Are you plotting with Colloni to bring about humanity's destruction? *Who* are you really?"

"Calm down." Dugan laid a hand on Rowan's shoulder. "I'm not helping just to save or destroy humanity, that's for sure."

"What for then?" Rowan gave him a cautious look.

"Freedom."

"So you're a slave of these elves, and you have to do their bidding until they release you?" Rowan raised his sword and attempted to shield Dugan from the others. "Step behind me and I'll—"

"You *do* remember that fight we just had, right?" Vinder had returned to the gathering, his pockets and pouches wider than before the conflict. "He just proved he can take care of himself. And he's definitely not about to be anyone's slave."

"Then we're *both* looking to stop the elves?" Rowan clearly was having some difficulty processing the information.

"That's how it would seem, yes," said Alara.

"But you're both elves," he continued, as if no one had noticed but him.

"And then there's the money," added Vinder.

"Money?" Rowan asked the dwarf.

"We're not knights—just looking to make a living," he replied. "And this job should fetch a pretty coin, that's for sure."

"So you're *mercenaries*?"

"*Adventurers*," Cadrissa clarified. "Adventurers looking to explore some interesting places."

Vinder gave a small snort before rolling his eye.

"And if you're going the same way, Rowan," said Alara, "you're more than welcome to join us."

"I'm no mercenary *or* adventurer. I'm a Knight of Valkoria, and I know my duty."

"That may be." Gilban tried keeping the Nordican's attention. "But you're destined to join us in our mission. Our goals are one and the same. If humanity *is* to suffer, it will do so under the lash of an Elyelmic Empire."

Rowan fell silent. It was the sort of thing that set Alara's nerves on edge. None of this was planned, and all of it opened up too many possibilities she wasn't sure she wanted to explore. Chief among them were the gathering crowds bravely inching closer for an investigation of their recent altercation.

"Are you with us or not, lad?" Vinder's tone was gruff and hurried. "The guards are bound to be here soon and I, for one, don't want to spend the night in jail."

"We won't be in jail tonight." Gilban spoke with an assured confidence.

"I don't feel like fighting any more guards either," the dwarf added for good measure. "That isn't going to end well for any of us."

"And you won't need to do any of that, either," said Gilban, keeping his focus on Rowan. "Everything will be fine." Rowan caught Gilban's eyes watching him, locking onto the empty white orbs in thought. "Everything," he repeated, more for Rowan's benefit than the others.

After a long moment, Rowan finally spoke. "Perhaps Panthora had our paths cross for a reason. And every high father has said we don't always know all her ways or reasons."

"So you're in?" Vinder sheathed his axe.

"Yes." Rowan gave a tentative nod. "If we're traveling the same way and for the same reason, I suppose I could join you . . . until I hear otherwise."

"Good!" Gilban smiled to himself. "And now we just have one more matter to attend to." His supposedly sightless gaze fell upon twelve Telborian guards making their way steadily for them. Their hands rested near the pommels of their short swords, chain mail shirts glittering in the moonlight.

"Great." Vinder scowled.

"I'm sorry," Alara heard herself telling Gilban.

"It will be all right," he reassured her. "You didn't do anything you weren't supposed to." Speaking to the others, he added, "Everything will be fine. Just let me and Alara do the talking."

"Fine by me." Dugan backed away as much as he could.

"I can speak for myself, thank you." Rowan sheathed his sword.

"Yeah, he's going to be fun to work with," Vinder muttered into his beard as he busied his hands flattening the conspicuous bulges scattered about his clothing and person.

"No more than you." Cadrissa's barb prodded some fresh ire from the dwarf, who muttered something in his native tongue before continuing his adjustments.

"The vision you had on the boat." Alara helped Gilban around the fallen bodies between them and the advancing guard. "Was it only about Rowan, or did you see something else?"

"I don't think this is the best time to discuss it." Once away from the bodies, he made for the guards with an uncanny accuracy.

"But you *will* discuss it, right? You know I don't like always being in the dark."

"And who says you're always in the dark?" She was going to press the matter but Gilban was already calmly greeting the guards. "Good evening," he said in as congenial a voice as he could muster. It was actually quite disarming, which was probably his intention. "You're probably wondering what happened here, and I'll be more than happy to explain."

CHAPTER 18

MERCENARIES ARE OFTEN LITTLE BETTER THAN
HALF-WILD DOGS. YOU HAVE TO CONTINUALLY REMIND
THEM WHO IS IN COMMAND AND TOSS OUT A FEW SACKS
OF COIN TO GO CHASING AFTER LEST THEY GROW RESTLESS
AND NIP AT YOUR HEELS. STILL, I WOULD TAKE THEM ANY DAY
OVER POLITICIANS, WHO ARE LITTLE BETTER THAN CATS.

—Chesterton Perkins, gnomish general
(300 PV–407 PV)

"**A**nd I think it would be faster if we traveled *around* the Marshes of Gondad." Rowan drained his goblet of its weak ale. "We could circle around and cut our time in half, and get to Taka Lu Lama that much sooner."

"I'm with Alara and Gilban," Vinder countered. The group was sitting around a circular table situated in an empty corner of the Mangy Griffin. "And they say we go *through* the marshes."

Rowan's concerned features were illuminated by the warm lanterns hanging from the nearby posts. "But we'd lose two, maybe three days if we—"

"I can't believe we're still *having* this discussion." Cadrissa's frustration was evident. She'd disappeared for a while after the guards' departure, returning some time later clutching the small chest she'd left on the sloop. Alara marveled at her bravery in heading out alone into the night after their recent skirmish, but Gilban assured her everything would be fine.

Alara sat across from the mage, remaining a silent observer. She'd done so for over half an hour, ever since they'd finished dealing with the guards.

Thanks to Gilban and the grace of the gods, they got through the encounter without incident. The three witnesses who sheepishly vouched for them also helped sway things in their favor. And while Rowan had said his piece on some things, he kept it simple, for which she was thankful.

In some ways it might have actually helped, though she doubted how much influence a knight from Valkoria really had over some Telborian city guards. But the less-than-sterling reputation of the dead men was really what helped their case. It appeared the guards were quite ready to look the other way if it meant removing such a thorn in their side. In the end they were just given a stern warning and the toothless threat of having an eye kept on them while they remained in Elandor. Basically not even a slap on the wrist.

She still was amazed at how quickly things had escalated. She'd acted in defense of another, thinking she could resolve things without much trouble, and they ended up killing nearly the whole lot of them. She'd taken some lives before back on Rexatoius, but not like this, nor like their previous encounter with the guards in Altorbia. Was that how it was going to be from here on out? It certainly seemed like it. She didn't relish the idea, but if she could do a better job leading, maybe the blood loss could be kept to a minimum. Maybe . . . But that wasn't her most pressing concern.

After finding a suitable spot at the back of the inn, she'd been looking forward to a simple meal, planning for tomorrow, and then some well-deserved rest. Instead, things escalated into an ever-growing debate. A less-than-promising start to what could be a trying set of days ahead. Gilban, seated on her left, was equally silent, calmly eating his stew and bread. On her right Dugan chomped away at the rest of a turkey leg as Rowan and Vinder continued their bickering.

"I'm simply stating the obvious," Rowan said in exasperation, glancing from Vinder to Cadrissa.

"This is getting us nowhere," Alara whispered.

"We still leave tomorrow," said Gilban, "according to plan."

"And they're still bleating away like angry sheep." She sighed.

Gilban's empty eyes fixed hard upon her. "Then maybe it's time for their shepherd to step in." Alara's shoulders felt the weight of his words.

"The *only* obvious thing here is that they're paying us to do a job, not try to rework their plans," said Vinder.

"Well *I'm* not being paid," Rowan shot back, "and I have orders of my own."

"Then maybe you should follow them on your own." Vinder's harsh challenge brought a threatening glare in response, which stilled the conversation faster than a slap to the face.

"Rowan, I understand your concerns." Alara quickly spoke up, trying to keep her voice soft but firm. "But it's all been worked out. And everything is moving forward just like it should. You don't have anything to fear." She still wasn't sure what to make of the knight, who seemed a mess of conflicting emotions. "Now, Gilban says you're meant to join us and you've been invited to do so, but if you want to go your own way, you can still do that too."

"Do you *really* want us to waste all that time?" Rowan's question was a mixture of a whine and an irritated growl. "The best way is *around* the marshes!"

Debate then rose anew as Vinder and Cadrissa engaged in another heated and rapid exchange with Rowan, who stuck firmly to his convictions. Curious, Alara eyed Dugan. The gladiator said nothing, only raised a questioning eyebrow that made the mountain on her shoulders even heavier.

"Maybe not so much bleating sheep," said Gilban, "as head-butting goats. But you've had practice with those, too, if I'm not mistaken." Alara took a deep breath.

"Listen up!" she almost shouted.

The others stopped their squabbling, snapping their focus squarely upon her. She was surprised herself at the strong tone she heard coming out of her mouth. "The plan was to go through the marshes, and that's what we'll do. Tomorrow we're going to get the rest of our supplies and horses from one of our contacts, and then we set off for the jungle. Now finish your meals and get some sleep. It'll be a long day on the trail."

She noticed Rowan was about to open his mouth, but she beat him to the punch. "The matter's closed, Rowan. Just make sure you're ready for tomorrow, if you still want to go with us." Then, without another word, she rose from the table and headed for a flight of stairs at the rear of the inn, pleased she finally was going to bed and putting this day behind her.

• ● •

"I think it's time for me to retire as well," Gilban said, slowly rising from the table, using his staff as a crutch for his stooping body. "It's been a long and eventful day." Stepping with the rhythm of his staff on the wooden planks, he made his way to and up the same stairs, without any hesitation or assistance.

"So you're all going to follow some blind elf?" Rowan asked once Gilban had left their sight.

"A boy should listen to the words of his elders," said Vinder. "It might give him some much-needed wisdom."

"A *boy*? I'll have you know, *dwarf*, I'm a Knight of Valkoria—newly pledged, but a Nordic *man* all the same! And a Knight of Valkoria is worth ten strong men."

"Hmph," Vinder puffed through calloused lips as Rowan shot up from the table and stormed up the stairs.

No sooner had he departed than Dugan stood. "Guess Gilban isn't the only one who's tired. I'll see you in the morning." Once he reached the top of the stairs, he locked his sights on Rowan, who was in the hallway leading to his room.

"Rowan, wait," he said as he grasped the knight's shoulder. Facing Dugan, Rowan's scowl melted.

"I knew you'd see my point. Now if we can just get the others to—"

"The plans are set, Rowan. I wanted to talk to you about something else." He watched Rowan closely as he spoke. "What can you tell me about Panthora?"

"As much as I know, but it would probably be better to speak in my quarters." He bid Dugan to follow him. "I'd be happy to answer any questions you might have, and then, when you're ready, I can—"

"Hold on." He caught Rowan on the shoulder again. "I'm not looking to join your religion, just learn more about it."

Doubt crept across the young knight's face. "All right. You just seemed interested, so I assumed—"

"Well don't. I just have some questions."

"Then I'll do my best to answer them." Rowan continued on for his room, Dugan following.

•●•

"First it was that gladiator and now it's this knight," Vinder told Cadrissa after Dugan's departure. "If I didn't trust the money being there, I would have left by now."

"I don't even know what we need with him," Cadrissa replied. "Who knows *what* he's really after? And why?"

"Like someone else I know." He drained the rest of his mug, spilling out a few amber streams into his beard before wiping them away with the back of his hand.

"So what are you going to accuse me of now?"

"I don't know. *Should* I be accusing you of anything?"

"Would it matter? You already have me marked as the end of the world walking on two legs."

"All right." Vinder shifted his chair for a better view of the wizardess. "How about this: you tell me what you're looking to get out of all this."

"Why?"

"I'm giving you a chance to prove your innocence."

"So then I'm on trial, is that it?" Cadrissa sat all the way back in her chair, needling the dwarf with her eyes.

"Or we could just be having a discussion."

Cadrissa sniffed at the idea. "And why do you want to know anyway?"

"If I'm going to be stuck in the Marshes of Gondad with you all for a while, I want to know what I'm looking at . . . should something *unexpected* happen."

"So you don't trust *any* of us—*including* Gilban and Alara."

"No, them I do—at least as far as their money obligates me," said Vinder.

"But you just said—"

"So why are you avoiding my question?" He began taking inventory of what remained of the others' meals.

"I could ask the same of you. I thought we already had a similar discussion back on the boat." She crossed her arms, adding, "What makes you think by helping Alara and Gilban I'm fulfilling some *secret* goal? I simply seek knowledge."

"Rubbish!" barked Vinder. "We all took this job on to gain something. That kid, Rowan—he's on some mission for his knighthood. Probably wants to gain prestige and honor in the bargain. We're just a means to that end for him. Dugan needed safe passage out of Colloni, and his freedom. He's probably sticking around now just to get some coin in his hand before he heads out to greener pastures."

Cadrissa suddenly became extremely interested in the contents of her wooden goblet. "I suppose this is where I confess the marvelous scheme of mine to use this venture as a steppingstone to bigger and better things? Like becoming a wizard queen?"

"A civilized person would." He began gnawing on the heel of his crusty bread.

"And you count me as civilized?" Cadrissa's eyebrows lifted with heavy sarcasm.

"They found you in a civil-enough place."

"Haven is far from civilized. They may act enlightened and behave like refined people, but trust me, they're far from it below the surface."

"Then what were you doing there?" He washed the dry bread down with the last swig of ale left in Dugan's mug.

"Knowledge," Cadrissa curtly replied. "Haven has a very large and well-admired academy of magic."

Vinder chuckled, spraying the remaining bread crumbs into his beard in the process. "You mean you were nothing more than a *schoolgirl*? Alara brought you fresh out of *school* with us?"

"You think wizards just instantly understand their spells and abilities? All wizards, no matter how great, are students first. Magic requires constant endeavor and study. The simplest misunderstanding or the most minute error can hinder wizards for the rest of their lives."

"So you learn your trade like a cooper or smith learns his?" Vinder was genuinely intrigued by the concept.

"I'm *still* learning," Cadrissa confessed. "It's a never-ending process, but a rewarding one. But it only comes after hard work and study, much harder work than the common thievery *you* practice."

Vinder's eye widened as Cadrissa drained her goblet of its last bit of wine. "Are you calling me a thief?"

"If dwarves consider robbing the dead thievery . . . then yes."

"How can you make such wild accusations?" He fought back the deepening heat in his cheeks and neck, hoping Cadrissa wouldn't notice. He'd been called many things in his life—all without much effect—but getting called a thief was like a knife to his heart.

"Oh, come now, Vinder, even Gilban could see you looting the dead after we dispatched them. You accuse me of foolish ambition, and I could accuse you of joining up solely to loot and pillage." She didn't let her gaze leave him, much to his dismay.

"Then you'd be wrong."

"Using the same logic, I could just as easily propose when we were all left to our own devices earlier today, you went to fence what you've found. Why load yourself down with more than is needed in the marshes, right?"

"I did nothing of the sort," he huffed.

"Then where *did* you go?" She was enjoying turning Vinder's argument around—far too much for his liking.

"It was a personal matter." He desperately searched for a way of flipping the conversation and focus back on the mage.

"See how easy it is to jump to conclusions before you know the facts?" She relented, though obviously satisfied with herself. "A good lesson for both of us."

It was at that moment Vinder found his opening and struck. "And what about you? Where did *you* go?"

"Not that it's any of your business, but I've made arrangements to take care of the books and scrolls I won't be needing for the journey. It's going to be hard enough bringing what I do require without having to drag another chest through the marshes too."

"That same chest you brought back from the boat?" he asked, putting things together. "Why not just leave it there?"

"You can't be serious," she half laughed in reply. "I only left the chest there as long as I did because Gilban said it'd be safe. I'm not going to leave it lying around where just anyone can get into it in my absence. The books and scrolls need to be protected and properly stored."

"Storage? For books? *That's* what you did all day?" It was hard keeping the doubt from creeping up his throat.

"*I* believed *you*," Cadrissa pointed out.

He was about to say something further when two burly Telborian men entered the inn.

"We're looking for a Cadrissa Dalon," said the shorter of the two.

"That's me," Cadrissa said, rising.

"We've come to pick up your merchandise for storage," the same man continued. Both were dressed in common shirts and pants, nothing out of the ordinary. And yet Vinder didn't think they were your common everyday laborers. There was a certain aura about them he found hard to place. If either of the men noticed Vinder's studious stare neither gave any indication.

"The chest's in my room." She made a motion for them to follow her upstairs, smiling with just enough smugness to ruffle Vinder's feathers. "Good evening, Vinder."

He grunted a reply. He'd gotten all he could from her for now. He'd just have to live with whatever might arise on the journey. Hopefully his *last* journey before putting the Diamant Mountains before him.

THE WIZARD KING TRILOGY

He was so close. So very, very close.

He fished out the necklace given him by Heinrick. He wore it around his neck and under his armor so it always remained close to his heart. After briefly studying the sacred image, he kissed the small figurine before returning it to its resting place. He then polished off what food and drink remained before retiring for the evening. Tomorrow would come soon enough.

•●•

"Is that so?" Dugan asked Rowan. They'd been discussing Panthora in great detail for the better part of an hour, and so far Dugan hadn't learned anything that could do him any good. Still, he kept asking questions and the knight kept talking. Rowan, like the rest of them, had been given a room—courtesy of Gilban and Alara—for the night. Dugan understood Rowan had another place he'd been staying. Given how simple and empty the room appeared, the knight apparently hadn't brought any of his belongings with him.

"Yes," answered Rowan. "The knights hold to a code based in part on the Sacred Scrolls."

"And this code . . . it makes you a stronger fighting force?"

"With it, we're united under one common goal to serve one common mistress—Panthora."

He could see the bits of dogma poking out of Rowan's logic—had all night, in fact—but he could tell he was finally getting closer to what he wanted to know. "Fine idea for an army maybe, but no way to live your life."

"It is if you're sworn to Panthora and the knighthood," Rowan offered.

"I guess." Dugan crossed his arms. "Where does Panthora stand with the other gods?"

"What do you mean?"

"What's her rank in the pantheon? Is she more powerful than, say . . . Rheminas?"

"Panthora's the mightiest goddess we humans have!" Rowan was quick in reply. "I don't know where she might rank with others, but I know she holds first place in my heart."

Dugan tried keeping his mild frustration from showing. "What else can you tell me about her?"

"Long ago Panthora was a mighty human warrior who united humanity into an army to challenge the evils of her day. She led them to a great victory, but soon the Telborians forgot her, though we Nordicans have honored her ever since. Because we held her in such esteem, the gods took notice, showing her great favor by granting her godhood. From then on we've celebrated her ascension, spreading her message and love to every human we meet."

"Wait." Dugan shook his head as if it would help shift all of what he'd been hearing this past hour into place. "A while ago you said Panthora *created* humanity?"

"Yes," Rowan cheerfully replied.

"Then how could she create humanity when you just said she was raised to *godhood* after being a *human*?"

As Rowan paused, Dugan waited, trying to keep his amusement in check. He knew Rowan held some strange ideas, but what he'd just heard made no sense whatsoever. It didn't even hold up to the most basic scrutiny. He was curious to see how Rowan would deal with it.

"The priests say she was a goddess before she was a human. They claim she formed humanity and then helped lead them before returning to her divinity." Dugan could do nothing but stare blankly at the knight. His humor had melted into a form of pity.

"Dugan?" Rowan leaned forward.

"That's a real interesting theory."

"It's not a theory, it's—"

"So what *really* brings you to these ruins? What do you plan to do once you get there?"

The young knight flinched at the statement. "I'm to stop the knowledge hidden in them from falling into elven hands. Same as you."

"Nothing else?"

"Nothing else."

"You must excuse me now, Dugan." It was Rowan's turn to be curt. "It's getting late, and we have a long journey before us."

Dugan got up to leave. He'd heard enough. Someone like Rowan wouldn't give him the answers he needed. Any devout follower would raise their deity above any others—he'd been told as much already. And anything they might be able to do would naturally be embellished to fit the high esteem their follower invested in them. Passing their evening talk off as folly, Dugan made for the door. Maybe there were others he could look to for answers.

CHAPTER 19

THERE ARE MAGES AND THEN NONMAGES
JUST LIKE THERE ARE PEOPLE AND THEN ANTS.

—Oserick the Cruel, Nordic wizard king
Reigned 600 BV–480 BV

Valan hunched over the Transducer's blue stone, caressing it with his thin fingers. Above him hovered the glowing globe, adding dancing shadow and light on the object he'd been obsessed with for months. Runes. Ancient, mocking runes. As always, they continued their soft purple glimmer—another hint at the true power resident within the ancient stone. Yet he was nowhere closer to discovering—let alone mastering—that power than when he'd first arrived. Then there were the hobgoblins: a thorn in his side worming its way ever deeper into his flesh.

How much longer could he endure them, or they him? It was clear he was reaching the end of his efforts. And if it was clear to him, it had to be at least vaguely clear to them as well. The Celetors had been a token gesture—a means at biding more time—but time to do what, exactly? He couldn't keep his attention continually divided between the tribe *and* the Transducer. Not if he wished to continue with any hope of success.

But what if he'd been wrong? What if the Transducer was flawed or broken in some way? Could he really be sure it was in perfect working order? It was here before the Great Shaking—even survived it, but maybe not completely intact. He'd read speculation about it possibly being flawed from the start. In his zeal he'd pushed such theories aside—partly because he didn't want to acknowledge them and partly because he couldn't verify their validity. But now that he'd spent some time with it and had conducted so many failed experiments . . .

The sound of heavy footfalls pulled him out from behind the stone column with his floating globe in tow. "What is it?" Valan could barely hide his annoyance at the sight of Boaz drawing near the fence.

"I thought I'd see how you're progressing." Boaz was calm, but Valan could see the anger blazing behind his eyes. "You've used up just about all of the humans."

"And?"

"There won't be any more."

"I figured as much," Valan said, making his way for the gate. "They were a rarity, but your tribesmen are workable too."

"There won't be any more of them, either."

"Afraid of taking up the lottery again?" Valan cleared the gateway, stopping a few yards from the chieftain, letting the tracking globe highlight Boaz's horns. The chieftain was yet another mystery he couldn't solve. His one success—of a sort—with the Transducer, which he could never replicate. "Unless, of course, you're feeling charitable." He mockingly invited the hobgoblin back inside the blue column.

"It might be time to make the same offer of you," said Boaz, watching Valan's brow furrow, and his eyes become glaring slivers. "The Basilisk Tribe has suffered you long enough."

"So you think to kill me now, is that it? You'd be a fool to try."

Boaz unleashed a leering smirk. "There are worse things than death that can happen to a man."

"An empty threat? Is that what you've been reduced to?"

"Who said it was empty?" Boaz turned back for the stairs. "When you've killed the last human you'll have worn out my patience . . . and your welcome."

"You've just doomed yourself and your people," Valan called after the hobgoblin.

"No, I've just saved them."

He watched Boaz ascend the steps without another word. This was the last thing he needed. More distractions. More opportunities to slow and stymie his work. Damn them all to the Abyss. Bull-headed idiot! If Boaz wanted more dead hobgoblins, he would be more than willing to accommodate. This time he'd send Boaz and all his subchieftains to the very gates of Sheol. Then he could make the ruins his own personal sheepfold.

"A temporary nuisance," he told himself, fixing his attention back on the Transducer. "It won't stop the progress, will it?" he asked the column—a habit he'd indulged in of late. One that only increased as the frustrating hours and days progressed. "And I'm close now too, aren't I?

"Yes." His fingers absently caressed the cold, blue stone. "Very close now. I can feel it."

•●•

"You're a weaker fool than I thought." Cadrith stood over the scrying skull, observing Valan's recent actions. He didn't like where things were going. It seemed his lingering uneasiness with the mage was well founded. The artifact had thoroughly gotten its hooks into him to the point of him becoming a liability. And Cadrith didn't need a liability when things were so close. But what to do? He didn't have any other alternatives, and it wasn't like he hadn't been looking.

Sensing a movement in the shadows, he shifted his attention to the corner of the room. "Sargis?" Cadrith called forth light from the skull crowning his staff, forcing the shadows to retreat into the farthest corners and crevices they could find. There was nothing there.

"Looks like the Abyss is finally getting to you," a feminine voice said, guiding his gaze to the window. Before it stood one of the more visually pleasing beings the Abyss ever produced.

"Hardly." Cadrith stood his ground as the woman named Tara gave the room a careful study.

"Still living like a beggar, I see." She slinked forward, folding her black swan wings behind her as she did.

"Not for much longer." He dimmed the light on his staff.

"So the mighty Cadrith Elanis is about to spread his wings at last."
Tara slowed as she drew near the scrying skull, sneaking a peek in the
process. Her tan skin and white hair contrasted her pure-black eyes. Taller
than Cadrith by shoulders and head, her strange form didn't detract from
her alluring curves and feminine graces. Not even the small ivory horns
poking out of her forehead could mar her unnatural beauty. "You won't
reconsider the offer?"

"You don't have anything I want," he said. "Neither you *nor* your patron."

"Sounded to me like she did."

"No. I'm going to succeed."

"Still bold and arrogant, I see."

"Confident," he corrected. "Just like I'm confident no matter how
much she tries, your patron won't succeed. And I'm not going to stay to
help her fail."

"Too bad," Tara pouted. "I think you would have enjoyed it." On any
other man her allure might have had some pull, but Cadrith was a lich.
There was only his spirit anchored to his dry old bones. Any temptations
the ocubus might have offered meant nothing to him.

"Are you at least happy to see me?" He watched her draw near. Her
measured steps showed off her legs through the slits in her form-fitting
skirt. Slit from the waist down, the brown leather fell just above her knees,
allowing her tall black boots to clearly be seen. She wore a thick black
belt lined with silver plates and fastened with a circular silver belt buckle
crafted into a crown of thorns. From it dangled pouches and a small
assortment of items, most notably two sheathed daggers—one for each
side—both within easy reach.

"I was beginning to think you might have lied," said Cadrith.

Tara was the last part in his plan, a fail-safe and a way of taking
care of other matters that might arise. After five years in the Abyss, he
managed to get in contact with her patron, someone not only
sympathetic to his cause but willing to help bring it about. At least that
was what he'd thought initially. But the days became weeks and then
months, until he thought he'd never hear from Tara or her patron again.

He might not have been too concerned if it had been any other matter—after all, the Abyss was full of liars—but he'd paid a dear price to secure what he sought.

"Did you now?" Tara crossed her arms below her breasts. Each wrist was adorned with a steel bracer, the two etched with the same twisting, thorny vine design.

"It's been over two months. So do you have it or not?"

Tara's hand went for her belt, where the few items attached there jingled until she raised her hand, opening her palm and revealing a small glass vial. "I think you'll find it was worth the wait." She placed the vial into Cadrith's waiting palm. He cautiously studied the green substance within the clear glass container. Only a cork stopped it from spilling, but he had no intention of letting a single drop go to waste. Next to his magic, this was the most precious thing in his possession.

"I wonder what Sargis would say if he saw us together?" Tara crossed to Cadrith's throne. "If he learned of what you were doing."

"Are you implying something, Tara?" Cadrith clasped the vial tightly in his bony grasp and watched her playfully plop into his seat.

"Just thinking out loud." She draped a naked leg over an armrest. Naked, that was, save for the dagger strapped to her inside thigh. "You *do* know how hard that poison was to come by, right?"

Cadrith ignored her antics. In some ways he supposed she couldn't help but act true to her nature. She was an abysmal incarnate after all—an aspect of the Abyss itself given sentient life and form. "And I trust my payment was *more* than sufficient."

"Oh yes, she's been quite pleased with your generous gift. It will go a long way in helping her efforts." The ocubus' eyes drifted toward the scrying skull once more. "But you're wasting it if you're still looking to only use it as you first intended."

"There are a few other kinks that might need some smoothing out down the road."

Tara raised both eyebrows. "Must be *some* kinks."

"I've allowed you a greater freedom than most, but only for so long."

"And here I thought you just enjoyed my company," Tara purred.

"Your patron has her payment, and I have the vial." He held up his clasped hand, emphasizing his point.

"Are you trying to get rid of me so soon?" Tara pouted again. "I was just getting comfortable."

"I'm sure you were." Cadrith's flaming sockets met Tara's pearl-like eyes. "But you can only stretch my patience so far. So unless there's anything else your patron requires . . ."

The ocubus surrendered the throne, pouting once more for good measure. "No, though I'll tell her you've turned down her offer."

"Fine."

"Having a wizard would have really made a difference, especially one who knows so much about crossing the divide . . . and Tralodren."

"She'll survive, I'm sure."

"Oh, she will, but I can't say the same about you," she replied, returning to the window. On her way she stopped and considered one of the tapestries fluttering in the faint breeze. On it was an image of a woman. The spiked red nimbus behind her head was still clearly visible despite the years. The image brought a smile to Tara's lips. "You're playing a dangerous game, Cadrith. I hope you know what you're doing, else we might see you back here faster than you'd like. And then you might not find my patron so accommodating."

"Then it's a good thing I'll have the vial close at hand." His icy words turned down the ocubus' heat. Flapping her wings, Tara leapt out the window and into the late afternoon air.

Finally. It'd been a dangerous and uncertain tradeoff, but now that he had the vial it all would be worth it. Had he still been able to use the small sample he'd acquired when he'd first met Sargis, he would have. But the poison had long dried out and lost its potency. This new vial, on the other hand . . .

He stood for a moment more before sitting on his throne. "Now what about you?" He peered into the scrying skull, returning to his previous quandary. He rested his staff beside him, letting its light fade. As the shadows ventured out of hiding, Cadrith pondered. He'd been grooming Valan for months—even *with* his apprehensions. He needed someone to cast a spell with the Transducer to create a force powerful enough to open a portal into the Abyss. The pieces were there, but his options were dwindling. And if he couldn't use Valan, who else was there? He had to choose quickly, lest Valan destroy the column or the portal before he could act.

Though Cadrith couldn't see or feel it, a dark shape gathered behind his throne as he pondered. Unlike Sargis, this form wasn't humanoid, rather a swirling mass of black tentacles. These same tentacles explored around the throne and over the lich, covering him in a writhing canopy. As he extended his hand over the scrying skull one of the tentacles went with it, touching the skull in the process. The action birthed a ripple across the surface just as Cadrith waved his hand above the ancient bone.

Suddenly, a new scene emerged: a group of people moving across the Grasslands of Gondad. It was nothing of great interest, but the skull had revealed them to him for a reason. There were three humans, a dwarf, and two elves. An interesting mix, considering the elves were Patrious and one of the humans was a Nordican, but beyond that nothing of any apparent concern or interest. But again, the skull had revealed them for some reason, calling for a closer inspection.

"And where might you be going?" he asked the image.

As if on cue, the Patrician woman at the lead began discussing their plans with a blind priest—of Saredhel, it appeared. They were discussing reaching the ruins in the jungles of Taka Lu Lama. Ruins Cadrith knew held the portal and the Transducer.

"Interesting." He leaned closer. "*What?*" He suddenly made the skull focus on the image of a golden-robed wizardess who'd crossed the viewing area just a moment before. He'd only seen her faintly from a distance, but upon closer inspection he thought he recognized a familiar connection.

"Could it really be?" Casting a simple spell upon the skull, he watched with growing interest as the image of the sable-haired mage shifted into an attractive blond Telborian woman instead.

"Seems you were a better survivor than you thought, Kendra." He watched the image fade back into the sable-haired mage. "And as fate would have it, you're going to help me finish what I started. But first we need to see how strong you are . . . as well as how useful you'll be *beyond* my return. And if you're anything like your foremother, I'm sure you won't disappoint."

The scene then shifted to the young Nordic knight in their company. "You might be useful too," he said, bringing the glass vial in front of his sockets. "Though finding the right venue for our introduction could be challenging."

Cadrith didn't like the way this new opportunity had seemingly come out of nowhere. But the scrying skull was doing its part: showing him anything of possible interest for his plans. It was just a little too coincidental, finding the new mage in the mix. But he wasn't complaining. He needed things to move quickly, and he was confident they still could after some slight alterations.

He sat back with a small degree of satisfaction. As he did the mass of tentacles behind him vanished, leaving him truly alone once more. Waving his hand over the skull, he brought the image of the wizardess forward, letting it dominate almost all the viewing space. She was young but so very close in appearance to her ancestor. He hoped that was all they shared. He didn't want to contend with the same temperament as well. Then again, he'd need someone of the same caliber once he was back on Tralodren. All the better to watch and learn while he could.

CHAPTER 20

I SWEAR MY ALLEGIANCE TO THE REPUBLIC AND EMPEROR,
WITH AEROTRIPTON ABOVE ALL.

—Oath of the Elyelmic army

Yornicus assessed the cohort's situation from the center of the elven soldiers. He didn't like what he saw. What remained of the first cohort of the Tenth Legion—forty men from the once one hundred strong—set themselves in place. Once more they'd mingle their blood with their approaching foes' in the Marshes of Gondad's murky waters.

"Keep at it." Adicus, their captain, sought to encourage his men from his position near Yornicus. They'd been battling a force of about fifty lizardmen who'd come upon them from the trees and underbrush predominant in the area near the jungle of Taka Lu Lama. Even with the lizardmen's simple weapons and near-naked frames, anyone could see the battle wasn't going the elves' way. Nothing had since they'd entered the marshes.

They'd lost sixty men so far, reducing the cohort to just four squads—a pale shadow of the glory they'd presented upon departing Claudina months earlier. Ruthless nature, having to tediously probe every inch of the terrain, and other matters like this surprise attack wore down the weary men. Though they had the numerical advantage, they didn't have the raw muscle of their opponents, and the longer they were forced to endure these additional trials without adequate food and rest, the more Yornicus saw their end creeping ever closer.

They'd already lost what remained of their supplies to another group of lizardmen a few days before. And that had followed their initial loss of supplies to another lizardman band shortly after entering the marshes. That encounter had forced them to take some unplanned and risky measures with equally damaging results.

"They're trying to surround us, sir." This was Ibrin, one of the four remaining sergeants. Like the rest of the elves, his formerly short hair had grown some since their departure from Claudina. None of the elves looked polished anymore. The pomp and pride in presentation had fallen aside in favor of gritty survival. And if they were to continue seeking the completion of their orders, it'd get grittier still.

"I know," Adicus shouted over the clamor of the battle. Yornicus, as well as the captain, could see the lizardmen fanning out and forming a circle around them. After corralling the elves tightly into a cluster, it would be easier for the lizardmen to close in and slaughter them like sheep. Any other time the lizardmen would have been sorely mistaken, but now . . . Well, now was a different story.

"Each squad take a point." Adicus motioned for ten men to divide into the cardinal directions. "Keep tight formation and hold the line." Adicus took to Yornicus' side, now in the middle of their number, seeking to take out whatever might make it through. The lizardmen, however, had other ideas. Their clubs and spears sought to draw more elven blood, but for now the elves' armor and swordplay were holding.

Along with a gladius, each elf carried a large rectangular shield with the crest of Colloni over a red background. Behind these shields each man wore a cuirass of segmented plate armor with matching pauldrons. A skirt made of leather strips, mimicking brigandine armor, flowed from the waist, and iron greaves were attached to the front of tall leather boots.

All wore the same open-faced helmet, save Adicus, whose helmet possessed a nose guard and bill at the back above the neck for added protection and distinction. Finally, each carried a brown cloth backpack with basic supplies. These had seen good use and notable depletion as a result of their numerous encounters.

"Savages," Yornicus muttered. He resembled the rest of the elves in all ways save for his round shield sporting the same crest. Even the gladius he tightly gripped was the same found in all the legions. He'd never adopted the custom of wearing robes like most wizards. He preferred the attire of the common elf over what he felt was too grandiose and impractical—not to mention restrictive—for his current endeavors.

"Feel free to help at any time." Adicus' sarcasm was rich and more than a little pointed. Yornicus kept his attention shifting from point to point, keeping track of the battle as best he could.

"I'm trying." It was hard seeing where he could step in and make any difference. There was too much going on, and Yornicus didn't know how much more he had left within, given all they'd already endured. He wasn't sent to fight battles, rather to relay messages and secure—and ultimately, take possession of—the lost knowledge they'd been sent to find. But since they'd entered the marshes, he'd increasingly been called upon to do little else but fight.

A few more lizardmen tumbled into the marsh with a splash but so too did a few more elves. This wasn't looking good at all. Yornicus sheathed his sword as he considered a possible option. It might not be the best, but given the circumstances, they really didn't have much choice.

"Keep your formation," Yornicus shouted. "Vestis mekola agris labrin . . ." As he cast his spell, a violet light rose from the soggy earth and covered the elves in a protective globe. Outside, the lizardmen snarled and snapped their jaws as they futilely banged away with club and spear at something that seemed harder than stone, though looked as thin and transparent as a fading mist.

"How long will that hold?" asked Adicus.

"Long enough to form a plan, I hope." He did his best to sound more confident than he really was.

"The men are exhausted, sir," Ibrin informed Adicus. "If we stay here to fight—"

"We fled before and look where that got us," Adicus snapped back. "They came after us, and in greater numbers."

"But, Captain"—this was Sabin, the youngest of the sergeants—"this isn't the best place to make a stand. We need solid ground to have a prayer. We're close to the jungle. If we—"

"Enough!" Adicus' shout silenced the men. "Are you soldiers of the first cohort or whiny children? We were chosen by the emperor to carry out this mission, and by Aero, we shall do it. We are soldiers of the Republic of Colloni—men of the Tenth Legion—and will act accordingly. Do I make myself clear?"

"Yes, sir," all the elves shouted in unison. All except Yornicus, watching the events while keeping an eye on the spell. He wasn't a soldier as his parents had wanted, but he'd found a means to serve in his own way when he studied magic at the Remolosic Academy. And it was a good thing he did—if these men's lives were worth anything.

The dome was holding despite the lizardmen's wild attempts to break it. But he knew it wouldn't hold for long. The spell was really meant for his own protection; he'd never cast it for so many people before. This was reaching into the depths of his training, pressing into what might lie beyond. And while in theory such efforts could be a worthwhile endeavor for growing one's skill, you didn't want to attempt such things while fighting for your life. His thoughts were interrupted by a rock-and-bast-rope bola slamming into the top portion of the dome, followed by a hollow cracking sound like broken glass or eggshell.

"Tripton's bow!" Adicus cursed and craned his head toward the sight, freezing everyone's blood. One of the stones managed to jab itself into the barrier and even beyond it, sending out a web of cracks in the process.

"I thought you said it would hold," Adicus growled.

"It is—or will for a little while longer." He tried his best to sound reassuring. "As long as they don't escalate their attacks, we should—"

"Captain!" Sejanus, the shaven-headed third sergeant of their cohort, directed everyone's attention to where he was pointing.

"Aero, be merciful," Ibrin grimly replied as he and the rest all spied a new group of lizardmen joining the others on their left flank.

"There has to be at least another fifty," said Sejanus.

"One hundred," Sabin said, pointing out their right flank, where another fresh group of lizardmen was swelling the enemy ranks—these about the same size as the first. As they joined, the fighting stopped; the lizardmen previously pounding away at the barrier were ebbing back, like a tidal wave gaining strength before its terrible return.

Adicus grabbed hold of Yornicus' shoulder with a painful grip. "You need to get a message to Claudina."

"There isn't any time."

"We'll give you time," Adicus said, releasing the mage with a shove. "You just get them a message. Tell them what happened and not to send any more men short of two legions if the emperor wants that knowledge." Yornicus found himself frozen as everything rushed at him at once. Adicus was putting everything on his shoulders. All these men. The mission. *Everything* rested on him.

"Can you do that?"

He searched the others' faces, each visage showing a resignation to the fate that lay ahead. "Yes." He gave a solemn nod. He couldn't stand by and do nothing. Even if he should join them in death, at least he'd die doing what he could to honor them and their mission.

"Listen up." Adicus returned to his men, who faced him with as much courage and dedication as they could muster. "We're going to buy Yornicus enough time to make one last report. We've done our best to honor the emperor. We've fought well, and I've no doubt, if not for this battle, we would have found what we sought.

"But fate has found us here, and Asorlok has come calling for our spirits. May we not be found wanting, but instead find ourselves in New Remolos before the day is done in a place of honor beside Aero and the heroes of old."

The reptilian wave outside the barrier rushed forward with a tumultuous roar. As one, they collided with the magical structure. Cracks and groaning creaks echoed in the elves' pointed ears as each one took a solemn stand beside their comrades in arms, awaiting the inevitable.

There was one more spell Yornicus thought he could try . . . but it didn't come without a few complications. Had their superiors been expecting more challenges, General Gallo would have sent a more skilled mage, someone better equipped for battle—not Yornicus. But that die was cast and now he and the others would have to do their best with what was left at their disposal. If they were about to give their lives for him, Yornicus could at least do his all for them.

"I have one more spell that could help," he said. "But it will take the barrier down with it."

"Do it," Adicus replied flatly.

Wasting no time, Yornicus began his spell.

"Eyes forward. Shields high," Adicus ordered. As one, the last of the first cohort of the Tenth Legion raised their shields and brought their gladii to attention.

"For Aero and Colloni!" Adicus raised his gladius in salute.

"Aero and Colloni!" The others took to beating their swords upon their shields. The thumping clap mixed with the crackling dome and snarling lizardmen, creating a frightful cacophony. As Yornicus finished his spell, the dome shifted from a violet light to a canopy of writhing flame, which exploded into the lizardmen with enough force to send them back a good ten feet. Many were severely burned or set on fire with the rest toppled by the jarring impact of having the others shoved into them.

"Run!" Adicus shouted at Yornicus as the elves pressed into their fallen foe, taking what advantage they could in the moment. Yornicus didn't look back, pounding his feet into the waterlogged earth for all he was worth, trying not to think of the duty he'd been given and how much blood would be paid to accomplish it.

He couldn't fail.

• ● •

Yornicus ran without thinking under the darkening sky. The terrain eventually rose into more solid ground, but he scarcely paid these changes any mind. He was focused on just one thing: running. The dense undergrowth sought to hinder his movement at almost every turn; roots entangled his feet, branches slapped his face and limbs. The humid air added to his plight, making it harder to breathe the longer he pressed on. But it didn't matter. He had to press on.

His legs felt like jelly, his lungs and throat burned in agony, yet he continued slaughtering his body with the effort. There were no other options left. He had to get as far from the marshes as possible. The thought to stop and send off his message would poke through his fear now and then, but he quickly shoved it aside. As much as Yornicus had a duty to perform, he had a tremendously strong drive to live.

Eventually he came to a stop against a tree. Sweat gushed from his pores, flooding his forehead and face, stinging his eyes, and dripping onto his lips. Catching his breath, the mage strained his ears for the sound of his pursuers. All he could hear was the pounding of his heart and his haggard breathing. Maybe he'd run far enough. Maybe the others were able to send the lizardmen to Mortis instead. He knew that was just wishful thinking. No, by now they were all dead. The first cohort of the Tenth Legion was no more. Their bodies would never be recovered, and their memory lost if he didn't complete his final duty.

Standing upright, the mage hurriedly started digging in his backpack as he let his gladius fall to his side. Pulling out a sheet of parchment, he awkwardly put it in his left hand, still holding his shield as he fished out a small vial of ink and a quill. Laying his shield down on the ground so that its concave surface faced him, he flattened the parchment sheet upon it. He unstopped the vial of ink, dipped in the tip of his quill, and started writing.

Yornicus Alcaran Ithiani to General Gallo:

It is with heavy heart I record that the first cohort has failed to complete their mission. I bear witness to them having made their way into the Marshes of Gondad, but the marshes have shown they wished to keep us back for as long as possible.

Lizardmen, Celetors, and the very terrain itself have taken their toll; I am all that remains. It has been advised if you do send more men that a greater number will be needed. For if we have only made it part of the way and failed already, then surely more will be required to complete the emperor's command.

He stopped. He thought he heard something behind him. Straining his ears, he waited a moment before resuming his work, only to stop again when the sound of a cracking twig brought him to his feet. Hurriedly, he brought to mind the spell needed to send the writing on its way to Claudina. As he spoke its words, Yornicus watched the text he'd just written turn a glistening bronze before fading back into the still-drying black ink. Breathing a small sigh of relief at having gotten the message off, he froze when another snapping twig—one much nearer than the last—filled the now silent area around him.

He threw the parchment, ink vial, and quill into the backpack, then slung it over his shoulder and picked up his sword and shield just as he saw the first lizardman make his way through the underbrush. Panicked, he cast the best spell he had for defense, sending a burst of lightning from his hand and down his sword, pointed at his reptilian aggressor. The creature flew back from the shock, but Yornicus knew nothing else.

Finding what reserves he had left, the mage pressed forward as fast as his sore legs could take him. While dodging short trees and low branches, he failed to notice a thick tree root that quickly ensnared him by the ankle. He tumbled to the damp soil with a huff.

Taking a deep draft of what reserves he had left, Yornicus madly leapt up from the moist earth. Steadying his weakened body, he continued his frantic run.

He ran on and on; his feet lost all feeling. His legs were powered by a heart he thought might burst with the next beat. Sweat flooded his eyes, continually blurring his vision. If he could survive long enough, he might be afforded some better options. He might be able to fully discover the others' fate, make his way back to Claudina, or maybe even continue on toward the ruins to try to complete the mission on his own. This was all predicated, however, on him making it through the night and staying out of the lizardmen's hands.

But though his will was strong, his body couldn't keep pace, and his weary frame fell. As he collapsed, Yornicus could hear his pursuers crashing through the jungle. At least he had gotten the message to

Claudina. One hundred men would get the honor they deserved for such brave and total service to the emperor and the republic.

"Aero, have mercy," Yornicus prayed before rolling to his side just in time for his face to collide with a wooden club.

CHAPTER 21

No matter how far or how long one walks the
path of knowledge, the temptation of power
stalks them, seeking to leap out and devour
them when they least expect it.

—**Sagarin Vonal, dwarven wizard king**
Reigned 670 BV–500 BV

C adrissa's chest heaved. Cold sweat poured down her forehead as she
hurriedly sought refuge. Fear chased her down the halls she'd been
running through for what seemed like hours, hounding her every step.
But it wasn't just the fear nipping at her ankles . . . It was something
else—*someone* else. She never dared look back, but she knew something
was there and it was getting closer, and when it did . . .

She found an open door to her left and ducked inside. Slamming it shut,
she did her best to latch it, then rested her back against it for added measure.
Alone in the dark room, she tried recovering her strength. After so long a
chase, she wasn't sure how much longer she could keep standing. She prayed
the door would hold and allow her some peace, even for just a little while.

She felt a chill seep in from the thick wood at her back and slide up
her ankles. An icy mist passed through the door and seemed to melt right
into her bones. Shivering, she backed away from the door. As the
moments passed, an azure light manifested, tracing the door's outline . . .
and then the individual planks composing it. The light grew more intense,
eating away at the wood. Cadrissa backed up further but knew it was no
use. She was trapped.

As more of the doorway was dissolved by the azure light, a black mist poured into the room. It seemed alive, eagerly reaching out for her as she continued inching backward. Finally, the door faded away altogether, leaving her completely exposed. The bright light dimmed, separating into two small azure flames floating in the midst of the swirling dark mist. As the tongues of flame came closer, she realized they were flickering inside the empty sockets of an evil-looking skull.

"Cadrissa . . ."

• ● •

Cadrissa woke with a start, bolting up from her makeshift bed like a freshly triggered trap. For a moment, something blazed in her memory like a white-hot iron yanked from the fire. It was important. She had to remember something. There was something she had to do. But what? In the ensuing heartbeats, that brilliant, urgent memory faded until she was left staring blankly around the camp with only the sounds of chirping crickets and the crackling fire rising over the swaying grass.

Once she'd gotten her bearings, she found herself staring at Dugan, who was eyeing her. "Just a bad dream," she explained. Though why she thought he'd be interested, she had no idea. He was sitting exactly opposite her, the fire between them—the lone sentinel watching as they slept. To her right were Gilban and Alara. On her left lay Vinder and Rowan. All slumbered soundly in their trampled-grass beds.

The horses were resting just on the edge of the fire's light, having taken their fill of grass before tomorrow's journey into the Marshes of Gondad. The grasses had nearly been taller than horse and rider when they'd first set out but had become shorter as the ground grew more moist and the air more humid. The journey thus far had been a safe and easy one. Of course, they weren't traveling in the marsh yet—which would have its own unique challenges. She was glad she wasn't lugging any extra weight and was enjoying the benefits of having the horses for as long as she could.

"Must be boring keeping watch all the time." She decided to strike up a conversation instead of letting the silence grow any more awkward.

"Boring can be good."

"Still. It must be hard trying to stay awake."

"Not really." Dugan poked the fire with the same stick he'd been using for the last four nights. "I'll get enough sleep once Vinder takes next watch."

"I've noticed Alara doesn't have Rowan joining you." She took in the knight with a casual gaze. He was close enough to the fire for light and warmth but far enough from the rest to allow a sense of independence.

"Or you." Dugan's reply brought a flash of crimson to her cheeks.

"I-I'd do it if asked. It's just—"

"You don't trust him." Dugan remained focused on the fire.

"I don't know if I'd go that far." Cadrissa sought for the right amount of shade to cover over the naked truth. "I'm just not sure why he's traveling with us. Frankly, I'm surprised he came along at all after the argument in the inn." She found her gaze drifting over Dugan's strong shoulders as she spoke, following them down the contours of his body. Though he was wearing his tunic it wasn't hard seeing things through it. He'd shed his mail shirt in the evenings, claiming it helped with his sleep—and apparently in keeping watch too.

"So why don't you trust him?"

"He isn't really part of this expedition."

He lifted his eyes from the fire. "Gilban seems to think so."

"Yes, but when I was hired, he wasn't part of the equation. Now here he is." She assumed Dugan's silence was a less-than-favorable appraisal of her thoughts. "Don't get me wrong, I'm sure he'll do fine—especially if Gilban thinks so. He seems a little different is all."

"You told me about the gods on the boat." There was a rather strong intensity to his stare as he spoke, making her all the more self-conscious. "What do you know about Saredhel?"

"Not a whole lot," she said, seeking escape from his deep, probing eyes. "You'd probably do better talking with Gilban."

"Still," Dugan softly probed, "what do you know?"

"She's a goddess of prophecy and helps people see the future."

"Does she ever appear to people herself?"

"I don't know." She wasn't sure how to take Dugan's sudden theological inquiries. "I suppose she does."

"Maybe like a collection of white light . . . or a swirling of black tentacles."

Now she was really lost. "I-I wouldn't know. I haven't really given the topic much study. My focus has been in other areas of late."

Dugan nodded and resumed his prodding of the fire. Cadrissa didn't know what else to do or say and so simply watched and waited until finally his eyes found hers again.

"So no other gods can see the future?"

"Not that I'm aware of, no."

"So you think Gilban knows more than he's letting on?"

"Weren't you the one just accusing me of not trusting people?"

"Yeah." Dugan's grin was as disarming as it was simple and went a long way in dispelling Cadrissa's former unease.

"I never really know how to read Gilban," she confessed, "but I trust Alara."

Dugan nodded, looking heavenward for a moment.

"The Two Lovers," Cadrissa mused aloud.

"What?"

"The Warrior contends with the Two Lovers," she explained, pointing out the constellations. "See, that's the Warrior," she said, indicating a group of stars forming the outline of an armored man with shield and sword at the ready. "It's rising now in keeping with the ending of Endaris and the start of Sharealia. And there are the Two Lovers." Cadrissa pointed out the other constellation, a young couple locked in a passionate embrace. The Warrior had the appearance of moving toward them, as if seeking to pry one from the other. "You can't have summer without them."

"You really do keep your head in the clouds," Dugan teased.

"I'm just eager to learn what I can while I can. You'd be surprised how knowing your constellations—and other astronomical information—can help when it comes to studying history and even magic."

"Stars affect magic?"

"There isn't a direct link, but they're helpful in dating things and keeping records. Since magic is also woven into the fabric of history, it's a good gauge to have. Sometimes the dates might not always match up. I'm sorry," she said, feeling a fresh wave of crimson rise up her neck and face. "I don't mean to bore you. Here you are trying to stay awake and I start rattling off all these—"

"You're not boring me."

"Oh . . . okay."

"I overheard you and Vinder talking about wizard kings on the ship." She braced herself with a small sigh as Dugan dug back into the encounter. "What was that all about?"

"He was just letting me know he doesn't like them."

"Why not?"

"When you start dominating the world and brag about being more powerful than the gods, it tends to ruffle some people's feathers."

"*Were* they more powerful than the gods?"

"Some came pretty close, if you can believe the texts. Of course that was right before the Divine Vindication—before they were wiped off the planet."

"What about today? Are there any strong wizards out there?"

"As strong as the wizard kings?" Cadrissa half laughed. "No, not even close. We've only now just started to come back to a greater understanding of magic. To reach those heights you'd have to pray you were lucky enough to come across some lost texts or artifacts.

"Of course," she added, "not a lot of mages are too faithful in their prayers."

"Not many gladiators are either." Dugan returned to his fire gazing. "Especially if they already know the answer." She didn't know how to take the comment so thought it best to let things rest for the night. She still needed some sleep, and she didn't want to pester Dugan any more than she had already.

"Well, I probably should get some more rest," she said, lying again on her simple bed. "We'll have a fun day in the marshes tomorrow, I'm sure." Dugan remained silent, keeping his eyes and thoughts locked on the crackling flames. As she closed her eyes, slumber quickly enfolded her in its embrace.

• ● •

"Walking can't be much slower than this," Alara heard Dugan say as he pulled on the reins of his cordovan steed, preventing it from stepping into one of the many pools of sucking mud covering the Marshes of Gondad. On top of the difficult terrain, the rotten stench permeating everything was only getting worse, increasingly souring her stomach. The animals were constantly sinking into the muck, their slender legs forced into the mire by their heavy bodies and the weight of the group's supplies. And then there were the mosquitoes vexing both horses and riders morning and night.

"We can hold out a little longer." Alara rode about five paces ahead of the Telborian. She, like him, had shed her cloak. The current terrain and climate had made it more burden than boon.

Gilban's hands rested around her waist as he rode behind her. His robes had changed to a dismal brown over their journey, and his head sprouted some white stubble, but otherwise he didn't seem any the worse for wear. Nor did any of the others, who were taking it all in stride. She prayed it would be the same throughout the rest of their journey. "When we get to more challenging terrain you'll see what a blessing these horses will be."

"*More* challenging terrain?" Vinder joined the conversation. "These beasts won't last a few more feet at their current rate." Most dwarves didn't ride horses—she wasn't sure he even knew how to ride one—but Vinder had done well in the grasslands and now in the marshes. Of course this might have something to do with him having to share his horse with Dugan, who was actually controlling the animal. Vinder was just along for the ride. Surprisingly, he didn't make much of an issue of it when she first presented him with the news, nor had he since. He was probably too busy trying to hang on as they rode.

They'd been in the marsh for two days following their four-day journey from Elandor. This gallop through the grasslands between Elandor and the Marshes of Gondad had been uneventful but trying for many of the mercenaries, who grew impatient with the apparently endless prairie leading up to the marshes. To gain as much time as they could, they'd pushed their mounts hard, allowing them limited rest until the marshes came into view on the end of the fourth day. Only then did they allow the beasts to walk; galloping through the soupy mess would have proven disastrous for both horse and rider. Since then, the marshes had become more wild, expansive, and fetid by the hour.

"How are you holding up?" Dugan called back to Vinder. Alara could clearly see both were uncomfortable with the extra layers their armor provided, but neither would discard it.

"Don't worry about me," Vinder gruffly returned. "I can handle myself." The dwarf grunted, catching himself on the horse's haunches as it slipped into yet another pool of muck.

"I want to apologize," Alara said over her shoulder, keeping her voice loud enough for Gilban's ears alone.

"For what?"

"I've been going over what happened back at the Mangy Griffin—with those men—these last few days. I shouldn't have been so quick to act. If I had stopped and thought things through I would have seen the odds weren't really in my favor and—"

"You did nothing wrong." There was no judgment, just his normal measured response.

"But I could have ended up causing some serious trouble—to everyone. And you were just sitting there on that bench and if—"

"You did what you were supposed to do," he continued. "You got Rowan's attention."

"And those guards too," she added.

"Who were dealt with, remember. No, everything is working out well. And you did well. Those men chose their own fate and were responsible for their own actions. As we all are."

"So they were fated to die?" She didn't know if she liked that idea, or even speaking it aloud. "Is that what you're saying?"

"I'm saying you did what was in your nature to do—you acted from your heart, and that's good. You were true to who you are. And truly good leaders have to lead with both their hearts and heads, the two complementing each other. If one dominates the other, things quickly go askew."

"So all that was just for Rowan's sake?" she asked, carefully swimming through the logic.

"And was it much different when finding Dugan?"

"It's just—I don't know. I just didn't envision all of this being so chaotic."

"Free will can do that to the best of plans." She could hear the smile in Gilban's voice.

Rowan glanced back, his eye catching Alara's before snapping his attention elsewhere. He'd been acting skittish around her since joining the group. He couldn't still be holding a grudge about taking the trip through the marshes, could he? He might not have been the most open and trusting when they first met, but now he was withdrawn, growing more distant and cold by the day. He'd yet to speak to her since they'd left the inn, and it troubled her. "Often it's the silent traveler who poses the greatest threat," an old Patrician saying went, and Alara couldn't agree more, especially since she'd begun noticing him staring at her almost constantly over the last few days. Staring but never saying anything.

"I'm also worried about Rowan," she confided in Gilban. "He's starting to act a little odd."

"It's the least expected place where the greatest of surprises arise," came his reply.

"What sort of surprises, though?"

"What kind do you expect?"

"If I had a choice, only good ones."

"Then keep your focus there. People have a tendency to rise to your level of expectation." A brief moment of silence followed before Gilban asked, "Is there something else troubling you?"

"It's nice to have another sword for our cause, but what do we really know about him and his knighthood?"

"I understand your fears, but the only way to solve your dilemma is to ask him. Otherwise your worry will eat away at your judgment, making you mistrust all those around you."

"Why can't *you* ask him?" She fought for balance as the horse uprooted itself from a particularly muddy spot. "*You're* the leader of this group."

"Am I?"

She twisted fully around, making sure she stared him right in the face—though what good it did she had no idea. "You're the one who got us all together and who had this vision in the first place. It's *your* lead I'm following."

"But *you* are the one who leads *them*. And remember—I'm a priest of another god from a different race. He's also been taught that humans are his chief concern. No, it's far better if *you* converse with him."

"But I'm not human, either."

"But you're more pleasing on the eye."

"And what's *that* supposed to mean?" She gripped the reins as the horse plodded through another rough patch.

"Nothing." Gilban quickly hid his smile. "Unless you wish it to mean something."

She hated not getting a clear answer when she needed it . . . which was just about all the time now since finding the others. Sometimes she wondered if he was doing this on purpose—as if it was some sort of game he enjoyed playing.

"If it will help, I can tell you how you and he have a destiny together—a future that will be made evident soon enough. The choice is still yours—but know what you do now will affect the outcome. Nothing in this world is free."

"We have a destiny together?" Swinging back around again, she asked, "Beyond this journey or just now?"

"That, again, is up to you." Gilban stared blankly ahead, making her ponder anew what good there was in facing him.

"Why even bring something up if you aren't willing to clarify it further?" She turned away with a huff.

"Faith and patience. Stay patient and keep your faith. It will all be made clear soon enough."

Knowing that was all she was going to get, Alara focused back on the marshes, noticing the muddy waters now reached her horse's knees. It was about time to dismount. As if on cue, Cadrissa's voice called from the back of the group as the mage splashed about in the water. The second to last in their number, she'd dismounted to help her horse out of the muck in which it'd become mired.

"It looks like horse and rider part here," Alara said, addressing the others as she dismounted and stretched out her hand to aid Gilban's descent. "Take it slow. We don't want to waste time fishing you out of a sinkhole."

Dugan offered Vinder a hand, who scowled at the gesture. "I can take care of myself."

"All right." Dugan waded to the front of the horse, his feet sinking into the mud just short of his knees. He picked up the reins and gave the horse a pull, urging the beast onward. The jolt rocked Vinder, who'd been climbing down from the horse, causing him to fall into the mud with a loud splash. Dugan rushed to Vinder's half-submerged body. He barely suppressed his laughter at the sight of the mud-caked warrior rising from the muck. "Need any help?"

"No." Vinder brushed away Dugan's offer with a muddy hand and attempted to pry himself out of the miry sea by placing his hands on the amorphous ground in front of him. Using them for leverage, he began pulling himself free, but instead found himself sinking face first into the brackish water—the marshy soil pulling his hands deeper the more he tugged in the opposite direction.

"Wo—" was all he could say before his head was swallowed in a covering of brown bubbles. Dugan reached down and retrieved the sodden dwarf with ease.

Vinder spat out a mouthful of mud followed by a series of coughs.

"I think it'd be safer if you rode the horse until we reached drier ground." Dugan began directing the muck-covered warrior in the animal's direction.

"I'll do no such thing!" Vinder huffed, crossing his muddied arms in defiance.

"Vinder, you'd be much safer if you stayed on the horse," Alara added with as much decorum as she could muster.

"She's right." Cadrissa spoke from behind the company. She held her golden robe above her pale knees, revealing the tall black boots just below them. "It'll be better for everyone."

"Not for me it won't," Vinder grumbled.

"We'll need someone fresh should anything come our way," Rowan said, advancing on the dwarf, his own horse in tow. "And from horseback you'll be able to provide a lookout."

"Well, that makes sense." Vinder wiped more of the mud off his embroidered patch and beard. "You go on ahead then, and I'll bail you out if you need it."

"All right. Let's move on." Alara smiled her thanks at the young Nordican. Rowan seemed startled by the action, as if he was unsure of how to respond, and instead grabbed his reins and continued trudging through the muck.

• ● •

As the rest of the group moved on, Cadrissa tried keeping up with the pace. She pressed slowly through the thick brown water with the soiled hem of her golden robe draped over her right arm, thankful her legs weren't completely naked. Suddenly she found herself tugging on the reins of her mare, which had stopped short without any apparent cause. No matter how hard she pulled, the horse wouldn't budge. It began neighing and became agitated, growing more defiant as she tugged.

"Come on, you stupid beast!"

"What's wrong?" Dugan asked, bringing his own horse to a halt beside her.

"This nag doesn't want to cooperate." Cadrissa wiped a tangle of sweaty locks from her forehead in frustration.

"Tug on its reins. Show it who's boss."

"That's what I'm *trying* to do!" she muttered through gritted teeth. "Besides, it's easy for you to say. You're as strong as a giant!"

Cadrissa continued pulling vainly on the reins, dropping her robes into the murky waters in the process. "*I'm* pulling, so *I'm* the boss," she informed the horse, who whinnied in response and leaned against Cadrissa's struggling attempts at gaining control. She watched the others wade onward and pretended to be winning the struggle, hoping maybe if she acted like she was, the horse would believe her.

"Look," she said sternly and stared the horse in the eye. "I'm the one in charge here, and I say we move forward!" The horse responded by giving a powerful yank of its own, causing Cadrissa to lose her footing and fall into the watery mud. She spat and spattered while glaring up at the troublesome animal.

"I don't want to hurt you, but we can do this the hard way or the easy way. The choice is up to you. I am a mage, you know." The horse paid her little heed as she pushed up her sleeves, preparing to cast a spell. As she did, she took a step back and tripped, falling once more into the muddy soup.

Something broke her fall. It felt like a slightly rotten log that kept her from sinking too far in the miry mess. Then she felt it move and shoot up after her as she struggled to stand. Suddenly, a pale, outstretched hand emerged from the mud, its decomposing fingers revealing the sharp bone underneath like some horrid claw.

Cadrissa screamed.

Still in fright's grip, she only barely registered Dugan rapidly wading her way, the others fast on his heels. Only Vinder and Gilban remained behind.

"What is it?" asked Dugan.

She said nothing, only pointed at the hand attached to a floating corpse, which was joined by two more bodies that had bobbed to the surface.

Dugan stepped closer for an examination.

"They're elves!" Rowan declared in disbelief.

"Elves?" Vinder was equally surprised and dismounted before carefully sloshing through the thigh-high water.

"They died in fear." Dugan prodded the bodies with his sword. "Look at their faces."

Cadrissa gave in to the suggestion and then quickly wished she hadn't. The flesh that remained was discolored and full of rot, worms, and insects—all of which had taken their grisly toll. She quickly sought something more pleasant lest she lose the meager meal she'd taken that morning.

"They look like soldiers," said Rowan.

"They are," Dugan added. "I've seen enough to know."

"Elven soldiers?" Cadrissa intently considered the others, avoiding the corpses between them. "If they've made it this far then they've probably beaten us to the ruins."

"No." Gilban's voice arose from behind them. "Not yet."

Alara neared the bodies, falchion in hand. "But if they're ahead of us we have some catching up to do."

"Not if this is what's left of most of their force." She yielded to her curiosity once more just in time to see Dugan move one of the corpses with the tip of his gladius. The whole bottom portion of the elf had been ripped away like parchment. Jagged edges of flesh and broken bone were covered in slime and maggots busying themselves inside the torn flesh. She snapped away from the sight before her stomach could fully turn over.

"Are those *bite* marks?" Rowan leaned in for a closer look.

"Looks like it, and big ones too." Vinder stroked some more half-dried mud from his beard as he joined them.

"My reading *did* speak of drakes that lived here," Cadrissa meekly offered.

"Drakes . . ." the dwarf pondered. "They're almost as bad as dragons." While Cadrissa had never seen an actual drake in person, nor a dragon for that matter, she didn't really think there was any comparison between the two. Drakes and dragons were both large and reptilian, yes, and might have shared some aspects in their build, but drakes were more bestial in a way—more a common animal. Dragons, however, were quite another thing altogether, with stories having some of them even capable of not only understanding speech but able to speak themselves.

"Do you think it is from a lizard?" Alara sloshed closer to Dugan.

"If it was, then he carried a club." Cadrissa peeked just enough to see Dugan point with his sword at a partially decayed skull on one of the bodies. Its bone structure looked normal enough except for a large indentation in the back where it had shattered inward at the force of some impact.

"I'll get Gilban." Alara started his way, but her arm was caught in Dugan's strong grip.

"A blind man can't help us here."

"He can help us by divining their fate." She pulled free from his grip.

"So they were beaten and *bitten* to death?" Cadrissa glanced nervously about, being sure her eyes never again fell on the bodies. Now open to the air, their rising stench added a whole new dimension to the marsh's putridity.

"Sort of looks familiar." Dugan's attention remained focused on the corpses.

"Familiar how?" asked Vinder.

"There were these big ugly things we fought in the arena that looked like a cross between a lizard and a man. Everyone just called them lizardmen."

"That's original," said the dwarf.

Rowan drew his sword. "How often do they attack?"

"Don't know. Whenever they're hungry, I guess. In the arena they often ate whatever—or whoever—they killed. But these elves are only half eaten."

"So what are you implying?" Cadrissa didn't like the conclusions being drawn. "That they didn't finish their meal and are letting these marinate or some such thing for later?"

"Maybe."

"Either that, or they didn't like the taste of elf." Rowan swept the surrounding terrain with cautious eyes.

"You think they're coming back?" Cadrissa started slowly making her way away from the bodies and the dark picture taking shape in her mind.

"Don't know." Dugan joined Rowan in his survey. "But they fight like men possessed."

"Dugan's correct in his assessment," Gilban informed them as Alara guided him to the bodies. His eyes were closed and his face was a wrinkled mask of concentration as his voice dropped to a monotone rhythm. "They were here several weeks ago. Lizardmen hid in the mud, laying traps for their victims. They designed a sinkhole . . . It captured these elves . . . The elves were not aware of the attack . . . They were set upon by the beasts and torn asunder . . ."

"Blessed Saredhel!" Gilban suddenly exclaimed. "They used these dead bodies as a lure! They're here and *waiting* for us! We've stepped into a trap!"

Cadrissa cringed while the others readied their weapons and wills.

"I don't see anything." Rowan kept scanning the marsh.

"They're out there," Alara replied grimly. "I'd stake my life on it."

"You just might do that!" Vinder idly smacked the butt of his axe in the palm of his hand.

"I should have just the spell—ouch!" Cadrissa felt a pinch on her neck, not unlike the mosquitoes that had been plaguing her throughout the trip. This time, however, there was a burning tingling to the bite.

She felt dizzy . . .

CHAPTER 22

TRIALS TO A MAN ARE LIKE FIRE TO METAL:
THEY REVEAL TO HIM HIS TRUE WORTH.

—Old Tralodroen proverb

Rowan watched Cadrissa drop into the mud, followed by Dugan and the others one by one, before feeling a pinch on his neck. He pulled out the object that had lodged just below the neckline of his leather armor. It was a dart. A simple, bone-tipped, down-fletched dart. His armor had kept it from poking him with the dark sap at its tip. This certainly was fortuitous—a blessing of Panthora for sure. He wasn't about to be killed in a marsh by some creatures whose favored meal apparently was elven flesh. But he needed to see this enemy first to beat them, and that required a trap of his own.

He dropped the venomous dart into the mud, then joined it, feigning unconsciousness. After a few heartbeats, he heard the muddy wading of an approaching group of feet that seemed to stop every so often, possibly checking over each of their victims. Moments later, he heard the guttural sounds of speech, which he could only imagine were the lizardmen arguing over who got the choice kill. The splashes drew closer, and a large, scaly foot—webbed between long, sharp toes—stepped in front of his partially submerged face.

Rowan closed his eyes enough to appear asleep and yet still be able to see. In this small field of vision, he saw strong, reptilian legs and tails covered in the same thick scales as their three-toed feet. It was as if common lizards not only had become the size of men but were able to stand upright like them as well.

The horses began panicking, whinnying nervously, but the mud held them fast, making escape impossible. Distracted by the commotion of the frightened mounts, the lizardmen used their heavy clubs to shatter the horses' skulls. He had to keep himself in check as his Nordic blood flared at the slaughter of such fine beasts. Thankfully, his training helped hold him in place.

He took advantage of the disturbance to get a better sense of his attackers. Their torsos were those of well-muscled men, but covered in dark green scales, with heads similar to what Rowan thought to be alligators—though he only had the rough drawings in old books he'd seen in his training as reference—and possessing a clawed hand with three fingers and a thumb. They even had the musky odor common to so many reptiles.

He partially closed his eyes again in an effort to keep himself calm and focused while forming a plan, but all he could see was the intelligent malevolence behind their yellow eyes. Even when they began savagely ripping apart the horses and eating them, he held his ground. He needed to wait for the right opportunity. He cleared his mind and continued to pray for an answer.

After the lizardmen finished with the horses, they ransacked their goods, taking their saddlebags and packs on their shoulders while others tied up their captives with crudely made rope. They bound each of their hands and feet with the rough cord, and then trussed the unconscious captives to wooden poles about eight feet in length. Soon enough, Rowan found himself dangling between two of the lizardmen as they braced the pole on their shoulders, leaving him hanging like a freshly killed deer. He let himself be disarmed along with the others but kept careful track of his sword's whereabouts. It fell into the hands of the one he guessed was their leader. The big scaly beast had fought off all his companions when the weapon was discovered, claiming it for himself. The others' weapons had been distributed among the remaining lizardmen more equally.

Once their captors had the entire party hoisted onto poles, they headed deeper into the marsh. Rowan was surprised by how little the marsh hindered them. Their webbed feet allowed them to traverse the slushy ground easily. Only on one or two occasions did walking appear difficult, which he attributed to the extra weight of their prey.

As they walked, he contemplated the group's situation and his ability to free them without a weapon. Hope dimmed as he realized he didn't have a real plan. Even Panthora remained silent. It was impossible to take them all on, and, now that he'd let them claim his sword and bind him, his chances were even worse. His only hope was in his faith that Panthora would aid him, believing her silence would break at any moment.

Daylight faded into twilight and then night, cruel and black. The lizardmen halted upon entering a clearing with dry, short grass. Crude huts made of thatch and mud were scattered about the area. Tree limbs and vines enclosed the camp in a rough fence. Elsewhere, small fires dotted the growing darkness, their smoke curling into the canopy. In the center of this gathering was a large open pit.

The lizardmen moved to join others of their kind. Even though those of the tribe were naked save for simple hide breechcloths, Rowan couldn't tell which were male and which female. Only a slight variance in physical size—such as height and girth—was noticeable, by which he assumed the females were the larger of the race, though he'd nothing but Nordic logic to make the claim.

He found the whole camp eerily fascinating. The lizardmen seemed a tribal people who lived under the rule of a chieftain, whom he could see standing near the lip of the pit. This chieftain wore an elaborate coat of leather, bark, and feathers, and carried a large stone axe. His body was also covered in paints and dyes, which made for an interesting collection of shapes and images as he moved about the pit's lip, growling orders at the ones carrying the bound captives.

He and the others were brought forward while the other lizardmen chanted and paraded around their victorious comrades with wild gestures and shouts. These celebrating creatures wore crudely constructed, fiendish masks and tossed bone axes in the air, juggling them like street entertainers. There were also torch jugglers, who wore even stranger and more menacing masks. Drumbeats reverberated as the performers juggled, matching the rhythm of the dancing lizardmen. Obviously, this was a ceremony, but what was *their* purpose supposed to be in it?

The chieftain shouted something while motioning erratically with his arm, indicating the placement of the captives into the pit. Rowan tried to glimpse more of his surroundings, hopeful of finding something to help with their escape, but his hope faded fast. He noticed more lizardmen pouring out of the sunken pit as he and the others were carried toward it.

One by one, Rowan and his companions were hoisted upright and pulled into the pit, where their poles were wedged hard into the earth with smaller pieces of wood pounded beside the poles—keeping them fast. As the lizardmen worked, Rowan noticed the broken branches, leaves, and other debris littered around the pit's base. His mind began racing as he realized their awaiting fate. Panicking, he quickly viewed the others, finding them unconscious, chins resting on their chests.

"Dugan. Cadrissa," he hissed. If they heard him, neither acknowledged it.

He scanned the area without hiding his consciousness. It was pointless continuing his ruse. He had to take action or die. The chieftain, noticing Rowan was awake, spread the lips of his maw in a sort of twisted smile, revealing a long row of glistening, sharp teeth.

He flexed his wrists and tried stretching the ropes binding his feet and hands to the pole, but to no avail. More lizardmen approached the rim of the pit, their clawed hands holding blazing torches, sputtering and spitting in the growing darkness like hungry asps. These began singing a savage, guttural song that filled the night with dread. When they finished, they threw their torches onto the pit. What followed was a scattered crackling, and then smoke that billowed upward as small fires appeared throughout the kindling scattered only a few feet from him.

"Have mercy, Panthora!" Rowan pleaded at the top of his lungs in his native tongue.

The smoke quickly thickened into a suffocating black wave. Rowan heard coughing. Turning, he saw Dugan choking on the smoke.

"Dugan?" Rowan shouted over the growing noise of the chanting lizardmen.

Dugan coughed again. "Where are we?"

"We've been taken captive by lizardmen. We're about to be burned to death. Can you break free?"

Dugan strained against the rope binding him to the post. The tendons in his arms bulged as he pulled his wrists apart, clenching his teeth with the effort. He groaned with the strain, but Rowan also heard the telltale creaking of the rope stretching away from his bloodied and bruised wrists.

"Almost there," Dugan said, gritting his teeth for another try.

"Hurry." Rowan continued fruitlessly struggling with his own bonds. "The fire's growing!"

Dugan wriggled his hands free and quickly untied the rest of the rope holding him to the pole, dropping down into the burning pit. The footing was unstable and rapidly being consumed by the growing fire, but there remained enough safe spots to run to Rowan.

"Hang on!" Dugan rammed Rowan's pole with his shoulder, sending it toppling backward. Part of it rested on the lip of the pit behind it. He did his best to keep from the rising flames as Dugan feverishly tore at the bindings on his legs. When he'd finished, Rowan slid himself to the ground, freeing himself of the bindings on his wrists by moving his hands down the uprooted pole.

"I'll get the others," said Dugan while running for Alara.

Rowan could hear the lizardmen's angry screams over the roaring flames. By the time Rowan had finished liberating his wrists, Dugan had freed Alara's limbs from their bindings and toppled her pole as well, slapping the elf's face as he worked on the ropes around her wrists. "Wake up!" After a few more slaps, Alara moaned.

In a flash she shot to her feet. Without pause, she shouted, "Gilban!" Dugan joined Alara in a race for the unconscious elf, dodging the rapidly increasing flames all the while.

Rowan passed them en route to Cadrissa, who remained unconscious, drooping like a rag doll. Lifting her singed robes in order to get at the biting ropes around her ankles, he shouted for her to wake up. The flames had become serpent-like, dashing in and out, eager to sink their fangs into his flesh.

"Wha—" Cadrissa said as she suddenly awoke.

"Hang on," he said and pushed against the pole.

She started to struggle as the pole fell backward, causing her to twist around and grind her hands against the wooden shaft. Rowan was right beside her, however, working her bindings with frantic fingers. A moment later she was free.

"I have you." He scooped up the mage in his arms. Cadrissa was silent while he carried her from the blaze, darting with sturdy strides across the burning branches. Above the pit, dozens of lizardmen swarmed about the lip, gripping simple wooden spears in their fists.

"What *are* those things?" He could feel Cadrissa's nails through the leather armor on his arms.

"Dugan's lizardmen."

"They're horrid!"

"And they have us pinned down. This might be our last stand."

"No, not yet." Cadrissa's face grew distant as her eyes changed from green to bright blue. "Not when I have just the spell for the occasion," she hissed in a frosty voice that was both her own but also the echo of another's.

"Are you all right?" Rowan's brow furrowed as he felt the shift in temperature about her frame.

"Perfectly fine!" she hissed, looking at him through those empty, bright-blue eyes in a manner more foreign and masculine than just a moment ago. "Now release me!" The command came out of her throat in a deep and powerful voice.

Rowan practically dropped her in his haste to comply. Instinct told him something wasn't right, and he'd best be as far from her as he could at the moment. Perhaps the ordeal had been too much for her. But before he could say or do anything further, he watched in awe as Cadrissa was enveloped in a glowing ball of aquamarine light. Within moments, the heat from the flames abated, and the fire disappeared completely, leaving only wafting tails of smoke rising up into the growing breeze. The lizardmen began crying out in frantic yips and shouts, retreating to their village in terror.

"I'll show them fear!" Cadrissa's voice echoed with a hollow tone that caused Rowan and the others to stare at the mage in slight concern. "Canga lorin mashan echeen!" the strange voice resonating from Cadrissa's lips continued. "Kotlin mia olo-bith!"

"She hit her head?" Dugan asked Rowan as she continued her spellcasting.

"No," he said. "Maybe it's part of the spell."

"Well, she's bought us some time." Alara made her way to the edge of the pit and scaled it effortlessly. "Let's use it."

Dugan hoisted Gilban by his waist up to Alara. He then gave Vinder a lift before turning back to Rowan. "Bring Cadrissa."

"I think you'll find she can take care of herself," said Gilban.

"Die!" Cadrissa screeched from inside the pit. The simple huts where many of the lizardmen had fled suddenly burst into flame. The eruption of the tiny shacks sent smoldering pieces of thatch and lizardmen into the air. The night became alight with the intense blaze, smothered with the heat, and sundered by the screams. The buildings burned fiercely, as did the lizardmen who had been hiding inside. The stench of burned flesh mingled with the aroma of choking smoke that further darkened the night sky.

Cadrissa shuffled to Rowan's side as if moving in a dream. Her footfalls were weak and misplaced, causing her to stumble and lose her balance. Rowan cleared the distance and caught her before she fell.

"We need to find our weapons and get out of here," said Alara, watching Dugan scale the pit in one graceful motion.

"Let's just hope they weren't in any of those huts," said Vinder.

"Can you walk?" Rowan asked, noticing Cadrissa's eyes were green once more. The old superstitions of his people reemerged, forcing him to suppress the urge to run her through right then and there. They needed her help, not only with their escape but for the rest of the mission. And she was a human in need. That meant he was obligated to provide what aid he could.

"Yes." Cadrissa shivered in his arms, her face pale and sickly. "What happened?"

"Later." Rowan helped her out of the pit and toward the others. Behind him, the lizardmen's village burned to the ground.

•●•

They ran into the thickening jungle, attempting to distance themselves from the growing inferno. The night was full of confusion and shadow. The village, and most of what surrounded it, had transformed into a monstrous bonfire, spitting sparks into the sky. Thankfully, the screams of the dying faded as the group stumbled through the chaos.

Vinder had managed to retrieve their weapons with the aid of Alara, who also gathered what she could of their supplies, distributing them as they ran. But while she had her sword, she hadn't located her bow or quiver. And neither of them had found Cadrissa's backpack . . . nor the precious scrolls and books inside.

Cadrissa was vaguely aware of her missing pack, and the hungry flames behind them had her fearing the worst. But such thoughts and concerns were jumbled with plenty of others as the night rambled on like some turbulent sea, splashing new awareness of her situation with every heartbeat.

Dugan and Rowan took the lead, directing the others through the tangled trees and vines. Cadrissa lurched along behind them like a drunk. Her mind whirled and her feet felt as though they were wrapped in lead weights. She still had no idea how she'd ended up running for her life. Worse still, she felt a deep throbbing in her head. The headache was so intense it clouded her vision, blurring the jungle into a big, dark green blob. But thankfully it was already loosening its grip. As the pain faded from her skull, she thought she heard a distant, frost-laced voice scratch at the corner of memory.

Soon we shall meet, it whispered before trailing into nothingness. She was reminded of her troubling dream a few nights earlier. She still couldn't recall what it was about but had a feeling the voice and what just happened were somehow connected.

The lizardmen didn't pursue them. If any survived the vicious attack, they'd scrambled for their lives in the opposite direction. That, she supposed, was a good thing. She didn't feel like taking on any more challenges. As they pressed on, small pools of water began forming beneath their feet. The smell of wet, decaying wood emanated from the soil as they ran.

"We're running back into the marshes," said Alara. The soft soil slowly sucked their feet deeper into the mossy ground. Slowed by the terrain and the deepening night, they stopped to catch their breath.

"Where are we going?" Vinder grunted. "We lost our direction in that mad dash."

"Do you know where we are?" Cadrissa asked Gilban. Her vision was better and she could at last think clearly again.

Gilban closed his eyes and stroked the Eye of Fate hanging from his necklace. Though he'd run with them, being dragged along by Alara for all of it, he didn't seem as worn out as Cadrissa and the others. Instead of heavy breathing, his lips mumbled a prayer.

"We are safe for now," he finally answered.

"Safe, but without direction," Vinder huffed. "I don't want to die here, so someone pick a direction and let's get moving again before any more of those things find us."

As he spoke, Cadrissa noticed Rowan staring off into the distance. She tried seeing what might have caught his eye, but there was nothing but the night-washed landscape. Letting the matter pass, she adjusted her thoughts back to the others.

"So where would you have us go?" Alara peered down at Vinder.

"I didn't say *I* wanted to choose, just that *someone* should . . . like maybe the *leader* of this outfit."

Alara's soft gray face grew hard for a moment.

It was then that Rowan spoke up. "I think I know where we are."

"How?" asked Dugan.

Rowan didn't answer at first, as if his attention and mind drifted through the night air.

"Rowan?" Alara's questioning tone brought him back to the present.

"Wha—"

"You said you thought you knew where we were?" Alara asked slowly, while Cadrissa examined the knight more closely.

"Yes." Rowan shifted under the scrutiny of so many gazes. "Something looks familiar here. I think we can get back to the path if we travel through the marsh in this direction."

"How can it look familiar when you've never been here before?" asked Vinder.

"I don't know. It just seems familiar . . . like I know just how far we are from where we're supposed to be." Rowan's eyes again grew dreamy as he stared off into the jungle.

"Really?" Vinder crossed his arms, axe in hand and ready for anything.

"You have a better idea?" Dugan asked the dwarf.

No one dared reply.

"I'm sure I know the way," Rowan continued.

"He will lead us to the right path," Gilban interjected. "I've foreseen it."

"Have you now?" Vinder chortled.

"Feel free to stay here if you like." Cadrissa was feeling better from the brief rest. "But Gilban hasn't been wrong yet."

"Just seems too convenient is all," said Vinder. "But I trust Gilban before I do the lad." He sheathed his axe.

"And it's better than running aimlessly through the night," she added.

"I just want to survive this trip," said Vinder.

"We all do," Dugan said, stepping toward the knight. "And that means we follow Rowan."

Vinder shrugged. "I don't really care *who* leads, just so long as I get out of here and I get paid. Personally, I think this heat and humidity is getting to everyone. First it was Cadrissa with the lizardmen, and now this sudden *epiphany* with Rowan."

"Yeah. What happened back there?" Dugan asked her.

"What do you mean?" Cold fear swirled in her gut at the question.

"Back at the pit with the lizardmen."

"Pit?" She grew even more concerned as she tried laying hold of a memory that wasn't there.

"Now isn't the time for discussion," said Gilban. "We must be on our way."

"Agreed." Vinder nodded. "But how are we going to complete this mission without our supplies and equipment? We've just got our weapons, and maybe a handful of rations. No more food or water, mounts, or anything but the clothes and armor on our backs."

"He has a point," said Dugan.

"It will all work out." Gilban seemed hurried, almost agitated in his speech and manner, which only served to give extra weight to the priest's words.

"The situation isn't going to improve if we rest for the night or try to retrace our steps," said Alara. "We'd still be out of gear and supplies. We have to make do with what we have. We're better off just following Rowan—if he says he knows the way—than trying to find another. If Gilban says it'll be okay, then I believe it will be—*if* we get moving."

"So then let's get moving." Rowan's words shoved them into action.

CHAPTER 23

Morning came with little conversation. The group devoured their meager rations while watching rainbow-colored birds flutter overhead, searching out their own breakfasts. Their songs blended with the melodious choir that began at dawn while marsh rats scurried back and forth among the underbrush, rustling leaves and splashing water. These were joined by all manner of insects, much to everyone's annoyance.

Cadrissa rubbed her temple, watching Rowan as he stood apart from the group. He continually peered off into the distance. Whether he was lost in thought or fixed on something she couldn't see, she wasn't sure. "I still can't believe I did all that casting just one spell," she murmured. "I don't remember any of it."

Vinder had filled her in on what took place the night before, but he might as well have told her about another person altogether. All she was able to recall was the dizziness, followed by Rowan shaking her awake and seeing the village burning. There *was* something about a fire . . . She'd been tied to a post, hadn't she?

"Well, you did," Vinder replied. "And it was definitely unexpected."

"For both of us." Cadrissa made a halfhearted attempt to smooth out her ruined robes. She didn't think they'd be worth saving when this was all over. "I don't plan on making it a habit."

She felt better than she probably looked and there was still the slight headache, but she could live with it. As long as she was able to keep herself from blacking out or whatever it was she'd done, she'd be content. She'd no desire to dwell on the swirling fears in the back of her mind. She'd enough to deal with as it was. Her energy and thoughts were better spent on the present.

"I hope not," said Vinder. "We have enough on our plate as it is." He indicated Rowan with a nod.

"He got us away from those lizardmen," she offered.

"But now we're lost. And might even be going in circles."

"You think you can do better?"

"I just wonder why he was ever allowed to lead us in the first place."

"A leader is defined by their followers," Gilban said, finding his way into the conversation. "You could have gone your own way." She'd almost forgotten he was there until he spoke. He'd lost his walking stick in the previous evening's chaos, which she assumed only made things more challenging.

"Fat chance there," Vinder huffed. "I just don't want to get any more lost than we already are."

"And who says we're lost?"

Vinder winced at the seer's question. "Don't you ever talk like a normal person?" he said. "You said it was going to be okay."

"I did."

"Then what's going on?" he continued. "I thought we were headed to the jungle?"

"We are." Alara stood and stretched her back.

"Well, this looks—and *smells*—like the marshes." Vinder swatted a mosquito on his cheek. Cadrissa did the same. She found herself doing so more as a reflex now than anything else. She wouldn't be surprised if she even did it in her sleep.

"He has a point." Dugan was still seated, eating the last of a dry loaf of bread. Like Vinder, he'd kept his armor on through the night. Rowan had done the same. She couldn't imagine how uncomfortable it was. The extra sweating alone made her happy she had only her robes.

"Thank you." Vinder nodded.

"Well, if I still had my backpack I might have been able to read up on some things, maybe even have found a better way forward. But someone went and left it behind in the flames." She tempered the anger in her words, but the better she felt the angrier she grew over what she'd lost.

"You thought I *purposely* left it behind?" Vinder was insulted at the accusation.

"Did you?"

"I *was* kind of rushed at the time." His words were measured. "There was only so much I could grab, and it wasn't all in one neat pile either. I took what was important and at hand."

"Well, those scrolls and books were important."

"You know Alara was helping too," he huffed. "You going to blame her too?" This caught the attention of Alara, who clearly didn't like the way the conversation was going.

"I'm simply stating a fact," she continued. "And if anything happens later I could have helped avoid—"

"We'll be fine." Alara finally jumped into the discussion. "What's important is we don't start—"

"Now that it's daylight, I'm even *more* certain the way can be found," said Rowan, intruding into both the camp and the discussion with an oblivious smile.

"I thought I heard that *last* night." Vinder gnawed on his last piece of hardened bread, clearly thankful for the change of topic.

"We're getting close." Rowan ignored the dour dwarf, focusing on Alara instead. "I can feel it."

"Close to what?" she asked. Rowan paused, his focus centered on Alara, who was clearly growing uncomfortable with the continued silence. And she wasn't the only one.

"You feeling okay?" Alara asked, returning Rowan to his senses.

"I'm fine."

"Then you want to tell me what's going on? You told us you knew where you were—"

"And you have nothing to fear," he was quick to reply. "I'm confident I'm being led the right way."

"*Led?*" Alara raised her eyebrow. "I thought you said you knew the way?"

"I do—or I will." Rowan shifted his focus back to whatever had previously commanded his attention. "I just need a moment to get my bearings."

"That's not all you're missing." Vinder's comment earned a cold stare from Alara.

"Finish getting ready," she said. "Once Rowan's set, we'll start walking again."

"You sure you want to do that?" Vinder slowly stood.

"I trust Gilban's judgment, which means we're following Rowan."

"It's going to be torture without the horses." Cadrissa did her best to work out the tiny kinks in her back and neck. She'd slept more awkwardly than she would have liked, but at least she had gotten some rest. The others keeping watch hadn't fared as well.

"We'll survive," Alara countered. "We'd have had to walk for part of the journey anyway."

"It's not just that, but the return trip as well." She sighed. "It'll take us quite a while to get back."

"One thing at a time."

"Well, the sooner we get going, the sooner we can get back." Vinder made the last adjustments to his person and peered heavenward with a hand over his brow. "And that sun isn't going to be any help once it gets higher."

"Rheminas' blessing, my eye." Cadrissa saw Dugan tense out of the corner of her eye while she finished her preparations.

• ● •

Rowan slogged through the soggy path as the hours passed, but he scarcely acknowledged them. He hardly noticed the others trailing behind him as the day faded into late afternoon. He was overwhelmed with the extreme need to reach his divinely appointed destination. He walked as though in a trance, his eyes constantly focused on the ghostly image of Panthora—he'd no doubt the faint image of the Nordic woman was her—always remaining just out of reach, leading him onward.

Come . . . Come . . . The feminine voice filled his head.

He couldn't help but obey the command. He'd first seen the vision the night before, beckoning him to follow. It struck him at once with its similarity to the dream he'd had back in the Broken Oar. He was sure it wasn't mere coincidence but something guiding him to the ruins and the hidden knowledge therein.

She appeared as a transparent woman crafted of glowing white light. In every way the perfection of Nordic beauty: the most splendid of women he'd ever hope to see in his lifetime. She wore her hair to her shoulders and was dressed in a long-sleeved tunic, a pair of pants, and tall boots. Her eyes, though, were what had caught and helped him the most. Bright and strong, they also radiated a welcoming love he found himself hard pressed to ignore.

Just as in the dream, he had a compulsion to trudge onward where she called. He'd become so enraptured with the experience he gave scarce consideration to anything else around him. There was only his goddess and her beckoning command. And so it had been for hours now, though to him it seemed only moments. And it would have continued if Alara's hand hadn't found his shoulder, breaking his trance.

"Are you sure you know the way?" He was startled by the voice, becoming suddenly aware of the oppressive environment once again.

"I-I know the way, yes." His gaze trailed from the elf, returning to his transparent guide.

"You just seem a bit . . . distracted." Alara eyed him cautiously. "And maybe a little bit . . . unsure of things."

"So you don't trust me anymore?" Rowan snapped. Alara withdrew her hand as if she'd been bitten by a snake.

"Is that what you all think?" He spun around, facing the others. "Don't you trust me, either?" He went from Dugan to Cadrissa, clearly seeing their reservations. "I'd expected as much from the elves and the dwarf, but not you two."

"We're not the ones who said he knew the way." Vinder was going to say more but Alara beat him to it.

"Rowan—"

"I'm telling you, I know the way!" He could actually feel the confidence in his voice. "Gilban even told you all to follow me. Are you calling the elf a liar?" Silence overcame the others as each sought Gilban, who remained still and detached from the conversation.

"Gilban *did* support you." Alara was measured in her reply. "And for that I was willing to give you a day to lead us to where you think the ruins are, but after seeing how it's turned out, I can't be party to it any longer—no matter what Gilban said."

"I see," he said. "So then I have until the end of the day?"

"A couple more hours, and then we make camp."

"All right," he continued, setting his sights once again on Panthora before pressing onward with a rapid gait. "We have to keep moving north."

• ● •

As the light faded with the hours, the ground grew more solid. The jungle was clearly reclaiming the area. Eventually, they found themselves at the base of a rocky hill.

"That's far enough, Rowan." Alara's comment retrieved him from the daze he'd been in for most of the day. "We can camp here for the night." She could tell he was just as tired as the rest of them but still willing to push on—maybe even to his own harm—just to prove a point.

"I'm confident if we just go a little farther—"

"It's been a long day." She made sure her voice remained calm and even. "Even *you* have to be tired."

"I can go on," he continued, clearly distracted by something on the hill. Something she couldn't see, no matter how hard she searched.

"You got us into the jungle again, and that's a good start."

"But if we just go a little farther—"

"Let it go, Rowan." She finally gave way to tired frustration.

"You want to give up when we're so close?" he returned with a mild contempt, taking her aback.

"We're not giving up," she replied, trying her best to sound reassuring. "We just need to rest. And this is a great place to set camp for the night."

Again his focus shifted back to that hill.

"What do you keep looking at?" she finally had to ask.

"Come with me." He suddenly had her arm and was yanking her to the top of the hill. He was stronger than she thought, forcing her to stumble along behind.

"What are you doing?" He was so frantic in his climb, it took all her concentration to keep from falling. He stopped at the crest, and his vision again became trance-like, taking in everything before them.

"This has gone on long enough," she protested, finally wrenching her wrist free of his grip. "Now—"

"Look!" He pointed ahead of them. "We've done it!"

Alara gasped. Beneath the canopy-filtered moonlight she could see stone blocks jutting out of the green carpet. Tall towers, some fallen, some leaning haphazardly, loomed above. The chunks of marble scattered around dense brush reminded her of crushed bone. Split and tumbled pillars resembled fallen logs, disintegrated by the weight of tumbled statues, while moss, weeds, and tree roots grew in the craters and crevices along broken battlements, storefronts, and toppled walls.

"We just needed to go a little bit farther." Rowan smiled, clearly pleased at the sight. Alara shouted for the others with the news, only to hear them galloping up the hill shortly after.

"I don't believe it," Dugan whispered.

"No dwarf quarried *those* stones," said Vinder, joining them with an amazed stare.

"We've found the ruins!" Cadrissa shouted with joy. She'd taken Gilban's hand on her shoulder, assisting in his ascent. Her green eyes shone with her obvious excitement. "But what do we do now?"

"We camp," said Gilban.

• ● •

Dugan strolled up to the low-burning fire and sat near the others gathered around it. As Gilban instructed, they'd moved their camp to the base of the ruins, hoping they'd find some rest in relative safety. With a sigh, he removed his armor and threw it into a pile on the ground. It felt good shedding it. If Vinder and Rowan wanted to keep theirs on, they were more than welcome, but he could use a break. The cooler air helped dry all the sweat.

He stretched, closing his eyes and trying to relax as best he could in the sticky air. No one would eat tonight, and they hadn't been able to hunt anything thus far. And when morning came they'd all want to keep going, making breakfast unlikely. He didn't blame them. The sooner they could find whatever it was they were supposed to find, the sooner they could get out of here.

As he rested, Vinder polished his axe until it reflected the firelight, while Cadrissa pondered the ruins. Alara worked on her falchion, rubbing what oil she'd salvaged into the metal, checking the grip and hilt. Gilban simply stared into the blaze, fingering his pendant in thought or prayer— Dugan wasn't sure which. Rowan was the only one outside their circle, standing a stone's throw from the camp and staring into the ruins with a forlorn appearance.

"If I had my bow I might be able to get us something to eat," said Alara, inspecting her blade with a practiced eye.

"Least you got your sword." Vinder turned his axe to and fro in the firelight. "I wouldn't want to be out here without *something* by my side."

"My father carved the wood himself," Alara replied. "He thought I needed something to help protect myself and the flocks." She shot Dugan a knowing look. "Course, it soon found its way into other uses."

"I can imagine," he said with a lopsided grin. He scanned the area around them, adding, "Doesn't look like anyone's been here for years. Maybe the elves didn't make it after all."

"No, they didn't," said Gilban. "These aren't the right ruins."

"*What?*" Vinder grimaced.

"You mean after all we've been through, we're still lost?" Cadrissa was less than pleased.

"In part." Gilban was solemn in reply.

"Great." Vinder sulked, returning to his work.

"What do you mean 'in part'?" asked Alara. "Where are we?"

"Gondad," said Gilban.

"*Gondad?*" Cadrissa nearly jumped out of her skin. "*This* is *Gondad?*"

"The very same." Gilban continued contemplating the fire.

"So what's Gondad?" Dugan asked Cadrissa.

"You mean you *really* don't know?"

"No."

"You're a *human* and you *don't* know?" she persisted.

"I don't get out much."

"Oh . . . right." A soft red fire played about the flesh of her cheeks and forehead. "Well, about four thousand years ago, during the Imperial Wars, this was a great glen. Old stories say Landis, the ancient Gondadian king, died cursing the land as it was taken by the elves of Colloni. The same legends say blood ran from his veins in great rivers of anger and sorrow—flooding his beautiful land with putrid water. That was how the marshes were created. All the peoples of this territory had to move away in order to survive, including the elves. Thus Landis was able to keep his land—but at a terrible cost. Gondad was destroyed, never to be rebuilt."

"So we've camped in a city cursed by a king?" Vinder rested his axe beside him. "How is *that* a good thing?"

"Don't worry. It's just a legend," Alara stepped in, calming any fears. "This city and the land around it are safe from any curse. Legends often cover up the full truth. We Patrious have a more accurate recollection of past events than most races.

"Gondad had an abundance of fertile fields due to the many tracks of irrigation running all over the countryside. In a desperate attempt to increase the city's defenses, Landis decided to turn the irrigation canals into a maze of moats. However, when he opened the floodgates to their fullest, he didn't take into account the effect of the force of so much water on the canals. The torrent eroded the stone waterways, flooding the land and destroying everything in its path. The floodgates could never again be closed. They were swept away, buried and ruined by the water. Since that day, the fields of Gondad have become a great marsh, with the city itself first becoming a corroding backwater and then finally a desolate ruin."

"So he destroyed his city to get revenge on the elves?" Dugan pondered aloud, not missing the irony of the action. It was something he could relate to—in part.

"That's what I was taught." Alara nodded. "Of course, revenge ran deep in Aero too."

"And still does with many to this day," Gilban solemnly added. His blind eyes rested on Dugan, who sat uncomfortably as the elf somehow peered right through him.

"Do you think he led us here on purpose?" Dugan indicated Rowan.

"Makes you wonder, doesn't it?" Vinder watched the knight carefully. "Maybe that was his plan all along."

"Not if what Gilban said was right," said Alara, attempting to squash the others' rising suspicion.

"He might have wanted us here too," Vinder was quick to point out.

"I want us to be true to our mission, wherever it may lead us," said Gilban, once more taken with the fire. "And right now it has taken us to this point."

"But for what purpose?" Alara asked what was clearly on everyone's mind.

"I'm sure we'll find out soon enough."

• ● •

Rowan didn't hear much of the others' conversation. In truth, he hadn't heard anything after he overheard they were standing in the ruins of Gondad. He knew from his training how the origin city was viciously destroyed by elven expansion, but to be here now? A human walking the streets of the once-great city? It was beyond amazing. And to think Panthora had led him to it. First the dream and then the reality of it playing out in the marsh and jungle. Now here he was in the very guts of that great city.

"Gondad, ancient Gondad . . ." he whispered in awe. After so many centuries of searching—even by people sent or supported by the knighthood—he'd been the one to find it, and on his first mission. As he pondered these things, the dream-like euphoria he'd been under the whole day took hold once again. Within its grasp, he heard an age-old melody echoing through the walls and flowing through the streets, from the rocks, trees, buildings, and even his heart.

> *Come into a great nation,*
> *Come into a great host.*
> *Blest from its first creation,*
> *And loved by gods the most.*
> *A nation of united, strong leaders of the land.*
> *Each day we hear our souls sing,*
> *And still our city stands.*

The melody and words welling up in him were as old as the knighthood itself, if not older. It was the ancient hymn of Gondad and was taught to all knights and Panians, for it was common knowledge all humanity had sprung from the blessed city.

> *There are none who would shelter*
> *Evil in our walls.*
> *Blest be the simple worker,*
> *And whom god calls.*
> *Our army is victorious,*
> *Ten thousand foes before them fall.*
> *Our nation will be forever*
> *For we are first of all.*

His spirit joined the hymn of praise, even as his feet began pulling him forward. Step by step he picked up speed, first a light trot, then a jog, and finally a mad run. He had to follow where he was led. It was obviously for a purpose—a purpose in dire need of discovery. In many ways it was like he was back in that dream again, only this time he was awake and closing on something great; he could feel it.

• ● •

Dugan noticed Rowan slowly walking for the center of the ruins. But before he could fully react, the knight charged into the night.

"Rowan!" Dugan jumped from his seat.

"Leave him," Gilban calmly advised. "He has come to find his destiny." Dugan fought back the urge to chase after him, reminding himself Gilban was probably right, no matter how he felt about it.

"Let's just hope he doesn't stir up any more surprises." Vinder's words echoed Dugan's thoughts. "I'm not in the mood for a fight right now."

"Will he truly be all right?" Alara asked Gilban.

"Yes." Gilban stared off into the horizon. "He has to meet his destiny alone. Only then will he return."

"*If* he returns," Vinder added under his breath.

"He *will* return." Gilban stared Vinder in the face, ending the discussion.

CHAPTER 24

OH, TO HAVE BEEN A WARRIOR FOR GONDAD!
WHAT HONOR. WHAT PRIVILEGE.
TO HAVE BEEN ABLE TO BEHOLD THE GREAT KINGS,
SEE GANDIA LIFTED HIGH, AND HEAR THE ORDER GIVEN TO ADVANCE.

—Harris Boralin, king of Romain
Reigned 1893 BV–1697 BV

After making considerable progress, Rowan stopped when a set of stairs caught his eye. Something called to him from them, something he wasn't completely able to define. The driving compulsion formerly gripping him had evaporated, allowing a moment of clarity in which he doubted the wisdom of his run into such a puzzling and potentially dangerous place. And yet he was drawn here for a reason.

The steps had been just like those he'd seen in his dream. He was sure of it. This was too much of a coincidence to not have meaning. In the dream he'd climbed them, but had also met up with an unpleasant surprise. Not wanting to make the same mistake, he cast his face toward heaven. "What am I supposed to do?"

No answers came.

Tentatively, he climbed the weathered stone until he approached the same dark doorway from his dream. He quietly drew his sword and entered the black portal. No sooner had his feet crossed the threshold than the previous dream-like grip returned, compelling him onward. His walk accelerated again into a run as he continued through the darkness of another decrepit hallway. The acrid smell of decay and dust clogged his nose and mouth, but it didn't matter. He could feel the very presence of ancient Gondad calling out from the shadows while the old hymn, now sung by ghostly voices, whispered in his ear.

For our god-sent leaders
Kept us sore oppressed.
Dreams crafted in marble
Lasted days at best.
Sorrow long and weary,
Tears freshly fell like rain.
And only an elf named Aero
Could take away our pain.

The haunting murmurs abruptly ended along with the compulsion, halting his steps. It was then a revelation set in. He was hopelessly lost. He'd no way of telling where he came from nor what lay ahead. Though the ruins were pitted with holes, they provided only faint pools of moon- or starlight.

As he cautiously made his way across the debris-strewn floor, he heard a great cat purring. Instinct drove his head to his right just as a dark gray panther appeared from the broken shadows. Unlike the one in his dream, this panther was of normal proportions, but there was still something supernatural about it. The creature's bright yellow eyes shone like lanterns as they stared at the young knight. After eyeing Rowan, the panther languidly proceeded down a nearby hallway. He kept watching it until it was almost completely swallowed in shadows. Curious and still lacking answers, Rowan followed.

Finding the creature was easy enough. And it apparently didn't mind him following, leading Rowan to wonder if this might be another sign of Panthora's guidance. The symbolism was fairly clear after all—the panther being a sign heavily tied to the Queen of Valkoria. In time, the beast slowed and then halted near a small wooden door, which had remarkably survived the assault of time, war, and rot. The panther's beefy paw slashed at its bottom half, then it crouched down, growling at him.

"I take it I'm to go in there?" Rowan pointed at the door. The panther made no response, only stared at him with its self-illuminating eyes.

"All right." Rowan gingerly edged his way around the great cat until he was facing the door. He gave it a small push. It fell with a loud crash, scattering dust, spiders, rodents, and other vermin. The panther's unnatural eyes lit up the space beyond just enough so he could clearly discern the fallen door dominating most of the small room's interior.

He slowly proceeded inside, breaking the ancient door into splinters and chunks under his heel. His attention was drawn to the unusual object ahead of him: a thick stone pillar upon which rested a small, rusted iron chest no larger than a hand's breadth and width. Again, he felt drawn to it and had sheathed his sword and reached out for it before he knew what he was doing. His hands gingerly handled the cold metal, seeking its opening. The old, delicate locks crumbled in showers of umber flakes when he lifted the lid.

In it, he discovered the same necklace from his dream: a strange, tribal-looking thing resting on a leather strap and sporting a small, shriveled paw along with some black and red beads. Experiencing it in the waking world, he knew the paw was from a baby panther. It was much smaller than the adult-sized ones he'd come to know growing up. He pulled it from the box for a better look, letting it swing back and forth on the leather strand as he did so. Why had he been led here? What was Panthora trying to tell him? Gondad. The strange panther. This necklace.

"The necklace is yours." A woman's voice suddenly filled the room.

Rowan jumped and nearly dropped the necklace and the small chest when he heard it. There was no doubt who'd spoken.

He knelt before the stone pillar. "Panthora, forgive me."

"For what?" The voice was far from angry. "I led you here to receive this gift."

"Thank you." He kept his eyes low. "May I ask why you did so? It seems as though you went to a great deal of effort to lead me to what would appear to be a rather simple necklace." Upon reflection, he quickly added, "I mean no disrespect. I simply wish to learn from your ways and become a better servant."

"Rowan, you've always pleased me." He took some delight at the pleasure he heard in Panthora's voice. "The gift is given for another time to come. When you're ready you will understand what this token of my favor has to do with you and your calling into my service. You have a great future before you. A future where this gift will be needed. Until then, wear it as a pledge of my favor."

"Thank you." He bowed his head. "I will do so always."

"I've been watching you. You've had a difficult time on this mission, but things will soon turn around. When they do, you will begin to see your true calling and your greater purpose. There are powerful and wonderful plans tied to you, Rowan. One day soon you will understand." Her voice was as comforting as a mother's, soothing the troubled waters in his spirit. "Until then, carry my gift with you and recall my favor toward you."

"I will."

"And don't doubt your heart. Listen to it, but don't be ruled by it—not yet." The words trailed off into faint whispers.

"What does—" His question was cut short by the panther's loud roar and the stark silence following it. Bravely raising his chin, he discovered the room was dark and empty once more. No panther. No Panthora. Nothing but the shadowy gloom. He donned the necklace, fingering the strange paw before shoving it beneath his armor, pressing it close to his heart.

"Hello?" Rowan drew his sword before slowly feeling his way out of the dark room. "Panthora?"

"Who are you speaking to?" A voice, no more than a whisper, floated past his ears. He spun in the direction but saw nothing but darkness.

"Who are you?" he called out blindly, finding the grip on his sword.

"I am a citizen of Gondad, but you are not. Yet you are human. How strange," the whisper continued.

"Where are you?" Rowan paced in a circle, his blade in front and eyes straining for any sign of movement.

"I mean you no harm," came the voice's reply.

"If that's true, then show yourself."

"Very well." A pale, translucent light shimmered into being before taking on the semblance of a human man surrounded by a glowing white aura. He'd obviously suffered a gruesome death: his torso was mangled by many open wounds, the result of being riddled with arrows and sliced through with swords. The worst, Rowan thought, was his face, which had a deep line cut diagonally through it, slicing the nose in half. This gash was so deep it exposed the bone of his skull underneath.

"What are you?" Rowan took up a defensive position.

"I have already told you," the ghost said softly. "I am a citizen of Gondad."

"Gondad's dead. It was destroyed thousands of years ago." Rowan held his stance.

"Yet I remain." The ghost hovered closer.

"Keep your distance . . ." He leveled his sword at the other.

"As I have said before, I am not here to hurt you. Be at ease. I am here to guide you."

"Guide me where?" He tried for more answers from the shadows, fearing ambush. "Who sent you? Panthora?"

"I have no knowledge of this Panthora you speak of."

"You don't know the goddess of the human race?" He was shocked.

"Yes, of course I do. Asora is the great creator of the human race," the ghost calmly replied.

"Maybe the elves who conquered you beat such thoughts into your head, but Panthora's the *only* goddess of humanity, blessing us with her protection and prosperity. And I'm one of her knights."

"Forgive me, I have angered you." The ghost bowed in respect. When he did so, a loose flap of skin fell over his face, returning to his scalp when he finished. "I forget I have not seen the world since my death. Much, it seems, has changed."

"You still haven't told me who sent you." Rowan lowered his blade, but remained ready for an attack.

"The king has ordered me to find you."

"You mean *Landis*?" Rowan quickly pieced things together. "*That's* who wishes to speak with me?"

"Yes."

He was truly amazed at how highly he was favored by Panthora. The gift of the necklace was one thing—but an audience with Landis himself? Though he wasn't sure why he was being called to the king's ghost, there must be a reason. Didn't Panthora just tell him he had a great calling to fulfill? Maybe it was going to be fulfilled faster than he thought . . . and with the ghost of the last king of Gondad, no less.

"Then take me to him, by all means."

"Very well." The ghost motioned Rowan onward. "Come with me."

He sheathed his sword and did as bidden. Together, he and the spirit traveled seemingly endless corridors and dark rooms. The ghost's illumination was almost equal to torchlight, and it easily led Rowan through the broken and twisted halls. He took it all in with a sense of awe. He was traveling the very passages the mightiest human kings had walked. He was in the presence of history! Though his surroundings were drab and decrepit, his spirit felt as though it was soaring in the heavens.

"We are here." The ghost stopped at an old cobweb-layered wooden door. Rowan placed his hand reverently upon its frame, amazed it still stood. Standing about ten feet high and seven feet across, it displayed a crowned lion's head whose profile faced right.

"The crest of Gondad," he whispered reverently. He gingerly traced out part of the raised wood, clearing away the grime and cobwebs.

"Yes." The ghost puffed his chest out with pride. "The sign of the mighty empire that would have gone on forever . . ." His chest then sank and his face grew sullen.

"The elves have much to answer for," Rowan told his guide.

"Some might say we have our own share for which we need give account."

He was about to ask what the ghost meant when he indicated the door. "But you have an audience with Landis. I would open it myself, but in my current state I fear I am no longer able."

Rowan gently pushed the door open. It creaked and moaned after generations of neglect, but still held true to its hinges and frame. He peered with hesitant wonder into the opening.

"How can I see if I have no light?"

The room suddenly lit up with a burst of flames from a row of empty sconces lining the side walls. Like spectral torches, they illuminated the interior in near-perfect light, allowing him a fuller understanding of just how empty the place was. Only a rotten wooden throne remained. And on that throne rested a skeleton draped in a few scraps of robe and some dull jewelry. Wisps of hair, no more visible than strands of spider webbing, draped from the skull's crest. A crusty green crown sat on its head, and a scepter of tarnished iron was still clutched in its left hand, which lay on its empty chest.

"Is that—" Rowan dared a look back and found the ghost had vanished as quickly as he'd appeared.

"Rowan," a faint voice called from a great distance. As was becoming the case, while he might have heard a voice, he didn't find its speaker. And then he saw a shadow near the throne shift slightly, followed by a figure who emerged from beside the decaying seat. Like the earlier ghost, the being was translucent and pale white. This new ghost, however, wore a death shroud as a cloak, which hid a great deal of his features as it twisted in an unseen wind sending out waves of frosty air into the otherwise warm room.

Rowan knelt before the throne.

"Rise, sir knight. Though I was once a king, I now come as a messenger to aid you on your quest." The spectral figure beckoned Rowan closer.

"You know of my mission?" Rowan cautiously did as bidden.

"Yes. You seek a ruined city built by the dranors, not far from here. There, you wish to bring honor to your knighthood by finding some ancient insight into what can make a nation great." The figure watched him stop a few feet from his throne. It was as far as Rowan dared tread.

"That's true, but you said you were a messenger. What is your message?"

Before Rowan could react, azure flames took over the spirit's eyes as his translucent hand shot out, gripping Rowan's wrist. Icy bursts of pain washed over him and he cried out, struggling for release. A heartbeat later he became receptive to the spirit, compelled to listen as its shape transformed into a skeleton draped in a ragged robe.

"Now listen, whelp. You're going to locate a tall blue cylinder in the ruins. Don't touch it, but instead, after the mage has cast her spell, you are to kill the demon who comes through the portal. Do you understand?"

Rowan nodded.

"Hold up your sword."

He did as ordered. The lich brought forth a transparent glass vial in his other hand. The bright green liquid inside was solid in comparison to the hand holding it. With a smooth motion, the lich pulled the translucent cork out of the vial and poured the thick green fluid over the blade. While careful not to use it all, he made certain the sword was covered from point to hilt before waving the same hand above the weapon. Green flames sprouted over the entire blade, wrapping around it like a shimmering emerald scabbard.

"Now listen very carefully. You will remember nothing of what was spoken to you here by me or the ghost who led you here. But when the time is right, you will recall all I've said and will do all I've told you . . ."

•●•

Following Rowan's departure, the others had sunk into silence, the long journey and dour circumstances getting the better of them. Dugan could have stayed awake a while longer, but decided he'd join the others trying for some rest. As he got comfortable around the fire, he caught sight of Cadrissa watching him, absently coiling a few black locks as she dared a peek. He pretended he didn't notice her admiring him as he shed his tunic in order to make a crumpled pillow, but he could feel her gaze upon him nonetheless. Opting for a quick peek of his own, he saw the slight smile flutter across her lips before her green eyes darted away.

"I think she fancies you," Vinder whispered from where he was preparing his own resting spot a few feet away.

"She's had her eye on me ever since Altorbia."

"Let's just hope you don't prove to be too much of a distraction. She has her head in the clouds enough already without having to daydream about you too."

"Well, I'm not leading her on," said Dugan.

"I don't think it takes much to get her going." The dwarf lay on his right side, keeping his axe sheathed at his left hip. "All the better *you* don't fancy her."

"There's just a few other things on my mind right now." Dugan arched his back and stretched from the day's hard trek. "Besides, there'll be plenty of time for all that once I get out of this jungle."

"I'll drink to that." Vinder grinned. "That is, I would, if we had anything left to drink."

"Still . . ." Dugan caught sight of Cadrissa pondering him yet again and couldn't resist a smile in response. "It's nice to know I'm not too sore a sight."

"Enjoy it while you can," said Vinder, brushing a stray mosquito from his cheek. "Eventually, you'll get to a point when they'll start thinking you're a grandfather."

"Speaking from experience?"

Vinder smiled. "More than you want to know." Their laughter was cut short by Alara.

"We're still going to need to keep watch—make sure we keep an eye out for Rowan when he returns. You up for going first, Vinder?"

"I suppose." He sighed.

"You were already in your armor," said Dugan, watching Vinder sit up. The dwarf hadn't removed it nor his weapon since they'd first met.

"Force of habit," he said. "I've learned it's better to be cautious than half naked." He gave Dugan a nod.

"I trust you'll be second, Dugan?" said Alara. "I can take third watch."

"Sure," he replied, letting Alara depart.

"Sleep fast," said Vinder.

A few hours later, the dwarf woke Dugan for his shift. He had just finished donning his tunic and strapping on his sword when the two paused.

"Did you hear that?" Vinder whispered.

Dugan drew his gladius. "It's coming from the west."

"Northwest, as I reckon it. Might be Rowan. What do you think?"

"He wouldn't be trying to be so silent," said Dugan. "Pretend to go to sleep. I'll check it out."

Vinder lay down, acting like he was readying for bed, as Dugan wandered over to some trees that had torn up the cobblestone streets with their corded roots. His nerves twitched and his muscles bunched. He could taste the keen tang of steel in his mouth; he was ready for anything. He went farther into the bushes, scanning through the dense growth, pretending he was preoccupied with emptying his bladder. He found nothing. Heard nothing.

Convinced it was the movement of an animal or even the wind, he turned to leave. As he did, he felt a blade press against his neck. Though it was crudely fashioned, he knew it was sharp enough to cause grievous injury if drawn across his throat. He struggled for a glimpse of his attacker, but could only make out an iron-tight arm of dark brown skin. At least he knew it wasn't Rowan who held him. His captor then shouted something next to his ear. The wilderness became alive with Celetoric warriors, who quickly encircled the camp in a mob of men too thick to count.

Vinder jumped into action. "We're under attack!" he shouted as a fierce, dark-skinned warrior rushed him.

•●•

A short time later Rowan found himself in the camp, bewildered as to how he'd gotten there. Just moments before, he thought, he'd been speaking with Panthora, and now here he was. Could it have all been another dream? And then he felt the hard object between his armor and his chest. The necklace and shriveled panther paw pendant were real. Whatever happened must have been real on some level—if not entirely, then at least in part. But now wasn't the time for working through such matters. He needed to get some rest and then . . . He paused, realizing he was the only one in the camp.

Where was everyone? The fire was spent, and there was no sign of anyone anywhere. Had they deserted him? He supposed it was possible. They'd made it clear they weren't too fond of him leading them here— even if it was Panthora herself guiding them. And he supposed his mad dash into the ruins might have been the final crack in the dam, convincing them to depart without him. He wouldn't put it past the elves. But where would they go in the darkness?

His moment of deliberation passed as a familiar twinge made the hairs on the back of his neck stand on end. Someone else was nearby. He could almost feel their breath upon his skin. He looked from his left to his right, making out shapes in the night, and caught sight of a dark silhouette. It appeared to be a man of normal height and weight, yet the figure was so swift he could barely discern him.

"Who goes there?" Rowan called out in Telboros. No sooner had he spoken than he was surrounded by spear-carrying warriors wearing nothing more than hide breechcloths.

"I mean you no harm," Rowan said in Abjula, the language of the Celetors. Rowan never was more pleased to know the language. Upon hearing their native tongue, the men whispered among themselves. Their conversation drew on for a few more moments until they allowed another Celetor to pass between them.

"How do you know the words of my people?" asked the other in the same tongue. He was dressed like the others—a simple breechcloth and bare feet—but he wore a green and blue feathered necklace with a bone bracelet about his left wrist. Like the others, he carried a spear, along with a dagger, at his side.

"I can speak all the human languages," said Rowan, "just like all knights in the service of Panthora."

"You honor Panthora?" The Celetors lowered their spears, taking a more relaxed stance while the lead Celetor stepped closer.

"Yes. The Knights of Valkoria look to serve her in all things."

"Then you're not with them?" The other pointed out a clump of trees where slumped, tied bodies could be seen in the darkness.

"Are they dead?"

"No, just sleep darts," the Celetor replied. "We didn't want to kill. Just question them. We thought they were coming to attack us like the others did."

"What others?"

"Like the gray-faced ones. They were not as pale but had the same pointed ears."

"Elves." Rowan's face darkened. "People like this attacked you?"

"Yes."

"When?"

"About two moons ago." Rowan's heart sank at the news. Were they already too late? Had the elves already reached the ruins and taken the knowledge? It was clear they'd made it into the marshes but how much farther had they gone beyond that?

"They came to steal our food and goods, but we ran them off before they could take too much. Ever since the yellow-skinned men, we've learned to keep better watch, especially at night."

"Yellow-skinned men?" Rowan's interest was piqued.

"Yes. Yellow-skinned men with pointed ears and clawed hands. They came about four moons ago—out of the jungle—and took many of the tribe away. My own brother, Ekube, was killed in the attack."

"May Panthora watch over him." Rowan made a solemn nod.

"Thank Panthora they haven't come back." The Celetor received Rowan's condolences and blessing, adding, "But we still keep watch each night."

"Yellow skinned and pointed ears?" Rowan thought aloud. "That sounds like hobgoblins." He moved for the unconscious bodies. The nearby Celetors tensed, but with a wave of their leader's hand, they relaxed. "Well, these people aren't here to attack you or your tribe."

The other pointed out Alara and Gilban. "And them?"

"They're not the same elves. And I've been with them the whole time. We haven't come near your tribe or you until just now."

The Celetor fell silent.

"What's your name?" asked Rowan.

"I am Nalu, son of Kabawa."

Rowan held out his hand. Nalu considered it. "None of us mean you any harm," he continued, regarding Nalu's stare.

"Your words have the weight of truth," Nalu said at last, taking firm hold of Rowan's wrist. "And I can sense you do hold reverence for Panthora." Rowan watched Nalu's previously serious expression transform into a toothy grin. "I shall be glad to call you friend." He motioned for the other Celetors standing by their sleeping captives to cut their rough bindings.

"They seem to respect and trust you. Are you their leader?"

There was a twinkle in Nalu's eye. "You may say so."

"You sound like a certain priest I know."

"I am not as wise or gifted enough to be a priest," Nalu stated flatly, not understanding Rowan's private joke.

"How long will the sleep poison last?"

"Not long," Nalu assured him. "We just wanted them to sleep long enough to get them to our village and question them there."

"Question them how? They can't speak your language like I can." Nalu simply stared at Rowan. Seeing he wasn't going to get an answer, he went for another question. "So they should be awake by morning?"

"If not sooner." Nalu's brown eyes shimmered in the starlight. "Where are you traveling?"

"To another set of ruins—even older than these. We thought these ruins were the ones we sought, but it seems this jungle is filled with them."

"Why are you going to these ruins?" Nalu's face wrinkled as he considered Rowan's answers. Rowan didn't know what—if anything—he should say in reply. Mindful of saying too much to someone he knew next to nothing about, he also was less defensive, since Nalu was a fellow human and Panian as well.

"We're looking to stop those elves who attacked you from doing the same to others." He was pleased with his reply. He hadn't lied, and he'd told him the basic meat of what this whole matter was really about.

"That is a worthy cause," said Nalu, "and I know those ruins well."

"You do? But this place must be filled with ruins—it *was* the heart of Gondad, after all."

"*This* is Gondad." Nalu gave the pavement he stood on a foot stomp. "All my people know of it, but there is only one ruin that is older than it, and I can take you to it."

"Panthora be praised!" Rowan exclaimed in delight. "It must be her will we crossed paths." The joy mingled with all the thin threads he was weaving in his mind. Being called out on the journey to begin with, the dream, the encounter, and now this. Truly Panthora was showing him incredible kindness and helping him more than he knew. Which could only mean she was making sure he got to the ruins before the elves did. It was clear he and his mission were highly favored.

"So it would seem. And perhaps it's her will that you look to deliver us from these troublesome people."

"It wouldn't surprise me if she'd have me help some humans along the way." Finally, everything was falling into place, thank Panthora. "Morning, you said, right?" Rowan gave the others another once-over. "I suppose we could get some rest and—"

"We leave now," said Nalu before giving out commands to the others.

"Wait." Rowan trailed behind him. "We'd do better to wait until daylight. In the dark—"

Nalu spun on his heel and faced the knight. "We have the stars to light our way, and we'll need to regroup with the others walking the wilderness."

"Others?" Rowan watched the rest of the Celetors begin picking up the elves.

"We keep watch around and outside the village," said Nalu, "in case more trouble seeks us out."

"Are you sure you're able to carry all of them?" The other Celetors erupted in laughter and slung the limp bodies over their shoulders.

"Come." Nalu made his way into the jungle. "Stay close, and you will do fine." Rowan quickened his pace, watching the night swallow Nalu whole.

CHAPTER 25

IT'S FAR BETTER TO ASSUME THE BEST THAN THE WORST;
YOU TEND TO GET WHAT YOU EXPECT.

—**Old Tralodroen proverb**

"You should have taken more sleep," Nalu said to Rowan in Abjula. They sat side by side observing the small fire. Both were sitting on the large stump of a tree the Celetors had felled a few days prior. Most of its trunk still rested a short distance from them, serving as a place to lay Cadrissa and the others. They still slumbered in what might have passed as restful sleep, none of them aware of the jungle or the Celetors around them.

Rowan had risen at dawn, the night trek to Nalu's camp not being as long as he'd feared. Having placed the others where they now rested, the twenty or so men took turns keeping watch. There was already some fresh meat on nearby spits when he woke, and the longer it cooked, the more his stomach growled.

"I want to be awake before they are," said Rowan. "They're bound to be a little confused, especially after how we parted ways last night."

"Parted ways?" Nalu tilted his head.

"It's a long story," he said. "I was sent here by my order and happened to cross their path after a bit of bad luck."

"Like you did with us?"

"You trying to tell me Panthora's guiding me more than I know?" He shared a smile with Nalu.

"No, I think you know that already."

"It's starting to look that way more and more. Having found Gondad was a great blessing. I'm humbled to have been allowed to see it."

"Why?" Confusion flashed across Nalu's brown eyes. "It rots like fruit cast from the tree."

"It's the birthplace of humanity—the origin city where all of us came from," Rowan stated with all the authority he'd gained from his training. "Didn't that priest who came to your tribe tell you anything about it?"

"Not like you. He said Gondad was of the past, but we are of the future." Nalu took note of Rowan's apprehension. "You do not agree?"

"Gondad is the *ideal*—the perfect example of humanity's greatest glory. It *is* our past, but it's our *future* too. And it would still be here—and be greater still—if it wasn't for the elves."

"Like them?" He pointed at Alara's and Gilban's prone forms.

"No, but close enough."

"I thought you said they were not dangerous."

"They aren't."

"But they're elves." Nalu continued the circular argument Rowan had started. In truth, he felt a bit dizzy himself trying to make sense of why he was still with them and how he was traveling with elves to stop some other elves. If it wasn't for Panthora leading and revealing herself to him he wouldn't be as confident doing what part of him felt was equal to turning away from all he knew was right and true.

"Rowan?" Nalu's questioning voice yanked the knight from his thoughts.

"These elves are different," he told Nalu. "Panthora wouldn't have led me to them if they were a hindrance to humanity."

"But you blame them for the ruined city?"

"I can't change history. The elves brought Gondad's glory to an end."

"And so you look to bring it back?"

"That's part of the knighthood's purpose." He let his focus fall on the fire. "We're to help humanity rise up and succeed with a glory Gondad was unable to achieve."

"How? It has long been taken by the jungle." Nalu did make a valid point. One he hadn't really given much thought to until just now.

"I'm just a knight. That's the sort of thing for priests to figure out." Looking to change the subject, he asked, "What about these hobgoblins? You said they raided your village?"

"Yes. We followed them to the ruins you're looking for but didn't go inside."

"Why not?"

"There were too many."

"*How* many?"

"We saw a great host—more than all our tribe. Against so many we could do little and so returned to the village. We now patrol the land between us. They will not get near the village again."

He didn't like this one bit. He wasn't expecting a tribe of hobgoblins, and he was pretty sure Gilban and Alara weren't either . . . though the seer seemed to have plenty of surprises up his sleeve.

"Were they all in the ruins?"

"Not all, some camped outside them."

"How long do you think they've been living there?"

"I do not know. We made our village over six moons ago and have only been attacked by them once."

"But they haven't attacked you until recently?" Rowan mused, trying to piece together a larger picture that was growing clearer and more encompassing the longer he spoke with Nalu.

"No."

"Strange." Rowan checked on the others again. Still asleep.

"It was the same with the elves," said Nalu.

"But you said you drove them back."

"We did, for they were few."

"How few?"

"No larger than our group here," said Nalu, motioning around the camp.

"I can't imagine they'd send so few for such an important mission," he mused.

"*Your* leaders sent only you," said Nalu.

"Well, that's different," said Rowan, straightening his spine. "I'm a Knight of Valkoria."

"You're still only one man."

"A Knight of Valkoria is better than ten strong men," he replied without even thinking. "You must have fought a scouting party."

For a moment Nalu seemed locked in some sort of contemplative stare. "All I know is once we fought the elves back they did not return," he said at last.

"So the elves are still out there somewhere . . . " And that was the troublesome issue in all this. Where *were* they? He was half expecting to run into them at almost any time, while his other half was casting down fears of them long having beaten them to the knowledge and already putting it into use. Eventually, one of the two scenarios would become reality. But which one . . . and when?

"At least we're close to the ruins. One silver lining is better than none," he said before their conversation was interrupted by some commotion from the fallen tree.

•●•

Alara's eyes opened on a slightly unsettling scene. It was no longer night, and she was in the midst of a rough camp—but it wasn't the camp she'd known in the ruins of Gondad. This one was in a small, open area in the middle of the jungle and occupied by a score of dark-skinned humans—Celetors. Each was barefoot, dressed in a simple breechcloth, and carrying a spear and dagger at their side.

Each of the Celetors was busy. Some tended a fire and a few spits rotating the bodies of a couple of large birds; others kept watch around the camp. The remaining took some sleep. In the midst of them all, seated on a large stump before another small fire, was Rowan. Another Celetor wearing a brightly colored feather necklace was with him.

"Rowan?" Alara only rose a few inches before the whole camp was alive with activity. As a group of Celetors hurried her way, she noticed Gilban and the others slumped against a fallen tree beside her. They were all asleep.

"It's okay," Rowan said, drawing near while she stood before a handful of curious Celetors. "You're safe."

"Where are we?"

"In another camp," he said, as the Celetors parted to allow him to pass.

"How did we get here?" She checked her belongings. She still had her falchion, and the rest of what she'd carried the night before was undisturbed.

"They carried you." Rowan's eyes looked over the others, adding, "They should be waking up soon. They just used a sleeping dart."

"Who did?"

"They did." Rowan indicated the Celetors. "It was a good thing I found you when I did."

"And why did they bring us here?" She watched the Celetor with the feather necklace come up beside Rowan.

"This is Nalu," said Rowan. "He's the leader of this patrol. I told him that we're looking for the ruins, and he offered to help take us there."

"He actually knows where they are?"

"Yes. Both he and some of the warriors of his tribe have seen them firsthand—and recently too."

"That's rather interesting." She kept her words measured, not wanting to voice the entirety of her skepticism just yet. She didn't like being so far out of the loop, nor that Rowan had decided to take the lead while they were unconscious. She hoped it didn't ruin what Gilban had already planned. More chaos. More free will.

"It's the favor of Panthora," said Rowan, smiling.

"Perhaps." Alara paused, mentally phrasing her next question carefully. "And you're sure they want to take us there?" She listened with some amazement as Rowan addressed Nalu in his native tongue, obviously relaying her question.

"Yes," Rowan replied. "Nalu's offer still stands."

"They *do* realize we don't have any means to pay them for their help." Again she waited for Rowan to translate.

"We share a common goal," Rowan replied.

"And what goal is that?" Alara considered the knight.

"The ruins have been nothing but trouble for them," he explained. "Any help we can give in lessening that threat, the better. They also want to see humanity blessed in the process."

"Wait." Revelation dawned on her. "They're Panians?"

"Yes." She noted the pride accompanying Rowan's answer. "The whole tribe holds to Panthora."

Alara shook her head. "What are the odds?" She felt Gilban chuckling to himself at all of this. Had he known this all from the start? From the vision in the sloop?

"What's going on?" Vinder's gruff bark brought all eyes to the rest of the mercenaries now stirring.

"It's all right," she informed them. "We're safe for now."

"And where are we exactly?" Vinder was on his feet, doing his best to assess the situation. "And what are *they* doing here?" He pointed out the Celetors keeping a careful distance.

"Rowan was just filling me in." She neared Gilban, helping him up. "I guess he's talked these Celetors into leading us to the ruins."

"Then it's a good thing he came with us after all," said Gilban.

"These are the same ones who attacked us, aren't they?" Dugan asked Rowan.

"They thought you were a threat, but I convinced them otherwise."

"And how'd you do that?" asked Vinder, not so much curious as leery.

"I found a common bond," he replied.

"Which is?"

"Panthora." It wasn't clear what Vinder thought of the answer.

"Why'd they bring us *here*?" Dugan went from Nalu to Rowan.

"To help you on your way." Nalu spoke in perfect Telboros.

"You can speak Telboros?" Rowan mirrored the others' surprise.

"The priest of Panthora did more than teach us the ways of our goddess," said Nalu.

Rowan considered the other Celetors. "So then all of you—"

"No, not all. But some, like me, have kept the tradition alive."

"Then why pretend you didn't understand us?" asked Cadrissa.

"To make sure he could trust us." Vinder didn't let his focus on Nalu waver.

"I've heard what I needed to from you by your own lips. Come." He directed them to the spits. "There's fresh food and water. Once you've eaten, we will leave for the ruins."

"Food and water sounds good to me." Cadrissa headed for the cook fires. "What sort of meat is it?"

"Parrot," said Nalu. "Very good for you."

While Alara had never had parrot before, it did smell fairly good and would be a welcome change from the survival mode they'd entered after the loss of their supplies. She shared her gratitude with Nalu. "Thank you for sharing what you have." She could only do so in Telboros but thought it would be sufficient. Nalu's shallow head bow made clear that it was.

"It sounds like there are some hobgoblins in the ruins too." As soon as Rowan conveyed the news, Alara's heart sank. There was never any talk about hobgoblins when they started making the plans back in Rexatoius. She wondered how many other surprises would cross their path before everything was said and done. Having yet another obstacle before them was something she didn't need, but it was good to know what else might get in their way.

"How many?" she asked.

"From what Nalu says, there could be a whole tribe."

"That's not something you want to run into," Dugan cautioned.

"No," Alara agreed, "which means we'll just have to be more careful going in."

"I think I might be able to help there," Cadrissa offered.

"How far away are the ruins?" Alara asked Nalu as they all came to stand around the roasted parrots.

"Not far. We will get there soon enough." He motioned for the others to take a seat on the flat ground. "For now we eat."

While they ate, Nalu and Rowan filled them in on everything. Alara had to admit, the more she heard of the previous night's events, the more she was impressed. Rowan had a lot of potential and showed himself rather quick on his feet. Hopefully this would become more common,

RETURN OF THE WIZARD KING

replacing his recent attitude and actions. As she listened, she kept an eye on Gilban. He'd secured a waterskin and was taking his fill. He looked well enough—as did the others. That was good. They all needed their health and wits.

If Nalu was right they could be facing the ruins in a matter of hours. But what then? A tribe of hobgoblins waiting for them, or worse? And then there was still the possibility of crossing paths with Elyelmic soldiers on the same mission. From what Rowan shared they might be weakened but still no less a threat. And then they still had to actually find the hidden knowledge. It had all sounded so simple before she and Gilban had left Rexatoius, but after seeing the scope and condition of Gondad, she was beginning to wonder if they'd end up combing every derelict building or rubble heap to find their prize.

Faith and patience. She heard Gilban's words in her mind. *Faith and patience.*

CHAPTER 26

WE'VE RISEN TO GREATER HEIGHTS THAN EVER THEY COULD
HAVE DREAMED. THAT'S WHY THE GODS FEAR US AND HAVE
STRICKEN US WITH THEIR CURSE. WE'VE SHOWN THEM—AND THE
WORLD—THE LIMITS OF THEIR MIGHT . . . WE CAN AND
SHALL BE GREATER. WE ARE DRANORS AND SHALL REIGN FOREVER!

—Marat, last king of the dranors

"You sure he knows where he's going?" Vinder watched Dugan hacking a path through the jungle.

"Yes." Rowan walked beside the dwarf. A few paces behind them, Alara swatted flies and mosquitoes while guiding Gilban through the twisted vines and roots that constantly threatened his balance. He was managing surprisingly well without his staff. Behind them was Cadrissa and then five Celetors at their rear.

"You know, they could be leading us into a trap." Vinder observed the Celetors from over his shoulder.

"Then they're sure taking their sweet time with it," Cadrissa grumbled. She hadn't been this miserable in all her life. The terrain was grinding heavily upon her. At this point, she was seriously considering turning around and putting this "adventure" behind her as quickly as possible. The sole, if small, consolation was she was closer now to the end than the beginning. Turning back now would actually take longer than seeing things through and heading back with whatever insight and fortune she'd amassed. It wasn't much in the way of motivation, but it worked.

"Nalu said we're almost there." Rowan stayed fixed on the path.

"I've heard *that* before," Vinder huffed.

"Just be patient," Alara counseled. "We'll get there soon enough."

"I'll be happy when this forest starts thinning out again," Dugan grumbled as the sweat ran in rivers from his temples.

"Nalu should be back soon," said Rowan. "Maybe he's found a better way ahead."

"Can you see anything?" Alara asked Dugan.

"Nothing but more trees and vines," he grunted, continuing his work. "Not even a game trail."

Alara wiped her brow with her sleeve. "Then I guess we can't do much else but wait for Nalu to return."

"*If* he comes back," Vinder muttered into his beard.

"The way is not much farther and is clear of all danger," said Nalu, suddenly appearing beside Dugan. One moment there was nothing, and the next, there he stood.

"How can you move through all this so easily?" he asked, amazed.

Nalu grinned. "It is not as easy as you might think."

"Well, you sure make it *look* easy."

"So how much farther we got now?" asked Vinder, swatting away some flies.

"We're almost there."

"Almost there." A sardonic smile accompanied the small nod. "Great."

"Patience," Alara admonished, helping Gilban over an unevenly cleared section of ground. "Just be patient." Gilban smiled at the comment.

Taking her advice, the others fell silent. Left with her thoughts, Cadrissa trudged through the jungle, following Nalu's lead and Dugan's sword strikes. A short while later, just as she was convinced there was no end to the choking greenery and sweltering heat, they came upon a large, hacked-out clearing. The sight was all the more unsettling when they saw burn marks everywhere. The scorched earth led toward a towering mass of pitted stones and mortar. It was a sign of concerted effort by a group of people—and a recent one. The clearing snaked around the half-crumbled outer walls, away from the deep forest, which was winning the war of dominance against the ancient city.

"Everyone, be on your guard." Alara kept her voice low. "Gilban?" She found the seer with his eyes closed, standing in focused concentration.

"It's still here." His voice was barely a whisper.

"Then we have no time to waste."

"Look." Vinder pointed at the ruins' skyline. Thin trails of smoke were rising from the interior.

Alara searched the horizon. "Well, we know they're still here."

"You didn't want it to be *too* easy, did you?" Dugan rolled his shoulders, apparently preparing for whatever came next.

"There's some powerful energy beyond the walls too," said Cadrissa. "It might be wise if we act as secretive as possible until we've assessed the whole situation."

"Agreed," said Alara. "Do you know of a way into the city that might not be guarded?" she asked Nalu.

He nodded. "I will take you to an area just behind the wall, but I will guide you no farther. Once I have taken you beyond, your lives are no longer in my hands."

"It will be enough." Gilban motioned for Alara's hand.

Together they slowly neared the city, Nalu scampering ahead, silently pointing to a large hole in the wall. The others followed, keeping constant vigil. Only Cadrissa took time to fully enjoy the view. To the untrained eye, it appeared as nothing more than a ruined wall, but to her it was a treasure trove of stories from long ago, when a different people lived on Tralodren—a people whose very commands brought forth miraculous wonders. A race who crafted a mighty empire with their willpower and magical might but were not, it seemed, immune to the power of Asorlok and time.

She couldn't believe she was finally entering a dranoric city! She wanted to stop and catalog it all, but time was against her. All she could do was stare at the old rock in earnest, occasionally running a hand along the pitted stones as she hurried behind the others. Oh, to have just an hour at her disposal . . .

Together they approached the hole, peering into an opening that burrowed through fifteen feet of rock and mortar. Immediately beyond was nothing more than fallen stone and the ruined shells of buildings. Beyond those, more solid-looking structures were visible.

To the north, Cadrissa saw two rows of four black obelisks rising from the jungle, each growing more complete until the fourth and final obelisks stretched a full twenty feet into the air. From where she stood, the ancient pillars could have easily been old burned tree trunks polished into a dull shine—out of place and intriguing. The east was littered with rough tents interspersed with rougher stone houses made out of salvaged debris. Small fires peppered the terrain with meat and other victuals roasting on low, smoky flames. The fires, though, were too far away to see who and how many tended them, but it was clear there were more than just a handful of people inhabiting the place.

"That's a lot of hobgoblins." Dugan stated the obvious.

"Just be as silent as you can. We need to get around the dwellings and into the center of the city," said Alara. "Gilban believes that's where we'll find the information."

"That's still a lot of hobgoblins." Cadrissa put on the best face she could even though she felt the blood draining from her cheeks and heart, pooling into her stomach.

"I must go, my friend." Nalu clasped Rowan's hand as the others decided on their next step.

"I understand," he replied. "You've helped us as best you could. Thank you, and may Panthora smile upon you."

"I will pray to Panthora to grant you success." Nalu waved goodbye. Rowan returned the gesture, watching him join the other Celetors.

"Ready?" Alara asked Rowan once he'd rejoined them.

"I was when I left Valkoria," he replied, ignoring Vinder's eye roll.

Moving as one, they stealthily glided past the decaying dwellings, all the while assessing the extent of their opposition.

"There must be well over three hundred there alone," Vinder said a hair above a whisper.

"Shut up!" Cadrissa hissed. "Do you want to get us killed?" The largest of the congregation was just a few yards from them.

But none of the hobgoblins appeared to hear them. They were too busy ravenously devouring their cooked meat. The mercenaries trekked farther inward, pausing only when a strange, eerie darkness—birthed out of thick, pitch-colored clouds centered on the heart of the ruins—fought for ownership of the afternoon sky. The black cumulus blanket fell fast upon them, absorbing all light. The strange phenomenon wasn't lost on either mercenary or hobgoblin—both taking in the development with growing unease.

"Those clouds aren't natural," Cadrissa whispered from behind Dugan. She could feel something behind their formation. Something that made her skin crawl.

"What's causing it?" Vinder observed the dark mass with growing concern.

"Nothing good, I'm sure," said Dugan. "But it can help mask us from the others."

"We should hurry." Cadrissa shivered. "I don't like any of this."

"Nor I," Gilban concurred.

They reached the interior of the complex using small puddles of light from the campfires and torches as guideposts. And as Dugan had said, the darkness not only helped cloak them from sight but provided a distraction for the hobgoblins, allowing them more freedom of movement.

Eventually, the group stood before two large buildings. One had been rebuilt with thick fortifications; the other was only partially completed. The two structures dominated the area like giants poised for a confrontation, overwhelming everything with their cold façades. A few hobgoblian guards—distracted by the growing darkness—patrolled the perimeter with leashed reptilian beasts that observed the area with sluggish glances.

"Basilisks," she whispered. The beasts' dog-like bodies were covered in thick, dark green scales, and their feet ended in deadly claws. "Don't let them bite you. Their saliva carries a toxin causing paralysis, leading to death. It's led to legends of them being able to turn people to stone."

"Pleasant thought," Vinder murmured.

"But they also have poor eyesight." She continued her short lesson. "So as long as we stay a fair distance from them, we should be fine."

"We're upwind too," Dugan added. "That should help. How well do they hear?"

"Fair enough, but their strongest sense is smell. They taste from the air."

"Then let's get moving while the wind's in our favor," Vinder advised.

Alara nodded. "Agreed."

"All right," said Dugan, "but which building? They're both well guarded."

Alara watched Gilban. Cadrissa did the same. "What we seek has no supernatural or magical properties—they're just scrolls and tomes of rare knowledge," Gilban whispered, "but they might be guarded by some powerful enchantments."

"Can you find where the magic is strongest?" Alara asked Cadrissa.

"I think so." She took in the whole scene carefully. Both structures were well repaired, except for a crumbled section of masonry on the southwest corner of the closest building. Double stone doors appeared to be the only entrance, and those had two rather mean and vigilant hobgoblins standing guard. The other building was a semipreserved structure with some of the original stained glass windows on the north and south sides remaining in place. It resembled some kind of temple. Frescoes and mosaics of long ago still clung to parts of the walls, while others littered the ground in crumbled shards. The temple also had a set of double doors. These, though, were unguarded.

Alara drew closer. "Is something wrong?"

"I can't tell which building has the strongest amount of magic in it." She shook her head. "It could be either one."

"Can you make a guess?" Alara pressed. "This darkness will make it impossible to see much of anything soon enough."

Something pulled at the back of her mind like cold claws, frosting her thoughts with their arctic touch. She forced herself to focus harder on the present—she couldn't afford any distractions.

"Cadrissa?"

"That one." She discovered she'd pointed out the building with the hole in the wall without thinking.

"Right. Now how are we going to take *them*?" Vinder studied the two guards. "There could be more inside. If we raise the alarm, we have a whole horde ready to come down on us."

"I have just the thing." Cadrissa dug out a handful of crushed quartz from a pouch at her side, thankful it still remained, unlike the rest of her possessions. She threw it at the others while chanting the ancient words she'd burned into memory.

"What are you doing?" Rowan fearfully watched himself and the others fade from sight.

"I've made us invisible." She threw another small handful of dust on herself and faded along with them.

"I can't see anyone!" Rowan's concern rose well above a whisper. "I can't even see myself!"

"Keep your voice down!" she cautioned. "It makes us invisible, not noiseless! Just as the spell makes us invisible to the hobgoblins, it also makes us invisible to each other."

"But how will we be able to follow each other if we can't see ourselves?" asked Alara. "We could get separated and not even know it."

"Don't worry. I have a spell to solve that too. Golrin hectin pressa." Instantly, they could see their hands, limbs, and each other once more— though all were translucent, like ghosts.

"How long will we be invisible?" Vinder inspected his hands, waving them madly in front of his face as if the action would return their opacity.

"Not long—only a few hours—but it should give us enough time to locate the information and hopefully get out of here."

"Then we need to be quick," said Dugan.

"And thorough," Alara added. "It'd be easier if we just slip into the building through that hole in the corner." She indicated the broken southwest corner of the building. "Vinder, you cover our backs. Dugan and Rowan will lead us in, and the rest will follow in the middle."

Cadrissa watched Dugan and Rowan slowly approach the hole. Upon closer view, she could see it had been caused by faulty masonry. Fresh stone was stacked near the damaged wall, which she assumed meant the hobgoblins were still at work on it. Thankfully, not today. Dugan waved the others forward as he and Rowan snuck inside.

Once inside the building's walls, the air turned stifling. Most of the heat from the jungle followed them in, making it feel as if they were climbing into the carcass of a freshly slaughtered beast. The light from outside was nearly gone, creating illumination equal to a starless night.

This hindered any chance of looking through the area in much detail. The interior was fairly large and blissfully empty. The only change to the bleak stone walls was a door made of new wood, located at the north end of the room.

"I'll check it out." Rowan crept close and put his ear against the wood. "I'm going to open it a crack. Everyone, be ready." The hinges were well oiled and didn't squeak as he peeked through the sliver he allowed between door and frame. "It looks like a hallway. There's some light from a few sconces, and it branches into two directions a few feet in."

"Well?" Alara asked Gilban.

"Saredhel's insight ebbs," said the priest. "This is where each of you must rise to your own strengths." He pointed to Cadrissa, who still found the pinpoint accuracy of the action eerie. "Ask Cadrissa. She knows far more right now than me."

Not enjoying all the questioning stares, she closed her eyes. The excitement of all the potential knowledge surrounding them nearly overwhelmed her. She needed to be sure and firmly set on what they were looking for. Focusing her will on a spell of detection, she saw two paths . . . Yes . . . One was more dangerous . . . Which one, though? It wasn't clear. Something was blocking her attempts to read more. But she had to choose quickly. From what she'd already seen, she wouldn't be surprised if the hobgoblins had a patrol set up in the building. And if they had basilisks outside, what might be inside?

"The path to the northwest looks the best, as far as safety is concerned." She opened her eyes. It was the best she could do. Hopefully it'd be enough.

CHAPTER 27

WHATEVER YOU YIELD TO WILL SOON ENOUGH MAKE YOU ITS SLAVE.
BUT IF YOU MUST BOW DO SO ONLY LONG ENOUGH TO PLOT YOUR REVOLT,
LEST YOU LEARN TO LIKE SHACKLES MORE THAN A CROWN.

—The Manual of Might

"**B**ut what do we do?" Ranak asked the other subchieftains gathered around Boaz's throne, their troubled features racked with concern. "We can't afford to wait much longer."

"I meant what I told him," said Boaz. "We're done paying tribute. When the Celetors are gone, it will be a perfect opportunity to show him his time here is over."

"But he isn't going to leave." Kaden stressed what no one else would openly admit. "We're in the same place we were before. Unless we deal with the column."

"Maybe worse than before," Morro added. "That is, if it's true—what I've been hearing of Valan growing more unhinged."

"So we bought some time and have nothing to show for it." Ranak's gloomy assessment wasn't acknowledged but wasn't disputed either.

"Why not send the whole chamber crashing in on him?" asked Nalis. "Be done with all of it?"

"How would we do that without giving him warning?" asked Kaden. "We'd have to weaken the floor, and with pick and shovel pounding we'd be sure to give ourselves away."

"Then it's back to destroying the column," Elek said with a sigh.

"It's better than trying to shove Valan in it"—Kaden shot Nalis a knowing look—"though we'd still have to face off with him."

"Not unless we coaxed him away from it." Nalis' face shone a bit brighter with the idea.

"With what?" Kaden's skepticism brought them back to reality. "And if he's really close to madness, our ruse might cause more harm than good."

"Poison," Ranak blurted out.

"I don't even know if he eats," said Morro. "And even if he did, how would we get it to him? And even then, would it kill him?"

"Hadek." When they heard Kaden's suggestion, the countenances of the others darkened. "He could get close enough to pass it on. And Valan trusts him."

"But do *we*?" Boaz's question silenced the room.

A moment later a hobgoblin burst through the doors. "Valan's gone mad!" the warrior shouted between heaving gulps of breath. "He's taking any hobgoblin he can find and putting them into the column!"

"*What?*" Boaz bellowed.

"When did this happen?" asked Kaden.

"A short while ago." The warrior tried speaking as clearly as possible through his desperate pants. "I killed those who tried to take me . . . and some others . . . but we don't know how to stand against the wizard."

"He's using *hobgoblins* to capture more test subjects?" Elek's voice was a mixture of shock and rage.

"Damn him and his column to the Abyss!" Boaz slammed his fist on the throne's armrest. "Each of you take some loyal men and secure the ruins." Leaping from his seat, he added, "If you find anyone trying to take captives, kill them."

"But what about Valan?" asked Ranak.

"He's mine," Boaz growled through gritted teeth.

"How?" asked Nalis. "As long as he's protected from our attacks—"

"I'm done cowering." Boaz drew his sword and gave it a practice swing. "I do this for the tribe's honor as well as my own."

"Let us come with you," Kaden begged. "If we have more swords, we might be able—"

"You have your orders. Now follow them." Boaz ran out of the room. Those who remained waited only long enough to claim a section they'd take over before following Boaz's commands, each mindful this might be the last day they drew breath.

•●•

Hadek's chest felt like it was being shred from the inside out as he raced through the hallway leading up to the hidden door of Valan's chamber. The door was no longer guarded, and there were signs of struggle and fights, along with a few dead bodies, peppering the area. He was sure the bloody scene would be repeated over the rest of the ruins soon enough. Valan had finally snapped, and it was time to run while he still had the chance.

After killing the last Celetor, the mage had fallen into a deeper pit of desperation about mastering the column. That desperation quickly turned into overwhelming madness as Valan began coercing any hobgoblin he came across to take on their fellow tribesmen in order to save themselves from being tossed in the Transducer. Hadek didn't know how wide Valan's actions had spread, but the mage had thus far stirred the beginnings of a very large skirmish between those doing the capturing and those attempting to liberate their fellow tribesmen.

Now was the time to run if ever there was one. Valan could turn on him at any moment. The tribe all hated him and wanted to see him dead. And then there was Boaz . . . No sooner had the thought arose than Boaz himself appeared at the end of the hall, charging straight toward him. Hadek nearly swallowed his tongue in amazed fright as the red-skinned hobgoblin closed the gap between them at a bewildering rate, sword drawn and a frenzied snarl on his face. Hadek didn't know what to do other than drop to his knees and cower.

"Mercy," he cried, letting his head fall into his lap.

Over the blood pounding in his ears he heard Boaz rush up to and then away from him.

Carefully raising his head revealed the chieftain hadn't even given him another thought, setting his sights instead on the secret door from which he'd come.

Not sure what was going on but not wishing to waste any time either, the goblin leapt up and continued his dash from the ruined temple. He might still have enough time to gather his meager belongings and take some provisions for his escape. And whatever he was going to do he needed to be quick about it. Once Boaz and Valan clashed, things would rapidly go from bad to worse.

As he scrambled out from the temple, Hadek stopped, noting the darkening sky. It should have still been daylight, but instead a thick darkness was rolling in. At first he thought it might be a thunderstorm, but the more he studied it, the more he realized something wasn't right. The darkness seemed to move almost by will—as if alive.

"This one too." He snapped his head to and fro, searching out the source of the strange voice he knew he'd just heard. He was still alone, yet he knew the voice had been as real as if it'd been spoken from right beside him. It was a strange voice too: not fully feminine but not entirely masculine either.

What was going on?

He drew a sharp breath upon spotting an unsettling sight in the thickening darkness. He thought he saw a collection of large tentacles swarming about the spreading pitch. Tentacles with snapping mouths at their ends. He blinked and the image was dark, rolling clouds once again. Yes, it was definitely time to go. Immediately, he renewed his run with more drive than before.

•●•

The chamber below the ruined temple had become little more than a refuse dump after Valan had started shoving as many hobgoblins as he could into the Transducer. Heaps and puddles of smoldering flesh dotted the floor around the column. Some of the blobs moved with sickening, twitching motions; others still had their former hobgoblian visage, but little else. Contorted and charred faces stared emptily into the swirling air, eyes reflecting the abject pain and horror they'd endured before entering Asorlok's gates.

Amid the carnage Valan danced with a wicked glee, his eyes bulging with the madness that had finally consumed him. His floating globe of light was always close at hand, helping guide his steps. He commanded two hobgoblins to shove another of their protesting tribesmen into the column's base. They did so without hesitation, knowing full well they'd take his place should they refuse. Once the victim was inside Valan gave the column a hard stare, thrusting an accusing finger forward and saying, "I'll master you yet. Do you hear me?"

The two hobgoblins exchanged a glance but did nothing more than take a few steps back while Valan began casting the spell. But before he could get more than a single word out the chamber was filled with the sound of a heavy thud followed by thunderous footsteps galloping down the stairs.

"*Valan!*" Boaz shouted.

Valan ignored the enraged chieftain, returning to the familiar incantation. He'd pulled his necklace out shortly after he'd used up the last Celetor. It was a preparation as well as a reminder that nothing could stop him from mastering the Transducer—especially that bellowing bull of a chieftain. The two hobgoblins didn't share the mage's boldness. Instead, they ran for their lives, disappearing up the stairwell as their chieftain passed them. No matter. He'd have more soon enough.

"Thoth ron heen ackleen. Lore ulter-bak ulter-bak . . ."

Boaz leapt from the steps. Valan continued ignoring him. His chant raised the magical energy in the room to a crackling charge as purple light emanated from the runes on the ancient column, filling the room with a fearsome brilliance. Boaz had barely landed at the base of the stairs when he lowered his head and set his horns for a charge. Valan continued as the familiar, deafening hum began gaining volume.

In the midst of the mayhem, a bolt of charcoal-gray energy hit Valan like a spear. He could clearly see during the flash it struck somewhere on his chest. But he didn't have time for any further investigation; the following moment Boaz was upon him. As waves of fiery agony burst up and over his body, it dawned on him Boaz had run Valan through with one of his horns. The attack had pierced his midsection, forcing his intestines out the other side.

"How?" he grunted as blood ran from the corner of his mouth. He knew this was a fatal wound. But how could it have been dealt in the first place? What had gone wrong with the necklace? Then he knew. The charcoal-gray bolt. It must have been a counterspell. But who was the caster?

"No!" An insane fire burned in Valan's mind and body. "I won't be beaten. Not now!"

Boaz shook his head. The horn cut deeper into the wizard's flesh. As he sank lower on the white bone, more of his innards spilled from the growing hole in his gut. Once Valan had slid the horn's full length, Boaz took hold of the wizard and violently pulled him off, throwing him on the floor.

"I'll cut you to ribbons and then feed you to the dogs!" Boaz raised his sword with a sadistic grin as Valan's eyes began glowing a bright silver.

Boaz stopped in his tracks when his bloodied horn burst into silver fire. Wherever Valan's blood had been spilled there erupted more wicked flames. These miniature blazes wouldn't go out, no matter how much Boaz pounded on his horn, head, shoulder, and chest. Enraged and screaming from the searing agony, he dropped and began frantically rolling around the floor. But it did nothing except spread the flames farther over his body.

Through the anguish, he cursed Valan and his magic, even cursed the gods: light, gray, and dark. He even cursed the very ground over which he rolled. Valan laughed at the sight, all the while trying to keep more of himself from spilling out. Boaz could only respond with a futile grunt as the last of his breath escaped through charred lips.

Valan groaned as he pushed himself up from the ground. Gathering as much of his intestines as he could, he shuffled toward the fence and column, the globe of light following. A simple motion opened the gate and a weary gesture dissipated the magical barrier at the column's base.

"Get out!" he ordered the trembling hobgoblin inside. The hobgoblin was still alive and shaken by the whole ordeal, but not a fool. He dashed from the spot, climbing the stairs with all his might.

Valan dropped to his knees and crawled into the column, leaving a trail of blood in his wake. The trail, like the rest of his blood, had been extinguished into cooling scarlet pools and splatters. The globe he left outside. It wouldn't do mixing magic in the vicinity. Once inside, he struggled into a seated position and brought the words of the spell to his pale lips. He closed his eyes and pushed through the pain. He had to focus. Focus.

"Thoth ron heen ackleen. Lore ulter-bak ulter-bak . . ."

He felt the magical barrier descend over the column's opening. The purple light of the column—which clawed right through his eyelids—overwhelmed him. The pulsating hum that followed soaked into him, shaking his bones en route to the very core of his being. Though his wound and the effects of the column distracted him, he fought hard in keeping his mind on the spell. This was his only—his last—chance.

Brilliant light blinded him and smashed into his head, twisting and tormenting his brain as fire and lightning coursed through his veins. Unbearable, unimaginable pain erupted from every pore. So great was the torment, he found the world fading into darkness. As he slipped into unconsciousness, the words of the spell faded and fumbled from his lips . . .

After a stretch of silent darkness had passed, his eyelids opened. There was no purple light and no droning hum. All was quiet and still. He was alive.

His hand went first for the wound. It was gone. Only the torn fabric of his robe spoke of its previous existence. The Transducer had healed him! He could see as well—that was good, as it meant he still had his eyes. He hoped they were where they should be and not scattered somewhere else about his head.

Taking in his hands, he saw he still had two of them, each possessing four fingers and a thumb, which he used in searching his face. He still had a nose and was in possession of his normal features. The pointed ears were new, but welcome. The dranors were said to possess them and he took them as a good sign.

Standing, he discovered he was taller than before—probably about half a foot if he had to guess. But everything else felt the same. No horns, no more pain, a bit taller. A promising start. His mind seemed clearer as well. More importantly, he was rid of Boaz. He couldn't have wished for a better outcome.

Another gesture dissolved the magical barrier around the column. He walked into the cooler area outside it. Like some loyal hound, the globe of light returned to its familiar position off the side of his head. By its aid he considered the scattered hobgoblian remains with fresher, saner eyes. There would be more coming soon. Word would spread of Boaz charging to face him, and when their chieftain didn't return, they'd come investigating . . . and in larger numbers. He needed to be ready.

And then he noticed how under the globe's light his hands had more of a yellowish cast. Another gesture summoned a swirling white oval of light. Dragging a finger across it made it mirror-like. With its aid, he took a good hard look at the image staring back at him with a growing scowl. He'd hoped he'd been able to ascend to the ranks of the dranors—his goal from the start. But it wasn't the reflection of a dranor staring back at him. His brown eyes now rested under a slightly protruding brow. And his skin clearly possessed a yellowish cast—almost the same shade as a ripe pear. Then there were the pointed ears and his black hair. A snarl revealed his sharp and more pronounced canine teeth.

In a fit of rage, he thrust his fist into the white light. It shattered like glass, sending shards of dimming illumination cascading to the floor.

• ● •

"He didn't die." Sargis raised his face from the scrying skull. "Was that because your spell was too weak?"

"The spell worked fine," Cadrith replied, referring to what he'd cast through the scrying skull just a moment ago. The charcoal-gray bolt had found Valan easily. "It removed his protection."

"But he didn't die," Sargis repeated. "I thought you wanted him dead."

"He'll be dead soon enough." Cadrith pulled a nearby chest closer to his side, always keeping his focus on the skull. His staff never left his possession. Valan's recovery, while annoying, wouldn't amount to much.

Not when the final pieces were falling into place. "This way he can suffer being changed into a hybrid of the very thing he despises."

"And you're certain these others are up to the task?" Sargis observed him. Cadrith took some delight in knowing how hard it was for the greater demon to discern his thoughts from his fleshless face. He knew Sargis was suspecting treachery. It was the way of life in the Abyss—a core aspect of every fiend and abysmal incarnate—but he had to string Sargis along a little longer.

"If I didn't, I wouldn't have summoned you." He continued playing the long-suffering man of integrity. He'd done it for so long it was almost second nature. "Actually, this can work in our favor far better than I first thought. With the chieftain slain there's now disarray, and with the others en route they should be able to finish Valan off—or at the very least wound him enough to allow the portal's creation."

"I'm not going to leave your side until it's finished." While it wasn't said as such, it was clearly a threat.

"Afraid I'd leave without you?"

"The thought had crossed my mind," Sargis coolly replied.

Cadrith sought a small pouch at his side. "If I have to tip the scales in our favor I'll need to act quickly." He sprinkled some dust he'd pinched from the pouch over the chest he'd lugged beside him, muttering a spell. The chest took on a faint violet illumination, then began shrinking. In short order it'd gone from half the size of a man to about a hand's width. Stooping to pick up the much smaller chest, the lich opened another pouch at his waist and stuffed it inside. "That means you'll have to trust me until everything is resolved."

"A world and a body," Sargis said, watching the scrying skull once more. "You promised me both."

"And you shall have them," he replied. "The magic in the portal will restore you. But we have to get through the portal first. Just remember, she'll cast the spell on the Transducer and then—"

"Why can't *you* cast it again?" Sargis popped his head up with a smirk in his voice, if not on his lips.

"That wasn't part of the plan." Cadrith knew full well the demon was having some sport with him again. But he wasn't going to give him any satisfaction.

"Because you've grown so weak?" Sargis continued. "Is that why that other mage still lives?"

"I can always make it so the portal only works for me. And I'd be more than happy to do so, too." That was a lie, of course, but he still said it with enough conviction even he was tempted to believe it.

"I wouldn't want you to change your plans on my account," said Sargis. "Just know that I'll be watching you—closer than ever before."

"Just be ready." Cadrith continued staring into the scrying skull.

CHAPTER 28

KNOWLEDGE IS A WEAPON. KNOWLEDGE IS A TOOL.
YET EVEN SO IT GOES TO WASTE IN THE HAND OF ANY FOOL.

—Old Tralodroen proverb

C adrissa kept to the middle of the group as they made their way through the murky hall. Dotted here and there were rough-hewn clay oil lamps forced into crevices and various nooks. A handful of anemic flames flickered among them, doing little to lift the hovering unease. Scattered debris marked a simple trail down the more solid areas of the floor, with a small collection of goblian graffiti appearing every so often. Here and there she also noticed clumps of dog and what was most likely basilisk scat. Some of these mounds were almost petrified, others more recently deposited.

As they moved on, they entered a ruined hallway littered with fallen masonry. Silently making their way around the debris brought them toward a set of stairs in the wall to their right. These they climbed with an abundance of caution—Gilban especially, who surprisingly kept up the pace without difficulty. At the top they found a hallway marred with gaping holes. The walls had been repaired, but only in part. And then they heard the barking echoing from another hallway on their left.

Everyone froze until Alara signaled they move on. As one they fled the landing, dashing into the damaged hallway. Through the holes, she could see the littered floor they'd just walked over moments ago. It remained empty—a good omen. Uneasily, they made it through the rest of the corridor until it connected with a solid wall.

"Where do we go now?" asked Alara. The barking had grown fainter but was still close enough to be worrisome.

"There was a smaller hallway I saw as we walked into this one, branching to the south," said Rowan. "It looks like the only way—"

"It *looks* like the only way"—Vinder grinned—"but I've found another."

"What do you mean?" Cadrissa didn't follow.

"Look here. This stone doesn't fit right, and when I push it . . ." Vinder pushed on the section of wall, demonstrating his point. As he did, an entire panel gave way, sliding aside to allow an opening to appear. "We have another way."

Dugan was impressed. "How did you find *that?*"

"I saw the different patterns in the rock." He shrugged his shoulders. "It's easy to see if you have the eye for it."

"Cadrissa?" Alara watched her, obviously eager for some more insight.

She closed her eyes again, focusing her will and tapping deeper into the spell. "I don't know. I can't discern anything about it."

"It's as safe as it is going to be!" Vinder pushed ahead of the others. "Standing around isn't going to accomplish much, and I bet those dogs can sniff out anything."

As if to emphasize his point, the barking grew louder, forcing them into the passage. Dugan protected their rear until they all passed through before moving into the hidden passage himself. The narrow walls forced them to snake in single file. They continued like that until they arrived at a massive crater in the floor. Here the hallway curved east. She surmised they were right where the building's corner had crumbled into the hole they'd seen from the outside.

"How do we get across?" Rowan peered into the hole. The chasm would definitely hinder their progress, if it didn't stop them completely.

"There." Dugan pointed out a shadowy ridge of rock hugging the wall like dried flesh clinging to aged bone.

"Oh no!" Cadrissa's eyes grew wide. "You've already got me crawling around this tunnel like a rat. I don't want to die like one."

"We don't have time for this." Alara was curt.

"I'm not going across that," she repeated.

"Oh yes, you are." Dugan picked her up over his shoulder and proceeded to carry her toward the ridge like a sack of wheat. She kicked and slapped his chest in protest, but he wouldn't relent.

"Do you want the whole city to know we're here?" He grunted under her weight. "And the less you struggle, the better my grip."

Instantly, she grasped the logic and limply complied. After she relaxed, Dugan skimmed over the ridge. Once across, he set her down carefully on the other side. No longer in a panic, she gave the gladiator a hard stare. Dugan couldn't suppress a grin. Cadrissa sheepishly discovered her own lips mimicking the expression as she watched the others join them. Gilban was the slowest of all, Alara leading him every inch of the way.

After they left the ridge, they came to a spot where the hallway ended again with a set of doors to the north. They were very old but still solid, carved with strange faces she couldn't easily place. While she might have enjoyed a closer study, they needed to keep moving. Dugan pushed his shoulder into one of the doors.

It didn't give.

He tried again.

"Stand back," he grunted. With muscles tensed, he ran straight into where the doors met, colliding in a thunderous echo of destruction. The point of impact exploded into splinters, chunks, and dust, while what remained of the doors flew open. After a fine cloud of dust settled, the interior came fully into view.

"I think they know we're here now." Vinder entered the room, coughing.

"All the more reason to hurry." Alara, with Gilban at her side, joined him. As they did, polished stone globes scattered across the walls began radiating a soft white light. The rest of the group followed.

"It's empty." Vinder busied himself trying to find anything of worth on the dusty floor or in the cobweb-filled corners. "What kind of a secret door leads to an empty room?"

"Maybe the elves got here first," said Rowan.

"No," said Gilban. "What we seek is still here."

"Well, I don't see anything." Vinder's aggravation was rising. "And now we brought down who knows *how* many hobgoblins on us."

"I wouldn't touch those," Cadrissa advised Dugan. He was about to tap one of the glowing globes with his sword. Each was cradled between a pair of brass wings affixed about eight feet from the ground. "They might be a bit unstable after all these years." He instantly thought better of the idea even as she became more fascinated with them. "Still, it's an amazing feat they've lasted this long. I could spend *days* studying them." She took a few steps toward the globe nearest the door.

"Well, I don't think we have an *hour*, let alone *days*." Vinder kept watching the doorway. The barking had stopped, but that didn't mean they were free from danger.

"He's right," Alara added. "If this isn't the place—"

"If this is where we were led," Gilban interrupted, "then this is where we should be."

"But there's nothing here," said Dugan, walking the large room with measured steps.

"Could there be another secret door?" Alara asked Vinder.

"Worth a look, I guess." He started searching the nearest wall. He didn't get far before Cadrissa spoke a word that sent a crackling arc of violet lightning from the globe she was standing under to the one on its immediate right. This in turn sent the lightning on to the next globe and so on, until it returned to the same globe from which it started. This was all done in a matter of heartbeats, the lightning racing through the globes and the room they encircled before anyone could react.

"What in Drued's name—" Vinder stopped dead in his tracks. "You trying to bring the ceiling down on us?"

"Cadrissa?" Alara was slightly more tactful but no less concerned.

"It's all right." She couldn't keep the excitement from her voice. "I figured out what they did."

"Who did?" Dugan was just as lost as the rest.

"The dranors," she happily replied. "I had a couple theories, actually. I guess I just got lucky on my first try. They used the globes as axis points in a spatial distortion."

"What?" Rowan cocked his head.

She composed herself, clearly needing a calmer mind and voice to explain. "They used the globes to hide what was in the room."

"Hide it where?" Vinder gave the area another look.

"Right in front of us."

"There's nothing here." Dugan made a sweeping gesture with his hand across the open floor.

"That's because of the spatial distortion. It's here, just not *exactly* here." Seeing she wasn't making any headway, she figured it was just as well to show them. "All I have to do is alter it just a tiny bit—"

"You really think you should be messing with all these things?" Vinder eyed her with a generous mix of suspicion and worry. "You already said they might be unstable."

"That was if you didn't know what you were doing," she replied. "But now I do."

"You do?" Vinder wasn't convinced.

"It'll be okay," she reassured him and the others. "The dranors were the ones who first used magic. It's just a matter of being able to match what they did to reverse the spell."

"And you can do that?" Alara was cautiously optimistic.

"That's what I was testing. If I couldn't, it wouldn't have arced like it did."

"All right." Alara nodded. "What do we need to do?"

"If you can clear out of the main area and stand behind me, that should be it."

"What's the worst that can happen?" Rowan joined the others migrating her way.

"Nothing. That's the worst."

"And the best?" Rowan cautiously inquired.

"We'll find out soon enough." Once all were safely behind her, Cadrissa focused her will, reached into her inner well, from which all mages cast their magic, and began working her spell.

"Masra morabi dalia. Haloth ra-rin kalora . . ." As she spoke, the polished stone globes became a mixture of swirling violet and white. An eyeblink later a beam of bronze light shot out of each globe, one to the other. With the link, the beams grew fatter and flatter, eventually forming a solid wall of bronze light from floor to ceiling. Next came a sudden alteration in the air that made everyone's ears pop. This was followed by a flash of bronze light, which returned the globes to their former glowing white state. But even though they'd returned to normal, the room was now quite different.

"Drued's sweet beard!"

"Where did all *this* come from?" Rowan, like everyone else, was awestruck by a room filled with open iron chests glimmering with copper, silver, and gold coins. Nestled amid these ancient coins were gems of all sizes and shapes; amethysts, moss agates, black opals, and rubies were but a few immediately visible. Dominating the rest of the room—these on the wall to their right—were nine lifelike, jewel-encrusted golden statues. These statues possessed faces similar to those found on the door Dugan had burst open, but of higher quality and with curled strands of beard fashioned of pure onyx.

Rowan dared a small step forward. "So where was all this before?"

"It was here, just not *exactly* here." Cadrissa attempted another explanation. "It's a bit complicated but if you're familiar with—"

"That gold real?" Vinder's eye had locked on a nearby chest.

"Yes."

"That's all I need to know." He hurried for it like a drunk to the bottle.

"So then the elves wouldn't have found this even if they tried," Rowan mused aloud, clearly pleased.

"Not unless they had a wizard with them," said Cadrissa.

"Are those dranors?" Dugan asked, making for the nearest of the statues.

"I think so," she said. Two short swords, a broadsword, and a shield lay next to the statue's base, along with a few small sacks of either gems or perhaps more coins.

"Consider yourselves paid," Alara informed the others. "Take what you wish, as long as you can carry it without slowing yourself down. But be quick about it."

"Aren't you going to take anything for yourselves?" asked Dugan.

"Just the information," said Gilban. "That's all we seek."

"But you lost everything in the marshes," he continued.

"Not everything," replied the priest in his usual cryptic manner. Not interested in any further back-and-forth, Dugan fixed his focus on the treasure. But Cadrissa was still taking everything in while watching Alara and Gilban out of the corner of her eye.

"So where is it?" Alara asked Gilban.

"*There.*" His blind eyes found a small, dust-covered chest none had noticed before. It was made of simple oak and absent any visible lock. Between one and two feet in length—half that in width and height—it appeared fairly humble, tucked in a corner next to so many other interesting treasures. Indeed, amid such grandeur, Cadrissa thought it was practically invisible. And apparently its mundane appearance had turned away the others' interest. Rowan now busied himself with the collection of weapons at the statue's feet, Dugan joining him.

"Isn't this like grave robbery?" she heard Rowan inquire.

"I don't see any graves." Dugan was matter of fact.

A round medium-sized shield caught Rowan's eye. It was decorated with a golden two-headed draconic wreath upon its black background. Bronze flames blasted out of the facing mouths, helping the continuous serpentine neck complete the circle.

She observed Dugan pick up two short swords resting near Rowan's shield. One was crafted with an emerald skull on the pommel. The other had a black opal set in the center of a cross hilt. He slashed the air, getting a feel for their weight, seemingly impressed with their balance and excellent craftsmanship. She also watched him scoop up a pouch of gems and tie it on his belt before continuing his exploration.

"Careful now." Gilban's words brought her back to Alara and the seer. Alara had reached the chest and was cautiously lifting its lid. Cadrissa held her breath. She had just enough of a vantage point to see three tightly rolled scrolls and two leather-bound tomes no larger than her hand and no thicker than two fingers resting inside the ancient wooden box.

Alara gently retrieved one of the tomes and opened it to a random page. "This is it, Gilban!" she exclaimed.

"Then things go well, indeed." A thin smile traced his lips.

Creeping closer, Cadrissa tried reading what was written but was too far away. She almost hurried over but stopped herself from intruding. As impressive as they may have been, they weren't for her. But anything else in this room was. And she only had so much time for searching. It was time she got to it.

Alara carefully packed the book back in the chest, closed the lid, and placed it into Gilban's waiting arms. "After all the trouble they took to hide everything else, I thought they would have hidden it better than this."

"Sometimes the most effective hiding spot is in plain sight." He held the box against his chest. "It's finished then. The Elyellium shall never rebuild their empire. Peace shall be preserved."

Cadrissa let everything else fade into the background while she searched. There was no shortage of things catching her interest, but there were also practical concerns, such as paying for more instruction at the academy. And for that the small mound of gems spilling out of a nearby half-ruined pouch caught her eye. When she retrieved it, a golden disk-shaped pendant attached to a thin gold chain spilled out with some stray gems.

The pendant was covered with strange carvings and symbols. And if what she'd learned in her schooling was correct the item could very well be enchanted. To what degree and with what abilities—if any—she wasn't certain, but it was a curiosity nonetheless. And it would certainly warrant further study. She quietly placed it into one of the secret compartments concealed in the folds of her robes and pocketed what she could of the gems in another.

"Let's go!" Alara's order roused them from their scavenging.

"It's a shame we have to leave them here." Vinder contemplated one of the statues. More than his fair share of the coins and gems were already bulging in his pockets, but his face clearly longed for a way to take the great statue back as well.

"How would you carry it out of here, let alone through the jungle?" Rowan placed his new shield over his left arm, testing its weight.

"I know." Vinder sighed in resignation. "Still, what a waste."

"We have to hurry," Alara continued. "We've already spent too much time as it is."

Cadrissa knew she was right, but this wasn't the only place she'd felt the presence of strong magic, was it? And who knew when—if ever—she'd be so close to something like it again?

"We need to go back to that other building," she informed them.

"Why?" Dugan sheathed his two new weapons behind his sword belt. "We got what we came for."

"I sensed a strong source of magic there; it might be important."

Vinder's eye narrowed. "To *us* or to *you*?"

"We should make sure we don't leave anything behind that could be salvaged." Rowan stepped in before she could reply. "It's what the knighthood would want."

All eyes fell on Alara, who in turn sought Gilban. But the seer said nothing, keeping the chest tightly under his right arm.

Alara sighed. "How much longer do we have with that spell?"

"There should be enough to get us there safely," said Cadrissa.

"*Should* or *will*?" Vinder crossed his arms. "I don't want to take any more risks than we have to—especially now when we're nearly out of this."

"Well, we're not gaining any more time standing around arguing about it." Rowan made his way for the door.

"Let's get out of here first and then we can look at what to do next if the spell still holds." Alara's decision wasn't what Cadrissa wanted to hear but did move them in the preferred direction.

CHAPTER 29

WHAT IS OFTEN OVERLOOKED TENDS TO BE
MORE IMPORTANT THAN ONE FIRST REALIZES.

—Old Sarellian saying

C adrissa watched Alara help Gilban through the secret door Vinder had discovered earlier. They'd been making good time with their backtracking. Their progress had slowed when they encountered the large hole again, but they made it through. She initially had some doubts with Gilban, especially after he insisted on keeping the chest in his possession. But he'd found his way safely across, chest under one arm and Alara helping guide him by the other. Rowan and Vinder had also managed well, but Cadrissa still wasn't too keen on the idea of walking such a narrow ledge. Thankfully, Dugan had helped her across, carrying her once more over his shoulders. And while the second time wasn't as nerve racking, she still kept her eyes closed for most of it.

While their temporary invisibility gave them a sense of freedom, they still remained intent on their surroundings. She hadn't heard any dogs since they left the cache and hadn't seen any other signs of life either. Even so, everyone remained focused—ears and eyes constantly alert for anything.

"Hey." Vinder stopped and stared at his hand. It was fading in and out like a flickering candle. "What's going on?" Cadrissa and the others observed a similar phenomenon.

"I guess we didn't have as long as I thought." She tried making it sound better than what it was: them becoming visible in the middle of a tribe of hobgoblins after raiding a cache of treasure. Even as she spoke she and the others fully returned to their normal state.

"We'll manage," said Alara. "From here on out, we rely on stealth and speed." It was then the loud barking rose from the end of the hallway.

"The dogs," Dugan grunted and drew his new blades.

"Hide!" Alara's whisper scattered them into whatever pockets of shadow they could find. No sooner had they done so than two large hobgoblins dressed in chain mail and carrying short swords turned the corner. Each had five vicious dogs with them—all leashed to wrought iron chains. Each of the chains was attached to a thick steel ring held tightly by the sentries' strong hands. The animals appeared to be a mixture of wild wolf and common hound. Their sleek brown and black bodies were covered in short hair, bristling around the muzzles and necks, their bared teeth shimmering a deathly white in the hall's limited illumination.

One of the hobgoblins said something in Goblin. His set of hounds were drawing dangerously near where Dugan was hiding. The hobgoblin peered closer into the darkness covering the Telborian. Cadrissa watched Dugan's body coil before he leapt from the shadows with a shout.

"Dugan—wait!" Alara exclaimed, revealing her own position.

The hobgoblins quickly recovered from their surprise, releasing the hounds from their master rings. Once loosed, they headed straight for the concealed intruders. The hobgoblin nearest Dugan charged him while his partner went after Alara.

The first hobgoblin swung at Dugan, who ducked and hit the other's arm with a return blow, causing him to lose his weapon. Spinning about, Dugan followed through with an arcing swing, slicing through a good portion of the hobgoblin's neck. The hobgoblin staggered back, gurgling something indecipherable before dropping. Before Dugan could react, three of the dogs were upon him.

The remaining hobgoblin grinned wickedly as he spied Alara. He gave his sword a couple of tight swings, trying to intimidate her. Alara stood her ground and studied his posture, searching for a weak spot.

She feigned a run to the left. The hobgoblin swung in anticipation and missed as she danced away to the right. The swing left the hobgoblin unbalanced and Alara took advantage of the situation, slicing through her opponent's neck. The hobgoblin collapsed, joining his partner in death.

With the hobgoblin dead, she readied herself for the two dogs that followed. The first one leapt, intent on marring the elf's face, but instead was greeted with a slash across the chest. The dog yipped in pain, retreating a few paces after landing, and leaving room for the second to pounce. Alara was faster on her feet, hacking the dog's head from its neck and then finishing off the other with a few focused strikes.

Cadrissa watched everything from where she'd hidden. She hoped for the best, but began thinking of ways she could better the outcome. She hadn't traveled so far and seen such wonders to die by a pack of dogs. Acting on self-preservation, she cast a brief spell upon herself. A soft white aura embraced her for a moment before fading from sight. As she kept watch she saw Gilban silently standing against a wall, apparently oblivious to the danger.

Vinder growled ferociously as he was set upon by two snarling dogs. Though the dwarf defended himself well, the faster beasts gnawed through his armor, drawing blood. This further angered him. His axe fell upon the first dog, lopping off its head with ease. On the upward stroke, the blade connected with the body of the second, cleaving it in half.

Meanwhile, the three dogs attacking Dugan ripped into his legs. He fought them off as best he could, driving back their snarling jaws as they leapt, eagerly snipping at his face. Through the chaos, he got his hands around two of the dogs' chain collars. He twisted them tight, doubling the chain and using all his strength to ram their heads together. The dogs collided with a wet thud and crack, before falling motionless to the ground.

The third dog made a leap for Dugan's throat, but he caught the beast's jaws before they got a grip. Grunting, he pushed back against the dog's hard press, getting a better hold on the animal. Once he had it, he broke its neck with a sudden jerk.

It was then Cadrissa noted Rowan was dealing with three dogs of his own. They nipped, snarled, and gouged his flesh wherever they could. His newly acquired shield blocked some of their attempts, but others still got through. Shouting in his native tongue, he unleashed a down stroke, then up, then down again, each time cleaving a dog's skull and brain.

In the short time since it began, the bloody din died away, leaving only the messy remnant of their work. Sloppy and cruel, it had been anything but quiet.

"Let's move." Alara led them forward, taking them up and around the corner. The twenty hobgoblins who greeted them stopped them in their tracks. Their leader shouted something in Goblin, urging the others on.

"Get behind me," said Cadrissa, working through the last parts of a spell in her mind. The others wasted no time complying. For a moment, as she closed her eyes and drew forth the energy from her well, there was a muffled clamor of voices, followed by silence. Oddly, she felt more powerful than usual, and the words to the spell slid from her lips with only the slightest effort.

"Darin lacara elkim! Soreen."

A hot blast of lightning shot off the tips of her fingers and into the hobgoblins. The deadly energy killed the first line and continued on toward the ones behind them. These convulsed in pain, dropping just like the others. In short order all had fallen, the lightning disappearing as rapidly as their lives.

Cadrissa leaned against the wall, steadying herself on weak legs and panting for breath amid the deafening silence. She knew she'd drawn deep into her well and would need time to recover if she was going to do anything quite as powerful again.

"That's one way to even the odds," said Vinder, impressed.

"But you didn't get them all." Dugan indicated a dark section of hallway from which the hobgoblins had emerged. A cowering bald goblin was slowly emerging from the shadows.

• ● •

Hadek had made some progress in his escape before he happened upon the band of hobgoblins, who'd detained him. They were taking him back to the throne room to await Khuthon knows what when they were sidetracked with the recent conflict. He'd no idea what was going on or why the dwarf, elves, and humans had come, and he didn't really care.

And while he could brave a run for it, the sight of the dead bodies around him gave him considerable pause. It was hard outrunning lightning. But he still might have a chance if he could just play the part right. Fate couldn't be tempted too much, he understood, but it sometimes could be helped along.

"Please spare me, mighty mistress." He fell on his knees, groveling in grating Telboros within sight of the wizardess.

"And who are you?" the dwarf demanded.

"My name's Hadek, and I mean you no harm." He crawled closer, putting all he'd learned about survival to use. "Please, don't hurt me."

The sandy-haired human in leather armor raised his sword. "He could be stalling for reinforcements."

"Hold, Rowan." The blind elf lifted a warding hand. "This one too has a fate intertwined with ours." Fate? Did he hear the elf correctly?

"You serious?" The larger blond human snorted. "Let's just kill him and move on."

The blind elf's face took on a serious cast. "He's a *help* to our cause, not a hindrance."

Again Hadek had to make sure he was hearing things correctly. *Him?* A help to these . . . whatever they were? And fated too, no less. What was going on? Why couldn't he just get out of here without running into all these distractions?

"All right." The elven woman eyed Hadek. "I'm in no mood to argue. Come over here." She motioned for him to join them. "If you can show us the quickest way out of here, we'll let you go free once we get out."

"With pleasure." He bowed politely before moving as close to the others as he thought appropriate. Not so close as to raise any discomfort but not so far away that they might think he was going to run at a moment's notice. Maybe things weren't going to be as difficult as he first thought.

"What about checking out that ruined temple?" Rowan's question caught the elven woman's attention.

"Ruined temple?" No. No. No. Keep moving. *Why* couldn't they keep moving?

"Yes," added the black-haired wizardess. "What do you know about it?" He could see where this was going and had to get out of it somehow. He wasn't going back there even if his life depended on it.

"It's too dangerous, Cadrissa," said the elven woman to the mage.

"Yes." He quickly nodded. "It's too dangerous."

"We've already had too many fights. We don't need any more." The elven woman started for Hadek. "We got what we came for, and I don't want to risk losing it on something even more dangerous."

"But there could be *more* hidden knowledge there," the mage pressed, stopping the elf in midstride. "It'd be foolish if we didn't check as long as we're here."

"Oh, there's nothing there you'd want to see," Hadek chimed in. "Just some old moldy books and—"

"Books?" He didn't like the way Cadrissa's eyes had widened. "What type of books?"

"Just moldy books—you wouldn't want them—so let me—"

"He *is* stalling for time." Rowan lunged forward, intent on running him through.

"No!" He jumped. "I-I, that is, you don't really want to go to the old temple."

"And why not?" The dwarf glared at him with more than a little dislike.

"Valan." Hadek lowered his head. He could see he wasn't going to get out of this, no matter how he tried. Best to speed it along as much as possible, hoping for the best.

"And who's this Valan?" asked the elven woman.

"He's a human—a wizard who's taken hobgoblins to use for experiments," he reluctantly continued. "He uses the books in the library to make his blue column work. It's best to just avoid the place altogether."

"Tell me more about this blue column." Cadrissa's eyes flashed a soft blue for a moment—he was sure of it—before returning to their previous green hue. Oh, this wasn't good at all. Why did he have to go and open his big mouth? He should have just kept to the shadows. They might have run right past him.

"There's a great blue column he believes can grant him power if he masters it. Even our chieftain was cast into it. He managed to survive, but the rest never came out alive." He dared another peek, relieved her eyes were still green. But they still seemed slightly lost—as if in deep thought. Or maybe growing slightly mad . . .

"How many books *are* there?" asked the elven woman.

"A few."

"We'd better check it out, just to make sure nothing's left for the Elyellium or anyone else."

The blind elf nodded. "I agree."

"But I thought you wanted to leave?" Hadek adopted an even more servile tone, making what he said next more a helpful suggestion than a desperate plea. "I'd be happy to—"

"How many guards are there?" the elven woman interrupted.

"It's too dangerous," he pleaded. "I can get you to the jungle, and then we can all be free."

"How many guards?" she firmly repeated.

He bowed his head in defeat. "None since Valan started his experiments again."

"Then we might have surprise on our side," she said.

"It's still *very* dangerous," he repeated. "*Valan* is very deadly, and the room has no escape." Maybe there was still hope—if he could just get them to see the idea was completely suicidal.

"No escape?" Rowan lowered his sword point to the goblin's chest. "You leading us into a trap?"

"I guess there is the portal . . ." The words jumped out of his mouth before he could close his lips.

"Portal?" Cadrissa's eyes blazed with even greater interest.

Hadek sighed. "There's a magical portal on the wall. It allows people to travel from place to place—at least that's how Valan got here." His head lowered with another sigh.

"If I could figure it out we might be able to use it to escape," said Cadrissa. "It'd be better than trying to walk all the way back to Elandor."

"And do you think you even *could* figure it out?" the elven woman asked the mage.

"I'd have to see it first," she replied. "But if it really was recently used, then it's working, and that could put things more in our favor."

"But we'd have to get through that wizard first," said the blond warrior.

"I could help distract him," said Cadrissa. "Between the six of us we should be able to handle him."

"You sure about that?" The dwarf was clearly not entirely convinced.

"If we can keep him from focusing for too long on anything, someone should be able to subdue him," Cadrissa replied.

"Subdue him." The dwarf didn't like the concept. "Why not just kill him?"

"He might have some helpful information we could use," said Cadrissa. "Like how to work that portal."

The dwarf snorted. "I'm not going to make any promises. If I get an opening I'm going to take it."

"I think we all will," the blond warrior agreed.

"But are you really going to trust a goblin, Alara?" the dwarf asked the elven woman. "I'd say you can't trust them any farther than you can throw them."

"If Gilban says he's a help to our cause then that means we can trust him." Alara was watching the other elf, but if he said or did anything, Hadek didn't notice.

"So what's it going to be?" The blond Telborian hurried things along. "We can't keep standing here all day."

"If there is any more information there, we can't risk it falling into the wrong hands." Alara wiped her sword on her pant leg.

"Agreed," said the leather-armored human. "We need to check it out."

"Are you sure?" Hadek dared for one last hope at sanity—at finally gaining his escape.

"Positive." Alara remained resolute.

So much for sanity.

CHAPTER 30

ONE IS EITHER WEAK OR STRONG: THE RULED OR THE RULER.

—**The Manual of Might**

"Where are the guards?" Vinder studied the temple. He and the others had been successfully—and rather rapidly—led there by Hadek. This was a feat in and of itself, since Vinder was expecting treachery at every turn. But their path was devoid of any trouble, letting them glide through the halls and stairs unopposed. But now, as they slowed their approach, he didn't like the way things looked.

"Gone," said the goblin. "I told you nobody wants to be anywhere near Valan now. You still don't have to go inside; we can—"

"Keep going." Alara prodded him with her falchion.

Hadek led them onward.

From time to time, the goblin waved his hand and sped them along whenever they lagged behind. For all his protests to the contrary, he seemed in a hurry to get there. He led them through a set of heavy wooden doors carved with an image similar in appearance to the statues they'd seen earlier. Except here its face and head had been destroyed by a vicious blade.

The figure held a sword in one hand and what looked like a holy symbol in the other, though who it honored Vinder couldn't say. Beyond the door, they traveled more ruined hallways lined with the bodies of dead dogs and butchered hobgoblins, like some demented meat market.

"This doesn't look good." He clenched his axe tighter.

"Stay sharp," said Alara, taking decisive steps around the bodies and debris. Gilban surprisingly managed his own way with the occasional hand from Alara, keeping the chest tightly under his arm.

Hadek led them up to and along the far wall of the temple, opposite the statues. As they moved deeper into the structure, they passed radiant, multicolored glass windows, most of which had been shattered by forces of nature or long-gone vandals. Some small scraps of glass still clung tenaciously to the windows' lead lining like dry leaves on dead branches. In some windows, clusters of color had been preserved, forming vivid pictures of glorious deeds and heroic battles. But as before, all the humanoid figures were devoid of heads or faces.

"We're almost there." Hadek maneuvered over the fallen mounds of flesh, nearly tripping over the cold arm of a large hobgoblin in the process.

"All these were killed by magic," Cadrissa said, grimacing as she skirted the bodies.

"You still think you can take this mage?" he asked Cadrissa.

"If he's been using so much magic already he might be weaker," she replied.

"Might?" Vinder didn't like the uncertainty behind her words.

The goblin perked up at the exchange. "If you're having second thoughts, there's still time to turn back."

"Keep moving." Alara dashed any such hopes as the goblin solemnly complied.

Together they came to rest at a statue standing at the far end of the temple. It resembled the many lining the walls: dressed for war but lacking a head.

"Push it open," Hadek said, gesturing with an outward rowing motion.

"*What* open?" Dugan asked, clearly not following.

"The door." Hadek motioned again. "Push it open."

"I think I know what he means." Alara motioned with her hand, saying, "Just push the statue aside."

Dugan moved to the side where Hadek had directed and took a deep breath, then began pushing. His muscles flared for a moment as the statue scraped against stone, revealing a doorway behind it as tall as the stone figure itself and just as wide. From that eerily silent opening wafted the smell of decay and death like some foul, plague-ridden wind.

"Down there," Hadek said, pointing.

"This better not be a trick," Vinder growled.

"No trick." The goblin's face paled.

"Everyone, be on your guard," said Alara. "Cadrissa, I want you to tell us the moment you feel any presence of this wizard or his magic. Rowan and Dugan, I want you up front. Vinder, you can cover our back."

Hadek started backing up. "I guess this is where we part ways."

Alara had other ideas. "You're going first to ensure a safe descent."

"But I thought you said if I helped you'd let me go free."

"You're not done helping us yet," she replied.

The goblin's eyes went from Dugan to Rowan to Vinder. All made sure he knew he had no say in the matter.

"All right." He sighed and started down the stairs. The rest of the group assembled into Alara's lineup, cautiously following.

• ● •

Halfway into their descent, Cadrissa and the others observed a soft white line appear on the walls, descending with the stairs. She surmised it was something used in navigating the staircase. But if it guided their steps it could also alert any others of their presence . . .

No one said a word as they descended into a large room lit with a purple light emanating from a tall column behind a square fence at the chamber's heart. Around it were toppled shelves and more corpses. She couldn't see much of the odd scrolls or books under the limited illumination, but the bodies had clearly been mutilated.

"What a horrid end," Alara uttered softly.

"What a horrid smell!" Vinder's nose wrinkled. All of them had cleared the stairs, inching deeper into the chamber.

"You're *sure* the wizard's alone?" Rowan found Hadek cowering behind Dugan, eyes darting to every shadow and mound of flesh.

"He was when I last saw him." Hadek's voice was small, almost reverential.

"Cadrissa?" Alara's question jolted her back into the present. She'd been momentarily lost in composing a mental inventory, seeing what was of immediate interest and possible importance. "Do you sense anything?"

"There's a great amount of energy emanating from that column, and . . ." She trailed off as her body shivered with a numbing cold. She fought it, but its flow through her was so strong she found herself lost in a dream-like state before knowing anything else. In it, her attention was directed at the circular mosaic dominating the chamber's far wall. It was constructed of azure and violet tiles blended together into a swirling vortex.

The portal. The words whispered across her mind.

"There's also some magic coming from that wall," she reported, hearing herself speak the words rather than knowing what she actually said.

"That's the *portal*," said Hadek.

"So where's the wizard?" Vinder took another tentative step forward, perhaps testing his luck.

"Cadrissa?"

Cadrissa heard Alara but remained lost in a daze. In it she saw the image of a skull with azure-flaming sockets staring her in the face.

"You okay?" Rowan voiced his concern.

She focused her will and shook herself awake. "Fine." She tried convincing herself as much as Rowan. "I don't think Valan's here."

"You don't sense him?" Alara continued her watch of the room, ready for any surprises.

"Discerning mages isn't the same as detecting enchanted objects," she explained, "but I'm fairly confident we're alone."

"Then I guess this whole thing was easier than we thought." Vinder began scanning the gruesome floor. "What are we looking for?"

"The same as before," said Gilban. "Ancient knowledge from the dranoric empire."

"You mean like all those books and scrolls?" Vinder jabbed his axe at the mess of parchment and paper around the column's cage.

"If what we seek is in there, yes."

"Well, *I'm* not going through all that to find *anything*," he scoffed. "We could have hobgoblins—or worse—coming down on us while we turn pages."

"Vinder's right," Dugan added. "We'd be like cornered rats in a fire if anyone does come."

"Maybe we can burn them," Rowan offered.

"*Burn* them?!" Cadrissa nearly shouted.

A solid mass suddenly dropped into their midst, making a sloshing sound similar to footsteps in melting snow. The flesh of the body was skinned away, exposing muscles and grievous wounds on the organs. The skull of its great head was exposed as well, and appeared a darker tint of bone than the set of bull-like horns protruding from it.

"Back up the stairs!" Dugan shouted.

"Way ahead of you!" Vinder joined Dugan's measured retreat while Rowan and Alara still held their ground.

"Boaz?" Hadek cocked his head, curiously observing the marred form.

"You know him?" Alara asked.

"He was the chieftain."

"And for all his boasting he still wasn't able to stand before me." A figure emerged from the shadows. "Just like none of you will be able to either."

While the others snapped into defensive positions, Cadrissa felt an intense chill rush through her. For a split second, the image of the skull with the flaming azure eyes again flooded her mind. It also came with a faint recollection. She had seen it earlier . . . and it had told her something . . . something she had to do. She shrugged the image off as quickly as it had occurred, along with the frigid air accompanying it.

But no sooner had she expelled the image from her thoughts than she fought against her neck turning to focus her face on the portal. No matter the strength of her will, her body still disobeyed. It took all her mental effort just pointing her eyes at Valan. But she was quickly losing that war. What was happening? An attack from Valan? Perhaps. Some sort of effect tied to the blue column? Maybe. No matter what it was, she'd be no good to anyone if she couldn't regain control.

"Valan?" Hadek was clearly confused.

"Hadek." Valan entered into the purple light. "I see you've brought me some new test subjects."

"I knew it!" Vinder huffed. "He was leading us into a trap all along."

"Not quite," said Valan. "But now that you're here I might as well put you to use. But first—" He let loose a crackling silver bolt, which crashed into Cadrissa. It felt like every pore of her body was on fire, and then she went numb. She was vaguely aware she was shaking, and then even that awareness faded as she dropped to the floor. She didn't feel any of it. Weakened and unable to move, she could only watch helplessly as events unfolded.

"Now then." Valan turned to the others. "Who wants to go first?"

Cadrissa watched Gilban beseech Saredhel for aid, then vanish from sight. Hadek did his best to find some spot to hide. The others ran forward, knowing they had to act as one—and quickly.

Alara swung twice, gaining the advantage of surprise. Valan cursed as Rowan swung high, Dugan swung low, and Vinder charged in. Dugan's new blades slashed deep into the wizard's ribs and thigh. Rowan's first swing was brushed aside by the wizard's spell, but the second swung true. Valan grunted in agony. Another magical burst of force saved him from Vinder's attack.

The wizard's eyes shone with a brilliant silver light. A spell on his lips, he hit Dugan in the stomach with such force the gladiator traveled about ten feet through the air, landing with a thud near the column's outer fence, where he banged his head against the wrought iron and sank into unconsciousness.

Taking advantage of the situation, Alara swung twice more. Valan tried ending her life with another silver bolt, but Alara gracefully dodged it. Enraged, the mage kicked Vinder as he readied for another series of strikes beside him. This sent the dwarf flying into the opposite wall; his body slid down the stone blocks, slumping at its base.

Rowan used the moment and opening provided to sink his sword deep into Valan's side, skewering the muscle over his left hip. The wizard retaliated with a silver burst of magical flame, but Rowan's new shield deflected it quite easily.

Throughout the battle, Cadrissa barely held on to consciousness, drifting in a land halfway between dreams and reality. In this cold void, she heard a voice calling out to her. A voice that came with a now familiar frosty grip.

Cadrissa . . . You need to help the others. The portal. You need to open the portal. Remember the spell I gave you. Cast it, and then you and the others can escape.

"The portal," she repeated to herself.

Yes. Now rise. Cast the spell.

She was unaware her eyes had become bright blue instead of their normal green. She felt the cold numbness about her, but she wasn't herself anymore. She could feel her body rising without having given the command. And then something like an icy hand slammed itself deep into her well. It was like taking a fist to the gut.

"Kelram Kor! Nuth-ral ackleem ishrem giltan giltan ock-roth!" She heard a strange voice speaking through her mouth even as the same words echoed in her head. The Transducer began shining a bright violet, blinding all in the chamber as the air thickened with magical energy. This same light shot from the top of the column straight for the mosaic before vanishing, leaving only a dim violet outline amid the circle of tiles before the entire chamber was again plunged into purple-tinted gloom.

"What have you *done?*" Valan lunged for Cadrissa but was stopped by Rowan jabbing his sword straight through the mage's chest. He gritted his teeth, forcing himself to stand as the blood poured more freely. But just as he opened his mouth for another spell, Alara's sword joined Rowan's, birthing a burst of fresh blood from his mouth before he could say anything further.

His final breath gurgled across his lips. Both withdrew their weapons, letting the wizard collapse. Once they were sure he was dead, each hurried to Cadrissa's side.

"What did you do?" She knew it was Rowan but couldn't move, remaining frozen in place like some statue.

"Cadrissa?" Alara was on her other side, careful in both her words and approach.

She shuddered and fell. She was too tired to move or even speak, but at least the cold was gone. She still wasn't in control of her mind and senses just yet, but she was alive. She hoped that was still a good thing.

• ● •

"The wall's spinning!" Rowan was stupefied by the swirling tiles. His heart raced as he watched them spin faster and faster until, with a bright flash, they became a pond of silvery light. And from that light emerged two figures . . .

The skeleton wore threadbare robes and hooded cloak, taking everything in as it entered fully into the chamber. Behind it a more frightful creature emerged. His fiery red skin covered a mighty frame, nearly twice the size of a human, wearing a black silk breechcloth.

Alara mimicked Rowan's statue-like manner. The scene was just too amazing. Thick black hair flowed to the back of his neck, framing the demon's monstrous face. The fiend's bright yellow eyes blazed with a cruel hate. His mouth was a toothy maw of destruction, glistening with yellowed teeth.

His back held two bat-like wings and a powerful tail. And Rowan made careful note of his cloven hooves and deadly claws, followed by the two sets of horns. One set was like a bull's, jutting out a foot from both sides of his head above his pointed ears. The other was smaller and goat-like, curving up from his forehead.

"Finally . . . a body." The demon looked around with satisfaction, resting a hand upon the pommel of the long sword belted at his waist.

"Yes," said the skeleton. "And here's where we part." The twin tongues of azure flame burning in the skeleton's eye sockets latched on to Rowan. It was then he remembered . . . there was something he had to do . . . something important. Neither he nor Alara noticed the green liquid bleeding out of his sword's blade.

"Seems you've held up your part of the bargain." The demon carefully wrapped his hand around his sword's handle.

"Of course." The skeleton ventured a few steps from the demon's side.

"Then we're done with each other." The demon slowly pulled the sword from its sheath. Unconcerned, the skeleton neared Cadrissa.

"Enjoy your brief stay," the skeleton said over his bony shoulder. "Now!" he shouted.

Rowan was racing for the demon before he knew what was happening. And apparently he wasn't the only one who was surprised. Before the demon could fully react, Rowan rammed his sword deep into the demon's bowels. By the time he did, the green liquid had thoroughly covered his blade.

Enraged, the demon slapped Rowan across the room like an insect, his shield unable to defend him from such a strike. "I'll have your head!" The blade still stuck in his gut as he charged the rag-covered skeleton, but just as suddenly he fell to his knees in agony.

"The poison will slay you in moments and send your spirit back to the Abyss."

"The poison . . ." the fiend sputtered, convulsing on the floor.

"I thought you'd enjoy it—for sentimental reasons. Though this time I've made sure it's fast acting.

"And you'll never find me again. I've made sure of that as well. Goodbye, Sargis." The skeleton laughed a hollow laugh and made a motion for Cadrissa to rise, which she did like a puppet jerked into action. Once she was on her feet, the skeleton's skull-topped staff glowed a bright violet, followed by the two wizards, who both vanished.

Sargis bellowed in rage before fading from sight. His passing closed the portal in a thunderous clamor accompanied with a massive explosion of light, color, and silver flames. These flames found homes on the books, scrolls, and bookshelves, along with some of the dead hobgoblins, setting them ablaze. Booming thunder shook the walls and cracked the mosaic. Falling dust and small chunks of debris from above increased Alara's concern.

"We have to get out of here!" she shouted to Rowan, fearfully watching the silver flames moving toward the stairs.

Thankfully, his recovery was rapid. His motivation for action was only accelerated by the realization that the chamber was burning.

"I'll take Dugan! You get Vinder!" He hurried into action as the ceiling gave another low moan. He ran for his sword first, sliding his shield across his back as he did so. Snatching it up, he made sure it was unharmed. From what he saw the blade was still clean and sharp. That was all he needed. Returning it to his sheath, he ran for Dugan. As he did he noticed Alara was already helping Vinder and Gilban—with Hadek's additional aid— toward the stairs. He must have missed the seer's reappearance in the chaos. Even better, the chest was still under his arm and whole.

Rowan reached Dugan and lifted him up. As they moved, the warrior became conscious. "We have to get out of here!" Rowan cried.

Dugan defiantly stopped and retrieved both of his weapons. Rowan could see the pain the effort of putting both under his sword belt caused, but the cold determination in Dugan's eyes never left him.

"*Now* we go."

Together, Rowan, Alara, and their burdens moved as fast as they could just as the ceiling began crumbling. They'd just made it to the top of the stairs and reached the hidden doorway when a large chunk of masonry landed on the column, cracking it from top to bottom.

A moment later, the ancient wonder exploded in a great whoosh of heat and purple light, sending chunks of stone airborne while further weakening the temple complex and surrounding area. This same stone would return moments later as flaming debris, raining death, fire, and destruction on all below.

• ● •

Hadek led the blind elf hurriedly through the streets. Alara had assigned him the task when she found him sneaking up the stairs when the chamber started collapsing. Given all he'd witnessed, he didn't put up much resistance. Beside him was the dwarf, whom Alara assisted as they hurried through the ruins. A few steps behind were the two humans, Rowan and Dugan.

The darkness he'd earlier watched spread across the sky now showed signs of relenting. Here and there a few patches of daylight were visible. It wasn't much but the extra light helped guide their path.

"We need to get to that field we passed through earlier," said Alara. "The one with the obelisks."

"Why?" Hadek asked.

"It's where we entered, and we have a trail already cut we can follow back through the jungle."

Hadek gave a nod. He could get them there quickly. But when everything was all said and done, what then? The tribe was gone now, either split up or destroyed by Valan and the flames. Even if he could find a small pocket of survivors, he wouldn't be welcomed with open arms, that was for sure. And did he really want to make his new life in the jungle? Alone, undersupplied, and unarmed, he was just inviting death.

He was shaken from his thoughts at the sight of a small band of hobgoblian warriors rushing past. But instead of fighting them, they hurried by without even noticing the mercenaries' presence. Everyone was looking out for their own hide. Whatever old loyalties they might have had were burned up in the growing inferno. As if emphasizing this point, a piece of fiery debris fell into a nearby section of wall, punching a hole through it while destroying itself in the process.

As they neared the two rows of obelisks, Hadek and the others slowed. A mass of hobgoblins were hurriedly packing up their dwellings and beating a hasty retreat into the jungle. In addition to the armed hobgoblins were panicked women and children, who added to the chaos.

"What now?" Rowan asked. "Do we try and go around?"

"There's no time," said Alara. "We just push through."

"But if we—"

"We keep going," she returned, moving forward. The others followed with only Rowan remaining behind until another incendiary chunk of masonry collided with one of the tallest obelisks. The impact roused everyone's attention—mercenary and hobgoblin alike. All froze, watching the obelisk crack at its base where the falling masonry had struck.

"That's not good," Hadek heard the dwarf mutter as the obelisk toppled like a felled tree. As it fell it struck its twin across from it with a massive impact, which in turn shattered and fell. Panic increased as the mass of hobgoblins rushed to get out from under the toppling pillars and raining debris. Some made it through, but many others were pounded into the earth with the crushing impact or brained from tumbling chunks of stone.

"Come on," Alara shouted, shaking the others into action. Renewed in his own commitment, Hadek made for the edge of the cleared jungle as fast as he could pull the blind elf along.

Finding where they'd first emerged, Alara directed the others through the opening, following herself only after all had made it through. This just left Hadek. He guided the priest ahead of him and took a final look at the ruins. A final look at his home. He could never go back even if he wanted. For the first time in his life he was truly on his own. Letting the past crumble into ash, he entered the jungle.

CHAPTER 31

Rowan joined the others watching the yellow claws of flame tear the memory of a faded civilization into cindery rubble. The uneasy darkness that had risen earlier had faded, but the sky was darkening again with the ascending strands of greasy smoke. Now that they were a safe distance away, standing in the open area around the ancient walls, the sight filled him with a sense of joy.

If they'd missed anything in their efforts, it would surely be destroyed. If the elves ever did make it here there would be nothing for them. Better still, they'd made it out safe and sound. Well, almost all of them. It looked like Vinder and Dugan would be all right. Their injuries weren't as great as he'd first thought. If it were Rowan who'd been hurt, he would have at least offered a prayer of thanks to Panthora, but apparently neither held to any god.

"A fiend and a skeleton?" Vinder wasn't sure how to take what Alara had just told them. She stood beside Gilban, who was still keeping the chest tight under his right arm.

"And if not for Rowan we might all have perished."

"Really?" The dwarf cast a curious eye his way. "*You* killed a fiend."

"I guess," he replied. "I don't remember all of it. One moment I was staring at him, and the next I was rushing him." And that was the whole of it as best he knew it. Everything had happened so fast he still had trouble with any finer details.

"You killed a *fiend*," Vinder repeated.

"Only by the grace of Panthora," he said. "She must have been guiding my hand."

"And then the skeleton just vanished." Dugan continued walking through the matter.

"With Cadrissa," Rowan added.

"But not us," said Vinder, making sure everything was still on his person. Once content it was, he asked, "So does that mean we're done here?"

"Our task is done." The fire danced across Gilban's mirror-like eyes. "We need only report back to the elucidator."

"But what about Cadrissa?" Rowan was amazed at the callous disregard of her fate until he remembered these were elves he was talking to.

"We can't help her," Gilban responded dryly. "She could be anywhere."

"And maybe keeping company with some more fiends." He wasn't too surprised by Vinder's reply, knowing how dwarves often sought their own interests over all others, but there was still one other human among them.

"And what about you?" he asked Dugan.

"I'm a free man with enough money for a new life."

"But what about Cadrissa?"

"What about her?"

He was amazed at Dugan's lack of concern. "We need to help her."

"We?"

"She's a fellow human, and—"

"I just gained a life," Dugan growled. "And I'm not about to go throw it away."

"That's *it*?" His tone turned indignant. "We risk our lives getting this information and lose one of our band in the process, and now you treat her like dirt?"

"One of our band?" Vinder snorted. "That's not how I remember your take on things earlier."

"Rowan . . ." Alara stepped hurriedly into the conversation. "We came here to complete a mission. We can't—"

"*I'm* not a *mercenary*. I'm a *Knight* of Valkoria—and I won't have a *human* woman being held captive by that . . . *thing* that took her."

"Do you even have a plan on how to find her?" Alara softly inquired. "Like Gilban said, she could be anywhere."

"Or dead."

He ignored the dwarf's dour comment. "I've heard talk of a wizard who lives in northern Frigia—maybe he could help."

"Doesn't sound like much of a plan," said Vinder.

"Well, it's better than just abandoning her."

"And what if the wizard doesn't want to—or can't—help you find her?" Alara's question was like cold water on a dying fire.

"And you have something *better* in mind?" He stared her down.

"Don't you have a duty to your superiors first?"

And then it hit him like a fist to the face. "You're right." He sighed. "That ancient knowledge needs to be dealt with."

"And until we get it back to Rexatoius, it won't be safe from the wrong hands," Alara continued.

"Wait. *You're* taking back the information?"

"Yes," said Gilban.

"But I need to bring it back to the grand champion."

"Oh boy." Vinder ran a hand through his beard.

"Worse than that, you're elves," he continued. "I was sent to keep the information from falling *into* elven hands." He didn't see Dugan and Vinder exchange questioning glances.

"*Elyelmic* hands," Alara carefully corrected. "And we're going to keep it safe from them too."

"But what are *you* going to do with it?"

"Keep it safe in the Great Library," said Gilban.

"Study it?" His hand fell on the pommel of his sword without even thinking. "You're going to use it to build your *own* empire."

"Calm down." Vinder stepped into the fray. "They got what they came for, everyone's alive, and we got paid. Just leave it alone."

"Not everyone made it."

"All right, have it your way," said Vinder, retreating a few steps. "I got paid. The job's done. If you want to stay and duke it out with the folks who let you tag along, that's your business."

"Tag along? I was already en route when—"

"We joined forces," Alara calmly interjected. "And we were successful."

"I came to keep that knowledge from falling into elven hands. I can't in good conscience leave without it." The uneasy silence that followed nearly strangled all present.

"Let it go," Dugan finally advised, but Rowan wasn't going to have any of it. He was in the right. Panthora had led him, and he had his orders. If they couldn't see that, it wasn't any fault of his.

"We can't do both." He kept his sights on the two elves, watching them closely. "Either that chest goes with me or—"

"What if *I* went with you?" offered Alara.

"What?"

"What if I went with you—back to your superiors—to verify our goals are one and the same?"

"Are you *insane*?" Vinder was obviously far from embracing the idea. "You don't owe him anything."

"I know, but if it helps resolve the situation, then it's worth it."

"You staying behind wasn't part of the plan," said Gilban.

"I thought you said we needed to be prepared for some acts of free will." She flashed him a small smile. "And we did invite him along, after all."

"Which he chose freely to accept," said Gilban.

"I know." She sighed. "I just—I just feel it's the right thing to do."

"I see. If that's what really is in your heart, I won't stand against it."

"You sure?" Apparently, Alara was expecting more resistance. "Are you going to be all right on your own?"

"Who said I would be on my own?" Gilban's eyes fell on Hadek. The goblin was standing a few yards from the others.

"*You're* still here?" Vinder frowned. "I'd thought you'd scurried away like the other cockroaches."

"Vinder!" Alara's reprimand was as pointed as a knife. "He helped us escape. You can at least *try* and be civil."

"You do what you believe to be right, Alara," said Gilban. "Saredhel has already seen to my needs. Come here, Hadek." He motioned for the goblin to join him. "You shall be my eyes until we resolve matters in Rexatoius."

"You're trusting a *goblin*?" Vinder was dumbfounded. "Worse still, you're taking him *with* you?"

"Great gifts sometimes come in unexpected packages. In fact, I sense he has yet a larger role to play in the days to come. There's a heavy weight upon him . . . a heavy hand that's—" He stopped his musings, releasing the goblin from his penetrating stare.

"You *sure* you want me along?" Hadek inquired sheepishly.

"You can always stay here."

After a rapid assessment of his surroundings, he asked, "Where are you going?"

"Rexatoius. The elucidator will want a prompt and accurate report."

"How far away is that?"

"Farther than you know," piped up Vinder. "Even longer with no horses."

"Actually, it's not as long as you might think." Gilban smiled another enigmatic grin, extending his hand to the goblin.

"Okay." Hadek accepted both it and the invitation.

"Wait a minute." Rowan narrowed the distance between them. "I'm not leaving without that chest."

"Rowan, we can work—"

"No." He brushed past Alara, keeping his right hand on the hilt of his sword. "Now hand it over."

Gilban stood calmly before him, his free hand gently fingering his necklace's strange pendant. Hadek cringed, his attention fixed on Rowan's still-unloosed sword. "Your destiny lies elsewhere, Rowan. And I won't keep you from it." Suddenly, Gilban and Hadek took on a lavender glow. "In fact," he continued, "I wouldn't be surprised if we crossed paths again." Both the light and their bodies started to fade.

"No!" Rowan rushed forward, trying to take hold of Gilban's shoulder, but closing his fingers over empty air instead. The elf and goblin had vanished.

"So they left for Rexatoius just like that." Vinder contemplated the empty space.

"The other priests blessed his pendant," said Alara, "providing us with a way home once we found the information or if we found ourselves in need of a rapid escape."

"So *you* would get out but not us?" Vinder blurted. "And if you could move across whole oceans and continents, why'd we have to take all that time with horses and boats and—"

"It was all part of the plan," she returned. "Which you agreed to—you all did."

Vinder made himself take a calming breath. "Yeah. We did. And now it's over. It's all over."

"The pendant was merely a precaution—for all of us," she continued, making sure everyone knew she was speaking the truth. "But thankfully, we didn't have to use it, and now the information is back in Rexatoius."

"And I've failed." Rowan's head dropped into his chest.

"Not yet," said Alara. "We can still go to Valkoria and talk to your superiors. I can assure them the knowledge won't fall into the wrong hands—we'll keep it safe and use it for the benefit of many."

"And why would they believe an elf?" The melancholy was seeping into his voice.

"You really are a thick one, aren't you?" Vinder shook his head. "She's willing to go all the way back with you to put in a good word for you. That's more honor than most would show you."

"And what do you know of honor?" Rowan growled.

"More than you might think," Vinder flatly replied, resting a hand over his chest, close to his heart. Rowan barely noticed or cared. Everything was falling down around him—he was being handed defeat right after achieving a great victory. And on his very first mission, no less.

"Where you headed?" Dugan asked Vinder.

"Back to Elandor. I have a few things that need attending."

"You mind some company?"

"I suppose it couldn't hurt." He took in the taller Telborian with a tolerant eye. "I won't be much for conversation, but the extra sword arm could help till we get into more civilized lands."

"Don't worry," Dugan returned. "I'm not up for much talk either."

"If you want . . . ?" Vinder indicated Alara was free to join them, but she declined the offer.

"Well, the sun will keep for a while longer, best use it while we can. Thank Drued that storm—or whatever it was—has passed."

"Thanks." Dugan gave Alara a passing nod.

"For what?"

"Proving me wrong." The small grin tracing his lips seemed almost alien on the normally serious terrain. "You're the only elf I've ever met who was true to their word."

"I pray there are others. Enjoy your freedom, Dugan."

"You up for a jog?" asked Vinder. "The more space we can put between us and any lingering hobgoblins, the better."

"Fine by me," said Dugan.

"Money-hungry warriors," Rowan muttered as he and Alara watched the two depart.

"But they're good men at heart," she added. "As are you." The comment caught him off guard, as did the sapphire eyes clearly showing she meant what she said.

"I'm sorry for what happened with Gilban." She spoke with such sincerity Rowan actually believed her. "It was for the best. I hope you'll come to see that before this is all said and done."

"Well, I can't do much about that now." He observed the smoky columns rising from the ruins. The fire would most likely continue for some time—probably well into the night and maybe even beyond. "I suppose you can come with me if you want, but I can't guarantee your safety."

"I'm pretty good at taking care of myself." The words and the confidence with which they were spoken caught his attention.

After realizing he'd been staring at her longer than he should, he ducked his head, pretending he was making some adjustments to his armor. "I suppose we should be off too, as long as we have some light. I figure we'll just follow the trail back to Nalu's camp," he said, daring a return to those calm eyes. "We could get some rest and supplies, and see about finding a way out of here without having to go back through the marshes."

"You really don't like those marshes, do you?" Alara teased.

"Never did." He found himself grinning for some reason.

"And yet if we hadn't gone through them, we'd never have found Nalu and been brought here."

"But we probably would have still had our horses and supplies." He found himself sinking deeper into those sapphire pools.

"So." Alara quickly broke away from his stare. "How far is Valkoria?"

"About a month's journey by ship—less if the weather's good." He scratched the back of his head, momentarily staring at his boots. "But the travel arrangements have already been made. By the time we get to Elandor a boat will be waiting to take me home."

"Good. Then we shouldn't have any trouble getting you back to your superiors."

"Why are you doing this?" he finally asked.

"I already told you."

"No other reason?"

"Should there be?"

He held his tongue, unsure of how best to answer that, or even if he should.

"Is there a problem with me coming along?"

"No." He spun on his heel, making for the same path Dugan and Vinder had traveled. "But if you change your mind along the way, I understand. You have an obligation to Gilban—to your people. Just like I do." He started walking.

"You really don't mind me coming with you?" She'd come up alongside him.

"I already told you it's fine." He kept his eyes forward, mind and body dedicated to navigating the path.

"I just don't want to—"

"It's fine." His words fell flat. The silence would remain until they reached the Celetors' camp.

CHAPTER 32

THE MORE KNOWLEDGE ONE GAINS, THE LESS ONE OFTEN DOES WITH IT.
THE TENDENCY IS TO GET MORE PUFFED UP AND PROUD
THAN BE OF ANY REAL GOOD TO ANYONE—ONESELF INCLUDED.
LET IT NOT BE SO WITH US.

—The Great Book

C adrissa became fully aware while materializing. Gone were the dark chamber, the bodies of the corrupted hobgoblins, and the stench of death. Instead, she was surrounded by ancient trees looming over serenely rolling green fields. It was one of the most beautiful places she'd ever seen. But deep inside, she felt something else disturbing the stillness: a bone-numbing chill radiating from her right. Turning, she froze. No more than a few inches from her was what she quickly deduced was a lich. He smelled of dust and age, of old bones and rotting fabric. He said nothing, uncomfortably staring at her with empty sockets, flickering with twin tongues of azure flame.

"Wh-where am I?" she asked, when finally able to speak.

"My island." Shivers raced up her spine as she watched the lich's jaw open and close. She saw no tongue inside, just a hollow skull. Yet somehow he'd spoken, just as anyone else would, and though he lacked eyes, she was sure he was able to see quite clearly too.

"Come. There's much to do." Cadrissa cringed as his bony hand clamped onto her forearm. It was colder than ice—a burning sort of cold. It flowed past her muscles and deep into her bones. She'd heard the cold was part of the process of becoming a lich—it helped preserve the flesh—but it was also a byproduct of the cosmic elements used in the spell's creation.

"And what if I refuse?" She tried sounding brave.

He gave a firm tug, adding, "Then your bones will be for the birds." She relented.

In the distance came the sound of thunder, which hurried the lich's step. All around them was the open wilderness, but if this was an island as he said, it couldn't go on indefinitely. She held her tongue from seeking answers, not wanting to put herself into any more danger than she already found herself in.

Together they moved through a meadow, fragrant with flowers of every color imaginable. The green leaves and manicured grass resembled the grounds of a temple more than wild countryside. The more they walked, the more she realized the land was still, quiet. Not even a leaf or blade of grass swayed, despite the rising breeze flowing through her hair. Another low rumble of thunder—this a little closer than before—summoned their gaze heavenward. It was thickening with thunderheads.

"Quickly now." The lich increased his pace, pulling her up a hill. She didn't know how much more of his touch her arm could take. It'd already gone numb. Just looking at him made her sick with fear, but at the same time she could sense the great well of strength within him—power that had kept him from the grave.

The spell for becoming a lich was one of the most extreme one could cast. It wasn't a popular option, given the enormous risks and costs. It was also rare. No mage had attempted it since magic's return to Tralodren. And Cadrissa knew of only a handful who'd dared it during the days of the wizard kings. In any case, successfully casting the spell required a great deal of skill, knowledge, and power. Some even said it walked the line between the divine and mortalkind.

He released her once they'd reached the top of the hill. She rubbed her chilled arm as she surveyed the terrain, making a study of her own. She'd a clear view of the greenish-blue sea surrounding them. For miles nothing else could be seen, save the island and water.

She knew there were islands on Tralodren but they were mostly in the west. Could she have been taken to one of them? If so, which one? If she could find some other clues, perhaps she could better place herself. There were a few trees nearby she could try climbing, but she doubted her captor would be so accommodating.

A sudden gust of wind ripped the gray hood from the lich's head, revealing a naked skull balancing on top of a spinal column. Between each of the vertebrae was nothing but air and a faint azure glow—a visible sign of the magic keeping all his bones in place.

"Come here." He pulled his hood back over his skull. She didn't think it wise resisting and cautiously drew up beside him. He whispered something under his breath. It was a spell, but she wasn't clear on what type. The grassy mound shook under their feet. And then the stone tower rose from the earth. It erupted with such vigor Cadrissa was violently thrown backward, rolling down the hill before encountering a rough stop. The lich, however, remained sure footed, despite his feeble-looking frame, studiously observing the structure's ascent.

Crafted of black marble, the few windows it had were all on the higher levels. And all of these were dark and empty. The ramparts were crowned in highly worked gems and gold. A ten-foot-wide golden door, carved with an impressive relief of two demons holding it shut, stood at the tower's base. Even from where she'd fallen, she felt the strength of its magic radiating outward. Such magical might in one place was unheard of in the modern day.

"Get up here," the lich snarled before speaking another word of magic at the tower. The great demons released their grip and the doors opened. The storm clouds were almost upon them. She shivered as the wind increased and the temperature dropped. The storm would be fierce.

She watched the lich enter the tower like some conquering king and scrambled behind him. Outside, the gap between the dark canopy and the blue sky narrowed. As soon as she entered, the doors slammed shut with all the comfort of a coffin lid. She was left in complete darkness with only the lich's flickering sockets revealing just how close she was to her captor.

A moment later light manifested across the tower's interior, flooding the ancient furniture, plush rugs, and relics with a cold radiance. The walls were covered with tapestries older than she could even guess. Sculptures of figures and forms from various races and times dotted the interior. She was taken by the wonders, never expecting she'd find such things here.

Yet even in the midst of these amazing sights, there lingered the scent of dust and decay, and of older, less savory things she couldn't quite name but recognized on instinct. Below these odors was the sensation of entering the heart of some giant, living thing . . . And it was watching her with hungry eyes. And then the storm was upon them. The tower shook as if struck by a strong fist.

"Come," the lich said, moving for the column of black marble stairs dominating the center of the room. For a moment she considered the doors. With the lich working his way up the steps perhaps she could—

"I won't tell you twice." He stopped, staring down at her. At least she assumed he was staring at her, given the angle of his skull. It was hard telling such things when there were no eyes to reference. Thunder clapped and the tower shook ominously.

"Are you sure it's safe?"

"The only thing you have to fear here is me," he said before resuming his steady climb.

Cadrissa fell in line, following a few paces behind the lich. Together they wound their way up to the top of the tower. The illumination that had greeted them at the door followed their ascent, dimming shortly after they'd moved on from the tower's lower levels. It was like walking in daylight and came without any torch or sconce. She'd heard of such spells, but, as she understood it, they always had to have an object upon which to be anchored for the light to shine. Here there appeared to be no anchor, save maybe the air itself.

Another deafening roar shook the walls. She felt as though every one of her bones had been rattled. It was as if the storm rested directly overhead—as if singling them out for this particular abuse.

"Inside." He motioned to the new door he'd opened as light rose in the room. Following his lead, she found herself in a study filled with books, charts, and scrolls. If forced to guess, she thought they were possibly a millennium in age. At least it smelled as such, with the musty odor blending with the rest of the tower's stale air. In the center sat an ancient tome, resting on the top of a silver podium that was crafted to resemble a hunched human skeleton supporting the weight of the book above it.

Cadrissa stood transfixed at the massive accumulation of knowledge. She'd thought she'd amassed something with her efforts but this—this was breathtaking. She felt as if she'd died and gone to Elucia—the realm of Dradin himself. The tomes alone could grant her insight into things she hadn't even begun fathoming—things she probably hadn't even known existed—and that was just what was immediately visible. But as amazing as such a sight was, it told her nothing of why she was here.

The lich hurried to the skeleton-supported tome as the tower again shivered with another clap of thunder. "It seems Endarien hasn't learned his lesson." Cadrissa watched him calmly turn one of the ancient tome's strange golden pages, sending up a small spray of dust in the process.

"En-Endarien?" She craned her head as if she could see through the stone ceiling into the raging storm beyond.

"He'll eventually give up. Just like last time."

"Last time?" Her wide eyes snapped back on the lich. He made no reply but simply continued reading. That wasn't good enough. None of this was. She was barely treading water in this sea of questions. She needed answers. *Something* that would at least serve as an anchor for the swirling chaos of her thoughts.

"Wh-who are you?"

The lich raised his head. "Cadrith Elanis, the last wizard king of Tralodren."

Chad Corrie has enjoyed creating things for as far back as he can remember, but it wasn't until he was twelve that he started writing. Since then he's written comics, graphic novels, prose fiction of varying lengths, and an assortment of other odds and ends. His work has been published in other languages and produced in print, digital, and audio formats.

He also makes podcasts.

chadcorrie.com | @creatorchad

Scan the QR code below to sign up for Chad's email newsletter!

"*Beyond the Blues* by Shoshana Bennett and Pec Indman is a very insightful, concise, informative manual that should be in the hands of all providers and new mothers dealing with postpartum depression. It is a fantastic book containing all the necessary questions and answers."

— **Shirley Halvorson**
   President, Depression After Delivery (North Carolina)
   Coordinator, Postpartum Support International (North Carolina)

"This valuable treatment manual should be in the pocket of every practitioner who works with women. It is well researched and indexed for quick and easy reference by healthcare providers as well as clients and their families. As a registered nurse and lactation consultant, I have found it invaluable in assisting new mothers to comfortably achieve the breastfeeding experience they want with their babies. Thanks for dispelling so many of the old myths!"

— **Pat Ross, RN, IBCLC**
   Kaiser Permanente

"Before I read this book I thought I was the only mother who felt this way. It was reassuring to know that I wasn't alone! My husband read the chapter for partners and he finally knew what to say to help me."

— **Patty B.**
   Recovering mother

"This book is an invaluable guide not only for women experiencing these disorders, but should also be mandatory reading for all who work with women during pregnancy and postpartum. It is a true breakthrough on the topic of prenatal and postpartum depression. This is the one book you should have on your shelf."

— **Lisa Nakamura, Postpartum Doula,**
   Nurturing Mother Postpartum Services

"I never knew you could be depressed when you're pregnant. I was told that the pregnancy hormones would keep the depression away. I was severely depressed two months ago and my mother found *Beyond the Blues* for me. Now I am eight months pregnant, and I can't wait for my baby!"

— **Carole B.**
Expectant mom

"I didn't know what to do when my wife started crying all the time after we came home from the hospital. The obstetrician handed me this book and finally things started making sense. It wasn't easy, but we made it through. The chapter for husbands was really useful for me because it told me what I should and shouldn't do to help my wife."

— **Jeff B.**
Husband of recovered wife

Also endorsed by

Sarah F. McMoyler, RN, BSN, FACCE Founder/Director, Sarah McMoyler's Birth University

Leslie Lowell-Stoutenberg, RNC, MS Director, Pregnancy & Postpartum Mood & Anxiety Disorder Program

Diana Lynn Barnes, Psy.D., MFT Past President, Postpartum Support International

Timothy A. Leach, M.D., FACOG

Beyond the Blues

A Guide to
Understanding and Treating
Prenatal and Postpartum Depression

Shoshana S. Bennett, Ph.D.

Pec Indman, Ed.D., MFT

Moodswings Press

Library of Congress Cataloging-in-Publication Data

Bennett, Shoshana S.
    Beyond the blues: a guide to understanding and
    treating prenatal and postpartum depression / Shoshana
    S. Bennett, Pec Indman. -- 1st. ed.
       p. cm.
    Includes bibliographical references and index.
    ISBN 0-9717124-1-7 51495

      1. Postpartum depression. 2. Depression in women.
    3. Pregnancy-Psychological aspects. I. Indman, Pec.
    II. Title.

RG852.B46 2003   618.7'6
           QB102-200725

Published in the United States
Moodswings Press, 1050 Windsor Street, San Jose, CA 95129-2837
www.beyondtheblues.com

This book is dedicated to:

Henry
by Shoshana

He suffered with me through two postpartum depressions. He brought snacks to the children upstairs, so I could lead groups downstairs. He supported my career change, and parented Elana and Aaron as I helped that career grow. He typed my doctoral dissertation, cooks and cleans more often than I do, hangs up my clothes in the bedroom, and is a really nice guy.

Ken
by Pec

With my love and appreciation for your support and encouragement of my passions. When I've flown off to attend conferences or teach, work evenings, or had meetings on the weekends, you've held down the home front. You are my partner in work, home, and play.

Acknowledgements

We thank Jill Wilk, a postpartum depression survivor, who generously donated her time to this effort as a labor of love. We also wish to thank Nely Coyukiat-Fu, MD and Jules Tanenbaum, MD for their review of the medical protocols. Betsy Miller and Maxine Granadino for providing our editing, and Arleen Virga and Dorothy Foglia from Foglia Publications.

To our husbands, Henry and Ken, thank you for your technical support. To our children, Elana, Aaron, Megan and Emily, for teaching us about being moms. And to our dear clients, who trust us with their deepest fears and greatest hopes.

Shoshana S. Bennett, Ph.D.
925-552-5127
www.PostpartumDepressionHelp.com

Pec Indman, Ed.D., MFT
408-255-1730
pec@beyondtheblues.com

Seminars
Training
Workshops
Consultation

Drs. Bennett and Indman offer consultation, lecture and training on perinatal illness to a wide variety of professionals and organizations. Sample topics include:

- *Assessment, diagnosis and prevention*
- *Psychotherapy models and techniques*
- *The latest research in psychopharmacology*
- *Consequences of untreated illness*
- *Resources to help suffering families*

They tailor their presentations to fit the particular needs and interests of the participants. Working individually or as a team, they can provide any type of program at your facility, from a brief lunch hour talk to a comprehensive two-day seminar. Please contact them directly for scheduling and fee information.

Their "Perinatal Mood Disorders" workshops are offered twice a year in the San Francisco Bay Area. Nurses, doctors, psychologists, marriage and family therapists and social workers can earn fourteen hours of continuing education units.

Watch for workshop and training dates on:
www.beyondtheblues.com

or contact Shoshana Bennett or Pec Indman directly:

SHOSHANA BENNETT, PH.D.   PEC INDMAN ED.D., MFT
www.PostpartumDepressionHelp.com   pec@beyondtheblues.com
(925) 552-5127   (408) 255-1730

10

About the Authors

Psychologist SHOSHANA S. BENNETT, PH.D. the mother of Elana and Aaron, founded Postpartum Assistance for Mothers in 1987 after her second experience with undiagnosed postpartum illness. Dr. Bennett is the President of Postpartum Support International. She is a noted guest lecturer, and her work has been the subject of numerous newspaper articles around the country. Dr. Bennett has been a featured guest on national radio and television shows, including ABC's "20/20". She hosts the popular talk radio show Mom's Health Matters on www.WorldTalkRadio.com where her presentations are devoted mainly to perinatal topics. For fifteen years prior to her current profession, Dr. Bennett was a college instructor in the fields of Special Education, Early Childhood Development, Rehabilitation Therapies and Psychology. In addition to three teaching credentials, she holds her second masters degree in Psychology and a doctorate in Clinical Counseling. Her office is located in the San Francisco Bay Area, and she offers telephone sessions to families throughout the country.

PEC INDMAN, ED.D., MFT has a doctorate in counseling, a masters degree in health psychology, and is licensed as a marriage and family therapist. Her training as a physician assistant in family practice was at Johns Hopkins University. Dr. Indman is a coordinator and trainer for Postpartum Support International. She is a member of the North American Society for Psychosocial OB/GYN  and the Marcé Society, and participates in annual conferences. Dr. Indman is an editorial advisor for OBGYN.net, and has been interviewed on national radio and for newspaper and magazine articles. Lecturing for a wide variety of audiences, Dr. Indman also provides trainings at hospitals and for organizations. She is in private practice in Santa Clara, California and is the mother of two girls, Megan and Emily.

12

Contents

Foreword

How appropriate it is that I am writing this foreword as I return from the 2002 meeting of the Marcé Society in Sydney, Australia. The meeting was fascinating though intense, and covered the newest research on psychiatric illness in mothers. There is cause for great hope for childbearing women! *Beyond the Blues* made excellent reading for the flight back. This fine publication fills the education void between sufferers of postpartum disorders (women, men and families) and healthcare professionals. Concise information is provided for all! Those of us who do clinical work and research in perinatal psychiatry define therapies, evaluate effects of medication for breastfeeding babies, explore preventive treatment, and much more — all very important endeavors. But the community of parents must be connected to well-informed professionals in order for even the most exciting of data to be put to use.

A very warm thank you to these two dedicated women for their commitment and sensitivity, and to Shoshana and Henry for their willingness to share the pain of their postpartum experience. It is my sincere hope that the countless people who read this book will benefit from your pain, thereby lessening the intensity of its memory.

Katherine L. Wisner, MD, MS
Professor of Psychiatry, Obstetrics and Gynecology and Pediatrics
Director, Women's Behavioral HealthCARE
Western Psychiatric Institute and Clinic/University of Pittsburgh
Medical Center
University of Pittsburgh School of Medicine

Preface

Postpartum depression (PPD), the most common perinatal mood disorder, is an illness that besets a significant number of women around the world. In the United States alone, over 3.5 million women give birth each year. Since the rate of PPD is between 15 and 20 percent, about 700,000 of these women will experience postpartum depression. The rate of gestational diabetes is between 1 and 3 percent and the rate of a Downs syndrome baby occurring in a 35-year-old mother is 3 percent. Curiously, we screen routinely for these conditions, which occur less often than postpartum depression, but we do not screen for postpartum depression, which afflicts up to one in five mothers.

While working in our communities, we have been asked numerous times to provide simple guidelines for assessment and treatment of perinatal mood disorders. Mothers and their partners have been asking the question, "Why is this happening to us and what can we do about it?" Many good books and journal articles have already been written on this topic. Our main goal is to summarize this information into a practical, easy-to-use format.

This book is not meant to be used as a replacement for individual counseling, group support, or medical assessment, nor do we intend it to be a comprehensive textbook. While this book will provide critical information for psychotherapists and clients alike, it is not specifically intended to teach psychotherapy techniques for working with perinatal clients. We want, instead, to provide the most essential and up-to-date diagnostic and treatment information as concisely as possible.

Introduction

I lost my wife, Kristin Brooks Rossell, to suicide following a four-month battle with postpartum psychosis. All the things one should not do in the treatment of this deadly disease were done to Kristin. *Beyond the Blues* is a step-by-step guide that would have saved her life.

The irony is that one of the authors, Dr. Bennett, lived less than ten miles from where Kristin worked and suffered daily. Kristin was even employed at a managed healthcare company with, supposedly, decent medical insurance. But not one of the professionals in charge of her care gave her the advice and counsel needed. This book should be required reading for every expectant mother, partner, and medical person charged with the woman's care.

Beyond the Blues is not long, yet its content is comprehensive and well written. I cried reading each page, knowing at each turn how this information could have been used to save Kristin, myself, and our families the pain and needless suffering we experienced.

The single greatest gift we have is the gift of life and creation of that life. It is an indictment of our patriarchal society that a disease which afflicts over 700,000 women each year in the US alone, is not routinely screened for. "Suicide is the most preventable form of death in the US today," stated former US Surgeon General David Satcher. If this is so, and I believe it is, then surely suicide as a result of poorly treated or untreated postpartum illness is the most preventable form of suicide.

I am still in therapy and have had support from family and friends in order to deal with the loss. By founding the Kristin Brooks Hope Center I have tried to make something good come out of my personal tragedy. The Hopeline Network

1-800-SUICIDE (784-2433) automatically connects callers —
people who are depressed or suicidal, or those concerned about
someone they love — to a certified crisis center. Crisis center
calls are answered by trained crisis line workers 24 hours a day,
seven days a week.

Never doubt that a small group of thoughtful,
committed citizens can change the world; indeed,
it's the only thing that ever has.

MARGARET MEAD

H. Reese Butler II
CEO & Founder, Kristin Brooks Hope Center
National Hopeline Network 1-800-SUICIDE
609 E. Main St. #112
Purcellville, VA 20132

· ONE ·

Our Stories

We arrived at this professional focus by very different paths, one through personal suffering, the other through social activism.

Shoshana's Story

My husband Henry and I happily awaited the birth of our first child. We enjoyed a wonderful marriage and had planned carefully for the addition of children to our home. We had both grown up in healthy, stable families with solid value systems. We were well-educated people with successful careers: my husband, a human resources professional, and I, a special education teacher. I had worked with children for years, beginning with my first baby-sitting job at age ten.

I felt quite confident taking care of children. The picture I had of my future always included children of my own. I prided myself on being a self-reliant person, able to manage well even under difficult circumstances. Henry came from a family of five children and had always planned on having a large family. We had many well thought-out plans for the future, and we looked forward with eager anticipation to being parents.

I felt terrific during pregnancy, both physically and emotionally. After childbirth classes, Henry and I felt prepared for the big event. There was one quick mention of C-sections and no mention at all about possible mood difficulties during pregnancy or after delivery. These classes were all about breathing techniques and what to pack in your hospital bag. On the top of every sheet on the note pad our teacher gave us appeared the words, "No drugs please." And it was also assumed, of course, that every woman would choose to breastfeed.

I endured five and a half days of prodromal labor (real labor, but unproductive), during which I could not sleep due to the discomfort. This was followed by another day of hard labor (still prodromal). My baby was transverse (sideways) and posterior ("sunny side up"), a position that caused severe back labor as well. I writhed as the sledgehammer-like pain hit to the front, then with no break, hit to the back. After not sleeping for almost a week, my insides were so sore and exhausted I thought I would literally die. At that moment a very strange thing happened. I suddenly became aware that I was hovering over myself, watching myself in pain. Although at the time I had no words to label that bizarre sensation, I now know it to be called an out-of body experience. Still not dilating, I was finally given a C-section.

My illusion of being in control was shattered. I had been a professional dancer, and my body had always done what I had wanted it to. The visual image I repeatedly had during this ghastly time was of a beautiful, perfect, clear glass ball violently exploding into millions of pieces. That was the self I felt I was losing. Hopelessness and helplessness replaced my previous feelings of control and independence. I was left with a posttraumatic stress disorder that haunted me for years.

I soon learned a skill that I would practice for a very long time — acting. I bought into the myths that I was supposed to feel instant joy and fulfillment in my role as a mother, as well as an immediate emotional attachment to my baby. As my daughter, Elana, was placed in my arms, I managed to say all my lines correctly. "Hi, honey, I'm so happy you're finally here," I said, wanting to feel it (as I did later on). Inside, I was numb.

Overwhelming feelings, fear, and doom intensified as my first OB appointment approached. While I drove to the doctor's office, my anxiety level rose to unimaginable heights. I pulled my car over to the shoulder of the freeway. Crouched over the steering wheel, I experienced my first panic attack. When I returned home and called to apologize for missing my appointment, I perceived only a tone of annoyance.

I had lost all the baby weight in the hospital, but just four months postpartum, I was forty pounds overweight. I had always enjoyed a wonderful working relationship with my OB, and felt that he respected me as an intelligent patient. Now, coming to his office as a hand-wringing, depressed mess, I felt embarrassed and vulnerable. As I sat in the waiting room surrounded by mothers-to-be and women cuddling their newborns, my feelings of guilt intensified. I became totally convinced that I should never have become a mother.

Though my OB was well-meaning, his technician-like manner was anything but reassuring. He focused primarily on my incision, not my huge weight gain or uncontrolled weepiness. With tremendous shame, I confessed some of my feelings to him, including, "If life's going to be like this, I don't want to be here anymore." I was shocked and hurt when he leaned back in his chair, laughed, and said, "This is normal. All moms feel these blues." He gave me his home number so I could call his wife, but he provided no referral. As my ten-minute appointment came to a close, I began to experience my first serious suicidal thoughts.

I did call his wife, who was convinced my problem was that the baby was manipulating me. I just needed to put her on a schedule. I also reluctantly joined a new-mom's group; since everyone was suggesting it, I decided to try. That was one of the most destructive actions I took. As I entered the room full of mothers cradling their babies with delight, I felt more alienated than ever.

Discussing "problems" in this group meant pondering the best way to remove formula stains from fabrics, spit-up management, and calming a fussy baby. When I mentioned that I was having a bad time, an uncomfortable silence fell. I learned later that my name had been removed from the group's baby-sitting co-op. Upon leaving the first and only group session I attended, I felt more inadequate and scared than ever. Now I knew I was the worst mother that ever walked the planet.

Another complication was breastfeeding. Although my daughter latched on easily, I was overcome with pain due to inflammation and bleeding. I had been one of the "good" students who had prepared her nipples before birth, just as the nurses had suggested — rubbing them with a washcloth to toughen them up. I asked a leader from a prominent lactation organization to help me.

While the representative proved to be very helpful with suggestions about relieving the pains of breastfeeding, her emotional support immediately ended when I divulged that I would be going back to work in six months and would have to discontinue breastfeeding. She abruptly left my home. At this point I made the decision to stop breastfeeding completely, feeling like a total failure.

Life at home was frightening and unbearable. I had full-blown postpartum obsessive-compulsive disorder. Terrifying thoughts of harming my baby plagued me. I could imagine every household item possibly hurting my innocent child. Accidently tossing my baby over the second floor railing, dropping her into the fireplace, or putting her in the microwave were common worries. I would not trust myself to be alone with her. Not even my husband knew about these horrible thoughts — I could barely admit them to myself.

If I could sleep at all, I awoke in the morning in a full panic attack, wondering if I could survive another day. The simple act of watching television could turn an already dreary day into a deeper depression. The commercials portraying mothers in wavy white dresses, with naked babies in arms, taking delight in changing diapers and smiling angelically at their bundles of joy, sent me further into the depths. These were subtle reminders of the differences between all other mothers and me.

When my husband left for work, I would beg, "Don't leave me, I can't do this by myself!" He would return from work to find me in the same emotional state as when he left. I still remember my husband peering in the front window each night with that worried look, trying to see how many of us were crying. If it was just one, it was me.

Henry was frustrated with me. His mother, who had been a postpartum nurse for twenty years and who had popped out five babies of her own without the least dose of the "blues," was feeding Henry unhelpful information like, "Shoshana is a mother now. She needs to stop complaining and just do it." My respite came each evening as I tossed Henry the baby, proceeded to the driveway, jumped into the car, and sat and cried for a half-hour. There was no laughter, no humor, no friends, and no plans. There was only despair.

My mother had come to stay with us for the first three weeks. She was wonderfully supportive but even with her therapist background, she did not recognize the signs of this serious illness. For the next year I continued on my downward spiral. I allowed no emotional or physical connection with my husband. I continued to be deprived of sleep due to insomnia and anxiety, ate without experiencing much taste, and just went through the motions with my daughter. I felt buried alive with no chance of clawing my way to the surface. I began seeing a psychologist, who never once requested any historical data on depression or anxiety in my family. All she did was probe for issues in my past, and if she couldn't find a real one, she would make one up. First she blamed my grandmother, then my sister. Finally she tried to convince me that having a Cesarean delivery caused my condition. I ended up feeling "crazier" than I did when I began. I swore I would never again open up to another professional.

When Elana was two and a half years old, my anxiety and depression began to lift significantly. "Maybe I can be a mother," I heard myself saying. My hair began to curl again for the first time since the birth. I began to enjoy my food and started seeing in color again, rather than shades of gray.

As with my first pregnancy, my second was flawless and without complication. I was enjoying my daughter by then, and the thought of a second child was a delight. After two days of prodromal labor, I decided on a C-section. The newfound enjoyment and relief from depression came to a crashing halt immediately after the birth of our son, Aaron. Although I could physically take care of him, my former "I'm incompetent" feelings returned. I would easily lose my temper at Elana, who was only three and a half years old. Having been a teacher and knowing child development, I could not find words for my shame and guilt at the way I was treating her. The brief amount of time she had her mom "all there" was suddenly ripped away from her.

In 1987, when Aaron was nearly six months old, Henry excitedly called me to look at a television documentary he was watching on postpartum depression. I was awestruck as the program described the disorder, its symptoms, causes, and possible cures. At the program's conclusion, I cried for an hour, looked at my husband, and said, "That's me!" The tremendous sensation of relief that someone had, at long last, described the turbulent agony I had been living, felt like a weight being lifted from my whole body. Equally important, I had finally heard that postpartum depression is diagnosable and treatable and that it can go away! If this condition is so common, I thought, where are all of us?

I started reading everything I could get my hands on, from all over the world, and realized that many countries were light-years ahead of the U.S. in recognizing and treating postpartum mood disorders. In my research, I came across Jane Honikman, in Santa Barbara, founder of Postpartum Support International. Jane generously offered me valuable information so that I could begin running a self-help group in the San Francisco Bay Area.

Although I was still depressed myself, I was excited about what I had been learning and wanted to share my knowledge with other sufferers and survivors. In contrast to the new-mothers' group I had attended, my group would be a safe place for women to discuss their depression and anxiety openly, without fear of judgment. I posted two flyers, one at a local supermarket, the other at my pediatrician's office. The response was thunderous! Calls came in from all over Northern California, and some from as far away as Hawaii. Every week my living room was filled with six to fifteen women, desperate for support and guidance.

I became convinced that postpartum depression needed the same support, psychological attention, and medical tools as other mental illnesses. I made the decision to begin a new career devoted to the study and treatment of postpartum mood disorders.

For the past eighteen years, the support groups which began in my living room have continued and flourished. As the President of Postpartum Support International, I am continuing to pursue my life's work.

Pec's Story

For as long as I can remember, I have been interested in political, emotional, and sociological issues as they relate to women. In the 1970s I trained as a family practice physician's assistant and worked in community-based family health clinics for a number of years. My interests varied, and my work took me to such places as women's clinics, an industry-based employee health center, a physical and fitness evaluation center, and weight management programs.

I entered a master's program in health psychology, and for the first time felt excited about school. I decided to continue and got a doctorate in counseling, getting my marriage and family therapy (MFT) license along the way. Many of my clients were referred by physicians, and much of my work with clients, particularly women, centered on issues related to health and emotional well-being.

One day, while in a physician's waiting room before a meeting, I came across a brochure from Postpartum Support International that described postpartum depression. I scribbled down the address, thinking, "I need to learn more about this." After receiving more information about PPD, I had a very mixed emotional response. I experienced sadness, extreme anger, frustration, and outrage. In all my years of training, I had learned nothing about perinatal mood disorders. I thought back to some of the women I had probably misdiagnosed. Why aren't health practitioners taught about PPD? My anger propelled me into action.

I have two daughters, and had a miscarriage in between. My second daughter was born when I was 40, after a work-up for infertility, a laparoscopy, and thanks to Clomid. My pregnancies went fairly well but both girls, each at 8.5 pounds, were delivered by C-section. The births were positive experiences. My older daughter was able to rock her new sister in a rocking chair in the recovery room as my husband, parents, and brother celebrated. I did have the "blues," yet they passed each time as my incision healed. I was fortunate to have a close friend on maternity leave at the same time, so we were together much of the time. All in all, my pregnancies, births, and postpartum experiences were positive. This only added to my outrage about PPD. All women should have the right to an emotionally and physically healthy pregnancy and postpartum experience!

My history of political activism served me well. I joined organizations and read books, attended conferences and trainings. Jane Honikman of Postpartum Support International told me about a woman in the East Bay, Shoshana Bennett, who was doing postpartum work. I called and asked if she would meet with me to make sure I was on the right track. She agreed, and we have been working together ever since.

This work has become my passion. I have never experienced so much personal and professional meaning and reward. I hope you will join us on this mission.

TWO

Pregnancy and Postpartum Psychiatric Illness

Perinatal (which we define as the time during pregnancy and the first year postpartum) mood disorders are caused primarily by hormonal changes which then affect the neurotransmitters (brain chemicals). Life stressors, such as moving, illness, poor partner support, financial problems, and social isolation are certainly also important and will negatively affect the woman's mental state. Strong emotional, social, and physical support will help her recovery.

Any of the six postpartum mood disorders discussed in this chapter can also occur during pregnancy. These perinatal mood disorders behave quite differently from other mood disorders because the hormones are going up and down. A woman with a perinatal mood disorder often feels as if she's "losing it," since she can never predict how she will feel at any given moment. For instance, at 8:00 A.M., she may be gripped with anxiety, at 10:00 A.M. feel almost normal, and at 10:30 A.M. become depressed.

Our clients who have had personal histories of depression tell us that postpartum depression feels very different (and usually much worse) than depressions at other times in their lives. One of Shoshana's postpartum clients is a survivor of breast cancer. At a support group, she beautifully explained:

When I had cancer, I thought that was the worst experience I could ever have. I was wrong — this is. With cancer, I allowed myself to ask for and receive help, and expected to be depressed. My friends and family rallied around me, bringing me meals, cleaning my house, and giving me lots of emotional support. Now, during postpartum depression, I feel guilty asking for help and ashamed of my depression. Everyone expects me to feel happy and doesn't accept that this illness is just as real as cancer.

Women who experience these symptoms need to speak up and be persistent in getting proper care. In the past, these illnesses have been downplayed and even dismissed. Research has shown how important it is to treat perinatal mood disorders for the health and well-being of the mother, baby, and entire family.

The Psychiatric Issues of Pregnancy

Contrary to popular mythology, pregnancy is not always a happy, glowing experience! Approximately 10-20 percent of pregnant women experience depression.

It can be confusing that many of the normal symptoms of pregnancy are very similar to symptoms of depression. It is easy to ignore or dismiss these symptoms as just a normal part of pregnancy. It is important that symptoms be evaluated and treated, if they are outside the normal range. Here are some guidelines to determine if symptoms are caused by pregnancy or depression.

Pregnancy	Depression
Mood up and down, teary	Mood mostly down, gloomy, hopeless
Self-esteem unchanged	Low self-esteem, guilt
Can fall asleep, physical problems may awaken (bladder or heartburn), can fall back to sleep	May have trouble falling asleep, may have early morning awakening and difficulty falling back asleep.
Tires easily, rest refreshes and energizes	Fatigue, rest doesn't help
Feels pleasure, joy and anticipation	Lack of joy or pleasure
Appetite increases	Appetite may decrease

When symptoms of depression or other mood disorders cause limitations in the client's ability to function on a day-to-day basis, intervention is necessary. This may include traditional (counseling and medication) or nontraditional modalities (such as Yoga or acupressure), or any combination thereof. The goal is to use whatever the individual woman needs in order to feel like herself again.

Depression during pregnancy has been associated with low birth weight (less than 2,500 grams) and preterm delivery (less than 37 weeks). Severe anxiety during pregnancy may cause harm to a growing fetus due to constriction of the placental blood vessels and higher cortisol levels.

Some women become pregnant while taking psychotropic medications for depression, anxiety, and other mood problems. Many of these medications are considered acceptable during pregnancy. A practitioner who is familiar with the current research about the safety of taking medications during pregnancy should be consulted. Often it is safer to continue a medication than risk a relapse.

The rate of relapse for a major depressive disorder (MDD) in women who discontinue their medication before conception is between 50-75 percent. The rate of relapse for MDD in those who discontinue medications at conception or in early pregnancy is 75 percent, with up to 60 percent relapsing in the first trimester. In one study, 42 percent of women who discontinued medications at conception resumed medications at some time during their pregnancy. Resources listed in the back of this manual provide helpful guidelines regarding the use of medications.

Mood Disorders

There are six postpartum mood disorders. This list details each of the principal disorders, some of their most common symptoms, and risk factors. It is important to note that symptoms and their severity can change over the course of an illness.

"Baby Blues" —
Not Considered a Disorder

This is not considered a disorder since the majority of mothers experience it.

- Occurs in about 80 percent of mothers
- Usual onset within first week postpartum
- Symptoms may persist up to three weeks

Symptoms

- Mood instability
- Weepiness
- Sadness
- Anxiety
- Lack of concentration
- Feelings of dependency

Etiology

- Rapid hormonal changes
- Physical and emotional stress of birthing
- Physical discomforts
- Emotional letdown after pregnancy and birth
- Awareness and anxiety about increased responsibility
- Fatigue and sleep deprivation
- Disappointments including the birth, spousal support, nursing, and the baby

Deborah's story:

For about a week and a half after my baby was born I would cry for no reason at all. Sometimes I would feel overwhelmed, especially when I was up at night with my son. Once I even thought that I had made a big mistake having a child. I felt resentment toward my husband since his life stayed pretty much the same and mine was turned upside down. When I started going to the mother's club at two weeks, I felt so relieved that all these other moms felt the same way.

Deborah's treatment:

Since Deborah was experiencing normal postpartum adjustment, she did not require any formal treatment. Her hormones were balancing out by themselves. All she needed in order to enjoy her new life was a combination of socializing with other moms, taking time to care for herself, and working out a plan of sharing child and household responsibilities with her husband.

Depression and/or Anxiety

- Occurs in 15 to 20 percent of mothers
- Onset is usually gradual, but it can be rapid and begin any time in the first year

Symptoms
- Excessive worry or anxiety
- Irritability or short temper
- Feeling overwhelmed, difficulty making decisions
- Sad mood, feelings of guilt, phobias
- Hopelessness
- Sleep problems (often the woman cannot sleep or sleeps too much), fatigue
- Physical symptoms or complaints without apparent physical cause
- Discomfort around the baby or a lack of feeling toward the baby
- Loss of focus and concentration (may miss appointments, for example)
- Loss of interest or pleasure, lower sex drive
- Changes in appetite; significant weight loss or gain

Risk factors

- 50 to 80 percent risk if previous postpartum depression
- Depression or anxiety during pregnancy
- Personal or family history of depression/anxiety
- Abrupt weaning
- Social isolation or poor support
- History of premenstrual syndrome (PMS) or premenstrual dysphoric disorder (PMDD)
- Mood changes while taking birth control pill or fertility medication, such as Clomid
- Thyroid dysfunction

Lori's story:

I was so excited about having our baby girl. My pregnancy had gone smoothly. I had been warned about the "Blues," but I just couldn't shake the tears and sadness that seemed to get deeper and darker every day. My appetite was non-existent, although I forced myself to eat because I was nursing. I lost about 30 pounds the first month. At night I was having trouble sleeping. My husband and baby would be asleep but I would have one worry after another going through my head. I was exhausted. I felt like my brain had been kidnapped. I couldn't make decisions, couldn't focus, and didn't want to be left alone with the baby.

I wanted to run away. I withdrew from friends and felt guilty about not returning phone calls. I couldn't understand why I felt so bad; I had the greatest, most supportive husband, a house I loved, and the beautiful baby I had always wanted. At times I felt close to her, but at other times I felt like I was just going through the motions — she could have been someone else's child. I thought I was the worst mother and wife on the face of the earth.

Lori's treatment:
Lori began psychotherapy and also saw a psychiatrist for medication. She was started on an antidepressant and the dosage was gradually increased. Initially she took medication to help her sleep as well. She began taking regular breaks to take care of herself. She also started attending a postpartum depression support group and met other moms with similar stories. After several months she felt like herself.

Obsessive-Compulsive Disorder

• 3 to 5 percent of new mothers develop obsessive symptoms

Symptoms
• Intrusive, repetitive, and persistent thoughts or mental pictures
• Thoughts often are about hurting or killing the baby
• Tremendous sense of horror and disgust about these thoughts (ego-alien)
• Thoughts may be accompanied by behaviors to reduce the anxiety (for example, hiding knives)
• Counting, checking, cleaning or other repetitive behaviors

Risk factors
• Personal or family history of obsessive-compulsive disorder

Tanya's story:
Each time I went near the balcony I would clutch my baby tightly until I was in a room with the door closed. Only then did I know he was safe one more time from me dropping him over. The bloody scenes I would envision horrified me. Passing the

steak knives in the kitchen triggered images of my stabbing the baby, so I asked my husband to hide the knives. I never bathed my baby alone since I was afraid I might drown him.

Although I didn't think I would ever really hurt by baby son, I never trusted myself alone with him. I was terrified I would "snap" and actually carry out one of these scary thoughts. If my baby got sick it would be all my fault, so I would clean and clean to make sure there were no germs. Although I had always been more careful than other people, now I would check the locks on the windows and doors many times a day.

Tanya's treatment:

After meeting with Tanya twice individually, her therapist suggested that her husband join her in the next session. Tanya needed reassurance that her husband knew she wasn't "crazy" and would never really harm the baby. She did not want to tell him the specific graphic thoughts, so she referred to them generally as "scary thoughts." After being educated, her husband's aggravation with her being "nervous all the time" subsided.

Tanya started taking an antidepressant and within two weeks the scary thoughts were occurring far less frequently. Her therapist suggested that she wait another few weeks to join a support group since she was still too vulnerable to hear about the anxieties of others. In the meantime, she was given the names and numbers of a few women to connect with who had survived this disorder.

Panic Disorder

• Occurs in about 10 percent of postpartum women

Symptoms
• Episodes of extreme anxiety
• Shortness of breath, chest pain, sensations of choking or smothering, dizziness
• Hot or cold flashes, trembling, rapid heart beat, numbness or tingling sensations
• Restlessness, agitation, or irritability
• During attack the woman may fear she is going crazy, dying, or losing control
• Panic attack may wake her up
• Often no identifiable trigger for panic
• Excessive worry or fears (including fear of more panic attacks)

Risk factors
• Personal or family history of anxiety or panic disorder
• Thyroid dysfunction

Chris's story:
At about three weeks postpartum I stopped leaving my house at all except for pediatrician appointments. I was afraid I might have a panic attack in the store and not be able to take care of my baby. I never knew when that wave would begin washing over me and I would "lose it." The windows had to be open all the time or else I thought I would suffocate if I had an attack.

The first time I had a panic attack I thought I was having a major heart attack. A friend drove me to the emergency room and the doctor on call told me it was only stress. He gave me some medicine but I was too afraid to take it. I went home feeling stupid, like I had made a big deal out of nothing.

Everyone told me that breastfeeding would relax me, but it did just the opposite. I never knew how much milk my baby was getting and that really worried me. Sometimes when my milk would let down I would get a panic attack. The first therapist I saw told me I must have had issues bonding with my own mother, but I knew that wasn't true and I didn't see that therapist again. On many nights I woke up in a sweat, with my heart beating so fast and hard. My head was racing with anxious thoughts about who would take care of the baby when I die. I thought I was going crazy. I was so scared.

Chris's treatment:

Chris had her first therapy appointment over the telephone since she felt she could not go outside. Her therapist talked her through taking a bit of the medication her MD prescribed, so Chris would know she had something that would help in an emergency.

Driving was too scary for her, especially in tunnels and over bridges. Her husband drove her to her next session, following a route that avoided those obstacles. Chris needed to sit near the door during the appointment just in case she felt the need to run outside for some air. Her therapist urged her to sleep for at least half the night, every night. Chris's husband began taking care of his baby for the first half of the night on a regular basis. Chris noticed immediately how sleep lowered her stress level. She attended a stress management class which also helped.

Psychosis

- Occurs in one to two per thousand
- Onset usually two to three days postpartum
- This disorder has a 5 percent suicide and 4 percent infanticide rate

Symptoms

- Visual or auditory hallucinations
- Delusional thinking (for example, about infant's death, denial of birth, or need to kill baby)
- Delirium and/or mania

Risk factors

- Personal or family history of psychosis, bipolar disorder, or schizophrenia
- Previous postpartum psychotic or bipolar episode

Mike's story:

My wife, Gloria, had a great pregnancy and a long labor. We were thrilled to have our first child, a son. But within days of his birth my wife began to withdraw into her own world. She became less and less communicative and she became more and more confused and suspicious. I almost had to carry her into the therapist's office; by that time she could hardly speak or answer questions, nor write her name on the forms her therapist gave us. I was told to take her to the hospital immediately.

When we arrived at the hospital, she became fearful and then violent. She ended up in restraints. Fortunately, she responded pretty quickly to the anti-psychotic medication, and was able to come home after about a week. She continued to improve, and when she was back to herself again, she slowly weaned off all the medications.

We had always wanted two kids, so we consulted with our therapist and psychiatrist. With careful planning, we now have our second child with a very different story to tell.

Gloria's treatment:

After being released from the hospital, Gloria continued therapy and saw the psychiatrist, who carefully monitored her medication. She worked to understand and process what had happened to her. Eventually she joined a postpartum support group which was quite helpful. Since there were no other moms present in the group who had experienced a postpartum psychosis, the group leader gave her the names and numbers of women who had "been there" and who wanted to help.

Posttraumatic Stress Disorder

• Occurs in up to six percent of women

Symptoms
• Recurrent nightmares
• Extreme anxiety
• Reliving past traumatic events (for example, sexual, physical, emotional, and childbirth)

Risk factors
• Past traumatic events

Jennifer's story:

During the delivery it all came flooding back. I felt terrorized and vulnerable. I thought I had already dealt with the abuse in my childhood. It seemed that all the years of therapy were a waste of time and money. I was so embarrassed for losing control during labor. I was angry that what happened to me as a kid was still affecting me after all this time.

My therapist told me the nightmares and flashbacks would go away but I just didn't know. It was so real — like the abuse was happening again over and over. I couldn't even leave my poor husband alone with my baby. I got the sick feeling that I couldn't even trust him. I was so messed up. I thought maybe I'd never be a normal mother.

Jennifer's treatment:

Jennifer hired a postpartum doula who took care of her and the baby for two months. Having this trusted female companion with her almost everywhere she went gave Jennifer comfort. She began weekly therapy sessions and eventually joined a support group. She and her therapist agreed that she did not need medication at this point.

Bipolar Disorder

• There is no available data about how often this occurs

Symptoms
• Mania (see appendix for description)
• Depression
• Rapid and severe moodswings

Risk factors

• Personal or family history of bipolar disorder

Tammy's story:

After my son was born I was happier than I'd ever been in my life. Everything felt wonderful. Everyone told me I should sleep when my baby slept, but I was too excited to sleep. I was really proud of myself that I kept the house spotless, took care of my baby and was still able to look great. My husband was pleased that dinner would always be ready for him when he came home. I was handling everything like a supermom, and felt on top of the world. After about two weeks my world started spinning out of control. I crashed. I started crying very easily and then a minute later I hated my husband and wanted a divorce. I started doing weird things like tape recording the baby all day so I could study his cries. I would also record my thoughts on tape since I believed they were profound and should be documented. My head would not slow down for a second. It was exhausting.

Tammy's treatment:

Tammy was prescribed an antipsychotic medication for a few weeks to sedate her enough to sleep at night when her husband was watching the baby. She was also put on a mood stabilizer. In therapy, she begn to understand what had happened to her, and set up realistic expectations for herself as a mother and wife. She started taking Omega 3 supplements which helped even out her moods. When she and her husband are ready to have another baby, she will discuss with the psychiatrist what the medical plan should be during pregnancy and postpartum.

Consequences of Untreated Mood Disorders

Maternal depression was placed at the top of the list entitled, "Most significant mental health issues impeding children's readiness for school" (Mental Health Policy Panel, Department of Health Services, 2002). There is a tremendous amount of data regarding the profoundly negative impact of untreated maternal depression on infants, toddlers, preschoolers, school age children and adolescents. There is an increased incidence of childhood psychiatric disturbance, behavior problems, poor social functioning, and impaired cognitive and language development. When a depressed mother goes untreated, every member of the family and all the relationships within the family are affected. The quicker the mother is treated, the better the prognosis for the entire family.

Perinatal Loss

No matter how a pregnancy is terminated, whether by nature or by choice, depression and anxiety commonly follow. Not only should grief be addressed through counseling, but medications may also be useful in reducing symptoms due to loss and hormonal changes.

When a stillbirth or neonatal death occurs, depression is, of course, to be expected. Counseling for the couple will be helpful, and medications may be needed to treat anxiety and depression. These women need to be monitored carefully for emotional symptoms in subsequent pregnancies and the postpartum period.

· THREE ·

Women with Postpartum Disorders

In the chapters to follow, we will discuss the role of practitioners, partners, and other family members in helping mothers recover. This chapter is for you, the sufferers.

Among the women we treat are those in the healthcare and educational professions, such as MDs, nurses, daycare and preschool providers, teachers, and therapists, to name a few. We often hear from these women, "This can't be happening to me! I take care of everyone else in crisis." What we tell them is that our hormones don't care what we do for a living! No one is immune. No matter what the educational or socioeconomic level, culture, religion, or personality, wherever women are having babies, the statistics remain consistent.

Women who suffer postpartum emotional difficulty experience their emotional pain in many different ways. Here are some of the common feelings they express:

No one has ever felt as bad as I do.
I'm all alone. No one understands.
I'm a failure as a woman, mother, and wife.
I'll never be myself again.
I've made a terrible mistake.
I'm on an emotional roller coaster.
I'm losing it.

Please know that each woman may experience these feelings at varying levels. Some may feel all of them, and others may feel only a few. You might also recognize some of your symptoms listed in Chapter 2.

Finding a Therapist

We encourage you to contact Postpartum Support International (PSI) at (800) 944-4PPD (944-4773) or www.postpartum.net to locate a therapist who has shown interest and commitment in the postpartum field. PSI, along with other organizations in the Resources section, provides specialized training in perinatal mood disorders. We have not found any graduate training that covers this material. Do not assume (as many insurance companies would like you to believe) that someone who has expertise in working with depression or other mood disorders is knowledgeable about perinatal mood disorders.

Sometimes an insurance company is willing to add a specialist to its provider list or pay for you to see one. If your insurance company will pay only if you see providers on their list, here are screening questions to help you determine their knowledge in this area. It's important to ask these questions, even if the therapist considers himself or herself knowledgeable. If you don't have the energy to deal with the insurance company or to screen professionals, ask a support person to do this for you.

* *What specific training have you received in postpartum mood disorders?*
* *Do you belong to any organization dedicated to education about perinatal mood disorders?*
Someone committed to working in this field should belong

to at least one of these organizations: Postpartum Support International, Marcé Society, North American Society for Psychosocial OB/GYN.

- *What books do you recommend to women with postpartum depression or anxiety?*
  Someone with expertise should be able to name several books listed in the Resources section of this manual.
- *What is your theoretical orientation?*
  Research has shown the most effective types of therapy for your condition are cognitive-behavioral and interpersonal. You are experiencing a life crisis; long-term intensive psychoanalysis is not appropriate.

If you are unable to find a therapist with expertise, interview until you find someone who is compassionate and willing to learn. If you do not think a practitioner is helping you, move on! Be a good consumer. Shop around until you feel satisfied that you are in capable hands.

The Truth of the Matter

As you face the challenge of a postpartum mood disorder, remind yourself of these truths:

- *I will recover!*
  We have never met a woman who, after proper treatment, did not recover.
- *I am not alone!*
  One in five women will experience a postpartum reaction more severe than the "Baby Blues."
- *This is not my fault!*
  You did not create this; it is a biochemical illness.

- *I am a good mom!*
  Even if you are hospitalized, you are still making sure your baby is provided for. The fact that you are trying to improve the quality of your life and your family's proves you are a good mom.

- *It is essential for me to take care of myself!*
  It is your job to take care of yourself so you can get better and take care of your family.

- *I am doing the best I can!*
  No matter what your current level of functioning, you are taking steps, regardless of how small they seem. Good for you!

Depression may interfere with your ability to believe these statements, so it is important to say them frequently, as if you really mean them. As you recover, this exercise will become easier.

Basic Mom Care

Finding Support People

Very often when we are in crisis, we overlook the people around us who can be of help and support. People can support you in different ways. Support may be physical; for instance, cooking, cleaning, caring for the baby, shopping, taking you for a walk or to an appointment. Emotional support may include sitting and listening, hugging, and giving encouraging words.

Even though the following writing task may feel overwhelming, it can serve to create your lifeline. This is a brainstorming exercise — write down everyone who comes to mind, regardless of the type of support they may be able to give you. If possible, do this exercise with a support person. Keep this list of supporters' names and phone numbers handy by your phone for times of need.

Here are some places where our clients have found people for their support network:

• Partner
• Family and extended family
• Neighbors
• Co-workers
• Religious communities
• Professionals (including doulas, lactation consultants, nannies, housekeepers)
• Hotlines
• Internet chat rooms (Warning: If you are anxious or obsessive we do not recommend)
• Postpartum depression support groups

Eating

Often women with postpartum depression and anxiety crave sweets and carbohydrates. If you can eat something nutritious, especially protein, each time you feed the baby, you can help keep your blood sugar level even. This will contribute to keeping your mood stable. We understand this may be difficult if you are experiencing a lack of appetite, so do the best you can. If you have trouble eating, try drinking your food — for example, protein shakes or drinks. Avoid caffeine.

Ask a support person to stock your refrigerator with things like yogurt, sliced deli meat and cheese, hardboiled eggs, pre-cut vegetables, and fruit. Better yet, if they are not already offering, ask people to bring you food. Don't forget to drink water-dehydration can increase anxiety. Appetite problems are quite common with postpartum depression and anxiety. Please tell your health practitioner about any appetite changes. It might be helpful to consult a nutritionist who is familiar with depression and anxiety when you have the energy.

Sleeping

Nighttime sleep is the most valuable sleep in helping you recover. Five hours of uninterrupted sleep per night is required for brain restoration because it gives you a full sleep cycle. The baby can be fed with breast milk or formula in a bottle. You need to be "off duty" physically, emotionally, and psychologically. You can either split the night with your partner or alternate taking a full night "on," then a full night "off."

If your partner is not home, you will need to enlist a support person to be responsible for the baby during this time. When you are "off" you should sleep away from the baby in another room, with earplugs. Many of our clients also use a fan, air purifier, or another appliance to block all baby noises. When your partner is "off," he can use the same techniques.

Remember, it is your job to take care of yourself. Even if you cannot arrange for this nightly, a few nights a week will help. If you are able to nap in the day, do so, but it does not replace nighttime sleep. Sleep problems occur frequently with mood disorders. If you are unable to sleep at night when everyone else is sleeping, please talk to your health practitioner. Medication will be helpful.

Exercising

Even a few minutes of brisk physical activity can help your mood. When you are physically able to be active, find something you are willing to do (for example, walking, dancing, or bike riding). Even if the thought of walking around the block is overwhelming, don't feel like a failure. It will get easier as you feel better. If you know you would feel better if you did the activity, but it is hard to mobilize yourself, designate a support person to encourage you and participate with you.

When you have insomnia or are very sleep-deprived, do not do intense aerobics — this can actually make your sleep condition worse. Wait until you have had at least a couple of weeks of good sleep before you resume or begin a heavy exercise program.

Taking Breaks

The myth is that if we really love our children enough, we don't need breaks from them. This certainly isn't the case! We've bought into the idea that taking time for ourselves is selfish and bad, and therefore we feel guilty when we even think we need a break. The truth is that all good mothers take breaks — that's how they stay good mothers! We strongly recommend that you get regularly scheduled time off at least three times a week for a minimum of two hours at a time. For every job other than being a mother, breaks are mandated by law, and you'd expect much more time off.

If you don't recharge your batteries, you'll be running on empty. You are not the only one who can care for the baby. Partners and family members, for instance, should be given alone time to bond with the baby too. This experience is important for the baby, and it can be done more easily with you somewhere else. Everyone wins.

If you're too depressed or tired to actually leave the house, go to another room and use earplugs or earphones. Or, maybe your support person can leave the house with the baby and give you alone time.

Going Outside

When we're depressed or anxious, the four walls feel as if they're closing in. Our world feels darker and smaller. We tend to fold in emotionally and physically (as in crossing our arms, hunching over, and fixing our gaze downward).

To counter this, go outside your home, look up at the sky, stand up straight, put your arms at your sides, and breathe. You don't have to actually go anywhere. Just go outside once a day, even if this means standing outside your front door in your bathrobe.

Taking Care of the Baby

Depending on the level of depression, you may need someone to do most, if not all, of the baby care. A support person can be with you when your partner is not, such as a family member, doula, nanny, or friend. Very gradually you can increase your participation with the baby care as your support person keeps you company.

Even though you may feel like a robot at first, just going through the motions without joy, it is still good for you to experience yourself doing "mommy" tasks. Your feelings of competence and confidence will increase, and eventually you will be able to enjoy your day.

Scripts

You may not know what you need when a support person asks, "What can I do?" It's all right to say, "I don't know what I need right now. I just know I feel awful." However, don't assume anyone can read your mind. You are most likely to get what you need if you ask for it.

Try giving your partner, family, and friends a script to guide them in how to best support you. For example, when you are experiencing anxiety, it will not be helpful to hear, "Just calm down and relax." Instead, try giving them suggestions of what to say and do:

I am sorry you are suffering.
We will get through this.
I am here for you.
Hug.
This will pass.

A script does not detract from the genuineness of caring and love. On the contrary, it will give your support people an effective way to give you what you need. People who love you want you to get better. They will be relieved to know what will help.

For Women with Anxiety or Obsessions

Be sure to avoid caffeine and keep your blood sugar level even (see section above on eating). For many women with anxiety or obsessions, information provides fuel for worry. Turn off the TV news, and don't read the news section of the newspaper. Don't read books, magazines, or Internet information about postpartum mood disorders if you find it makes you more anxious. If you go to the movies, select comedies. Find activities that can soothe or distract you, rather than those that stir up anxiety.

Stimulation

When the usual sights, sounds, and daily activity feel like too much, it is important to adjust your surroundings. Remember, you are in recovery. Treating yourself with "kid gloves" can greatly boost your recovery. Don't push yourself. If, for instance, going to a family event (even if you have had fun at this event in the past) seems overwhelming, you probably should not go. Trust yourself. As you recover, you'll be able to handle more.

When very anxious, perinatal women often feel hypersensitive to stimulation of all kinds — visual, auditory, and kinesthetic (touch). If this is happening, it may be soothing to lower the light in your house. (If you are feeling more depressed than anxious, try brightening your house with more light — open your curtains and add lamps, for example.) As long as you can hear what you need to, try wearing earplugs or earphones during the day to muffle unnecessary noise. You may become more sensitive to touch — for instance, clothing may rub, scratch or itch. Be compassionate with yourself and do what you need to in order to be comfortable.

Myths About
Nursing and Bonding

Myth: *"I can't be a good mom unless I nurse my baby."*

The truth is there is no one right way to feed your baby. Whatever works for you and your family is the right way. There is a tremendous amount of pressure on new moms in our society to nurse exclusively, regardless of physical or emotional obstacles. We believe that one size never fits all. Whether you feed your baby breast milk or formula has no relationship to how much you love your child or what kind of mother you are.

There are advantages and disadvantages to both breast-feeding and bottlefeeding, and some combination of the two may work for you as well. For instance, having a support person bottlefeed with formula or breast milk so you can be off duty is a responsible choice for your family's well-being. Don't allow yourself to be guilt-tripped!

Be prepared for intrusive and inappropriate questions and comments about how you're feeding your baby. This may happen anywhere; for example, out in public, at your health practitioner's office, a mom's group, or at a family gathering. If any person, whether lay or professional, seems judgmental about the plan you've chosen, remind yourself that you have made the best decision you can for you and your family. You can ignore the question or comment or change the subject. Alternatively, you can say, "It's none of your business," "I can't breastfeed. I have a life-threatening illness," "I chose not to," or

"My doctor told me I can't."

Remember, you are entitled to respond any way you need to in order to get inquisitors off your back. You have nothing to apologize about. Good moms make sure their babies are fed. Period.

Myth: *"My baby won't bond if I don't nurse."*

If this were true, there would be whole generations of adults who never bonded with their mothers! Some women actually begin to bond with their babies when they stop breastfeeding. For women who are experiencing anxiety or pain related to breastfeeding, bottlefeeding may allow this time together to be more relaxed and enjoyable. There are no rules about how to bottlefeed. If you desire skin-to-skin contact, you can bottlefeed bare-chested.

Myth: *"My baby can sense my depression or anxiety."*

Your baby cannot read your mind! Your thoughts or feelings will not damage your baby or the relationship with your baby. What babies can sense is temperature, hunger, wetness, and physical contact. Your baby will feel close to you regardless of depressed or anxious thoughts running through your head.

Myth: *"Bonding happens immediately at birth."*

No adopted children would ever bond with their adoptive moms if this were true. There is no one magic moment of opportunity when bonding must happen, and no reason to worry about bonding if you were unable to touch or hold your baby immediately after delivery. Even if your depression or anxiety has made it difficult for you to care for your baby, it's never too late. Bonding is a process of familiarity, closeness, and comfort that continues for years.

Recovery

What will help each woman recover from postpartum depression depends on the reason(s) for her illness and her preferences for treatment. Whatever helps you get better is what we recommend. In Chapter 7 we outline a few different treatment options which you may choose to do separately or in combination. Since medication is among the most common treatments for these disorders, we've listed a few of the questions we hear most often.

Antidepressant
Questions and Answers

Question: *I'm afraid medication will change my personality.*

Answer: Depression and anxiety change your personality — people who are usually easygoing and stable may become irritable, moody, withdrawn, or worried. As the medication begins to work, you will begin to feel like yourself again. In a sense, medication restores you to your "old" personality.

Question: *How long will I have to take the medicine?*

Answer: Treatment length varies, and is a decision between you and your prescribing practitioner. If this is your first episode of depression/anxiety, the general recommendation is to take a dose that gets you "back to yourself," then continue on the medicine for a minimum of six months. If you have a history of depression or anxiety, your practitioner may suggest a longer course of treatment. Staying on the medication for the recommended time is critical to reduce your chances of having a relapse or reoccurrence of illness.

Question: *Will I become dependent on the antidepressant?*
Answer: Antidepressants are not addictive or habit-forming.

Question: *What if I have side effects?*
Answer: Many people experience no side effects at all. If side effects do occur, they are usually mild and temporary, lasting less than a week (nausea, fatigue, or shakiness, for instance). If you experience a decrease in sex drive, it may persist through the course of treatment. If you feel more severe side effects or side effects that do not clear up after a week, contact your practitioner. Some women need to try more than one antidepressant before they find the one that works best for them. To reduce the likelihood of side effects, it is helpful to start at a very low dose and slowly work up to the correct therapeutic dosage for you.

Question: *Which antidepressant is the right one for me?*
Answer: In general, most people do well on most of the medications. If you have previously been on a medication that was helpful, or if you have a blood relative doing well on a medication, that one would probably be the first choice. If you are anxious, a medication that may have a calming effect might be chosen. If you have fatigue, a medication that is energizing may be tried. The most important indicator is whether you begin to feel better.

Question: *When will I feel better? How will I know if the medication is working?*
Answer: Most of the newer antidepressants begin working within two weeks, while the older medications can take four to six weeks to work. Here are some comments we have heard as the medicine begins working:

I'm not crying all the time.

I have more patience — my fuse is longer.

I'm singing in the shower again.

My husband noticed I seem happier.

I feel more motivated — I'm cooking for the family again.

I'm enjoying the baby more.

I'm not worrying as much — the little things aren't getting to me.

Question: Won't medication be a crutch?

Answer: A crutch is a temporary tool that you use until you no longer need it. If you broke your foot you wouldn't think twice about using crutches to support you while your foot heals. Medication restores your brain chemistry to a normal state, allowing you to get back to feeling yourself and back to your life. As you become well you will wean off the medication.

Question: *I want to breastfeed but I don't want to take anything that will harm my baby. Can I take medication and nurse?*

Answer: According to the professionals who have dedicated their careers to studying the safety of antidepressants and nursing, the answer is yes. When infant blood was examined, few, if any, metabolites of medication were found. Babies exposed to medication through nursing are as healthy and normal in all ways as babies not exposed.

It's clear from the research that it is more important for a mom to receive proper treatment than whether she feeds her baby breast milk or formula. So if you think you will worry too much about your baby if you continue breastfeeding while taking an antidepressant, it is better to wean (slowly) rather than to go without treatment. Remember that the best gift you can give your baby is a happy, healthy mom. Often the anxiety about nursing while taking a medication goes away once the medication starts working, since the anxiety can be caused by the mood disorder itself.

Question: I am pregnant and really depressed. Do I need to feel this way for the rest of my pregnancy?

Answer: About 10-20% of women experience depression in pregnancy. Getting treatment is important for both you and the baby. Researchers have begun looking at the harmful effects of untreated depression and anxiety on the fetus. Also, if you are depressed or anxious in pregnancy, you may not be eating or sleeping as well as you should. This is not good for you or your developing baby.

Counseling alone may be sufficient, but often medication is necessary. SSRIs (selective serotonin reuptake inhibitors) have been shown to be helpful for both depression and anxiety. No increased risk of miscarriage or malformations has been shown to result from taking these medications, even in the first trimester. Depression in pregnancy also puts you at high risk for postpartum depression. Being on medication through pregnancy and postpartum will significantly decrease this risk.

Question: I am embarrassed and ashamed about taking medication. Am I weak because I need a medication?

Answer: There is a stigma in our culture about people who take psychotropic medication. This stigma is based on ignorance. Somehow it is presumed we can control our brain chemistry. If you had diabetes or a thyroid disorder you wouldn't expect (and no one would suggest) that you could will yourself to make more insulin or thyroid hormone. It's a strength to get help when we need it, not a weakness!

Taking medication is a personal choice. You are not required to share this information with others. Being private is not the same as being ashamed. However, once our clients begin to tell close family or friends, they are often surprised to find out how many of them are also on medication, or know someone who is. Whether you choose to take an antidepressant or not, find people who will support your choices for wellness.

• FOUR •

Partners

This chapter is designed to provide support to you, the partner, regardless of your gender or marital status. To avoid confusion, we sometimes refer to the new mother as "wife." The sooner you become involved in the recovery process, and the greater your involvement, the more you both will benefit — together and separately. The more you understand what she is experiencing, the better supported she will feel. That will, in turn, expedite her recovery.

Things to Keep in Mind

- *You didn't cause her illness and you can't take it away.*
  Postpartum depression and anxiety is a biochemical disorder. It is no one's fault. When her brain chemistry returns to normal, she will feel like herself again. It is your job to support her as this happens.

- *She doesn't expect you to "fix it."*
  Many partners feel frustrated because they feel inadequate or unable to fix the problem. She doesn't need you to try to take the problem away. This isn't like a leaky faucet that can be repaired with a new washer. Don't suggest quick-fix solutions. This isn't that kind of problem. She just needs you to listen.

- *Get the support you need so you can be there for her.*
We frequently see the partner becoming depressed during or
after his wife's depression. You can avoid this by taking care
of yourself and getting your own support from friends,
family or professionals. You should make sure to get breaks
from taking care of your family. Regular exercise or other
stress-reducing activity is important, so you can remain the
solid support for your wife. Provide a stand-in support
person for her while you're gone.
- *Don't take it personally.*
Irritability is common with postpartum depression/anxiety.
Don't allow yourself to become a verbal punching bag. It's
not good for anyone concerned. She feels guilty after saying
hurtful things to you. If you feel you didn't deserve to be
snapped at, explain that to her calmly.
- *Just being there with and for her is doing a great deal.*
Being present and letting her know you support her is often
all she'll need. Ask her what words she needs to hear for
reassurance, and say them to her often.
- *Lower your expectations.*
Even a non-depressed postpartum woman cannot realistically
be expected to cook dinner and clean house. She may be
guilt-tripping herself about not measuring up to her own
expectations and worrying that you will also be disappointed.
Remind her that parenting your child and taking care of your
home is also your job, not just hers. Your relationship and
family will emerge from this crisis stronger than ever.
- *Let her sleep at night.*
She needs six hours of uninterrupted sleep per night to
complete a full sleep cycle and restore her biorhythms. If
you want your wife back quicker, be on duty during this time
without disturbing her. Many dads and partners have
expressed how much closer they are to their children because
of nighttime caretaking. If you can't be up with the baby
during the night, hire someone who can take your place. A
temporary baby nurse will be worth her weight in gold.

What to Say, What Not to Say

Say:

- *We will get through this.*
- *I'm here for you.*
- *If there is something I can do to help you, please tell me.* For example, care for the baby, run her a warm bath, put on soothing music.
- *I'm sorry you're suffering. That must feel awful.*
- *I love you very much.*
- *The baby loves you very much.*
- *This is temporary.*
- *You'll get yourself back.* As she recovers, point out specifics about how you see her old self returning; such as, smiling again, more patience, or going out with her friends.
- *You're doing such a good job.* Give specific examples.
- *You're a great mom.* Give specific examples, such as "I love how you smile at the baby."
- *This isn't your fault. If I were ill, you wouldn't blame me.*

Do Not Say:

- *Think about everything you have to feel happy about.* She already knows everything she has to feel happy about. One of the reasons she feels so guilty is that she is depressed despite these things.
- *Just relax.* This suggestion usually produces the opposite effect! She is already frustrated at not being able to relax despite all the coping mechanisms that have worked in the past. Anxiety produces hormones that can cause physical reactions, such as an increased heart rate, shakiness, visual changes, shortness of breath, and muscle tension. This is not something she can just will away.

- *Snap out of it.*
  If she could, she would have already. She wouldn't wish this on anyone. A person cannot snap out of any illness.
- *Just think positively.*
  It would be lovely if recovery were that simple! The nature of this illness prevents positive thinking. Depression feels like wearing foggy, dark, distorted lenses which filter out positive input from the environment. Only negative, guilt-ridden interpretations of the world are perceived. This illness is keeping her from experiencing the lighter, humorous, and joyful aspects of life.

From a Dad Who's Been There

This was written by Henry, Shoshana's husband, for Shoshana's newsletter, soon after her first depression had subsided:

You've just come home from a long day at work, hoping to find a happy home — and what you find makes you want to get back into the car and leave. Your wife is in tears, the baby is crying. The house is a mess, and forget about dinner. By now you know better than to ask how her day was. Her response is always the same. "I hate this 'mother' stuff. I don't want to be anyone's mother. I want my old life back. I want to be happy again." You shrug, go to hold the baby, and wonder why your wife is feeling this way, why she's not as happy as you are about the baby, and when she will snap out of it.

You're not alone. I lived with this scene every day for two years. Every ounce of my patience was tested, but I kept hoping that things would be "normal" again. I focused on my baby daughter, the one in the midst of this mess, and kept telling myself I'd be there for her.

Slowly, slowly, my wife recovered from the illness. Today, we have that happy home we both always wanted. Be patient and tolerant. Remember, it will get better.

FIVE

Siblings, Family, and Friends

After the birth of a baby there are many changes that occur in a household. Although older children may expect some of these changes, they probably will not be expecting Mom to be different. Even siblings who are too young to understand the concept of depression will most likely notice that their mother's behavior has not been normal.

Children usually notice if Mom is, or has been, crying. They will notice if Mom yells or gets angry over little things. Perhaps they will notice that Mom stays in bed more, does not have the energy to take them to the park, or does not seem to laugh much lately. Maybe they see her staring blankly into space, not paying much attention to them. Children can tell this is not the Mom they used to know, and they need honest, clear explanations about what is occurring.

It is crucial that the path of communication with children is open. Whenever possible the mother herself should talk with her children. The partner or another adult can help to reinforce the information. There are several important guidelines in communicating with children about what is happening.

Communicating with Children About Postpartum Depression

- Even adults are often unclear about words like "depression" or "anxiety." Instead, use descriptive words like "sad," "cranky," "tired," "weepy," "worried," or "grouchy."

- Reassure them often that they did not cause Mommy's illness or problem; this is not their fault, nor could they have done anything to prevent it.
- Let them know it is not the kind of illness caused by germs. She did not catch it from anyone, nor can she pass it on to them.
- Let the children know that Mom is getting help: seeing a doctor or counselor, taking medicine, and she will get better soon. Let them know Mom may have some good and some bad times as she recovers.
- Ask the children how they can help Mom. Perhaps they can draw a pretty picture, leave "I love you" notes around the house for her, and offer to help with age-appropriate tasks.
- Tell the truth. Children know if Mom is not "herself," so don't tell them she is fine when she is not. Mom should be direct and honest too. For instance, when it is apparent that she is feeling sad, she can say so. Sadness is just a feeling; it does not have to be logical or rational. Feelings are part of being human. To hide sadness (for example, saying, "Oh, these are 'happy tears'"), gives the message that it is not permissible to be sad.

What we can teach our children by showing feelings is how to express ourselves in appropriate ways. This will not damage them. On the contrary, it can model behavior that will serve them well in the future. And by getting help we teach our children that when there is something wrong we can do something about it.

Here is an example of what a mother could say to her child/children:

You may have noticed I have been crying and getting mad a lot lately. Some of the chemicals in my body are not working right, and it has been affecting how I feel and how I act. I want you to know I love you very much, and I love the baby, too. I also want you to know that this is not your or anybody else's fault. I am taking good care of myself and getting help so I can get better as fast as I can. I am probably going to have good times and bad times, but I will get better and better until I'm completely well. I am looking forward to taking you to the park again. I love you very much.

Family and Friends

Whether related by blood or marriage, the reaction of family and friends to the new mother's depression can critically affect her recovery.

Sometimes a depressed mother feels too scared to tell her partner about uncomfortable feelings, fearing disapproval. This mom may open up to you first, if given an opportunity. But even if she is talking openly with her partner, having the right kinds of support from those including her parents, in-laws, grand-parents, siblings, and friends, will provide her with the best environment for recovery.

When we become mothers, even if we aren't depressed, we often crave the company and approval of our own mothers. If the woman's own mother is deceased, or if their relationship is strained, it will be extra important to have another woman who can help fill that void. Because depressed mothers are, in general, even more vulnerable than non-depressed mothers, they will need substantial reassurance from those around them, especially from adult females.

New moms in general are sensitive to criticism. Moms with postpartum mood disorders are typically even more sensitive. Compliment her frequently on her mothering and avoid negative comments, especially those related to her parenting.

Things to Keep in Mind

- *You will not be able to cure her.*
  You may feel frustrated that postpartum illnesses cannot be cured in the same way as other conditions. The course of this illness, even with medication, is different from that of an ear infection, for example. Where most common conditions get steadily better until they disappear, postpartum illnesses fluctuate during recovery.

  Typically the woman advances two steps forward and feels better, and then drops one step back and "dips." She may feel hopeless when these dips occur, since depression robs her of a perspective that she is getting well. She may voice that she is back to square one and that she is not getting better.

  It is important that you remind her that the dip is only temporary, she is getting better, and her moods will get back on track. A dip is not a regression — it is simply part of the process. Remind her that as long as she is going in the right direction overall, that is what is most important.

- *Encourage, do not insist.*
  Women suffering from postpartum depression often feel incapable of finding the words to communicate their feelings. While it is positive to encourage her to share her thoughts, it is unhelpful to demand it. Let her know you are willing to listen without judging her.

  Trust that she will open up when she is ready and feels what she has to say will be treated seriously and respectfully. Even just being there in total silence together can be a great support. Your presence alone is tremendously helpful, even if she cannot or chooses not to speak.

- *Stay in the here and now.*
  With her up and down moods, the recovering woman cannot trust that the good times will last. She never knows when her brain chemistry will shift and her moods will drop. She may be reluctant to share the good times with you for fear that you'll think she no longer needs your support.

  Eventually the good times will last and the dips will go away, but this process can take several weeks or even months. Reassure her that you understand she will be riding some waves in mood for a while, and that your support won't be suddenly yanked away before she's ready.

- *Don't let looks fool you.*
  Postpartum depression is a hidden illness. These women often appear normal to the outside world. They can look "put together," complete with makeup, jewelry, and even a smile, and be deeply depressed at the same time.

  Sometimes the more depressed a mom feels, the more she overcompensates for it on the outside. For instance, if she feels ashamed, she may try to act perky in order to hide her true feelings. It is important to ask the mother how she is doing and never assume based on how she appears. So if you hear another family member say, "But she doesn't look depressed," you can teach them that looks can be quite deceiving when it comes to postpartum illness.

What to Say, What Not to Say

Say:

- *I'm here for you.*
- *I'm sorry you are suffering. That must feel awful.*
- *You're doing a great job.* Be specific whenever you can.
- *You're a great mom.* Give specific examples, like "I love how you smile at the baby."
- *You're a great... (sister, daughter, aunt).* Be specific.
- *You will get well.*
- *Would you like me to do... (insert task)*
- *I went through this, too.* If you truly did — remember, this is not "Baby Blues" and will not go away in a few days.

Do Not Say:

- *Just buck up and tough it out.*
  Not getting adequate treatment puts women at risk of chronic illness and relapse.
- *I don't get what the big deal is.*
  Depression makes everything feel like a big deal. She's overwhelmed.
- *You have so much to be happy about.*
  She knows that already. She feels guilty that she is still depressed despite those things.
- *You just need more sleep.*
  Sleep is important, but is usually not all she needs to be well.
- *You just need a break from your baby.*
  Breaks are crucial, but usually not all that is needed.

- *I went through this too.*
  This is not "Baby Blues." Don't minimize her experience by saying you've "been there" unless you really have suffered with this illness.
- *Women have been having babies for centuries.*
  And a certain percentage has been getting depressed for centuries!

What you can do to help

- Make dinner.
- Watch the baby (or her other children) so she can take a break.
- Do the laundry.
- Do the dishes.
- Make lunch for her.
- Sit and listen.
- Clean the house.
- Take a walk together.
- Go shopping or do errands for her.
- Write thank you notes for her.
- If her partner is not home, be on duty at night so she can sleep.

SIX

Health Practitioners

The fact that you are reading this book clearly indicates that you are a caring and concerned professional. Your guidance during this critical time will significantly impact the mental and physical well-being of women with perinatal mood disorders. It is important not to underreact or overreact to these women's symptoms. Just treat them as matter-of-factly as you would any other common perinatal experience, for example, gestational diabetes.

This chapter contains answers to the questions that we have been most frequently asked throughout the years regarding signs, symptoms, and treatment. Because a distressed woman's contact with a professional office includes the receptionist and nursing staff, it is imperative that the entire staff be knowledgeable about the information in this book. We have created sections for primary care providers (family practitioners, internists, osteopaths, chiropractors), pediatricians, OB/GYNs and midwives, psychiatrists, birth doulas, postpartum doulas and visiting nurses, lactation consultants, childbirth educators, new parent group leaders, and adjunct professionals.

Please remember that warning signs of distress are not always obvious for a variety of reasons. Shame, guilt, or fear of judgment may cause the woman to hide her feelings. She may present more "socially acceptable" complaints such as fatigue, headache, marital problems, or a fussy baby. Just because a woman is smiling or well groomed, don't assume she is not suffering silently. Postpartum depression is a hidden illness. Although there are risk factors to help predict postpartum depression, there is no particular "type" of person who becomes afflicted. We appreciate that you may be apprehensive about asking questions that could open a Pandora's box. She might feel accused of being a bad mom, and become defensive. But once she hears your matter-of-fact tone, and understands no shame is attached to postpartum illness, she will be able to accept the information. In the long run, you will be saving time and providing quality care.

Culture and Language

Although the prevalence of perinatal mood disorders appears to be generally the same throughout the world, reactions to these disorders vary among cultures. Where shame is a great personal threat, for example, women may be more reluctant to discuss their symptoms and will require considerable reassurance.

Those assisting women with these disorders should take into account that nonverbal communication varies among cultures as well. For instance, a nod could signify either understanding or acquiescence to authority. It is also important to make clear what your role is in order to avoid unrealistic expectations.

Sociocultural factors and literacy levels should not be overlooked when taking a history or completing an assessment. The perception of stress, types of stressors, as well as coping styles, differ across cultures. These will affect the woman's response to recommendations on which treatment methods to use or to avoid.

The level of simplicity or sophistication you use should be attuned to that of the patient, but do not assume that an educated woman will automatically understand her condition better than a woman with less education. For instance, avoid raising questions of self-diagnosis, such as, "Do you think you have postpartum depression?" even when a patient is highly educated. She may have a preconceived idea of what that term means. Instead, ask specific questions about her mood and behavior, which will elicit this information. These questions are outlined later in this chapter.

What to Say, What Not to Say

Say:

- *These feelings are quite common.*
- *This is treatable.*
- *You will get well.*
- *Here is some information that will help you.*

Do Not Say:

- *Join a new mom's group.*
  If a mother is clinically depressed or anxious, this may be a damaging suggestion, depending largely on the leader of the group. A depressed mother is already feeling different and inadequate compared to other new mothers. Attending a "normal" new mothers' group may intensify her alienation.

  If you know that the leader of the group is sensitive (such as those reading this book) and discusses mood problems, this mom will be fine. Ideally, she should join a group specifically designed for mothers with postpartum depression and anxiety. Many of our clients belong to both types of groups: one to discuss the normal new mom stuff and the other to openly express more difficult feelings.

- *Take a vacation with your husband.*
Although a change of scenery may be nice, the depressed mother takes her brain chemistry with her! Her anxiety and depression level may actually increase due to the financial investment, leaving her baby, and guilt that the trip did not "cure" her.

- *Exercise.*
These mothers are feeling overwhelmed. Some have barely enough energy to wash a bottle, let alone go to the gym. Suggesting exercise to the chronically sleep-deprived mother can actually backfire and cause insomnia. Endorphins only work temporarily. Exercise will not cure her depression. When she's able to leave her house and take a short walk, she can be encouraged to do so. But, until then, this is just another setup for failure.

- *Do something nice for yourself.*
This is always a good thing, but again, it will not be enough to regulate the depressed mother's neurotransmitters. This suggestion should be used only as part of a much larger treatment plan, not presented as a quick fix.

- *Sleep when the baby sleeps.*
Even a non-depressed mother may have difficulty sleeping when the baby naps during the day. Especially for those mothers with high levels of anxiety, this will be an impossibility. What is most important is that she sleeps at night when her baby sleeps.

Screening

We recommend whenever possible using standardized screening surveys, such as the Postpartum Depression Screening Scale or the Edinburgh Postnatal Depression Scale. For your immediate use, we have outlined informal screening tools. We use the term "perinatal psychotherapist" to indicate a psychotherapist who specializes in the field of perinatal mood disorders.

Prenatal Screening

Several prenatal screening inventories have been developed. They are listed in the resource section. If time is too limited to use screening questionnaires, the questions in the **Pre-pregnancy and Pregnancy Risk Assessment** should be asked. At the bare minimum, the questions associated with highest measure of risk must be asked, noted with a ★. These are the questions relating to personal/family history of mental illness, previous postpartum mood disorder, and severe premenstrual mood changes.

Given prenatally, the Edinburgh Postnatal Depression Scale has been found to effectively identify women at risk for postpartum depression.

PRE-PREGNANCY AND PREGNANCY RISK ASSESSMENT

Warning Signs

- Missed appointments
- Excessive worrying (about her own health or health of fetus)
- Looking unusually tired
- Crying
- Requires support person to accompany her to appointments
- Significant weight gain or loss
- Physical complaints with no apparent cause
- Flashbacks, fear, or nightmares regarding previous trauma
- Her concern that she won't be a good mother

Questions to Ask   ★ *These indicate high risk.*

Note: Even if your clients/patients have experienced these disorders, they may not be aware of this fact if they were never formally diagnosed. You may need to ask about their experience with the symptoms of the disorders as opposed to using diagnostic terms in order to adequately assess.

★ **Have you ever had depression, panic, extreme anxiety, OCD, bipolar disorder, psychosis, or an eating disorder?**
Women with a personal history of mood disorders need to be educated about their high risk for a perinatal mood disorder. They should be referred to a perinatal psychotherapist to help them develop a plan of action to minimize their risk. Those women with a history of bipolar disorder or psychosis should also be referred to a psychiatrist for

medication evaluation and observation during pregnancy and postpartum.

★ *Are you taking any medications (prescription or nonprescription) or herbs on a regular basis?*
Women who are self-treating for insomnia, anxiety, sadness or other symptoms that may indicate a mood disorder, should be evaluated by a perinatal psychotherapist.

★ *Have you had a previous pregnancy or postpartum mood disorder?*
Women answering yes to this question are at extremely high risk for another perinatal mood disorder. They should be referred to a perinatal psychotherapist in order to develop a plan of action to prevent or at least minimize another occurrence.

★ *Have you ever taken any psychotropic medications?*
If yes, educate them about their risk of developing a perinatal mood disorder. Observe them carefully during pregnancy and postpartum.

★ *Have you ever had severe premenstrual mood changes (PMS or PMDD)?*
Women whose moods are affected by hormone changes are clearly at high risk during pregnancy and postpartum since there are dramatic hormonal shifts. Educate them about their risk, and observe them carefully during pregnancy and postpartum.

★ *Do you have any family history of mental illness?*
If yes, educate them about their risk, and observe them during pregnancy and postpartum.

• *Do you have any personal or family history of substance abuse?*

- *Do you smoke?*
- *If pregnant, how have you been feeling physically and emotionally?*
- *Do you feel you have adequate emotional and physical support?*
- *Have you had a birth-related trauma (or other traumatic incident such as rape or sexual abuse)?*
- *Are you experiencing any major life stressors (for example, moving, job change, deaths, financial problems)?*
- *Have there been any health problems for you or the fetus?*
- *Do you have a personal or family history of thyroid disorder?*

Postpartum Screening

Two postpartum depression screening inventories are available (see Resources). Either one can easily be completed in a waiting room.

The Edinburgh Postnatal Depression Screening Scale (EPDS) was developed in 1987 in Britain, by Dr. John Cox, et al. It is a 10 question self-report test. It has been translated into many languages and is used all over the world. It can be found on many Internet sites.

More recently, Dr. Cheryl Beck has developed the Postpartum Depression Screening Scale (PDSS). It has been found to accurately screen for both postpartum depression and anxiety. The PDSS can be administered in either a short or long format. The total score can be broken down into seven symptom content scales when using the long format. An elevated score in a particular symptom area indicates a greater amount of distress than average. The symptom scales are: Sleeping/Eating Disturbances, Anxiety/Insecurity, Emotional Lability, Mental

Confusion, Loss of Self, Guilt/Shame, and Suicidal Thoughts. In comparing the PDSS with the EPDS, Beck found that the PDSS has higher combinations of specificity and sensitivity than the EPDS in screening for major postpartum depression. Additionally, the PDSS was more likely to identify women with symptoms of sleep disturbance, mental confusion, and anxiety. If you have assessed that a woman has a postpartum mood disorder, here are some basic "do's and don'ts."

POSTPARTUM RISK ASSESSMENT

With your postpartum patients who were not screened pre-natally, ask the first six questions from the **Pre-pregnancy and Pregnancy Risk Assessment** (the questions marked with ★), as well as the **Postpartum Risk Assessment.**

Warning Signs in the Mother
- Missed appointments
- Excessive worrying (often about the mother's own health or health of baby)
- Looking unusually tired
- Requires support person to accompany to appointments
- Significant weight gain or loss
- Physical complaints with no apparent cause
- Poor milk production (could indicate thyroid dysfunction)
- Evading questions about her own well-being
- Crying
- Not willing to hold baby or unusual discomfort handling or responding to baby
- Not willing to allow others to care for baby
- Excessive concern about baby despite reassurance (for

example, eating sufficiently, development, weight gain)
- Rigidity or obsessiveness (for example, regarding the baby's feeding or sleeping schedules)
- Excessive concern about appearance of self or baby
- Expressing that baby doesn't like her or that she's not a good mother
- Expressing lack of partner support

Warning Signs in the Baby

- Excessive weight gain or loss
- Delayed cognitive or language development
- Decreased responsiveness to mother
- Breastfeeding problems

Questions to Ask

- *How are you doing?*
  Have good eye contact with her while you ask this question.

- *How are you feeling about being a mom?*
  Women who feel like they're doing a bad job or who generally don't like the job, may be depressed.

- *Do you have any particular concerns?*

- *How are you sleeping (quality and quantity)?*
  Five hours minimum of uninterrupted sleep per night is required for a complete sleep cycle, necessary to restore brain chemistry.

- *Can you sleep at night when everyone else is asleep?*
  Insomnia is a symptom of every mood disorder.

- *How is the baby sleeping?*

- *Who gets up at night with the baby?*

- *Have you had any unusual or scary thoughts?*
  If yes, refer woman to a perinatal psychotherapist for evaluation. Some thoughts may be normal, however others may indicate OCD or psychosis.

- *Are you receiving adequate physical and emotional help?*
  A good support system of family and friends can make a significant difference.

- *Is your partner sharing the responsibilities of household and parenting?*
  Remind her that these jobs do not just belong to her, even if she is the primary caretaker.

- *Do you generally feel like yourself?*
  Women with postpartum mood disorders often report not feeling like their usual selves, or having a different personality.

- *How is your appetite?*
  A significant change in appetite is a warning sign.

- *What and how often are you eating and drinking?*
  See section on eating in Chapter 3.

- *If breastfeeding, how is it going?*
  Poor milk production may indicate a thyroid dysfunction or be a result of anxiety.

- *If using formula, when and how quickly did you wean?*
  Abrupt weaning can precipitate a mood disorder.

- *When was your last period?*
  First menses after delivery can be a precipitating factor.

- *Are you taking any medications or herbs on a regular basis?*
  Women who are self-treating for insomnia, anxiety, sadness or other symptoms which may indicate a mood disorder, should be evaluated by a perinatal psychotherapist.

- *Are you feeling moodier than normal (tearful, irritable, or worried)?*
  This is common in mood disorders. Refer to Chapter 2 for a more complete list of symptoms.

- *Have there been any health problems for you or the baby?*
  These factors increase the risk for mood disorders.

- *How are you feeling toward your baby?*
  Ambivalence and anger are two examples of feelings that may indicate postpartum depression.

Primary Care Providers

As a primary care provider, you may have a longstanding relationship with your patient. You have a good sense of her mental and physical health history. This puts you in an advantageous position to evaluate her pre-pregnancy risk, and provide appropriate direction. Your office may provide a safe haven should a pregnancy or postpartum mood problem arise. Please have information from the Resources section available, as well as referrals to local professionals trained in perinatal mood disorders.

A woman taking psychotropic medications who is pregnant or planning a pregnancy should be encouraged to consult a psychiatrist specializing in perinatal mood disorders in order to determine whether to continue her medications. Recommendations will differ based on each woman's history and chronic problems. Women on medication for a bipolar disorder or psychosis should definitely be referred to a psychiatrist to develop a medication plan. These women need careful monitoring throughout pregnancy and postpartum.

Use the **Pre-pregnancy and Pregnancy Risk Assessment** on ALL women who are pregnant or planning a pregnancy. Even if she is feeling fine early in the pregnancy, she may not later in pregnancy or postpartum. She should be screened periodically throughout the pregnancy.

With your postpartum patients who were not screened pre-natally, ask the first six questions from the **Pre-pregnancy and Pregnancy Risk Assessment** (the questions marked with ★), as well as the **Postpartum Risk Assessment.**

Use the **Postpartum Risk Assessment** on ALL women during their first year postpartum.

Pediatricians

The well-being of your patient is largely dependent on the well-being of the primary caregiver, usually the mother. It is well documented that the mental health of the mother has a tremendous impact on the emotional and physical development of the child. While the focus of the pediatric visit is primarily the baby, the health of the mother is a crucial component that must not be overlooked.

In addition to the obvious milestones, the mother-baby relationship must be assessed. She will need your reassurance if she wishes to nurse while taking an antidepressant. Have referrals to local professionals trained in perinatal mood disorders and information in the Resources section available.

If you have the opportunity to screen the woman before her baby is born, ask at least the first six questions from the **Pre-pregnancy and Pregnancy Risk Assessment** (the questions marked with ★).

Use the **Postpartum Risk Assessment** at every well baby visit throughout the first year postpartum for ALL your patients' mothers.

OB/GYNs and Midwives

Your office has been a source of comfort and advice throughout the pregnancy. This intimate relationship makes it likely that a woman with postpartum distress will come to you for help if she feels depressed or anxious. However, many women will not be forthcoming with negative feelings or concerns unless specifically asked. Have referrals to local professionals trained in perinatal mood disorders and information in the Resources section available. Please follow up on a regular basis.

A woman taking psychotropic medication who is pregnant or planning a pregnancy should be encouraged to consult a psychiatrist specializing in perinatal mood disorders to determine whether to continue or change her medication. Recommendations will differ based on each woman's history and chronic problems. Women on medication for a bipolar disorder or psychosis should definitely be referred to a psychiatrist to develop a medication plan. These women need careful monitoring throughout pregnancy and postpartum.

Use the **Pre-pregnancy and Pregnancy Risk Assessment** on ALL women who are pregnant or planning a pregnancy. Even if she is feeling fine early in the pregnancy, she may not later in pregnancy or postpartum. She should be screened periodically throughout the pregnancy.

With your postpartum patients who were not screened prenatally, ask the first six questions from the **Pre-pregnancy and Pregnancy Risk Assessment** (the questions marked with ★) as well as the Postpartum Risk Assessment.

Use the **Postpartum Risk Assessment** on ALL women during their first year postpartum.

Psychiatrists

Since you are the professionals who work most closely with psychotropic medications, many perinatal women will be referred to you for assessment and treatment of mood disorders. You play an integral role in this treatment team.

Research findings and recommendations about medications in pregnancy and lactation are constantly changing. There have been some important findings recently in the area of medication management of perinatal mood disorders, which will be discussed later in this text. If you are only providing medication management, make sure you give your patients the name of a psychotherapist trained in perinatal mood disorders.

Use the **Pre-pregnancy and Pregnancy Risk Assessment** on ALL your patients who are pregnant or planning a pregnancy.

Use the **Postpartum Risk Assessment** on ALL women during their first year postpartum.

Birth Doulas

Studies show that the use of a doula contributes to the reduction of postpartum depression. As a birth doula, you are in a unique position to screen prenatally for risk and to watch for early warning signs of emotional problems. If, for instance, when administering the **Pre-pregnancy and Pregnancy Risk Assessment**, you discover the woman has suffered a previous traumatic delivery or childhood sexual abuse, she may experience flashbacks during the upcoming birth. Have referrals to local professionals trained in perinatal mood disorders and information in the Resources section available.

A woman taking psychotropic medication who is pregnant or planning a pregnancy should be encouraged to consult a psychiatrist (specializing in perinatal mood disorders) in order to determine whether to continue her medication. Recommendations will differ based on each woman's history and chronic problems. Women on medication for a bipolar disorder or psychosis should definitely be referred to a psychiatrist to develop a medication plan. These women need careful monitoring throughout pregnancy and postpartum.

If you are interviewed before employment, you can ask her if she has any particular concerns about birthing or postpartum. She then may share some information which could give you clues about her mental health. Let the woman know that one of your strengths is sensitivity to the various emotions which can occur during birth and postpartum.

Use the **Pre-pregnancy and Pregnancy Risk Assessment** on ALL women who employ your services. If you continue to see these women postpartum, use the **Postpartum Risk Assessment.** Keep in mind that this information can be gathered quite informally, simply through chatting. Be familiar with the questions and the pertinent information you need in order to screen.

Postpartum Doulas and Visiting Nurses

You have the opportunity to observe the home and social environments of the mother, which can give crucial information about her well-being and that of the family unit. For instance, if you notice a lack of partner support or signs of marital conflict, she is at greater risk for a postpartum mood disorder. If her house is unusually neat and clean, you will want to find out who is doing the housework. If she is, for example, obsessively cleaning or awake in the middle of the night vacuuming, this is not normal. Have referrals to local professionals trained in perinatal mood disorders and information in the Resources section available.

If you are just meeting women postpartum, you have not had the opportunity to screen them prenatally. Ask the first six questions from the **Pre-pregnancy and Pregnancy Risk Assessment** (the questions marked with ★), as well as the **Postpartum Risk Assessment.**

As long as you are familiar with the questions and understand what information you're trying to gather, this screening can be accomplished very informally through chatting.

Women should be assessed throughout the first year. If your last visit to her is before one year postpartum, make sure she has referral information in case she needs it later.

Women already on medication, or those who you assess need a medical evaluation, should be referred to a psychiatrist specializing in perinatal mood disorders.

Lactation Consultants

The role of a lactation consultant may superficially appear to be one-dimensional and relate only to the mechanics of breastfeeding. However, as we know, you are also providing tremendous emotional support. You may be the first professional to see the mother and baby during the initial postpartum weeks.

Your intimate relationship with the mother at this vulnerable time allows you to observe and listen for potential emotional problems. Postpartum moms listen carefully to what you advise and are quite trusting of you. It is so important that you help each woman decide what is right for her.

If her physical or emotional health is declining, it is obviously not good for the baby. You have a great deal of influence as to whether new mothers give themselves permission to take care of themselves (for instance, five hours of uninterrupted sleep at night). Sometimes this will mean partial or complete weaning.

Difficulty breastfeeding is associated with postpartum depression and anxiety, and also thyroid dysfunction. When a woman is weaning her baby, make sure she weans her own body very slowly even though her baby can wean "cold turkey."

Abrupt weaning can precipitate a mood disorder, especially when a woman is predisposed. If she is already suffering, abrupt weaning can greatly exacerbate her symptoms. Especially if a woman is depressed and not feeling good about herself, there can be a great amount of guilt if at any point she cannot or should not continue breastfeeding. What you say or do not say at that time can make a big difference regarding how she feels about herself as a mother.

Many professionals are unaware of the current research regarding nursing and psychotropic medications. It is important that you are informed so you can advocate for women who want to nurse while taking medication. Have referrals to local professionals trained in perinatal mood disorders and information in the Resources section available, including a psychiatrist who has experience prescribing medication during lactation.

Your assessment of ALL women not previously screened should consist of the first six questions from the **Pre-pregnancy Risk Assessment** (the questions marked with ★), plus the **Postpartum Risk Assessment.** As long as you are familiar with the questions and understand what information you're trying to gather, much of the screening can be completed quite informally through chatting.

Childbirth Educators

So often we hear the lament, "Why didn't anyone warn us in our birthing classes about mood problems during and after pregnancy?" Even though your primary focus is on labor and delivery, you have a responsibility and opportunity to educate couples about perinatal mood disorders. This might be a difficult topic to discuss since no woman wants to think it could happen to her.

If you know a professional who is an expert in this field, you can invite her or him to speak to your class. If not, bring the subject up in a matter-of-fact manner, the same way you would any other common pregnancy or postpartum experience.

The rate of depression in pregnancy is about 15-20 percent. Therefore, we can assume some of the women in your classes are already suffering and are at risk for a postpartum mood disorder. Your participants will not bring up this topic, so you need to. There is no danger in giving information, and there is great danger in omitting it. You have a captive audience with both members of the couple. The partner might be soaking up this information even if the mother-to-be is not. It is often the spouse who later recognizes the symptoms and encourages his wife to seek help.

Hand out some information from the Resources section and the name and number of a professional trained in perinatal mood disorders. At the class reunion ask about participants' feelings about the challenges as well as the joys of parenthood. Be sure to call participants who did not attend the reunion. They may not be doing well and could be trying to avoid an uncomfortable situation.

New Parent Group Leaders

If there are ten women in your group, remember that, statistically, at least one of them will have postpartum depression. Rarely will this woman be brave enough to disclose her feelings, since she will most likely be experiencing guilt and shame. She will be aching for someone to open the door to this discussion and give her permission to express how she is really feeling. If spouses and fathers are present, ask them how they are doing.

Encourage discussion about the normal feelings accompanying adjustment to parenting and the relationship to oneself, partner, baby, friends, and family. You can easily work in some facts about moods and behaviors that fall outside the realm of normal adjustment.

For each new group, make sure this topic gets explored in a nonjudgmental manner. If you prefer, you can invite a professional with expertise in this area to lead a discussion. In any case, use the information in the Resources section and the names and numbers of local professionals trained in the area of postpartum disorders.

Adjunct Professionals

There are many other wonderful professionals who touch the lives of pregnant and postpartum women. For example, physical therapists and instructors in prenatal and postpartum exercise should mention the possibility of mood disorders, since you are encountering suffering women all the time. Above all, making the information in the Resources section available will support the pregnant and postpartum women with whom you work.

SEVEN

Treatment

Prevention

Prevention of postpartum depression is, of course, the ultimate goal, and research is beginning to evaluate preventive methods. What follows is the information currently available.

Women who have a personal and/or family history of depression, and especially those who have had a previous postpartum depression, are at increased risk. One small study looked at nondepressed women who had a previous postpartum depression. After having another baby, 41% of these women developed postpartum depression. Most of these women developed symptoms in the first two weeks after delivery. The rest of the women, except for two, developed symptoms by 28 weeks postpartum. Several studies have demonstrated that there are preventive measures that reduce risk.

In a Canadian study, women at high risk for PPD were offered an extended postpartum hospital stay (up to 5 days) in a private room. Their babies slept in the nursery at night, so the moms could sleep without interruption. Additionally, the moms met once with a member of the Women's Health Concerns Clinic during their stay. This study highlighted the importance of uninterrupted sleep and support, as these women had a reduced incidence and a reduction in severity of PPD.

Not only is psychotherapy an effective treatment for PPD, there are also studies showing that psychotherapy can be effectively used for prevention. Interpersonal psychotherapy groups and psycho-educational groups during pregnancy reduce the occurrence of PPD.

What about medication? A study found that women at high risk who started Zoloft (sertraline) within 15 hours after delivery significantly reduced their incidence of PPD. All new mothers need a postpartum wellness plan, because all moms need nurturing. This is not a luxury — it is a necessity! If a woman is at increased risk for PPD, she should meet with a knowledgeable psychotherapist while still pregnant to create a postpartum plan. Some areas included in this plan should be follow-up appointments with professionals after delivery, sleep arrangements (to ensure blocks of uninterrupted sleep), food and eating (who will shop and cook), and getting breaks away from the baby during the week. If PPD does occur, a wellness plan will be in place that will support and speed recovery.

Information and education are critical components of treatment. Depending on the severity and cause(s) of her symptoms, sometimes this is all a woman needs in order to recover. She needs to know her illness has a name, and is treatable. This information may come from professionals, non-professionals, or both.

Alternative Therapies

Studies are currently being conducted regarding the treatment of depression in pregnancy and postpartum which do not involve medication.

For instance, the therapeutic effect of massage on depression in pregnancy and postpartum is beginning to emerge in the data. Morning bright light therapy is already being used both in pregnancy and postpartum either as an alternative or in conjunction with medication. Exciting evidence about the effectiveness of the Omega-3 essential fatty acid DHA (docosa-hexaenoic acid) in both the prevention and treatment of prenatal and postpartum depression is also apparent. Taken while nursing, the baby's neurological development may also be enhanced.

Some therapies are not yet found in the literature as proven treatments; however, many of our clients have used them, including acupuncture, homeopathic remedies, chiropractic, Yoga, hypnotherapy and types of spiritual and energy healing. We advocate using the therapy or combination of therapies (including medication) which is the most effective for each individual. In other words, use whatever is safe and works!

Women seeking treatment often try to reduce symptoms on their own before seeking the advice of a professional. This self-treatment may include potentially risky substances, such as alcohol or untested herbal or drug remedies. Twenty percent of pregnant women smoke, 19% use alcohol and 6% use illegal drugs as a way to reduce symptoms.

Herbs can be wonderful but they can also be dangerous. Little research has been done on the safety of herbs such as St. John's Wort during pregnancy or nursing. They are powerful medicines, often produced with little or no regulation or safety monitoring. Some herbal remedies and illegal drugs have been associated with serious harm to both mother and child, including birth defects, infant death, and liver toxicity. On the other hand, quite a bit of research has been conducted regarding the use of certain prescription medications during pregnancy and lactation that effectively combat perinatal mood disorders.

The most immediate goal of treatment is to alleviate suffering as quickly as possible. While it is generally prudent to start medication at a low dosage, it should be increased as rapidly as possible to whatever the therapeutic dosage is for that woman. Undertreating can lead to chronic problems and increase the risk of relapse.

What follows here are guidelines only. All treatment must be individualized. For medication management we recommend the woman see a psychiatrist with expertise in treating perinatal mood disorders.

Since brand names may vary by country, we are including both brand and generic names of medications.

Pregnancy

I have spent the last 10 years of my career worrying about the impact of medications. I've been wrong. I should have been worrying more about the impact of illness.

ZACHARY STOWE, MD
ASSISTANT PROFESSOR, DEPARTMENT OF PSYCHIATRY, EMORY UNIVERSITY

Current thinking regarding the use of medications in pregnancy has evolved over the past few years. Researchers who have spent years investigating the potential effects of medication on the fetus have shifted their focus to the harmful effects on the fetus when maternal mental illness goes untreated. These experts agree that maternal depression and anxiety must be evaluated and treated to maximize a positive outcome for the baby.

Pregnancy causes alterations in metabolism and blood volume; therefore, higher doses of medications may be required to reach therapeutic levels.

Antidepressants

Studies of selective serotonin reuptake inhibitors (SSRIs) or tricyclics (TCAs) used in pregnancy have revealed no increased risk of physical malformations, neonatal complications, miscarriage, or impairments in neurobehavioral development. At seven years of age exposed children tested normally on IQ and development tests. These data include first trimester exposure.

Based on current research, the preferred choices during pregnancy are Prozac and Sarafem (fluoxetine), Zoloft (sertraline), Paxil (paroxetine) and Celexa (citalopram). The top researchers maintain that there is no reason to change from one medication to another; go with what works and gets the quickest results. In 2005 the company that makes Paxil issued a warning about its use in pregnancy. They looked at past information from small unpublished insurance company databases. They reported a slightly increased rate of heart abnormalities in the infants exposed to Paxil. These findings are different from other studies that show Paxil, along with other SSRI's, do not increase the risk of major malformations.

In 2004 the United States FDA (Federal Drug Administration) and its Canadian counterpart issued warnings about using SSRI's in the third trimester of pregnancy. They reported symptoms in newborns including shakiness, restlessness, increased muscle tone and increased crying. None of these symptoms were serious and they all went away by themselves, sometimes within hours. Discontinuing an antidepressant before delivery, a time which is high risk for depression, can be quite serious. Since we know the effects on the infant are uncommon and do go away without treatment, it is not recommended to stop medication in the third trimester. Speak to someone who knows the research before you make any changes in your medication.

Electroconvulsive Therapy (ECT)

ECT is considered an acceptable treatment for severe depression or psychosis in pregnancy. It may also be useful in treating bipolar disorder during pregnancy. ECT is not an appropriate treatment for prenatal anxiety, panic, or obsessive-compulsive disorder (OCD).

Antipsychotics

Conventional high-potency antipsychotics, such as Haldol (haloperidol), are recommended over low-potency or atypical agents throughout pregnancy.

Mood Stabilizers

Recent research shows that the risk of Ebstein's (cardiac) anomaly with lithium use in the first trimester is only about 0.05%. A fetal cardiac ultrasound between weeks 18 and 20 is recommended for those with first trimester exposure. No significant neurobehavioral or developmental problems have been noted.

Lithium maintenance throughout pregnancy should be considered for women with severe bipolar disorders, since the risk of relapse is high. A study of bipolar women who discontinued mood stabilizers when they became pregnant was reported at a recent American Psychiatric Association meeting. Within three months, half of the women relapsed, and by six months, about 70% had relapsed. Reintroducing lithium after discontinuation in the first trimester does not protect well against relapse.

Other mood stabilizers, such as Tegretol (carbamazepine) and Depakote (valproic acid), increase the rate of neural tube defects and are not recommended during pregnancy.

Antianxiety Medications

The literature regarding antianxiety exposure in utero is limited and confusing. First trimester use has been associated with cleft palate. However women with anxiety or panic disorder should be treated. SSRIs, while not specifically antianxiety medications, are effective in treating these disorders. Ativan (lorazepam) is used for short-term relief of symptoms. The lowest effective dose for the shortest period of time is recommended.

Sleep Aids

If sleep is impaired due to depression or anxiety, medication may be necessary. TCAs such as Pamelor (nortriptyline) or Elavil (amitriptyline) may be useful at bedtime. Deseryl (trazadone) also has a sedative effect. Ambien (zolpedem) has a faster rate of onset and is considered acceptable in pregnancy.

Postpartum

Thyroid

At least 10 percent of postpartum women will develop postpartum thyroiditis. In the early stages of thyroiditis, women may experience anxiety or depression. Sometimes this condition is temporary, and will resolve without treatment in about six months. But for others it can lead to chronic thyroiditis and hypothyroidism (Hashimoto's thyroiditis).

Since thyroid disorders can cause depression and anxiety, thyroid dysfunction must be ruled out. The suggested time for testing is between two and three months postpartum. The following tests are recommended for all women with post-partum mood complaints: free T4, TSH, anti-TPO, and anti-thyroglobulin. It is important to check for the anti-thyroid antibodies (anti-TPO and anti-thyroglobulin) since there have been many cases where the T4 and TSH levels were within normal ranges but the anti-thyroid antibody titers were elevated. We recommend that the woman be evaluated by an endocrinologist if she has thyroid abnormalities.

Hormone Therapy

Hormone therapy for postpartum depression is still being evaluated for effectiveness. Research with estrogen holds promise for treatment of postpartum depression and postpartum psychosis. Taking estrogen, like any medicine, has certain risks and needs to be evaluated on a case-by-case basis. Women sensitive to hormonal shifts, including those with postpartum depression and anxiety who choose oral contraceptives (birth control pills), need to be monitored closely for mood changes. Women may experience fewer mood problems on a monophasic birth control pill as compared to a triphasic birth control pill. The monophasic pill delivers the same ratio of estrogen and progesterone unlike the triphasic, where the ratio changes weekly.

Women with a history of increased moodiness on oral contraceptives should consider alternate methods of contraception. Synthetic progesterone (progestin) including the "mini-pill" has been associated with a worsening of symptoms. Depo-Provera (medroxyprogesterone acetate), a long-acting progesterone injection, is not a good option since it cannot be discontinued should it aggravate mood problems. Hormone therapy is not currently recommended as sole treatment for postpartum psychiatric disorders.

Medications

A woman who is not nursing has many choices of medications available to her. If this woman, or a blood relative, has had a positive experience with any particular medication, that would be the first choice.

Few studies have been done on the efficacy of particular medications in the treatment of postpartum depression/anxiety.

One study found Effexor (venlafaxine) to be effective in the treatment of postpartum depression. Wellbutrin (bupropion) for postpartum women with depression but without anxiety seems to be energizing and also reduces the likelihood of sexual side effects.

There is not one medication that, in general, is better than the others for treating postpartum depression. In our experience all the SSRIs work well. Each woman has her own individual chemistry which will work better with certain medications than with others. It is recommended that SSRIs be started at a low dose with regular follow up, increasing the dosage until an adequate therapeutic response is achieved. She should report feeling back to "herself." Undertreating can lead to chronic illness and increased risk of relapse.

Medications and Nursing.

Antidepressants

Of the most commonly used antidepressants, Zoloft (sertraline) and Paxil (paroxetine) were undetectable in the infant. Prozac (fluoxetine) and Celexa (citalopram) were found in small amounts in the infant's blood and no significant problems were noted in the infants. It is generally felt that it is safe to nurse while taking SSRI's. The first choice for every woman should be a medication that has worked for her in the past or one that has been used successfully with a blood relative.

The benefits of nursing far outweigh the theoretical risks of medications. Behaviorally and developmentally these infants and children are normal.

Mood Stabilizers

Tegretol (carbamazepine) and Depakote (valproic acid) are approved by the American Academy of Pediatrics (AAP) for breastfeeding mothers. Lithium is not recommended.

Antipsychotics

High-potency antipsychotics, such as Haldol (haloperidol), are used for nursing moms.

Sleep Aids

Ambien (zolpedem), Restoril (temazepam), Deseryl (trazadone), Pamelor (nortriptyline), or Elavil (amitriptyline) are frequently prescribed for nursing moms.

Antianxiety Medications

Low doses of short acting medications such as Xanax (alprazolam) or Ativan (lorazepam) can be used on an occasional as-needed basis for anxiety, panic, and sleep.

Electroconvulsive Therapy (ECT)

ECT is considered an acceptable treatment for severe depression or psychosis postpartum, including for nursing mothers. It may also be useful in treating bipolar disorder postpartum. ECT is not an appropriate treatment for postpartum anxiety, panic, or OCD.

Medical Protocols

The chart on the next page suggests treatments based upon the woman's history. Treatments should be followed in sequence, with Treatment 1 tried first, followed by Treatment 2 if necessary.

Although the treatment protocols that follow refer only to depression and psychosis, they are also effective in the treatment of OCD, anxiety and panic.

SSRIs are usually the first line medications in the treatment of OCD, anxiety and panic. For OCD, Luvox (fluvoxamine) and Anafranil (clomipramine) are second choices. Although Anafranil tends to have more side effects, it seems to be acceptable during pregnancy and lactation. Luvox has not been as well studied for use in pregnancy or lactation. It may be helpful to use low dose anti-anxiety medications on a short-term basis for anxiety and panic.

Pre-Pregnancy		
History	**Treatment 1**	**Treatment 2**
One episode of major depression if on medication + asymptomatic for 6–12 months	Taper off medication + psychotherapy (monitor closely for relapse)	Resume medication + continue psychotherapy
Severe recurrent prior episodes	Continue medication + psychotherapy	
Mild major depression	Psychotherapy	Psychotherapy + medication
Severe major depression (first episode)	Medication + psychotherapy	
Bipolar disorder	Continue or switch to lithium + monitor closely by psychiatrist + psychotherapy	Switch to high potency antipsychotic if lithium-resistant or intolerant + continue psychotherapy

Pregnancy (including first trimester)		
History	**Treatment 1**	**Treatment 2**
One episode mild major depression, currently in remission	Trial slow tapering medication + psychotherapy	Resume medication + psychotherapy
One episode severe major depression, currently in remission	Maintenance on medication + psychotherapy	
Mild major depression, first or recurrent	Psychotherapy	Medication + psychotherapy*
Severe major depression, first episode	Medication + psychotherapy	ECT + psychotherapy
Recurrence or relapse of depression if off medication if mild major depression	Psychotherapy	Resume medication + psychotherapy
Severe major depression, currently symptomatic	Resume medication + psychotherapy	ECT + psychotherapy
Psychosis in any trimester *Note: do not rely on psychosocial interventions alone; requires hospitalization.*	Antipsychotic + psychotherapy Add mood stabilizer or antidepressant if needed once stable Or ECT + psychotherapy	

If this is not successful, further treatment of ECT + psychotherapy should be considered.

Postpartum		
History	Treatment 1	Treatment 2
Mild major depression	Psychotherapy	Psychotherapy + medication
Severe major depression	Psychotherapy + medication	Consider ECT
Postpartum psychosis *Note: hospitalization required. Do not rely on psychosocial interventions alone.*	Antipsychotic + psychotherapy Add mood stabilizer or antidepressant if needed once stable Or ECT + psychotherapy	

Prevention of Postpartum Depression in Women with History of Depression, Anxiety, Other Mood Disorder, or Prior PPD		
History	Treatment 1	Treatment 2
First pregnancy	Meet with psychotherapist when risk identified (pre-pregnancy or pregnancy) + psychoeducation for woman and partner	Intervention (refer to pregnancy treatment protocol) if symptomatic
Prior postpartum depression	Psychoeducation for woman and partner as early as possible + start antidepressant 2–4 weeks before delivery + psychotherapy Or start anti-depressant immediately after delivery + psychotherapy	
Prior postpartum psychosis	Start lithium upon delivery + psychotherapy	

EIGHT

Resources

Organizations

Family Mental Health Foundation
1050 17th Street NW, Suite 600
Washington, D.C. 20036
website: www.ppdhope.com
Helpline: 1-877-PDD-HOPE (1-877-773-4673)

The Marcé Society
PO Box 30853
London, England W12OXG
www.marcesociety.com
International organization dedicated to scientific research in the field.
Annual conference.

National Hopeline Network
609 E. Main St., #112
Purcellville, VA 20132
(800) SUICIDE (784-2433)

North American Society for Psychosocial OB/GYN
409 12th Street, S.W.
Washington, DC 20024-2188
(202) 863-1628
www.naspog.org
Annual conference.

Postpartum Support International
927 N. Kellogg Avenue
Santa Barbara, CA 93111
(805) 967-7636 or 1-800-944-4PPD (944-4773)
www.postpartum.net
Telephone support and international directory of members.
Annual conference.

Websites

Baby Center, Postpartum Depression
www.babycenter.com/refcap/227.html

British Columbia Reproductive Mental Health Program's
Reading Room
www.bcrmh.com/disorders/postpartum.htm

Canadian Pacific Postpartum Support Society
www.postpartum.org

Center for Postpartum Health
www.postpartumhealth.com

Depression Central
www.psycom.net/depression.central.post-partum.html

Doulas and Postpartum Caregivers
www.childbirth.org/doula123.html

Doulas of North America
www.dona.org

Husbands and Dads Support
www.postpartumdads.org

The Marcé Society
www.marcesociety.com

Massachusetts General Hospital, Center for Women's Mental Health
www.womensmentalhealth.org/

Medlineplus Health Information
www.nlm.nih.gov/medlineplus/postpartumdepression.html

Motherisk
www.motherisk.org

New Zealand, Bounty Services
www.bounty.co.nz

North American Society for Psychosocial OB/GYN
www.naspog.org

Postpartum Assistance for Mothers
www.PostpartumDepressionHelp.com

Postpartum Depression Online Support Group
www.ppdsupportpage.com

Postpartum Education for Parents
www.sbpep.org

Postpartum Resource Center of New York, Inc.
www.postpartumny.org

Postpartum Support International
www.postpartum.net

Pregnancy and Depression Medical Articles
www.pregnancyanddepression.com

Ruth Rhoden Craven Foundation, Inc. for Depression Awareness
www.ppdsupport.org

South Africa
www.pndsa.co.za

UCLA Mood Disorders Research Program
www.npi.ucla.edu/uclamdrp/pregnantpostpart.htm

Books

Beck, Cheryl, and Jeanne Driscoll. *Postpartum Mood And Anxiety Disorders:* A Guide, Jones & Bartlett Publishers, 2005.

Cohen, Lee ed. and Ruta Nonacs ed. *Mood and Anxiety Disorders During Pregnancy and Postpartum,* American Psychiatric Publishing, 2005

Fran, Renee. *What Happened to Mommy?* (Can be ordered for $7.95 payable to Renee, from R.D. Eastman, P.O. Box 290663, Brooklyn, N.Y. 11229 or on Amazon.com)

Hanson, Rick, Hanson, Jan, and Ricki Pollycove. *Mother Nurture: A Mother's Guide to Health in Body, Mind, and Intimate Relationships.* New York: Penguin Books, 2002.

Honikman, Jane. *Step by Step, A Guide to Organizing a Postpartum Parent Support Network in Your Community.* 927 N. Kellogg Ave., Santa Barbara, CA 93111.

Honikman, Jane. I'm Listening: *A Guide to Supporting Postpartum Families.* 927 N. Kellogg Ave., Santa Barbara, CA 93111

Kendall-Tackett,, Kathleen. *Depression In New Mothers: Causes, Consequences, And Treatment Alternatives,* Haworth Maltreatment and Trauma Press, 2005.

Klaus, Marshall, Kennell, John, and Phyllis Klaus. *The Doula Book: How a Trained Labor Companion Can Help You Have a Shorter, Easier, and Healthier Birth.* Cambridge, Massachusetts: Perseus Publishing, 2002.

Kleiman, Karen. *The Postpartum Husband.* Philadelphia: Xlibris, 2000.

Kleiman, Karen. *What Am I Thinking? Having a Baby After Postpartum Depression,* Philadelphia: Xlibris, 2005.

Miller, Laura, ed. *Postpartum Mood Disorders.* Washington, D.C.: American Psychiatric Press, 1999.

Misri, Shaila. *Pregnancy Blues: What Every Woman Needs to Know about Depression During Pregnancy.* Delacorte Press, 2005.

Nicholson, et. al, *Parenting Well When You're Depressed; A Complete Resource For Maintaining a Healthy Family.* Oakland: New Harbinger Publications, Inc., 2001.

Robin, Peggy. *Bottlefeeding Without Guilt: A Reassuring Guide for Loving Parents.* Roseville, California: Prima Publishing, 1996.

Rosenberg, Ronald, Greening, Deborah and James Windell. *Conquering Postpartum Depression,* Lifelong Books, 2003.

Sichel, Deborah, and Jeanne Driscoll. *Women's Moods.* New York: William Morrow and Co., 1999.

Journal Articles

Perinatal

Abramowitz, J.A. Obsessive-compulsive symptoms in pregnancy and the puerperium: A review of the literature. *Anxiety Disorders.* 2003: 17; 461-478.

Bodnar, L. and Katherine Wisner. Nutrition and Depression: Implications for Improving Mental Health Among Childbearing-Aged Women. *Biol Psychiatry.* 2005; 58:679-685.

Freeman, M., et al. Selected Integrative Medicine Treatments for Depression: Considerations for Women. *JAMWA.* 2004; 59:216-224.

Gavin, N., et al. Perinatal Depression Prevalence and Incidence. *Obstet Gynecol.* 2005: 106(5).

Jain, A.I. and Timothy Lacy. Psychotripic Drugs in Pregnancy and Lactation. *J of Psych Practice.* 2005: 11;177-191.

Lindahl, V. J.L. Pearson, Colpe, L. Prevalence of suicidality during pregnancy and the postpartum. *Arch Womens Ment health.* 2005: 8:77-87.

Ross, L., et al. Sleep and perinatal mood disorders: a critical review. *J Psychiatry Neurosci.* 2005; 30(4).

Yonkers, K., et al. Management of Bipolar Disorder During Pregnancy The Postpartum Period. *Focus.* 2005; 3:266-279.

Prenatal Screening

Beck, C. A checklist to identify women at risk for developing postpartum depression. *J Obstet Gynecol Neonatal Nurs.* Jan-Feb 1998; 27(1):39-46.

Posner, N., et al. Screening for postpartum depression; an antepartum questionnaire. *J Reprod Med.* 1997; 42:207-215.

Postpartum Screening

Beck, C.T., and Gable, R. Postpartum Depression Screening Scale (PDSS). Available through Western Psychological Services (800) 648-8857.

Beck, C.T. and Indman, P. The Many Faces of Postpartum Depression. *JOGNN.* 2005: 34:569-576.

Boyd, R.C. et al. Review of screening instruments for postpartum depression. Arch Women Ment Health. 2005; 8(3):141-53.

Cox, J.L., et al. Detection of postnatal depression: development of the 10-item Edinburgh Postnatal Depression Scale. *British Journal of Psychiatry.* 1987; 150:782-786.

Derosa, N. and Logsdon, M.C. A comparison of screening instruments for depression in postpartum adolescents. J Child Adolesc Psychaitr Nurs.. 2006; 19(1):13-20.

Freeman M.P. et al. Postpartum depression assessments at well-baby visits: screening feasibility, prevalence, and risk factors. J Womens Health. 2005; Dec; 14(10):929-35.

Tam L.W. et al. Screening Women for Postpartum Depression at Well BabyVisits:Resistance Encountered and Recommendations. *Arch Women Ment Health.* 2002; 5:79-82.

Postpartum Depression

Cohen, L.S., et al. Venlafaxine in the treatment of postpartum depression. *J Clin Psychiatry.* 2001; 62(8):592-596.

Hendrick, V., et al. Postpartum and nonpostpartum depression: differences in presentation and response to pharmacologic treatment. *Depression and Anxiety.* 2000; 11:66-72.

Hibbeln, J.R. Seafood consumption, the DHA content of mother's milk and prevalence rates of postpartum depression: a cross-national, ecological analysis. *J Affective Disorders.* 2001.

Nonacs, R. and Cohen, L.S. Postpartum mood disorders: diagnosis and treatment guidelines. *J Clin Psychiatry.* 1998; 59 (suppl 2):34-40.

Stowe, Z.N. and Nemeroff, C.B. Women at risk for postpartum-onset major depression. *Am J Obstet Gynecol* 1995 Aug; 173(2):639-644.

Stuart, S., O'Hara, M.W., Gorman, L.L. The prevention and psychotherapeutic treatment of postpartum depression. *Arch Womens Ment Health.* 2003; 6(suppl 2):57-59.

Wisner, K.L. Prevention of recurrent postpartum depression: a randomized clinical trial. *J Clin Psychiatry.* 2001 Feb; 62(2):82-6.

Wisner, K.L. Timing of depression recurrence in the first year after birth. *J Affect Disord.* 2004; 78(3):249-52.

Depression in Pregnancy

Bennett, H.A., Prevalence of Depression During Pregnancy. Systematic Review. *Obstet Gynecol.* 2004; 103(4):698-709.

Berle, J.O., et al. Neonatal outcomes in offspring of women with anxiety and depression during pregnancy. *Arch Women's Mental Health.* 2005; 8:181-189.

Cohen, L.S., et al. Relapse of Major Depression During Pregnancy in Women Who Maintain or Discontinue Antidepressant Treatment. *JAMA.* 2006; 295:469.

Field, T., et al. Prenatal depression effects on the fetus and the newborn. *Infant Behavior & Development.* 2004: 27: 216-229.

Hendrick, V. and Altshuler, L. Management of major depression during pregnancy. *Am J Psychiatry.* 2002 Oct; 159(10):166-173.

Marcus, S.M., et al. Dpressive symptoms among pregnant women screened in a obstetric settings. *J Womens Health.* 2003; 12(4):373-380.

Oren, D.A., et al. An open trial of morning light therapy for treatment of antepartum depression. *Am J Psychiatry.* 2002 Apr; 159(4):666-669.

Spinelli, M.G. and Endicott, J. Controlled clinical trial of interpersonal psychotherapy versus parenting education program for depressed pregnant women. *Am J Psychiatry.* 2003; 160(3):555-562.

Van den Bergh, B.R., et al. Antenatal maternal anxiety and stress and the neurobehavioral development of the fetus and child: links and possible mechanisms. A Review. *Neurosci Biobehav Rev.* 2005 Apr; 29(2):237-58.

Medications During Pregnancy

Altshuler, L., et al. Pharmacologic management of psychiatric illness during pregnancy: dilemmas and guidelines. *Am J Psychiatry.* 1996 May; 153:592-606.

American Academy of Pediatrics. Use of psychoactive medication during pregnancy and possible effects on the fetus and newborn. *Pediatrics.* 2000 Apr; 105(4): 880-887.

Barki, J., Kravitz, H., Berki, T. Psychotropic medications in pregnancy. *Psychiatric Annals.* 1998 Sep; 28:486-497.

Baugh, C., and Stowe, Z. Treatment issues during pregnancy and lactation. *CNS Spectrums,* 1999 Oct; 4(10); 34-39.

Chiu, C.C., et al. Omega-3 fatty acids for depression in pregnancy. *Am J Psychiatry.* 2003; 160(2):358.

Cohen, L. Bipolar disorder, drugs, pregnancy, and lactation. *eOb/Gyn.News.* 2003 Sept; 38(17).

Cohen, L. Drugs, pregnancy and lactation: update on bipolar disorder. *www.womensmentalhealth.org/topics/pregnancy_lib_bipolar_update_06.02.html*

Cohen, L. Pharmacologic treatment of depression in women: PMS, pregnancy, and the postpartum period. *Depression and Anxiety.* 1998; 8(suppl 1):18-26.

Cunningham, M., and Zayas, L.H. Reducing depression in pregnancy: designing multimodal interventions. *Soc Work.* 2002 Apr; 47(2):114-23.

Freeman, M., Omega-3 fatty acids: an ideal treatment for depression in pregnancy? *Evidence-Based Integrative Medicine.* 2003:1(91)43-49.

Koren, G., et al. Is maternal use of selective serotonin reuptake inhibitors in the third trimester of pregnancy harmful to neonates? *CMAJ.* 2005; 172(11).

Kulin, N., et al. Pregnancy outcome following maternal use of the new selective serotonin reuptake inhibitors. *JAMA.* 1998; 279(8):609-610.

Malm. H. et al. Risks Associated With Selective Serotonin Reuptake Inhibitors in Pregnancy. *Obstet Gynecol.* 2005; 106:1289-1296.

Moses-Kolko, E.L., et al. Neonatal sighs after late in utero exposure to serotonin reuptake inhibitors: literature review and implications for clinical applications. *JAMA*. 2005; 293(19):2372-83.

Nonacs, R., Cohen, L.S. Depression during pregnancy: diagnosis and treatment options. *J Clin Psychiatry*. 2002; 63 (suppl 7):24-30.

Nordeng, H. and O. Spigset. Treatment with selective serotonin reuptake inhibitors in the third trimester of pregnancy: effects on the infant. *Drug Saf*. 2005; 28(7):565-81.

Nulman, I., et al. Child development following exposure to tricyclic antidepressants or fluoxetine throughout fetal life: a prospective, controlled study. *Am J Psychiatry*. 2002 Nov; 159:1889-1895.

Nulman, I., et al. Neurodevelopment of children exposed in utero to antidepressant drugs. *NEJM*. 1997; 336 (4):258-262.

Pinelli, J.M., et al. Case report and review of the perinatal implications of maternal lithium use. *Am J Obstet Gynecol*. 2002 Jul;187(1):245-249.

Sanz, E.J., et al. Selective serotonin reuptake inhibitors in pregnant women and neonatal withdrawal syndrome a database analysis. (see comment). *Lancet*. 2005; 356(9458):482-487.

Wisner, K.L. et al. Pharmacologic treatment of depression during pregnancy. *JAMA*. 1999; 282:1264-1269.

Medications and Lactation

Birnbaum, C. S., et al. Serum concentrations of antidepressants and benzodiazepines in nursing infants: a case series. *Pediatrics*. 1999; 104:11.

Burt, V.K., et al. The use of psychotropic medications during breastfeeding. *Am J Psychiatry*. 2001; 158:1001-1009.

Chaudron, L. When and how to use mood stabilizers during breastfeeding. *Primary Care Update OB/GYNs.* 2000; 7(3).

Chaudron, L., and Jefferson, W. Mood stabilizers during breastfeeding: a review. *J Clin Psychiatry.* 2000; 61:79-90.

Llewellyn, A., and Stowe, Z. Psychotropic medications in lactation. *J Clin Psychiatry.* 1998; 59(suppl 2):41-52.

Newport, D.J., et al. The treatment of postpartum depression: minimizing infant exposures. *J Clin Psychiatry.* 2002; 63 (suppl 7):31-44.

Stowe, Z., et al. Paroxetine in human breast milk and nursing infants. *Am J Psychiatry.* 2000; 157:185-189.

Suri, R. A., et al. Managing psychiatric medications in the breastfeeding woman. *Medscape Women's Health.* 1998; 3(1).

Wisner K.L., et al. Antidepressant treatment during breastfeeding. *Am J Psychiatry.* 1996; 153(9):1132-1137.

Weissmann, A.M., et al. Pooled Analysis of Antidepressant Levels in Lactating Mothers, Breast Milk, and Nursing Infants. *Am J Psychiatry.* 2004; 161:1066-1078.

Psychotherapy

Appleby, L., et al. A controlled study of fluoxetine and cognitive-behavioural counseling in the treatment of postnatal depression. *BMJ.* 1997; 314:932-936.

Beck, C.T., A meta-analysis of predictors of postpartum depression. *Nurs Res.* 1996; 45:297-303.

Field, T., et al. Prenatal depression effects on the fetus and the newborn. *Infant Behavior & Development.* 2004; 27:216-229.

O'Hara, M.W., Stuart, S., Gorman, L.D., Wenzel, A. Efficacy of interpersonal psychotherapy for postpartum depression. *Arch Gen Psychiatry.* 2000; 57(11): 1039-1045.

Segre, L.S., Stuart, S., O'Hara, M.W., Interpersonal Psychotherapy for Antenattal and Postpartum Depression. *Primary Psychiatry.* 2004; 11(3):52-56.

Spinelli, M.G., Interpersonal psychotherapy for depressed antepartum women: a pilot study. *Am J Psychiatry.* 1997; 154:1028-1030.

Effects of Maternal Depression on Children

Beck, C. T. Maternal depression and child behaviour problems: a meta-analysis. *J of Advanced Nursing.* 1999; 29, 623-629.

Field, Tiffany. Emotional care of the at-risk infant: early interventions for infants of depressed mothers. *Pediatrics.* 1998 Nov; 102(5) (suppl):1305-1310.

Field, Tiffany. Maternal depression effects on infants and early interventions. *Preventive Medicine.* 1998; 27:200-203.

Gelfland, D., Teti, D. The effects of maternal depression on children. *Clin Psychol Rev.* 1990; 10:329-353.

Glover, V. and O'Connor, T.G. Effects of antenatal stress and anxiety: Implications for development and psychiatry. *Br J Psychiatry.* 2002 May; 180:389-391.

Goodman, S. H.,et al. Mothers' expressed attitudes: associations with maternal depression and children's self-esteem and psychopathology. *J A Acad Child Adolesc Psychiatry.* 1994; 33:1265-1274.

Hammen, C. and Brennan, P.A. Severity, chronicity, and timing of maternal depression and risk for adolescent offspring diagnoses in a community sample. *Arch Gen Psychiatry.* 2003; 60:253-258.

Miller, L., et al. Self-esteem and depression: ten-year follow-up of mothers and offspring. *J of Affective Disorders.* 1999; 52:4-49.

Orr, S.T., et al. Maternal prenatal depressive symptoms and spontaneous preterm births among African-American women in Baltimore, Maryland. *Am J Epidemiol.* 2002; 156:797-802.

Appendix:
Medical Terms and
Healthcare Professionals

Medical Terms	
Bipolar Disorder	Also known as manic depression, this is a chemical imbalance in the brain characterized by moodswings from manic (see "mania") to depressed. Many researchers believe there is a strong genetic component to this illness.
Cognitive Behavioral Therapy (CBT)	With CBT, the therapist takes an active role in the therapy process and provides a clear structure and focus to treatment. Behavior therapy helps the client weaken the connections between situations and the negative habitual reactions to them. Cognitive therapy teaches the client how certain thought patterns or beliefs create symptoms such as depression, anxiety or anger. The therapist works with the client to help develop new positive ways of thinking and acting.
Cortisol	Called the "stress hormone," cortisol is a hormone released by the adrenal glands during anxious or agitated states.
Delusion	This is a false belief. One may fear being pursued or think she is someone other than herself. Often there is religious content to the thoughts.

Beyond the Blues

Depression	A common disorder characterized by sad mood, irritability, sleep and appetite disturbances, loss of pleasure, fatigue, and hopelessness. Depression can be caused by a variety of factors, including biochemical, emotional, and psychological.
Etiology	The cause or origin of a disease or illness.
Hallucination	Something one sees or hears that others do not. Hallucinations often have religious overtones, for example, hearing the voice of God or Satan.
Insomnia	Inability to sleep.
Interpersonal Psychotherapy (IPT)	IPT is a brief and highly structured psychotherapy that addresses interpersonal issues. IPT helps the client solve problems, for instance, disputes, feeling isolated, adjusting to new roles, or grief following a loss. The therapist works from a collaborative framework.
Mania	A symptom of bipolar disorder (see above) characterized by exaggerated excitement, hyperactivity, and racing, scattered thoughts. A person in a manic state feels an emotional "high" and often does not use good judgment. Speech may be rapid and she may feel little need for sleep or food. Thinking is usually confused and she may act in sexually, socially, and physically unhealthy ways, for instance, inappropriate sexual behavior or shopping sprees.
Mood Instability	When moods fluctuate and change rapidly. Mood may swing from happy to sad, for instance.
Neurotransmitter	Chemical released by nerve cells that carries information from one cell to another. This type of chemical transmits messages in the brain. Some neurotransmitters are serotonin, norepinephrine, and dopamine.

Obsessive-Compulsive Disorder (OCD)	Occurs in about 1 in 4 people. OCD is associated with a chemical imbalance in the brain. This condition worsens in times of stress. Obsessions are thoughts which occur intrusively and repetitively (for instance, thoughts of the baby being harmed). Compulsions are repetitive actions which often take the form of cleaning, checking (for instance, the locks on the door or the baby's breathing), or counting (for instance, the number of diapers in the bag). A person may have only obsessions, or a combination of the two.
Panic Disorder	During a panic attack, the person may feel symptoms including intense fear, rapid breathing, sweating, nausea, dizziness, and numbness or tingling. Sufferers often fear having the next panic attack and may develop behaviors to avoid situations thought to put them at risk.
Perinatal Mood Disorder	A mood disorder (for instance, depression or anxiety) beginning during pregnancy or during the first year postpartum.
Phobia	A persistent, irrational fear of a specific object, activity, or situation. This fear usually leads either to avoidance of the feared object or situation, or to enduring it with dread. Common phobias include fear of heights, flying in airplanes, fear of small places, and spiders.
Postpartum	After a mother gives birth.
Posttraumatic Stress Disorder (PTSD)	PTSD can occur following life-threatening or injury producing events such as sexual abuse or assault, or traumatic childbirth. People who suffer from PTSD often experience nightmares and flashbacks, have difficulty sleeping, and feel detached. Symptoms can be severe and significantly impair daily life.

Premenstrual Dysphoric Disorder (PMDD)	About 3 to 8% of women experience severe mood changes around their periods that create a significant impact on relationships and lifestyle. There are now specific diagnostic criteria that define this disorder.
Premenstrual Syndrome (PMS)	A combination of symptoms that appears the week before a menstrual period, and resolves within a week after the onset of the period. Common symptoms include: bloating, cramping, irritability, fatigue, anger, and depression. About 75% of women experience some degree of PMS.
Prenatal	During pregnancy.
Psychoanalysis	A form of psychotherapy that focuses on unconscious factors affecting current relationships and patterns of behavior, traces the factors to their origins, shows how they have changed over time, and helps the client cope with adult life. The client talks and the therapist is primarily a listener. Usually therapy takes place four or five times a week, and can continue for years.
Psychosis	An extreme and potentially dangerous (suicide, infanticide) mental disturbance which includes losing touch with reality. The psychotic person displays irrational behavior, has hallucinations and delusions. Hospitalization and medication are required.
Psychotropic Medication	Medication that affects thought processes or feeling states by acting on brain chemistry. Antidepressants and antianxiety medications are included in this category.
Relapse	To return to a previous state of illness. To become depressed or anxious again after having been well for a period of time, or to experience a worsening of symptoms after having improved.

Healthcare Professionals

Note: Licensure varies from state to state. Also, information about perinatal mood disorders is not a routine part of most training programs. See section in Chapter 3 on finding a knowledgeable therapist.

Certified Midwife (CM)	A CM is an individual educated in the discipline of midwifery, who is certified by the American College of Nurse-Midwives. The CM provides primary healthcare to women including: prenatal care, labor and delivery care, care after birth, gynecological exams, newborn care, assistance with family planning, preconception care, menopausal management and counseling in health maintenance.
Certified Nurse-Midwife (CNM)	A CNM is a licensed healthcare practitioner educated in nursing and midwifery. She provides primary healthcare to women of childbearing age including: prenatal care, labor and delivery care, care after birth, gynecological exams, newborn care, assistance with family planning, pre-pregnancy care, menopausal management, and counseling in health maintenance. CNMs attend over 9% of the births in the United States. Many CNMs are able to prescribe medication.
Clinical Psychologist	Mental health professionals who have earned a doctoral degree in Psychology (either a Ph.D., Psy.D, or Ed.D). They have received extensive clinical training in research, assessment, and the application of different psychological therapies. Clinical psychologists are concerned with the study, diagnosis, treatment, and prevention of mental and emotional disorders. They are not able to prescribe medication.

Doula	The doula's role is to provide physical and emotional support to women and their partners during labor and birth. Some doulas are also trained in postpartum care. The doula is not a labor coach. Her main role is to provide emotional reassurance and comfort. Doulas do not perform clinical tasks such as vaginal exams or fetal heart rate monitoring. Doulas are not trained to diagnose medical or psychological conditions or give medical advice.
Endocrinologist	A physician (MD) who specializes in treating problems related to hormones. Endocrinologists frequently treat thyroid problems.
Lactation Consultant	Trained, often certified, specialist who provides support and education about the process of breastfeeding. A Lactation Consultant can provide help regarding nursing, pumping, bottlefeeding, and weaning.
Licensed Clinical Professional Counselor (LCPC)	An LCPC is a masters level mental health professional. LCPCs are not able to prescribe medications.
Marriage and Family Therapist (MFT)	A masters level license in California, MFTs are similar to LCSWs and LCPCs. They are trained in individual, couple, and family therapy. MFTs are not able to prescribe medication.
Midwives, other *(See Certified Nurse-Midwife & Certified Midwife)*	Some women practice midwifery without a license. Be sure to ask about training and licensure.

Psychiatrist	These mental health professionals have earned the MD (Medical Doctor) degree. Advanced training focuses on psychiatric diagnosis, psychopharmacology (medication management of mental health issues) and psychotherapy. These physicians are the experts in prescribing psychotropic medications.
Psychiatric Nurse (APRN)	Registered Nurses who seek additional education and obtain a masters or doctoral degree can become Advanced Practice Registered Nurses in a specialty (APRNs). They provide the full range of psychiatric care services to individuals, families, groups, and communities, and in most states they have the authority to prescribe medications. APRNs are qualified to practice independently.
Psychiatric Social Worker	These mental health professionals have earned the MSW (Masters in Social Work) degree and are trained to be sensitive to the impact of environmental factors on mental disorders. LCSW designates Licensed Clinical Social Worker. These professionals cannot prescribe medication.
Psychotherapist	A person who practices psychotherapy: either a clinical psychologist, psychiatrist, professional counselor, social worker, or other mental health professional. Unless this person is also an MD (medical doctor), he/she cannot prescribe medication.

INDEX

QUICK ORDER FORM

Beyond the Blues
A Guide to Understanding and Treating
Prenatal & Postpartum Depression

Order by Internet:
www.beyondtheblues.com
Credit cards accepted over the Internet

Order by mail:
Send your check or money order to:
Moodswings Press, 1050 Windsor St., San Jose, CA 95129-2837

Name: _____

Address: _____

City: _____ State: _____ Zip: _____

Telephone: _____ Email: _____

English – Quantity: _____ @ $14.95 per book $ _____

Spanish – Quantity: _____ @ $14.95 per book $ _____

Sales Tax:

California residents please add 7.25% $ _____

Shipping:

Add $3.00 shipping for 1 book, $ _____

then $1.00 for each additional book $ _____

Total Enclosed: $ _____

PLEASE ALLOW 7-10 BUSINESS DAYS FOR DELIVERY

CONTACT US FOR BULK DISCOUNT RATES
books@beyondtheblues.com • Fax (408) 253-8277

Notes

Notes

Notes

Notes

Notes